"Colum's unique take on the "real" agenda behind Brexit makes as much sense as any explanation I've heard on the News - and more sense than some but this is more than just a novel about the next-door-nation descending into chaos. It's a tragicomic rollercoaster ride that takes you from the murky world of oil & gas prospectors off the Irish coast, to shady goings-on in the vicinity of Knock - and who doesn't love a rollercoaster?"

EDEL BROSNAN author & TV writer: *EastEnders/ Casualty*

"Brexit's ulterior motive ? Or the Empire's endgame? Gazillion is so funny, so thought provoking, its language an unending polka of energy. Utterly charming. Epic. Completely brilliant."

SIOBHAN CLEARY: Opera/Film composer

"Shimmering between alternative history & speculative conspiracy, Gazillion is a galloping, playful road trip through contemporary Ireland's energy industry. It's peopled with brilliantly original, wonderfully odd characters, peppered with startling real details that are delightfully hard to distinguish from the wonderful inventions, this deftly woven tale is funny, thought provoking, engrossing, all packaged in prose that is fresh, crisp and excitingly inventive."

KEVIN HOLOHAN author of *The Brothers' Lot*

GAZILLION

COLUM STAPLETON

SMIRSH LTD

GAZILLION

First published in 2019

Smirsh Ltd, The Gyreum, Corlisheen, Riverstown, County Sligo, Ireland

Copyright © Colum Stapleton

WEBSITE **gazillion.ie**

Cover design/ desktop publishing Paul O'Connor, Judo Design, Sligo, Ireland

ISBN 978-1-9993718-0-7

COVER Image provided by Marine Institute INFOMAR team. INFOMAR is the Irish national seabed mapping programme funded by the Irish Government through the Department of Communications, Climate Action and Environment, managed jointly by Marine Institute & Geological Survey Ireland.

CHAPTER ONE

The entry code for the *Bord Sol-athair Peitriliam* sector within the Department of Energy, Seascapes & Bawneens is a guessable four digits, one - seven - three - zero. The sieve-brained or hung-over can simply google former socialist energy Minister, Justin Keating's birth date, gringo the month, meaning reverse the 7th for the January and presto they're in. Keating was born at the height of the Irish answer to the Great Depression. An industrial i-spy mind could do said gooh-gell but she'd first have to have managed to limbo dance beneath Terrence Duffy's security desk at front of Department House, Adelaide Buildings, facing Adelaide Street, Dublin 2. The wealth of the nation of Ireland was as sound as a nest of genuine Fabergé cuckoo eggs in the innerest panic room of this Topkapi.

"Air side" of the energetic Department's turnstile is a thirty eight metre foyer wall, walk it in the company of a long drawn out abstracted, heavy metal map of Ireland, her deep seas enormous, jaggeding westwards, north westwards and a Porcupine of a snout south bent. Terrain Ireland is done in top brass, its shallower seas with deprecating pewter. Half arsed sea monsters in oxidised bronze in turn guard and sink. The expansive monotony of the pewter, once majestic, has tarnished. Despite its enormity this artwork is a miniature; scale-wise a small widow's knitting needle to a man sized cock o' hay. The real Land and Sea that it mimics combined are the best part of one million square kilometres of ocean; that's the span of Egypt, the sway of Nigeria. Imagine one million big ones, an unimaginable million more or less square, if undulating kilometres of ocean; as up for grabs as same sized gassy Bolivia. If an alien landed and had not an ounce of education; he'd swear Ireland was a clout of a country, her shoulder pads titanic, her strut into the Atlantic cocksure.

Anton Fruen is bang on his ritual twenty five minutes early, heaves through the five bomb-proof panes of the Department's swivel door, nods to Terrence, Terrence nods, reading specs mid nose, no need lowering his yesterday *Herald* (headline GHAWAR DEATH TOLL:1270). Face recognition accomplished. Anton traverses the metal detector, *ke-peep*: toe-caps and a prince albert, not bad for a fellah at home with being forty. Anton mooches past abstract pewter Ireland, gains the coded door, does the 1 - 7 - 3 - 0 and he's within. The Swiss bank of a door *shklumps* behind him. He is as good as in the dragon cave mounded with gilty coin the size of dinner plates. Yet all Anton half sees is dodgy decor, all the same mauve since Duran Duran's *Ordinary World* was in everyone's head; stringy early Haughian hessian, furlongs of the stuff. Burglars could be fooled by the humbling, crumbling decor but in that Department's bowels were descries 'n' treasure maps of the riches of the Irish oceans and depending on how 'tense the suck o' yer Dyson, some weighed, that beneath the sea bed, you'd not be short changed the full shilling of a trillion li-*quid*s, others said upward of a gazillion big ones were *waiting* as Madonna'd have it, *waiting*.

Anthony St. John Sullivan Fruen's mum had cut the ad from *The Indo*. There was little a graduate of geography and social studies could grasp of a life bar taking the next *Ulysses* to Holyhead. Nine years on, a full head of red curls on him yet, jammy gym membership, canteen discount and ample savings to have the best part of a month holidaying per annum and the half of 36 Homefield Road, Harold's Cross, Dublin 6. All that for a career he adored. As a child he assumed adults got waged according to how much they disliked their job. First division have-have-have soccer ace gets hundred grand the week, all smiles striker, Anton de Seven-year-old weighed but his invisibling Dad was paid some too many notches below the industrial wage for making double yellow lines along the streets of the wards of Fingal. The thrill of the precision of those buttercup coloured, parallel parking codes, little Anton imagined, wore thin with time. The then Venerable John Sullivan was prayed to so that premature Anton could survive his early arrival. The hero's journey beckoned, thus he foresook the womb early. He felt grand but Dr. Anthony Johnston thought safety first and he was placed for seven magic weeks in a slightly scratched womb-tomb c-thru perspex thing at The Coombe Children's hospital, paediatrics answer to orgon accumulation, a steep learning that, made a man of him, even with his wide eyes shut, gasping in pouts and assessing the clinical planet and his visit's reason with Eastern Health Board regulation oxygen.

Anton's remit was tight-as, yet central; he deciphered the 3D and 2.5D and 2D seismic data from the furthest droops and troughs of Ireland's Continental Shelf to the near shores of the wet Atlantic from Malin to Slyne to Carnsore to Cooley. He had little truck with the comparably ungiving onshore. 'D' as it often does, stands for dimensional; there are at least seven of them. Seven of Anton's actually nine if not ten hours in his work day were unmingled joy. While his lunch food was tasty, the sometimes lonesome enough hour dragged and at 1:42pm the clerical officer would be likely back among his charts of wet yet deep contours. Sometimes people asking obvious questions with difficult accents would call his phone and that was a good 17.25% of his day in some space between a panic and a fluster. Sometimes these callers would try to trick information out of him but he could call their wiles even midst their misused prepositions and unnecessary tense.

Today's undersea data had arrived by secure courier from Stavanger, from Grog International. There might be all imagined secure clouds but what could "be peachier than the ole memory stick and flappable pages," über-boss, Secretary-in-General of the Department of Energy, Gulls & Causeways, Dr. Jarlath Duhallow, would repeat at Anton, whose face never got the blues from clichés. "The internet is just too NSA-able." The new data had cost a pretty penny and yet would hardly dent the vast ignorance of the million square kilometres of Irish undersea, "a quarter of a gazillion hecky-tares," Duhallow would song and dance about. Seemingly the boss liked repeat gags. Anton bore it, and as said sort of smiled round the reflux.

This early Winter's day 2022 there was that new clerical officer wanting attention. Anton had Tanya grab a tea first and then took not a short while explaining the basics: "the ocean acreage of Ireland is divided into a grid five thousand, one hundred and forty blocks, each the size of say a County Longford, each and everyone portrait shaped, give or take, they're 30km long and 20km broad." The gape on Tanya reminds Anton of his own once green horns. Anton showed her some examples of blocks and more blocks on a nineties looking flip chart; 'not exactly Jedi training' Tanya Electra FitzGibbon sighed. Anton could only imagine as he flipped the pages that some blocks have enough oil or oil 'quivalent in their deep recesses, that surfaced 'n' shored 'n' even at market worst could yet be the purchase of all of a year's beef of Ireland and its sheep, its pigs, its fine breeds of horses, notwithstanding its poultry and game. 'Where is this slippery, black bullion?' imagined Anton for Tanya and so reading her assumed thoughts he fell silent and nervous and could not answer, would not answer. Anton had so become his seismics that he no longer could see Ireland as Ireland-shaped. Then he excited: "Tanya Electra; this is a grand empire" and with a sweep of his strong hand and click upon click of his Hewlett Packard presented clefts after clefts, seaworlds with their own sea-hidden *sliabh*s 'n' reeks, dells 'n' planes, prospect dreams no less or greater than the whin-hidden Aughties, proud Galtees, low Blooms 'flecting the meadows of the Huguenot, the empty Silvermines, the Blue Stacked Mountains and the broke bachelors about said slopes.

Imagine Anton's aunty Anne even till he was fifteen and the mocks round the corner gave him religiously annually an advent calendar with the cheapest chocolate hiding behind teeny cardboard flaps for each day. This is how Anton sees the great hydrocarbon shindig; wise men with treasures incomparable. If only the periodic table looking grid of Ireland's oceanic empire hanging by his desk could offer much needed national serotonin with each flipping of its seemingly humble Longford sized flaps. Imagine Anton's office is the only place in Ireland and on Earth where all the blocks are in-equal in the eyes of God. Every oily blackguard would love a rasher of Anton's brain. Tanya doodled a three legged milking stool of an oil rig as Anton described licensing policy changes since 1998. 'May the force be with you - and also with you.' She kanoodled in her nod.

Anton took the lift down to floor three for his morning peppermint tea and Kellogg's yoghurt bar. He needed a break from the Tanya's lack of engagement; she'd let slip she'd been going "stead" six months already. Anton's middle of the line manager was seated by the window engrossed in chat with a man Anton'd not seen before but was demonstrative, sure and brown. Between them was a woman sat, her back toward the cafeteria, her *hijab* purple and black. There was a sweet aroma from the table; it co-mingled with a perceptive wind, soughing eastwards, through the opened window, shaking some tall lemongrass, that appearing fake, wasn't. There was no Kellogg's yoghurt bar so Anton knew that would bring on mild sugar withdrawal issues and sure enough the idea was enough to start that yen as he moved beyond the cash desk and he vented his upset in a dislike in the meddling middle manager's direction, Dots Dingham by "name." Anton got a bad attack of aversion; he dwelt his resentment on Paul 'Dots' Dingham, 'meritocratic chief swine, the typique parachuted in from the private freckled sector sort, cute as the proverbial whoor with shored up handsomeness, bottles and bottles of definitely not Nivea lotion 'n' aftershave deep, sunk.' At forty eight Dots Dingham's energy could power a remote town. Anton did not then know his very own strength and him eight years less to Dots and to all intents and purposes a dozen votes better looking than the dynamo. Dot's home place was Llanpumsaint, a clutch of a village in the slate quarry vales, his parents both sorts of Munsters, hence the instant Zelig from Welsh to Irish to Plum accent according to the champion's league of survival table Dots was sitting at. His freckles much bigger than Anton's became him but did not counterbalance his retreating, remaining dark ginges of hair. Today middle manager Dots was not Irish and not so Welsh but at his best, upper-lip Plum-awse because in front of him was the round Malay of a face-off, the very first cousin of the Sultan of Selangor. Kualagas, the Stately Oil company of the United Kingdoms of Malaysia was seeking new prospects further south than their present, near exhausted fields off Cork and they were cutting the ice with the government body they imagined were charged with divvying the gas blocks.

Dots caught the eye of Anton as the clerical officer moved across the cafe to his comfort zone. Dots smirked his 'Mainland' smirk at Anton, the one that meant stay away with the 'f' word not far behind. Anton got the message and went sat after his habit, observed his resentment and tried and succeeded in stopping it by putting his perfect intention on removing the pyramidal Avoca peppermint sachet from its mug. So he sat there with no Kellogg's yoghurt bar. The scant learning from his new app for meditation guidance and panic monitoring was being sorely tried. It was called 'mindfulNess' and its simple logo was said monster peeking above the meniscus of his lock-in**.** Sitting this far south from the group of three, Anton was within side swipe eyeline of the hijabbed woman. He stereotyped her as P.A. to the smoothy older chap but she had sharp encompassing eye that could assess over distance. The foreign lady liked the look of Anton but culturally she'd've been incapable of divining that Anton suffered from an advanced form of Kertbeny syndrome. Then the party of three became animated gesticulating this and the other. Sharp words were likely attached. Dots said something calming then hailed Anton, near as clicking his strong rugby fingers to win his attention.   Anton obeyed and hurried over. Dots, was an able hooker and even on a wet day was the most reliable for conversions, at the obliquest of angles even.

"This is Anton Fruen de Bruin," said Dots Dingham. Anton was only Fruen but Dots the Dig reckoned Anton affected, effected with exceeding and incurable Kertbeny syndrome and hence the aristocratic nonce 'de' suffixation. Kertbeny syndrome makes its sufferers go weak at the knees if confronted with their own sex. It was discovered in 1868 by a German Hungarian. Hijab woman woke up to a smell of importance and gave a wee tilt of her fabricated head: "Mister de Bruin. Excellent. Excellent," and she offered the delicate hand of friendship but Dots cut the crap so fast their hands grazed only.

"Anton we need seismics on blocks 3149, 3148, 3152. Do-able? Today-wise!"

The Sultan's emissary reminded "and 3154 mister Paul please."

Anton had a little think and saw waves crashing against the pride of rocks about the Fastnet. "3148 is in the public domain. The other three from memory have 2.5D seismic. 3154 had a later 3D survey done by Loude-Abiliter in 2009," Anton deprecated to the consultant to the Sultan. "As the instigators and bank rollers of the survey, L & A are the only ones privy to that material. It'll be in our domain in three years..... Sir."

Turning to Paul 'Dots' Dingham, Anton was not sure how else to fill a silence that for him was long "Mr. Dingham. There are some positive indications from the data back from Stavanger."

"Stick to the point Anton."

"Well...." Anton found it difficult to public interface with oil magnate types. He preferred reams of colourful data spewing from his A'0' Canon printer. The zigzags of the seismic needle, divine doodling, spiking 'n' flattening. Pinning these on the wall, scrolls of potential, wondering what squiggle hid what cavernous bauble, what basalt, what microshist oodles of calor and beneath it slumped in its ooze from tropical primordial the black concentrate, sweet molasses almost, giant perhapses, a world only fathomable by people of immense certitude. "Non Formal Sector stay the feck clear," Dots had once bitch slapped him with. That really hurt and was and remained in his top ten loopine negative mantras for quite some time.

"Will it suffice after lunch?" put out Anton.

"His Excellency could use it by noon, if your Gracie Fields is not too busy" and Dots behind the eyes of the Malays mimed a camp filing of nails while raising his eyebrows with the matters of facts, a gesture only manageable by those not born in Ireland these hundred years. Anton of a sudden with six eyes at him got the gist. 'Job for life. Job for life my ass. Slave to the rhythm more like' and without bowing, without dredging his peppermint, nor scraping his parting he hastened out of the canteen and descended flights of steps to see what *Bord Sol-athair Peitriliam* had on blocks 3149, 3148, 3152 and the ever popular 3154.

The filing system is much changed from the old ledger of the 1960s that sits like a *Book of Kells* in the foyer of the Department of Energies, Puffins & Bloss. The ledger beneath a glass box, a page turned once a month had columns representing zones moving away from Ireland's coast. There were no "here be monsters" illustrations but as good as with plenty of undiagnosed '*Terra Incognita*s.' The locating and legalising of gas 'n' oil had gone from flint shards to the hydrocarbon version of dianetics in two half sleeping generations. Anton strode along the noughties era shelving and stopped in the 3000s that covered all the region that Secretary Duhallow wagged as "the south sea bubble.". Anton span the shelving wheel of the three point two metre high, light grey shelving like he was a caravel captain Horn bound. Anton, tall yet slim, slipped into the made gap. 'Imagine getting squished to death in here.' No matter how many times in his day he hamned his way into these grey sandwiches he always shuddered at the trap factor, like getting pressed like a hyacinth in an unforgiving naturalist's tome. "Hhhmmmmmm box 3148." Anton opens it. There were its scroll of seismic, gorgeous, its pen drive, its notes, its geological snap summary, its scant Lidar, its Special Area of Conservation (S.A.C.) report, 'notes on mating porpoises.' All ready and correct. Next box. 3149 had had a pencil survey done in 1959 by Madonna Oil which wound up as Longrun. In 1966 Longrun, all lead plumbs and Neolithic sonar had implored Hope and tried Luck so they drilled and they drilled but hardly a squirt through their half inch pipe, even at 700 bar, hardly a spurt along its two and one half miles. Move on twenty years their initial report was first in the pouch, sat beside a 2.5 dimensional seismic survey from 1988 that showed signs of a crude potential bauble in the crosshairs of blocks 3148, 3149, 3078 and 3079. A further 3D survey in 2002 sent hopes and share prices tumbling; the bauble had long ago crumpled, some ancient fissure showed up and the cathedral of gas had farted away and a faintest slow fade of oil over millennia slicked off south to Biscay. Anton then removed the metal box for 3152; the usual plus a 2.5D survey that was low key and wouldn't wake curiousity. 3152 shared the same basalt substratum as 3148 and 3149 so there was the case that none of 3148, 3149 or 3152 had ever been penetrated seismically beneath 2,700 metres below the bedrock. Anton took mental note. The Malays must be interested, not just because it conveniently, roughly adjoins their present declining prospect and its pipeline to shore but they must believe that there is Deeper with a capital 'D' potential. But little proof. 'You'd need some sort of a Uri Geller of a divine with twigs and coat hangers out on the high seas to proficy the black drops to have any of your wildest Southforks come true in that neck of the woods,' asserted Anton. Anton opened metal box 3154, a box no larger than a royal compact and uncommonly light, not as spacious as a piratical trunk with its maps of islands of buried potentiality, caches found after much lyrical hints and not a little gore and planking. 3154 was empty; neither a treasurable map nor a winking doubloon.

Anton assembled all and only the information that could be allowed for the first cousin twice removed of the Sultan of Selangor and his woman. In modern terms it was scant, like offering a sextant to an iphoney teenager and challenging him to locate Diego Garcia. Dots Dingham cut through Anton's apologies on the shortcomings of the materials stating "This will be of exceptional benefit to your assessment of those blocks."

"And 3154?" intruded the distant aristocrat framed in his Gucci cooh suit. His woman, an actual hydrologist from Putrajaya

University, Faculty of Oil Concentrate, adjusted her hijab and rose her brows at Anton. Anton was about to say "3154 is ...." but Paul 'Dots' Dingham dove in "not a sausage" which was rich said to Moslemites, "not a bean or a bubble, not a jot of data beyond the shape of its deep and hidden cliffs" which was Public School for 'trust me, end of story, our meeting's concluded' with a peppering of 'I'm white and you're virtually Bornean brown and that's the way this cookie crumbs and you're not exactly the Shilton o' Brunei whose Islam we forgive 'cause he has a *boyng boyng* mink-coated 737 to gad about in for the wives.'

So all four stood and there were six actions of handshaking. The low cost royal Malay felt progress'd been made, the woman as a modern belle recognised the waspic put-down. Anton wondered if some rule was being broken, and if so what number was it, or subsection, then counted to ten the number of days to his holidays. Dots Dingham kicked inwardly himself for being so callous as to have left Anton stumble on the empty box and worse still to have left it so. He assumed Anton's in-diagnosable Assburger's could contain suspicion.

CHAPTER TWO

A mean time thirty four years ago in Amsterdam in the scorch of July 1988 two real queens were thinking of tea and a nice smoke away from the city's kafuffle. One was north of middle middle aged, not used to the unseasonal torpor, the other was only just adjusting to being a queen and her clothes' colours were more subdued than the flamboyant lettuce greens of Her older 'Sister.' They drove past several coffee shops and stopped at the *Dam* Palace and went inside.

  Tea was brought for them, a rarefied Burmese green, great for the complexes and those with intact livers. The recent IRA bomb at Nieuwbergen was full of itself again across the newspapers, both Dutch and English, placed with military precision tip to tip about a silver tea tafel. Much about sad RAF better halves bleary, mourning sick; Queen Elizabeth took memo-note of their names. The Dutch queen glanced, sped read and knew it was not her territory. Queen Elizabeth was not used to being so left alone with new if known person but She knew She should say something. The younger Dutch queen eased: "the acacia honey brings out the tanning perfectly. I dislike process sugar. Try some!" and she tipped a tiny silver spoon into the tiniest ever bowl on four legs, with the House of Lippe insignia 'graved across it and withdrew a curling of the densest of honey on her wee wooden honey gadget catcher. The English queen was captivated by the device and its non drip but wasn't ready for a lecture-ette on product design should She inquire.

The room was fifteen hundred times their size, with long white shutters that got whiter as noon struck on the *Dam* Palace campanile.

DONG and the older Queen pulled Her skirt to cover Her choice knees. DONG and a leftward leaning, lame, male pigeon flew toward their window, landed safe and regarded in through the perfectly Hollandic square squares at the aging queens. DONG and a clock on the mantle started a pertinkling DING that was yin to the DONG and the Dutch queen remembered that there were twelve dongs or was it eighteen to the *Angelus* and that a Spanish queen had told her the *Angelus* was a dozen or more dongs too many, three times per day; 6, 6 hours later and 6 eventide. DONG the Dutch queen offered a red Rothmans to the older English Queen. They sorta sprung from a flat gold box with a silver, sugarcane busy embossment. DONG "thanks We will." So seven thumps of the bell to rest. DONG. A waiting man manifested and lit the English Queen's cigarette. He was dismissed. DONG. The Dutch queen lit her own red Rothman with her manly hands. The door slammed to. The queens alone, thrown upon themselves. DONG   Both queens inhaled and looked to the gazing pigeon who had awoken in a gutter off the Prinzengracht and had never cross-eyed two queens at once, nor witnessed meaty history making. DONG "I only smoke in the afternoons," lied the Dutch queen. DONG   "We only smoke in socially situations. We take so little......." DONG ".......interest in them they often turn to ash on One," said the English Queen truthfully. DONG "Inhaling is marvellous to balance the nerves in our giddy world" and the much talked about Dutch queen elevated the most emaciated ever made cup of China in all of The Two Hollands & Frisia and reached it toward the English Queen who rose Hers too. DONG "To our Glorious Revolution" and They pinkled without breakages their cups.

Some fraternal and familiar laughing from the chambre outside the queen's apartments is noted.

"Pip and Klaus appear to be good buddies." The Dutch queen nodded towards the door, a riot of pink with baby blue Casters and Polloxes doing various acts of kindness and seduction.

"I don't know how they keep all the facts in their head; so much to know and one cannot put it to paper." The English Queen regarded Her beige handbag.

"Well now you've brought it up; let's sort the bare bons." The Dutch queen had such lofty, fruitful English yet betimes she went Dutch like the tongue could slip on ice: 'bar bons,' observed the English Queen as the Dutch queen placed an A2 sized map, a privateer's sepia in tone upon the table and cut to her chestnut.

"S.N.A.K Oil's CEO had his top hydrologist draw up this map for us. It is the only copy in existence. "

"Oh it is lovely. Beautiful tones and contours. What are those oranges under Iceland?"

"They are the already sure fire 'gushers' relinquished but dubbed mediocre" said the Dutch queen testing her rough oil derek lingo.

"Gushers" repeated the English Queen reassuring, careful not to droplet Her green tea on the map least it be misinterpreted.

"And they are in what will be Irish waters." The Queen of Holland said it like she'd just traded trinkets for five caravels of nutmeg and the natives are caught staring at their glint.

"How unfortunate! Scotland's productivity is on a steep decline curve, steep from the point of view....." The lovely newness of the map mesmerised the older Queen who stretched Her delicate index across the map from Rockall to just west of the Shetland Islands, then down to the I'll-Have-Man, and down dropped Her hand till it dawdled to a stop about Bannow Bay, dusting Hook Head. "The Shetland basin is an unknown and commercial finds in less than five hundred feet of depth are so far......" The English Queen counted out seven on Her fingers. "Seven" she enunciated and to press Her point rose Her left hand like pledging troth plus Her two fingers of the right Hand like how She recalled Churchill did for victory but She had them arse-ways. "Seven paltry wells." The Dutch queen smirked at being given the peaceable two fingers from an older richer "Cousin" and sought clarity: "paltry?"

" Paltry means damn all." Her own version of a smirk pursed.

"We need Irish friendly waters for this to work." The Dutch Queen swivelled on her wee stiletto. A tall woman.

The English Queen found words hard to assemble, but had a go at an answer: "We are at a sort of war with them." And she gestured with Her chin towards the newspapers but then She remembered "Philip said that needed to end but We've not worked out the details."

"A milestone of ten years should do that. It is surely obvious and essential that your United Kingdom is a non belligerent when the pipes commence to flow. Ireland not Scotland is the landfall for the East Atlantic. Can I park that with You?"

The English Queen was impressed by these words and re-assured at how little thinking was required of Her in the heat. "Yes of course. That will be easier when Mrs Thatcher hoofs off. We imagine it so. Philip and Klaus can work that out. Perhaps We can offer her something or that enterprising husband of hers."

"If there's no peace it's not the end of the world but it makes piping and refining less troublesome. We don't need more bleedy bombers" and the Dutch queen gestured toward that day's *De Standaard.* "S.N.A.K. reckons it's not Saudi sized but more Gulf, Mexican Gulf sized." The Dutch queen lit a new red Rothman off her butt. The English Queen ever so mildly revolted looked toward *Dam* Square like She were no sizing-up queen and eventualied:

"Yes possibly, but the drill bits, rig leg parts need to cut the mustard. Deep, deep water."

"Twenty five years off. "

"Oh My. Technology best get her skates on."

"Factoring all improvements; reach shoreline for Your 70th coronation year party. What might the proverb barrel of oil fetch uz then; hhmmmmmmm?"

The two Queens laughed at that gag and the Dutch queen only stopped laughing as she made a kazoo of her mouth and tooted the first bars of *God Save the Queen.* Both laughed a little longer but less sincerely and then touched fingers in a really lovely "sisterhood" kind of Chalet School fidget.

Queen Beatrix of the Netherlands, Malukas and Antilles and Arubans among Others pressed a bell beneath the cornice of her House of Orange throne-lette and presto like electronics the double doors open and in walks the Duke of Edinburgh and Prince Klaus, Count of Lippe. The two were sort of giggling.

The Duke went to the *Dam* window and looked at a gaggle of Italian tourists awaiting a red light on the zebra crossing by the top of Kokryngstraat. He noted the colour coordination of their whites and the girth of their shoulder pads.

Prince Klaus behind his wife, rested his right hand in troth on Queen Beatrix's chipless left shoulder.

"Is this North?" asked the Duke to fill the air.

"No Philip it is sort of east" corrected Koningin Beatrix with a grin she shared up at Klaus.

The Queen of England, Scotland, Wales, Ireland and France pushed the ashtray away from Her Person.

"We were just discussing how best or better to celebrate the Glorious Revolution,'The 300' I believe they're calling it."

The Duke leans his spine into the casement: "my eye you were." He regards the black gleam of his Chester Le Broq shoes. "Prince William of Oranjeboom was a shameless fag."

"Careful Pip," chided QE2. The Prince turned away from the window light.

"Prince Billy landed on a Saturday at Brixham sixteen eighty something....."

"1688 dear."

"...... and paraded his camp army lead by the blackest of black men of Aruba in feathers that hot, hot afternoon in celebration of His peaceful landing. Glorious Revolution. First ever Pride march in Hampshire more like."

Prince Klaus stared back at Philip, unsure of his new found buddy's obscurantism. Klaus was more businessman and could not utter a hooting as to what the past entertained. All it mattered was that he was a Prince on the back of it. "We must soon be on our way. Garden party at Huit den Bosch. Have you lovely Ladies settled on departing time?" Deferring to Philip with the weeniest klick of his *Obersturmführer* heals: "Don't worry Philip. Small affair. No raff riff."

Queen Elizabeth Saxe Coburg Gotha caught a gloom: "We must make a speech about the Glorious Revolution?" Like She asked her own royal We, and not the three other humans *per se* in the room.

Queen Beatrix broke the gathering vagueness. "Philip honey, join us. I'll speech; don't you worry."

The Duke sat next His Queen, a bold teenage twist about his Aryan face, his shoes shifting on the Louis Xiii tapis. Prince Klaus rummaged in his man hand bag. He appeared not to be finding his need. His Queen regarded him with disdain that could shape shift to sheer house wifely familiar love-in in a twinkling.

"Our Klausy ever the German must have his affairs about him." Prince Klaus removed a little box and with no deferring took a pinch of powder the colour of cayenne and took a mighty sniff, one severe in-snort. Philip was appalled by the lack of apology at the inhale and the faggotry of the man-bag..

"*Mein Gott, lernt man jeden Tag eine neue Marotte*?" exclaimed Edinburgh's Grecian Duke towards Klaus.

Queen Beatrix laughs a rather acted protracted laugh.

Queen Elizabeth feels sidelined. "What did he say?"

"You learn each day a new...... foible," cares Queen Beatrix.

Queen Elizabeth is seeking niceness and says to Queen Beatrix: "Pip here, We mean Philip of course and your father, Bernhard, best of pals."

"Of course, of course." answers Klaus for his wife who has momentarily slid into "am I talking with plebs mode ?"

"Of course," adds Beatrix to wake herself out of broad smiles and meaningless communication.

The Duke of Edinburgh was getting bored, reaching toward the coffee table for a hand bell, a golden Sikkhamese dorj of a treasure, once touched by Younghusband but not stolen by him. As he was about to dingle it he beckoned with his eyes permission of Beatrix. She was put out, less than startled by such an affront beneath her own regal ceiling.

Beatrix had simultaneously pressed her button, the royal *Flesopener* to the Crown of Nassau was so quick to them, as if teleported.

"A bottle of your best Irish whiskey," demanded Philip. Then he did his Paul Daniel's impersonation, raising his arms and enthused: "now your majesties what is this Glory Revolution plan or were You possibly talking beastly in-vesty-ments? You girls never waste a Florin of a moment's second."

Philip turned to Klaus admiringly: "Prince Klaus has all the balls of your father, Beatrix. It's his plan, not mine. Ireland is to become Scotland 2, on steroids by the sound of things. While we may be in our sepulchrae before we reap the benefit. Our two baby Williams will be overseers of the bounty."

Prince Klaus interrupted, ever with the air of clarifying, even in situations that were obvious. "The first stage has succeeded. The royalties to the Irish government has been made zero seven months now." He flicked his fingers wizard like towards Philip, smiling.

"Oh my Pip well done,.." The Queen of England tactlessly saw through Philip's modesty in deferring the plan's scheme to Klaus. Klaus looked at the Britvic Queen and recalled seeing once a jigsaw half done of her coronation self in a glowing playroom, bodiless, head and shoulders. "you're no fly zones..... both of you" She added approval toward Klaus and began to fidget. Sirens blared outside the Dam palace and the *Flesopener*, out of breath, returned with four Waterford crystal cut tumblers and a decanter of twelve year old Middleton. He'd run to and from the bottle shop on Verkiehsvvaard and purchased their only better Irish.

"Come on man, the bottle. I like to read what I'm drinking." Immediately exasperated by his own edginess, he recanted as he decanted, "oh leave it then."

The Queen of England retrieved Her hand bag, a sign that leaving was imminent. She worried when drink interrupted a predetermined afternoon. She sought some finality.

"And the taxes to Eire's government they are still a tad..... normal?"

Klaus knelt oddly by Philip, "*Wie lange bis zu dieser Steuer die meisten gelöst?*"

"Our Austin, Texan man is working overtime. But hour and day and date we cannot presuppose. It is dependent on bounty remaining hush hush of course. The royalties are locked down and a way lower tax is in the offing but both are rather dependant on who is watching the pipe at landfall. We don't fancy Paddy'll be much on duty."

Prince Klaus asked "how many know the plan ?"

The Queen of England without looking up from a rummage for Her lip stick pronounced "eighteen, and that includes our chap in Ayr? Are We correct?"

"Yes Ma'am," said Prince Philip taking a giant gulp of booze. "Nineteen. Undersecretary at Mi6 had to be briefed. Details. Details. " Philip, son of a nun, raises his glass "Let us cross the shallows of the Boyne in victory one more time."

The Dutch royals rose to Philips crispin challenge and jounced their see through crystal grenades, clunking more than clinking. Queen Elizabeth the Second remained seated a short moment pondering the enormity of the heist and its hydra headed risks and then remembered not to Overthink.

CHAPTER THREE

Knock proper is some while south of Knock the Airport. It's in Knock proper that a particular seventh son of a seventh son lives. Not knowing he is the seventh son of a seventh son doesn't affect the inherited powers. He lives five houses up from the Apparition chapel in the not so shiny town of Knock. His name is Lar Ewing and at some point every day he wonders among his atheist thoughts - why of all the Marian Shrines of Greater Europe had this Irish Mary apparition kept mum and what variety and how sophisticated a jack-o-lantern or other outlandish spectrograph might yet have been invented by 1879. Flanked by two bearded gents the self styled Mother of God hovered in brilliance in that August of '79 up 'gainst the gable in a Time before a brownie or selfie could've vouched Her. A spectrograph if they'd been invented could have broken the light of Her into logic but Dublin was a good eleven hours by train from Claremorris and then by hobble trap from Claremorris, a camera, let alone a spectrograph would be destroyed if not late. Mother Mary said nothing, neither admonition, nor gag in the odd hours she dallied and hundred and sixteen people saw Her. In mainland Europe it tended to be gawpy young kids who saw the shining Our Ladies, scampering home to be unbelieved.

In Irish Knock would be like driving through a place called Hillock, but Knock became *Cnoc Mhuire* which means 'Bit of an Aul Hillock o' Mary.' Now almost a rough century and a half has mooched by since the so called Mother of Jesus had appeared flanked as said by two Parnellite looking gents in the frocks of bishops who the locals concluded were two of the particular apostles. The Polish Pope had visited Knock for the hundredth anniversary of the apparition. He was emphatic that Mary of Knock was not only Queen of Heaven but also of Ireland. As he descended out o'heaven that day in his holy chopper - that very moment was the same moment he discovered a flaw in his fate; happens a lot at Knock.

The nomenclature for Knock Airport is NOC. As nobody in the world knew where Knock 'City' might lie; the elders of the local *Chambre* of Commerce of the district changed its name to Connaught Regional Airport which meant it could boast being the only airport in the known world whose aviation code was arse-wise. Then it turned out nobody'd heard tell of Connaught, soon to be the richest of Ireland's five provinces, thus while remaining Knock, the airport's initials became IWA, Ireland West Airport or as one inconsiderate security man had wagged at a lock-in in Baile Cathal "Mary Incontinent Airport !" and got thumped for it and that was the last drop of drink units that 7th son of a 7th son took, and despite his battles with the One Being of the Father, Lar Ewing, agnostic turned atheist, to his defence wore a pioneer pin since the day of the slur. Pioneer pins are loud and clear.

Lar's customs security shift work at the airport allowed him chunks of time for his own devices, Mrs. Ewing notwithstanding and thirty seven years married. Herself, a fortnight older than Lar, first of a third daughter, boasts the tidiest garden along the entire Knock drag. It doubles as a B&B. Mrs. Ewing had had an American Monsignor guest bring a particular set of seven dwarves from Akron, Ohio, specially to populate the garden. Normal sized but luminous in the night. Tripadvisor comments often gave them a mention. Pilgrims to Knock who suffer with unusual curiousity might venture beyond the shrine zone and passing Ewing's often are taken aback by Flo Ewing's gerenia, her single black tulip, the sad foils bobbing the drizzle off themselves in the frequent gusts. The *jardin's* centrepiece has a former bronze strumpet with her Scythic' amphora of plenty pouring water into a pond of stunted piebald carp who ate the golden fish some time before the flood. The seven dwarfs laugh at that tragedy and/ or the insufferable pounding of the Multiverse.

The Ewing garage is a convert. Here there's a small kitchen even, that Lar Ewing need hardly vex his wife with his "idle" world. He only works six hours at the most on the trot at the airport. Here he hides mid stacks of rolls of paper and there hanging almost religiously where once a holy object might have hung was Lar's pendulum, a wee plumb line of an effort, dangling against the paisleyite wallpaper ready to yay, nay but never a possibly, such was its surety in the great farm-labourer-alike hands of its swinger.

Mrs. Lar Ewing had her own name, as said, Flo. She kept mostly pilgrims as guests but only when Philo'd send them her way. Philo lived nine doors north and Philo'd pack off her extras, an excess of widows, or too many Priests at once or even earnest young Polish - off they'd go to Flo and Flo would afford them a lot more attention than Philo.

Knock Airport had quietened down. The winter set into its best worst and the pipes of the ill prepared B&Bs on the Knock drag froze. Mrs. Ewing had no swinging sign, announcing accommodation and her sat in her orange rind kitchen, the wood frames bright ambur and all itself west-looking. So even when the sun wasn't going down; it was always going down. In a kind of a sort of a casement she kept her snow shaker selection, squat to tall, round to the ovaliest, holiest, profane and fay. Her favourite was *Cristo Redentor*, because she knew it'd never snow on the *Corca Fhada*. It was a gift from a Sister Cruzeiro Delfina

Summit, a beautiful slightly Portuguese nun devoted to the Yanumany with specialist devotion to Our Lady of La Salette. She visited Knock each Olympic year La Salette, Fatima and Medjugorje being her cardinal other points. She could prove Lourdes was a fraud; if you'd the time to spare.

Mrs. Ewing startled from a worry, her fifth worry in so many minutes. *The Bells of the Angelus* theme tune shook her Samsung across the table. She grabbed its possession. "Yes. Who is it?"

"Flo. You're dozing."

"Auh Philo. Great."

"Flo, what's your water story?"

"We've the moving fish pool in the garden. We're grand. We can bucket through the ice hole Lar made. Jokin' apart. Our pipes are grand."

"There's a gentleman has rung me. He sounds very mannered. Out of the blue."

"I see; a priest."

"I have all my en suites all vacant and aired but he asks for a nice garden aspect. In particular."

"Odd."

"He googled his self a street view and must have found you and thought it was me."

"Gardens."

"He loves gardens but as he hadn't your number I supposed he tried me through the guide book or more googles. He said he was a coeliac."

"What order are they?"

"They don't eat bread."

"Those strange and unusual orders. They're the ones oftener than not the ones that, you know, get the worst so-and-soes."

"Mrs E. Really ! He sounded a gem and he'd like to stay five days and dinners for sure and if lunches were no trouble; them too."

"Has he experienced Knock himself before?"

"Not that I am aware of. I sensed not."

"I can put on the infrared for the box room. When's he wanting.....?

"Today. Late afternoon flight from East Midlands FR5067. By the way. We missed you the other evening."

"What's the book for February then? Lar'll find it in the Amazon."

"*The Aquitaine Conspiracy.* It was Des Murtagh's choice."

"Typical. Is it long?"

"It looks it but Olive said it's pacy but repeats itself a lot."

"Thanks for letting me know."

Mrs. Flo Ewing folded her arms on the brushed oak table and worried that the guest would be awkward, then silent, then unrelenting, then religiously overzealous, downright dirty but three hundred and fifty two euro, lunches aside, would put a mighty dent in her mauve hide suite. She wasn't née Cash for nothing.

The King Charles spaniel's name was Ryan. Chief Inspector Ryan weighed nine kilos most of the time. Like all airport security dogs conceived in Taurus he was extremely conservative, right of right if there were canine Christian Democrats. As he aged he became more dogged but less precise in his differentials. Before Christmas rush at NOC he'd assumed marzipan was semtex and in the same week that some yellow cherry tomatoes on the stalk was weed. His conservative assumptions were his back up to his nose which more and more went on the blink. On All Saint's Day a shabby scaffolder returning from Leeds had a roacheen of a spliff in his baggy excuse for pants but it was his gaupy gait and Primarks got Ryan yapping at him "yrrp yrrrrp yrrrrrp" and then a snarl directed at his flittered docks. The poor gom had forgotten utterly the splifflette in his sports wear and his P turned out, had no THT, his blood pure; he was released without warnings.

Fourth in Command of security was Lar Ewing. He believed in feeding dog Ryan amply before duty, a fetid lamb chop left over at Boggans o' Charlestown. Ryan sniffed it like it was a test then swallowed it in two chomps.

"Bing bong" went the announcing, then the Ballaghaderreen strip of a girl of a voice announced "Delayed Flight FR5067 will tempt another landing. Passengers awaiting the return flight to East Midlands please remain patient in de-parting lounge. They have the snow ploughs out over. Over. Caution required." She yet had the eensiest Lancashire about her Mayo tone.

'Who'd want landing in our West Midlands from their East Midlands on a blizzard of an ill conceived Tuesday.' Lar Ewing took in the nineteen women and fifty seven men, at the thirty five baptised Catholics, four Protestants, three Moslems and an array of shape-shifters. He didn't like this dog job, preferred to stand behind the counter nodding a hundred thousand welcomes. Ryan strained on the leash, not aiming for anybody, simply feeling underutilised. To placate him only as he'd not had his walk, what with the minus five without, Lar marched Ryan as far as the terminal entrance in a straight line, not bending adjacent to the poor Treblinkin' stream o' humans shuffling to exit. A finely dressed man with a purple silk scarf tied up after the Paris fashion and an angora coat caught Ryan's attention. "Respect," beamed the dog at the man. For the sake of stretching the retiring dog's small black and white legs further, Lar skirted along side the passengers hurriedly till he regained the Garda point and sure then why not walk back along it and Ryan stopped then and sniffed shamelessly snootily but it was only toward the fat goose-be-bumped legs of some traveller women, their feet stockingless and slanted by high heels, kicking their pink and black holdalls along the floor. Lar pulled Ryan on and they marched towards the end, Ryan's royal face up-tilted as if to vouch for all the settled decencies of the others. Then from silence began a most sharp yammering and snarling, almost unprofessional it was that ferocious aimed at an LV bag. When Ryan rose his head to view the owner he did a head stagger and Lar full taut with the lead to keep Ryan from GBHing the landed looking fellow, as suave as after shave. But instinct was instinct no matter how flagrantly decent the bag's carrier. Ryan dog struggled between his politics and his nose.

The stranger stepped this way and was gracious without perturb, was told his rights and remained silent. Ryan regarded him yet with wonder as first the purple scarf and then the coat came away to reveal the crisp cotton of the Cloth. The over-detoled hospital of a searching room was windowless, lit by drunken fluoroes.

"I am Lawrence Ewing, duty officer at the Ireland West. Please I need to search your bag and person..... Father."

As the LV bag was lifted on to the aluminium table Ryan again got excited and snarled so wide his double nicotine fangs were plain to see. It appeared he was emphasising the bag as the guilty all night party, not the respectable....

"Your name. And please your passport."

"Reverend Father Ayrton, Ayrton Van der Op."

"As in Senna."

The priest held down his puffed under-eye, playing to feign youth: "you flatter."

The passport which was crispy despite many stamps of admittance and farewell had a lovely snap of the cleric trying to keep a laugh to himself.

"You fairly like the travel."

"My parish allows me that. I have an energetic curate."

"I, with Officer of the Garda will now commence the search." A lovely Guard came in and slouched by the door keep. Lar nodded to him. The Guard stepped to the table. Lar scanned the suspect. He brought to mind those priests who hover in the 460s of Sky, on American Catholic channels, with production values too high for the dredgery of the content, speaking about the power of regular recitals of rosary with gleaming studio and shady guests and dove logoes and 'logos' this or that.

The handsome though podgy fingered Garda went through the bag's pockets, in one of which inside a plastic kinda tube of a bag was some white powder. The brand or stuff of the bag said Xylitol. Lar placed it on the counter. Ryan's wet nose took little disinterested sniffs at its 250 grammes.

"What is this white stuff ?   You've a right to remain silent, Father." Lar speaks like he is the blushing Guard's ventriloquist.

"It is made from the bark of a birch tree." The priest says.

"It will require analysis."

"Taste it."

Lar takes in the priest with small mounts of atheistic bile. His regard said: "I do the ordering here; afterlife or no afterlife."

"We imagine birch to be silver. Birch are common in Russia. Where did you get this bag?"

"Eindhoven."

"Where's that?"

"Nayderlanz."

"Ah Dutch. Where precisely ?" Lar eyed the purply front of the priest's passport with a coat of arms that looked what he imagined but had forgotten the Windsor's had.

"Conan Creek Neither Lands. Hhmmm." Lar reads the front of the passport.

"Apotheek Keyser on Michelangelolaan. They had Xylitol on special, selling for €5.99. Usually closer to the tenner." The latter said like he'd gone to slang class.

The Guard who was rummaging at the base of the LV seeking hidden concealments had by now piled one surplus, one alb, one tupperware of wafers with IHS stamped about their middles. One oldy worldy Bible, three pairs of Calvin Klein undergarments, all a similar light grey, black ecclesiastical pyjamas, one candlestick, a silver chalice and some already dog smelt altar wine contained in a 100ml. fake tan sort of bottle. The Guard spoke for the first time his mind.

"I assumed Father that the Dutch were Protestants."

Lar gave the Guard a sideways eye and well nye in apology

"but there's the Spanish Netherlands. ."

"The South is 'dominantly Catholic. I am from Den Boss We're the wilder ones, the Burgundaisies." said Vater Van der Op laying on the implication of good craic with trowels.

Lar put on his 3:2 glasses and read that Xylitol was 'Nature's Answer to Sugar and was suitable for diabetics.'

"Are you a diabetic, Father?"

"Partially. Hence the powders you see in your hands," said the Priest contritely. "I'm also a coeliac"

Lar placed his whetted index in the granules and proffered a tincture for Chief Inspector Ryan who sniffed quickly and licked it approvingly, wagging his tail.

"Would you mind stepping away from your bag a moment, Reverend...." Lar regarded the passport: "Father Op."

Vater Ayrton Van der Op obeyed. He was elbow ushered by the Constable to an adjacent yellow wall which held one poster of offending Class 'A's in not at all stylish light and one poster of disallowed weapons: antique Samurai swords, Damask scimitars, Macau flick knives. Lar had Ryan decide the LV. In human comparison the 84 year old spaniel gave each sector an exhaustive, exhausted nasal audit and came away wagging. Was the fellow gone awry? One minute all snarls, the next wag, wag away. Lar brought the dog to beneath the priest. Lar made twice with his nose a faint "sncf sncf" noise. Ryan took command. A quick sniff of the left ankle sock, a lengthier one for the right. Left shoe no study. The right shoe got thorough attention. Ryan imagines all the spayed and bollock-sure Eindheavies, and Den Bossy bitches. Ryan looks up and catches Op's eyeline and boy does he growl his growliest without the indiscretion of fang baring. Lar must act upon the suspect suspicion. He progresses to a touch search. He locates an iphone in pocket left, a crumpled cloth kerchief in pocket right with the simple darning: 'OP.' The fellow had no money but in his wallet was an ABN Visa Gold Card with Ayrton Van Der Op expiring July 2031. As Lar fumbled across the Priest's shirt, he could not but notice how firm were his pectorals and there'd be a six or even an eight pack surely about and above the navel.

"Quite the athlete for your age," he said aloud.

Father Op smiled his fifty two year old smile. With that Lar said "pack your things unless you have something about your person you wish to declare. Admit and there'll be no need for further probing."

Father Op showed neither relief nor candour. He placed his hand inside his breast pocket and ever so slowly removed a slither of beef jerky and wiggled it in front of the discomfited Ryan who snapped it in a blink, gone, one scoff and with his aged tongue hanging forth he gave off joyfully like he'd sorted every dastardly hound of Baskerville that'd ever dared Knock.

CHAPTER FOUR

The snow generalised early that late 2022 and then a late
November warmth from the South disappointed both real and
inner children. In the East particularly those who had rolled up a
snow man in haste the evening before were faced with thin pale
ice dukes that dawn, their leprous carrot excuses for noses
haunting and dripping.

Anton Fruen tested his D6 *cul-de-sac* for black ice and went
fetched his twenty one gear mountain bike and implanted his
luminous green nano-ears. Two Didos, a Plexi and a Pet Shop
Boy later he was in the bike zone of Adelaide Buildings. His legs
felt great and in two days he'd be stretched to the sun in
faraway-land. Despite his freckles he had the Vi-kingly gene that
meant his skin sort of gilt edged, rather than burnt in proper resort
sun.

Anton had so hurried he failed to note a lovely looking foreign
woman who was viewing the hammy display of old curios about
the Department's foyer. She strolled her lovely legs in the
gentlest clack and another so polite clack, taking in the history.
She was stalled in front of a glass case that told the story of
Madonna Oil in less than a square yard just with faded *Evening
Press* clippings. (Madonna were the first to dare wonder that
there might be more than whale blubber in our waters to light our
lanterns.) Central in the display a dotty snap of some glistening
Texans grabbing Premier of Ireland, Sean Lemass's hand. They
all looked well oiled. 1958 was how far back it looked. The
lovely lady removed her Jackie Ohes and made plane to klep eyes
at Anton. 'Maybe she is speed memoring the entry code,' he

thought 'and what an odd tourist to find out our hydrocarbon museum so early in the morning.'

In the busiest day of his then life Anton physically restacked all the 3D material plus inputted into the "Oil Conference: 2023+Beyond" spreadsheet all possible potential zones of all the untaken blocks of all of Ireland's gazillion half quarters of hydrocarbons. He parcelled all the duplicates and requests re. blocks from within eyesight of the British Rock o'Rockal to the gannet dark skies o'er Macdara Basin, not a million miles from Moneygold and from the thin pickings of oil pockets between Saltee and uncertain Hook and, from the bounty of Corrib Erris to the great unknown seabeds, vast and nameless, underworlds the size of Munsters, play named be bored Tolkien reading size-mologists, wizening Dereks 'n' Niges sorts in the depth charging tugs of the mid 80s: Mordor, Erdogan, Isengaard and precious little Golum a far far cry from Loop Head: these were the names clept to the precious possible oil seems neath the whale-lanes, so far so invisible from the solid sheer o'landmass. 5pm Friday, December 2nd 2022 was the date set for this free-for-all stake your claim of an Oklahoma of a gas 'n' oil conference. St. Helen's Hotel in Stillorgan was chosen as it could be locked down for protests; if any cared to. The extravagance of the conference and the extraordinary terms it promoted was the giddy wild card of the then exiting, acting Minister for the former Energy, Gravity & the Smattering o' Pass Irish Department. In lesser thinking oleos industry circles it was seen as a daring-do gauntlet. The dumber runts of the oil sisterhood believed they saw through the veiled bluff calling, like's if they were hearing a loud challenge "Here Yee. Here Yee. Is there a feck load of gas 'n' oil or feck all in our grey mermaidless world ?" being shouted out from the pent upper office of Adelaide Buildings. "Yee've all that fancy finding technology so go do your can-do," said like an after shock from the rural auctioneer TD turned minister of yahooing. If you yahooed the detail and had your small print specks on you'd see that submissions could be altered right up to the last day of said Conference, highly unusual.

"The terms for the winners are really shocking favourable. It's a bit more scientific than just choose your red or black square, you know on the roulette. It is all about info and the has-info chaps versus the has-nots, this round gonna be extremes-mega-divided." Anton half gist-recalled Paul 'Dots' Dingham whisper shout to a lawyer-in-law or someone's sister one day on an off the record sounding phone call.

The flashest wing in all the post downturn dreer of the Department of Energy, Fastnets & Cliffhangers is The *Bord Sol-athair Peitriliam* itself. It has a water cooler with fizzy Italian water even. The *BSP* was entering its slackest time. For the fortnight or so in advance of the licence for exploration application date there was a moratorium on information. Neither latter day JD Rockefellers, your Yamanis, nor hanky-standing Hugheses, nor the minowy prospectors in classy glassy offices from Ranelagh to Thorgaardlaan, Stavanger, not even the able bodied fracking gunslingers could disturb staff at the Ministry with 3D this question or who owns that rusty rig I saw on me Google Mac Mercator the other week. No more phoney war like silence and a click and then ring ring again; some Mr. Minnow in short pants "I got cut off, got caught short...... the other last thing who, who's relinquished that bubbleen of once hopeful so seventies slick out there beyond the golf lanes of Ballyconneely, in the lee o' Slyne.....?" That kind of copper faced pub talk nine to five.

This slack period was exactly when Anton went got a shed load of Vitamin D, oftener than not, without his more than civil partner. They took a week for sure early Summer in Sitges for first anniversary, Cap d'Ail the second, Mykonos the third but that caused jealousy accusation ructions, all rainy early 2020; such venom and loaded silences till Padraic 'ventually kissed Anton on his favourite tender side of his neck and forgave him; genuinely and proposed full blown marriage and since then rosy round the door-ville.

Dark as, four forty and Anton had still to send thank-you update to Grog Instruments in their head office in downtown Stavanger. Anton's never been there but imagines it like a cold version of Waterford and oily seabirds, squalling and desperate, and sixty K plus Saabs keeping up with each other. Grog's 3D-ing had come up with some gorgeous roundels of rock formation between Fanore and the edge of the precipice the industry had at first jokingly called *Tir na nOg*; it was that far out. Anton's eye was caught by a light coming on in the co-eval building floor opposite. His right brain only noted that he had never seen a light there before. His left brain busy ticking off an endless list of Anton-only-knows-things, things that needed resolving before evening or the Irish hydrocarbon universe would do a lemming on herself.

Between Adelaide Buildings and its southern shadow was a car park for who knows who, parking ever in shade, then a yellow brick wall giving out to a stinky Victorian garden not tended since George V, then a five story building, all tall and casements. There, there it was again, a shadow in the light. Anton was drawn to the window. A second light clicked on in the far window left and then the non descript silhouette turned itself sideways and Anton gasped - there was only one torso without shoulder pads of that extent. He bet himself: P 'D' Dingham. Anton came away from the window and his first thought was extended late lunch breaks, second thought was often enough he'd espied Dingham about the Canal area ways after Dingham claimed to be heading home or squashing a chum. Anton caught the lift to the lobby.

Terrence the Security said "G'nite Anton. Enjoy," and buzzed the palpitating clerical officer out.

Anton turned right, right into Battered Wives Lane and then some short steps and right along a canal skeined with ice and saw angry ducks dumbfounded, their webs not liking the ice one bit. There was a refuge of a bench facing the canal. Anton sat in minus two, looking over his shoulder at suspect building. In its front same light, a dimmer, if trendier light, not so fluoro-storagie as the room facing the Department of Energy, *Inish*es & Lend-Uz-a-Tenner. To be not so nosey, Anton took in the hungry ducks. He was lucky that he was wearing his Banana Republic pilot jacket. Furry collared. He decided to man up the stake out. Perhaps the bell markers or some top brass plate might hint at what affairs went on beyond the sunfade, dead salmon matt door o'26 Herberton Parade. Perhaps he was simply tired, only deluded that P.D. Dingham was moonlighting or whoring or double jobbing. As the light above stayed on and highlit nobody, Anton summoned Chance and strode across the road. The set of bells were bedsitty dingy, a faint 'D. Halpin, a 'Ben Hammoud' or 'Hammond,' a 'Burlington Corps,' a 'MacDiarmaida,' a 'Dos Santos Exports,' and top most, 'E flat' with its light broken and its piece of paper blotted and damp. Anton turned away from the door and returned toward his bench and the unflappable ducks watched him in case he was dangerous or himself hungry. Then Anton turned to regard again the window and SNAP his eyeline was zip-lined with the head turn of Dingham whose head the previous nano-second had been possibly pored-over paperwork. An impossible glare. They knew each other too well. Anton bent to feign a lace tying, fumbled and quick paced back left, left, left and pale as snow enters the Department of Sapped Energy, of Land, of Dust.

Anton bleeps his pass at the turnstile. Terrence Duffy has his hush puppies up on his round lobby desk and is hidden behind his *Herald.* Anton could be anybody inputting the 7 1 3 0. Wrong 1 7 3 0.

"You again ? Don't work too hard !" says Terrence lowering the headline: MECCA SIEGE: DAY 2.' "The *Hutis.* Jayzis could you credit them," says Pundit Terrence. Anton agreed that you could not credit them; just to be on his way and hasted toward the basement imagining a toilet visit to be a remedy. Too bewildered to pee, he went whetted his face once, thrice. He placed his wet hands in the fake Dyson and hated its jet loudness. He was drawn to the data vaults which were nearish the toilets. Here were the towering swivel shelves and he made straight for the 3000s and unwound them, ran among them: "Don't squash. Don't squash me. Please. Please." 315.. 3150, 3152, 3153.... 3154. Many boxes were missing. He was drawn to 3154. It was different, tilted some. Opening it, there was the pen drive. He regarded the 2.5D seismic data and knew it was amiss, the writhing lines across the green coloured graph paper were altered some or downright made up, their usual ample lines were flat, meaning hopeless, not a suck o' diesel. Steps, footsteps clacking along marble. The 8 foot tall vault zone door, opened. Footsteps came closer, the 0000s, the 1000s, the 2000s, the 3....... Anton saw the Slieve League of shelving move as if towards him, then towards him, as if the cliffs of Hades were going to make pastrami of him. "Cripes." Then they stopped.

"Terrence told me you'd come down here. What brings you here so late?" Dingham seemed to have his hand idling on the shelf swivel.

"I.....I'm returning something."

"Aha!" and he stepped in front of the shelf corridor. "Anton. Do you often loiter about the canal after dark?"

Anton only had to put one two and two together: he'd rapid reasoned that Dingham was having an affair with for example an iffy Ukrainian, a size 38 Bulgarian and that he'd rented E flat for same liaisons and good luck to him but he also felt that, that Dingham's mooching about was in a space that was neither apartmental nor all-because-the-lady-loves-Milk-Tray in terms of soft lighting and some decent heating beyond a Super Ser.

"So you're tired of your lovely darling that you dawdle in the cold." Dingham clanked the shelf swivel and narrowed Anton. "Are you inventing a new cruising ground?"

"No I am trying to understand why this box here was empty, was not logged in the log as empty and now it has some of its contents back, not all of them, but this material is not correct and there are other boxes missing and others not in the correct...."

".....not creckt." Dots tries to imitate Clondalkin Talkin.

"3154......"

"3154 is no concern of yours."

"Why were the Malayans not given due access?"

"Why do you think ?"

"You're trying to keep its potential to yourself or inside trade it or ..... You were so obviously blocking them. It was clearly very obvious."

"Look seriously, Anthony. It is not so stealthy. The Minister is seeking to encourage another party, closer to our national interest to vie for your precious 3154. Let's leave it at that."

Dots Dingham leaving much unsaid swung about and stepped briskly to the stairwell. Anton half dawned that 3154 was an iceberg's tip of a wider shenanigan but was so relieved that his *1984* pet terror moment once arrived, had abated. The shelves were unmoving.

"You so deserve your break Anto," echoed Dots going up the wide bare stairs. "Kisses to all them future Mizz Tunises isn't it ?"

As far as Anton could recall he'd not informed a single coworker where he was away to that very night, not even Tanya, least of all the Dots Dingham and just then his CouchSurfing App pinged on his 9S and he received a *'Si Amigo'* from a Noim in Tunis.

CHAPTER FIVE

Vater Van der Op was learning his ropes. He had performed the
Knock's outdoor Stations. A brisk icy drizzle hurried him from
one to the next. Grundtvig D154 satellite kept apace of him and
noted at 9:39am and seventeen seconds precisely he entered the
sacristy. Vater Van der Op is visible on CCTV. Even sacristies by
now have the CCTV. Silverware is very feckable. Op decides to
wear his surplus with no trousers, kisses the alb before donning
it. A Mr. Payne, a volunteer sacristan, who himself had been
abused, saw the kiss and managed to make his face wrinkle,
nearest a smile as he could achieve, while yet manoeuvring the
Dutchman into his tight fitting chasuble. Op ran his finger across
the missal to get the timings right and come to terms with any
O.T.T. ecclesiastical terms. If Sector H of Dutch Secrecies knew
the lengths of his method they'd've the first and last chortle were
he to get the Oscar for most supportive priest. Secrecies are
housed in a non describable dull Le Corbusier pastiche of a
fensterless building in the 'burbs of Hilversum. A note for
Compare & Contrast: the Dutch secret service's vectors is as good
as invisible unlike their British counterpart lording it in their
Apocalypto-Aztec of a temple-upon-Thames, there be Vauxhall.

   Mrs. Ewing loved ten mass at the Apparition chapel, She felt
the done up Basilica still a hangar for some concrete yet uncertain
sky god. Though its walls had been softened by the gorgeous
mosaic, by tapestries of Ireland's triple patrons, otherwise ones
prayers got blocked somewhere in the sextangle of a where-house
of the place. Lar had not argued faith and reason these long years
with his wife. His principle principles were softening that he

could now enter a church to share the matches and despatches. He loved the *bonhomie* of the uninvited of a funeral but a stocious marriage was good pendulum time wasted. This blue sky freezer of a day Lar accompanied his wife as his shift wasn't till the Liverpool take off at 13:40. Mostly he attended as he was curious to see the Dutchman interact with the God. He was grateful that he'd not gone the full monty of the latex probe with a gent who'd be housling his wife's tongue. Mrs. Ewing was right and fitting old fashioned, not given to hands on bread of Life.

The Apparition Chapel is on the south, south west face of the real 1840s chapel of Our Lady. Mother Mary came to where she was welcome and known. On a typically pouring August 21st 1879 the Our Lady spent two hours beaming at an ever growing gaggle of well wishers some time just about sunset or so or hard to tell it was that overcast. She said barely nothin' or actually nothin.'

Vater Van der Op cat walked out in a Bunratty green vestment swish for swish Vatican Calendar 2023 material - minus a sorrowful decade or so. He had put it in Mrs. Ewing's head to encourage Lar to attend his mass and was delighting to see Lar five seats from the top, quite an affront for borderline peasantry registered Op, himself a minor 'risto, a Brabant, though illegitimate. When he got to the *Confiteor* he made his first quite loud *faux pas.* Instead of 'I believe in one god' he said 'we believe' but then again the Netherlands was a clotted population of a place and the mostly Mayo congregation forgave. Privacy would not be easy in such a country and they'd had brutal schisms and religious wars over much worse than pronouns reckoned the mostly pension age crowd. The first reading was about Abraham hearing voices to kill his son and then at the last minute he got sense and a two yearling scruffy yoh got killed in his stead and was feasted on after the episode. The Op had invited Mrs. Ewing to do the Second Reading and the Responsible Psalm; she said yes and it was years since she'd had a mic tilted toward her apple red lips. "The Lord is Our Countenance and Protection." The only thing Lar picked up on as he day dreamed was the word chrism which sounds like prison and he wondered what kind of stuff was it made from - he reckoned it was some kind of resin found under deserts in the roots of some thirsty cactus there out beyond and before Palmyra; wherever that was. His Eir cell was on plane mode so no googling during mass he told himself. The Gospel concerned the convertible tax collector.

Despite the weekday Op gave a sermon. Another *faux pas*: he thought all masses had sermons.

"I'd like to thank you all for letting me honour Our Lady by saying your mass here for you today. Netherlands has never had an apparition of Our Blessed *W*irgin. Our nearest is among our cousins the Flamz.

"At the time here in Knock there was much rebellion and land agitation particularly about here in May-oh." said he with his long drawn out 's-Hertogenbosch drawl. "Fr. Cavanagh was P.P. here at that time and he was adamantly against the land reforms that would give land from the English landlords to the Irish peasantry. He was a very big fan of *status quo*."

Lar became alert.

"Now at the time there was some touring circus type troop doing their summer circuit of Ireland. They were a mixed bag of jugglers, fire eaters but among them a Mr. Ernest Diano had a cumbersome contraption. Now I remember; their names was THE SWIRLING BILLERICAYS. The hefty contraption was what we'd term a jack-o-lantern, like for primitive image making. It is known for sure that they performed in Headford Town on August 18th and again in Castlebar on August 19th so might we wonder where were they on the night of August 21st 1879. We know that like our lady of Knock in particular, a Jack Lantern image doesn't portend, it was silent. The ripple effect of the Apparition here was not immediate. Within a few years devotion gathered a pace and it calvinised the plain farming people to their mother church, that the Mother of God had deigned to appear in this wet farmland sent the people back to their beads, renewed their faith. Davitt's Land League reforms played second fiddle with a thin bow about the bauh-hogues. Five generations on of Irish people, look where we are" and he poised for effects and there were few. "Look where we are," he repeats and Lar wonders how the Dutch National could make such a quick Mick of himself. The congregation were long used to listening to their heads and not their priests when sermons were non-modulating so the news that Goddess had been a figment of some bizarre panteloomed roaming pack had gone angel like over their heads. Mrs. Ewing caught the lion tamer's name, Ernesto and recalled IMPORTANCE OF BEING EARNEST and wondered how a tot'd survive time in a handbag. A large portion of the other mostly widows copped quick enough that this contrarian Dutch hunk o' priest must have tipple issues. Lar could hardly articulate a gathering worry that this icy enough priest of Holland must be bipolar.

".... and of course millions have been healed in soul and body visiting here. I'm hoping for my own miracle and he eye-lined Lar. "Right now there is a low murmur I hear, of a new agitation and it is about hectares of sea and who owns their bounty. If all the seas and land of Ireland were combined then divided equally between every northern woman, every deep southern modern man, every babe and twink of this island; all would have a wee holding of 55 saltwater acres apiece; but is that a likelihood? There has been no believed out-of-the -ordinary since 1879. The new Jack Lantern's are the make believe of Sky and the Fox" and like he was playing charades Op created an air rectangle, his great hands coming out from his nun-sewn sleeves to emphasise some top of the range wide-screen. "Ignore at your peril. In the name of the *Vater, Zohne* and holy ghost."

Lar returned from his airport shift to find Vater Op supping a little sherry in front of the ominous swirls of Vecta fake coals. He was reading he couldn't see what, sat in Lar's florid chair.

"Your wife says you have a second job, correct me if I am wrong, water divining." and he doesn't even up tilt from the VIP magazine; its cover has Queen Katherine receiving a bouquet of hepatica from a gat-toothed Kiribati boy.

"That is half sort of right. Not much, just when there's a call for it, outlying planning."

"Are you working on a divine nowadays? I'd love to see it work. It is a science; heh? Do you use the twigs, the rods?"

"Neither. " he didn't want to reveal his jujube.

"Plumb line?"

"Pendulum" Lar decided perhaps if he took the Dutch man out for a divine, even a proxy one, he'd keep him away from Mrs. Ewing.

Lar shuffled. "Would you mind sitting over this side." Lar pointed to his wife's less florid chair. The priest obeyed. That reseating act of chess assertion sent them into a spell of man silence.

"There's a site on the slipway out beyond Ballyhaunis road turn. There's a good water supply there surely but where is the question."

"Many wheres yes; I'm sure." For a man who had so clearly promoted a line of discussion; he could maggot enough disinterest when it went suited him weighed Lar but he kept with the humouring.

"I've an ole ordinance of the site, inch to the mile and I have already divined it but I double check usually; after a feed we can go out."

"To what degree of accuracy is your ...... craft?"

"I don't need really go to the site at all. I can go figure from the map or chart of a thing.'"

"Highly unusual."

"For appearances sake I walk the land with the owner but to save time I go to the patch where I know drilling should take place."

Op, hardly without a hhmmmm or a haw but with the gungho of a citizen of a doing land barks, "I must to accompany you on your next occasion." Lar turns to fake coal watching to not answer right then but eventualies, "you were lucky there was only the widows about this morning, huh?" He gives the priest an air elbow dig.

"Excuse me."

"You're a rare sort of a priest. Your few words at mass today weren't the typical."

"You were the only one to notice. God the others didn't bat....."

"Why did you do it?"

"Testing. Testing. Testing." and the artifice of a circular priest impersonates a CB trucker while knuckling his left brain. "I said my sermon because in my kurt research it seemed to be true. The British Crown dreamt up all sorts of means to confound the enemy."

"Are you a radical, Father?"

"Perhaps at this age when we are meant to buy the red Maserati, I have become a little contrarian."

"The menopause." and Lar blushed with the obvious stating.

"In the 1870s the British Office of the Interior that Palmerston had long while before set up set out strategies to regain control of rural Ireland. Parnell and Davitt were succeeding; they were too, too intelligent."

"A fake Virgin? That's stretching the bounds."

The Dutchman then told the by now infamous legend of the final collapse of the Zulu warrior empire. "The British bribed a soothsayer to prophecy that when the moon covered the sun, the grains, the cattle, should all be destroyed, must be and only then would the white man be rolled up and spat out from Zululandia. Within weeks the eclipse came. The Zulus had been told that the burning of their crops and slaughtering their cattles would be the needed action for their gods to spit out the British fellows." Lar listened as the imaginary flames of the Vectra swirled infernally. "A famine ravaged the Zulu lands and the British astronomers congratulated themselves and the military doubly much and a land as great as Upper Egypt and bounty with plenty and the Zulus became the underground people, extracting gold for the hon-key."

"Sure the Brits; yarrah you know. So did you come here on pilgrimage to tell us that, that the Virgin o' Knock's a jack-in-the-box ?"

"I came here for a break. I am not only a pastoral priest but I'm a lecturer in Leiden Catholic University. I lecture part time in the anthropology of religion."

"Lies, more like." Lar is confused whether he is dealing with proper cloth or a socialite with delusions of some sort. Op is a little put out that his Brit-bashing is gaining him no kudos.

.

Lar and Vater Van der Op bonded oddly the next day during the divining. Lar hadn't known it but the owner had the drillers

Brody 'n' Brody special up from the Midlands to bore. So the water-divine and the doing were done in one single mid afternoon.   At two hundred and thirty foot, Brody's Texan-looking driller-killer of a truck struck a rich stream, three hundred gallons an hour and sweet. Brody the Senior's mouth was his Chemistry Set and taking the dirty heavy gauge lock o' pipin' he diverted a gush o' the hose to his gaping perfect teeth and declared it "the best stuff." After this triumph Op says to Lar let us get "varm and wittled at the International."

  Mrs. Ewing's book club was Thursdays so Vater'd thought to invite Lar to dine. Lar ordered the soup, a main of the supreme and a winter amphitheatre of a soufflé drizzled on by a royal purple coule of forest fruits. The man o'the cloth snapped and fussed that he'd need a glutton free dish and the only hope was an auspiciously large terrine of indescribable Ocean creatures which he slithered into himself at the pace of Lar's three courses. Tina from the grotto office's way younger sister Megan served them with child in oddly high heels reckoned the double Dutch agent. She liked working winters at the International Hotel 'cause the coach tours didn't come then. When the second carafe of lime water arrived Op overcame the insecurity of the security man.

  "Today Lar not only did you know the spot to drill, but you predicated the rate of flow. How's that done?"

  "It's not difficult. Flow is easy. Rate of flow I mean.   Three hundred gallons. Not bad." and Lar napkined his gravy lips.

  "And you can achieve it simply from the map?"

  "There's a greater swing on site, but the answer's the same." Lar mattered little the facts.

  "You must be in demand."

  "Not so much. The odd word of mouth. I am not my own best publishist. Put me foot in it, Flo says."

  "So water's your thing !"

"80% of the time. Yes."

"So you do other stuff, like....?"

"I do sidelines but very much to try myself, pinpoint things, sometimes at great depth."

"Lost pets?"

"The odd mutt."

"That's it?"

"Well no."

"Not quite?"

"I can locate pet-or-il. Imagine," Lar whispers that others in the restaurant should not hear his stupidity.

"Well. Well. How interesting."

Tock tick, tock tick, tock tick. The occasional B&B which would be starred 'n' tripadvised as middlin' good, lower middle class, their doilies for example might be a tad too cream, the rubbers of their fridge seals somewhat fungal yet same could have some Class A gentry heirloom that creates an atmosphere. In the Ewings it was a grandfather clock from the 1870s and its tock was the score of the ground floor, up to the landing.

For Lar divining was as simple as making O_2 into CO_2, what's called breathing. Lar knew he was himself a seventh son. One time he had pondered it but that thought never doubled nor got into trouble beyond his working out that his own father was a fifth son and that was that. Nobody'd past down that twin male identikits, wannabe or would-be uncles for Lar, had stillborn in Tuam maternity on the 5th of November 1949. A Spinster aunt in Cleveland Ohio did remember remember the fact and wrote it up in a family history that was never ever read by anybody else, that Spinster is now rested in the Calvary Cemetery looking toward Lake Superior. The family history is chalk boarded over in a loft refit done by a very extended Vietnamese family who needed extra in-law space above the Spinster's *hygge*-bare house.

Lar then is the seventh son of a seventh son of a seventh son of a third son but he does not know the fact. Key to each of the gifted ancestral seventh sons of seventh sons was the ability to defy liquid through solids, even if same solid was itself and foremost beneath liquid, even a distant part of an ocean could be sized up. Finding was seemingly natural and effortless for this Mayo man. Oddly it was Lar's great grandfather Pious Ewing (seventh son of a third son), who was maundering across Poker's Field on that pissing night of Our Lady's apparition, had past the mountebank's wagon which had a great girth of wheel, riveted together against the bockets of the zaggy lanes about *Cnoc*-without-Mary-in-the-Mire. The clutch of circus sorts were drunk since leaving Slattery's public house in Roundfort. Pious took a long enough time to divine what he was looking for, using just two hazel fronds. When he succeeded he returned south and his better eye's attention was tweaked by a so called light against the gable of the Knock church, phosphor bright by the time it caught the wile in both Pious' eyes. 'What could it be only but something to ask of later.' "What was that light about half past six or later? Why in Heavens so bright like's if Fenien Froncy'd borne his plump albasters, breaches about the calves?" That it was the Nazarene's tele-pathetical Mother busy with her appointed hypnotherapy was not a first conclusion for Pious who was glad three farthings richer for locating a lost sheep in a fairly Biblical thicket of blackberries. His success was a clear two fingers to the loveless sodding excuse for that most sodden Summer of '79. Pious hid the coppers in the giant tock-tick clock, itself twice half door sized.

The same clock that Lar Ewing dusted every other month in the hallway. Fr. Op and Lar had retired to the Ewing garage study of a potential granny flat for a cocoa before bed. Fr. Op thought the tock 'n' tick of the clock asymmetrical, loud enough through closed door and he chose the 'outbreath' of the tock to say:

"That's a strange map of the sea Lar."

"Huh !"

"That on the wall."

"Yes, a big sway of sea. Well I'm ready for the shut eye," and he rises from the chair. Lar recalled some garbled reference to the Ocean made by the so called Priest in his sermon. The Priest's tilting at Lar's windmills was starting to make Lar queasy.

Op blue-eyed him. "There's said to be a lock of oil out there or gas, out there," says the hot about the collar Lowlander with his colloquier-than-thou Connaught regional.

"Yes there's an awful amount. I been saying it for years."

"Who to ?"

"To myself, " and that was as near as Lar could get to a determination.

"You know from the pendulum; don't you?" and Op held Lar priestly by the elbow. He had risen.

"Nothing a priest should think much on. Sleepy now father ?" Lar for the life of him couldn't quite recall how Op had wheedled him into his study. The rich and lengthy dinner had taken his energy.

"Beg you a moment. You said that you can divine water remotely. Could you also do oil?"

Op trod over a mess of foolscap and pointed to a marine map on the wallpapered wall. He chanced his Navy Seal fingers across the lats and longs of a vast western Ocean, then dropped the hand, South. Lar'd drawn some faint pencil lines over the map.

"Here. How about it *au hazard*. This place. This, I don't know how you refer to them?"

"Block."

"Block. Yes."

"Block three one" and Lar tilted his bifocals, "block three one five four. I haven't done that boyho yet but some of its neighbours."

"And why has your skills skipped it?" asked Op loudly, needing to zap the sloth of unworked out reluctance from, in Op's eyes, a man who was clearly part Firbolg.

"I am working my way round the coast clockwise going outwards, like *arron-dise-ments* and it is just that I have not reached that one yet."

Mrs. Ewing knocked on the door. Op grimaced.

"Fancy a top up and look glutton free HobKnobs?"

"Yes. In a while. In a while. I, we'll come out. Just in a moment." Op answers like he could *ex-cathedra* rude as he pleased in not his own house.

The door hardly reshut and Lar pipes up low "I'm not a circus trickster."

"Meaning."

"Means, I can't, well won't just go at it."

"So do it in private. I respect that."

"Take your drink and come back. Watch yourself some telly."

The Basilicas lights turned off as it was ten on the dot and the village fell devil dark. Half those asleep were dreaming steadily, others drew blanks and remained oblivious and half serene. Those still at their wide screens were mostly on *Prime Time* a fuss about a misappropriation had become ads and part two a long winded tribulation to the just dead, well severed King of all the Saudites.

Op was pale with the telly or as Mrs Ewing saw it, in the telly glow. Op was rude with disinterest in her pink dressing gown gabbling. He could've hit her to be quiet. You'd swear the King Saudi was his cousin and he was the last to know of his demise.

Seeing that the TV was more pertinent to the priest than her ailments and cold predictions Mrs. Ewing commented that the bearded king had the longest name surely ever. Op knew he must now faster than fast track. He needed seven deep breaths, to his usual two and that allowed him settle his head a moment - at least for now the first semi-unsuspecting step had been made and Mr. Lar is doing some beneficial Yuri Geller on some needling point in the heavy neap swells off Galley Head. 'I must keep him safe,' thought self styled Op and he outstretched his clasp of fingers and his knuckles made mighty crix.

CHAPTER SIX

Jarlath Duhallow, Anton's boss was only one of two top civil servants invited to the 8 a.m. on the Q.T. round table meeting held at the Cabinet room, notionally the least bugged of the *Dáil* rooms; the third 2022 Committee in as many weeks.

"Wake up. Sir."

A trail of black hybrid Lexi slished through sleet and silently made a cavalcade of high self importance passed Barclay's, up Molesworth Street then through the security gates of power into Bowl 5 of Government Buildings. Duhallow woke to and jounced his cranium on the bazooka proof window. The chauffeur borrowed from the Minister of Justitia opened the Secretary of the Department of Energy & Strand's door and handed him a thin dossier with a harp on its front, top, middle; all held together by a paper clip, an offensive pink.

The meeting was mostly Cabinet; those already arrived were making their rackets in couples and threesomes, suited to the nines. Scant women of import clustered with their fellows. This was all about final touches to the fast approaching ceremonies to celebrate the Century of Self, one hundred years of the State of Independence, to backslap free flowing rivers and all those tributaries babbling and overflowing the girth and length of all her twenty six counties plus the six new reluctant shall-bees. Duhallow wasn't sure why he was there apart from being a wise guy and if he could be cajoled to opine usually his very not Barrys-Town-tone made dubious quarterly actions appear long term and wise.

A Junior Minister, 'for what, ah yes Youth Suicide appeared to be chairing, responsible for that laughable campaign a year back or more '*nobody wants to die, nobody wants to come back.*' Duhallow could not recall his new portfolio but he was famous for highlighting the numbers of young dead males about his constituency that is cleft along the Suck Valley. Bored Duhallow wondered how the chap'd look when he'd fully grey and he'd make the right looking district-court-of-a-judge-alike. The racketeers came to, sat in front of their brass badges. DR JARLATH DUHALLOW sat at his with a dreamy view over the roofs of Freemason's Hall. Well he knew it and 'neath its slates the Egyptian Lodge's loft of pillars and sphinxes. Duhallow scanned the agenda without specs: 'Bored Gosh Theatre RIVERS RUN FREE three hour special, the parade route, the invitees, and non-invitees, seating protocol.'

His neighbour Minister for Inefficiencies said "did you hear; did you hear Jarlath, King William's responded to the invite through Merrion Road that his wife Kay Windsor, Queen of, would attend the after party at Dublin Castle. Snub snub eh! No more no less."

"Snub double; despite our rejoining the blinking Commonwealth to keep our fucking ducks in order," retorted Duhallow with a golden tone that softened the expletive. "I assume he is catching some early ski action at Grimentz."

The Suck Valley right honourable as if overhearing their chat announces as starters that the King would not be attending THANK GOD but the "Crown Prince George would attend with mummy, not the parade but kind of nondescriptly in the back door for a five course banquet at Dublin Castle."

"George'll get his green jelly," digs Duhallow to his neighbour then reckoned: "they should have sent and we should have invited the two bit Edward of Wessex and his Royal Beardess," and he asides to his other neighbour, again half whispered: "herself a descendent of the "Barons" of Rossport and Polly-Thomas in upper west side Mayo." That neighbour had no idea what chortlings Duhallow was at.

The district-court-judge-in-waiting-stand-in-alike though yet so young was already *Opus Dei* jowly as Duhallow was comparable high degree Royal Arch and his own chin tripling on occasion. The Chair spoke a high pitched middle East Connacht and spelt out the details of the length and duration of the Century of Self parade and an able summary of who'd be sitting to the left or right or arse-ways of the Prime Minister. "The Vice President of the United States was now a security consternation and certainty."

Duhallow regarded the seating plan in his dossier - the Chinese ambassador fifth row back and way left of centre. That wouldn't do; behind the scenes, 'I'll get her her due.' He jovialled to the entire table: "Pity about Kate Middleton, la Wind-sore. She should have been sat under the Prime Minister but then again she's gotten so thin lately she'd hardly guard a bullet for him." The Deputy Prime Minister gave Duhallow the evil eye of Fatima and a tart smirk. So on and so forth and all the meeting did was endorse what was known and make everybody feel connected to Momentousness.

On his way down the blue soft stairs his elbow gets grabbed by the Junior Minister for Insecurity and Nail Biting. She was a strong woman from east Cavan, a lyrical Virginian timbre in her blather. She was Sugar Freddy, *Sinn Fein* in lamb's outfit. She said to him; I've had murmurs at me of recent, something about our seas. That is you isn't it ?"

"Not everything is my fault."

"Not by half," she says meaninglessly. "Listen to me," and she sidles him into a nook. "The Brits are getting wile active these past weeks; their shipping; their navy even, up and down Rockal to Fastnet, on the go. My own clutch of Ass. Principals say to me 'not a bother Junior.' They would wouldn't they. Is there clear protocols for who is up to what in our pond, Jarl.....?"

"Yes and no; what being Commonwealth all over again means is not worked precisely out yet in terms of friendly visits egg setra egg zetra. There are of course the never ending where does our blessed EU begin and end." He moves to disentangle from the Virginian. He gets a step away and was so glad his face was not facing her when she asks.

"And Jarlath any jabs at this: something by the name of 'Fat One;' what might it mean; might be an operation or an exercise ?"

"Pronounce it again." He turns with half regained composure.

She sees she has scared him so she jabs his paunch with her spikey violet wedding finger nail. "Fat One. Fat Fellah. Like that. That is it, up and about the "deep" net-waves. Some god knows chatter is all it might be; Fat One."

"Maybe something the *Garda* are at; they use funny ole names for their cocaine swoops; don't they," Jarlath answers as stupidly as he can muster like he is himself the fat pike of ignorance half clobbered on the bank o' the Suck itself.

Our most hero, Anton Fruen's first Monday waking up for work after his week off. He had two resolutions from his holz: he was going to figure out mindfulness so as not to be such a scatty bee and he was going to really practise loads more assertion; or learn methods of how to fake same. He wrote in his diary:

'Sunday 27 November, 2022: *lgbt swim this evening at Markievicz pool. Glad Padraic stayed clear so I could test tan shamelessly. Interesting the body factor, a lot of the attraction/ repulsion issue. Some serious gorge bods as well as pasty floaters. The breathing that is so important in meditation helps me swimming. I can be mindful of my breaststroke and the breathing it requires to not get so jaded.'*

Anton had grown a stylish stubble, a sign that could be wrongly interpreted as holliers affair. It gets removed before his roughened up self causes aspersions to be cast. He returns to the bedroom from the *en suite* and in the winter dawn light a version of his lengthy other half diagonaled on the bed and snoring a snore of conceited sleep, though so considerate bi day. Anton did wonder sometimes. Padraic would catch a gooh of an ample woman's breasts and rest on them. What a dark bristling face perfect husband, the pale Shinrone calves, the twice county club champion, quiet the hunter and himself the Gathering. Sat on the bedside he sent him golden light of contentment after a Buddhist fashion he'd learnt from the Triratnas on James Joyce Street.

The rigour of the cycled streets o' sleet to work woke him and prepared him for his day. He shook his Gore-Tex in the lobby aggressively.

"You've been gone so long - we'd forgotten the look of you." says Terence at Security.

"Grand spell." says Anton. Thinking and vigorous action not his specialism.

The i-memo on Anton's desk advised his being at the Secretary in Chief's office sharp zero nine thirty. Dingham's separate frosted glass corner office appeared empty and unlit. Anton could not figure what to do nor what to wonder about Duhallow's wanting him so he went as mindful as was manageable, his in breath through the left nostril and out his right and he continued this till nine nineteen then went to the water cooler, village pump *per se*, where Aoife Shaughnessy née 'Dildo' in Dot's Dingham's parlance mind and Anne-Marie Patel discussed *Prime Time*, discussed the frocks of the women who had been talking about answerabilities with regard to appropriateness. Anton pressed the blue presser and half filled his empty cup, then the white presser and filled the half full cup a degree or three. The women's attraction to him vexed and mesmered him, so he pulled away with a polite grunt but one held him by the arm. Aoife, the first born, said to him:

"It's true isn't it ?"

"What's true ?" and Anton wobbled his plastic cup.

"You'll be in the corner office by Christmas at least or before," added Anne-Marie her tuppence.

"The corner office ?" says Anton emphasising his ignorance

"Anne-Marie, which little bird was it told you ?" and Aoife's arm dove for Anne-Marie's funny bone and set off a charge.

"Dot," says Aoife.

"Rumour, real or pretend?" Anne-Marie wagers.

"Cross his heart and hope to....." and Aoife impersonates unwittingly the fifth element of the ritual of initiation of the 19th Degree of Royal Arch Freemasonry be the ancient Scottish rite.

"What are you two maggots on about ?" Anton camps.

"Pro-motion," they jinxed him.

"Be Seated." Anton's enviable legs stretched across the LIDL blue of the what must be an inch and half high weft of carpet, a moor of weaving stretching to the four walls of the Mussolini of an office. The focal point of the carpet was behind Anton, a semi-abstracted sea eagle positioned as if at home in the Oval Office but a lot less certain. Duhallow standing, had his back to Anton and was watching live porn. As he would not pay attention to Anton's arrival Anton must watch along. Without the window, precarious on the sill, was apparent in the drizzle an awkward threesome, attempts and more attempts, coy again, strut, and start the piggy back, back and flutter the slick mother of pearl of the male feathers, then the girls got fed up and flew off north leaving the plump male eejit on his tod, up and down, pace pace, then up he fluttered to glide all dude o' the hood across to the sill where Anton had foreboded Dot Dingham's other life but a week and an half earlier. The bird luck got tried again with other fed up to the teeth females. 'Pigeons and straight men can be so unthinking,' Anton managed to think despite the edgies.

"In ancient Rome. Augurs read much in the action of doves." The Secretary in Chief sat back in his heavy chair, kept a further eye on the fifty shades of grey without then revolved like an impressed 'Voice of Ireland' judge. Duhallow looked beyond Anton at the abstract bird of prey in the carpet's weft. The Secretary of the Department of Energy & Fledgling Puffins spoke from the lip as he leant his unnecessary leather elbow patches on the bog oak Cosgrave era-een of a desk.

"The sea eagle has a greater wingspan than our woolly fellow here." Secretary Duhallow lent further across the enormity of the desk, almost Opel Commodore sized. "Our *olar na mar*, our sea eagle friend can spot its prey from a Slieve League away, a herring beneath a weight of water is hopeless." Mr. Duhallow made fowl claws of his enormous hands grappling the thick fictitious fish. The exertion sent him back to the leather squeak of his provincial throne and Anton wondered why the Secretary in Chief's much younger wife was prone to leaving him; 'surely Jar-Du must, with those huge hands, have matching preferment in the zip zone. All he'd need was a peppering of ole arginine on his meat two veg to overhaul that department, or sneak it on his dippy egg and he'd be back bang buck.' Still the Secretary would not speak so Anton saw the boss in a different light, locks greyish, henna tinted likely, darkly badly and some too many washes unreplenished. He saw him in his bathroom tinting with a Wisdom toothbrush or could his imagined, if occasional wife see fit to help him, to stifle age, and abet in making him young, he-man him again; her Doctor Do-little.

"Are those eagles extinct?" Anton eejitted.

"They're this ten years re-introduced along the cliffs of South Donegal." Mr. Duhallow, fisherman's son, had grown up some miles east of those cliffs between the rapids of the Inny and the ottering of the Oily River. His accent had the mildest benevolence of Donegal but the added sonarity of the oaken refinements of the Kings Inns, long years without ever putting a phrase afoot in the proverbial. Anton felt very Dublin South West Ward in the face of him.

"Anton Fruen. Thanks for taking time out from, from......"

"Re-aligning blocks in the outer West areas in relation to Gardiner's processes and new findings in relation to United Nations Law of the Sea updated 2009 and applying same definitions to more well define the precise location of our Continental Shelf, Sir, Mr. Sec......"

"Jarlath from now on."

"But Mister, Sir, Du. That's not my pro-rogative."

"Well there's some shuffling of the clubs and hearts round here." and he points to the middle of his desk. "So call me Jarlath. We'll be seeing much of one another."

"Jar."

"Two syllables Jar-lath." The Secretary let out a right Bilderberger of a chortle, sort of a chortle that in a month of Sundays the likes of Anton'd never muster.

"Anton, Mr. Dingham has left us. Private sector. Happens to our best. We can't compete with their added zeroes," and making spectacles from the zeros of his fingers Duhallow looked eagily legally through them and half states, half asks: "I want to try you in his place."

"That's two, that's actually three promotions beyond my pos....."

"Jigs and reels. Anton, we have an unusually sensitive and difficult material to make plane in the next eensy short time. The 2023 Expo showcase thingummy is a fortnight off....

"......less than."

"Very inconveniently it clashes with the bloody Centenary shenanigans."

"And Mr. Dingham had charge of the conference."

"You're the only one who knows what he knows."

"I beg to de-fer."

"Explain."

"Nothing. I know the stuff but I am in the backdrops. Will I get help talking to people? What do I need to know that I don't know now."

"Masses Anthony."

"Anton, Sir."

"Just let's get you across the coming rough fortnight, Antinoös."

"Of course. So I should ditch what I'm doing."

"Yes prioritise the blocks that are non licensed according to top down in terms of value or knowledge or both. You know the records backwards. Come to think of it; present them backwards."

"The records going back how far?"

"From the top, Longrun and before."

"To Madonna?"

"Well that's Stone Age where we're concerned"

"But Madonna gave birth to Longrun and the schematic of their twelve mile zone, limit still holds in certain cases....."

"From 1973 onwards. I will, and only I will filter other zones to you over the next fortnight; Jesus a lot less than. Let us keep them between you, me and these listening walls." The tone had grown odd and Anton could read some waver, a shake to the usual bustle of certainty.

"You can have Mr. Dingham's office," got said in an okay-sort-it sort of a tone but Anton got one of his inner mumblings that had to out.

"Jarlath. Has our Department some archive or access in that building across?" Anton pointed over at the questionable building where the male pigeon was fluttering near a mound of guano, two decades worth by the look of it. A building of no importance.

Mr. Duhallow's eyes glared into his paper weight as he pressed his buzzer and leant into the 1980s intercom "Ms.English. Prepare the new shelf maps info for Mr. Fruen. Find him his new zip key thingummy."

The paperweight was a lump of condensate from the Mississippian deltoid formation off Loop Head. It was Jarlath Duhallow's charming lodestone. In it resided his daemon that gave him his self possession. It was a gift from a large American gentleman with systolic 180 blood pressure. He'd come at him sideways at some gaseous conference of the imprecise noughties, the great lump in his hand like he'd caught an asteroid fragment while out for lunch. The lump's story been faxed him. Not long after that his troubles began.

"Good day and congratulations, Principal Officer Fruen. Attention and Commence." At that Duhallow rose saluted like he was white suited military in a tough love remake of a C movie that'd surely wind up in a monumental court case presided over unlikelilly by a black judge, even a black woman judge lording it over the disputants and a wee David o'righteousness winning the day by the last moment's turn up for the best. Anton turned at the door as Secretary decidedly coughed artfully.

"Your new position might involve some secrets acts stuff that you need to keep mum on. It is in the H.R.'s small print. No big deal."

"Jarlath. I get you."

No Dealz that home going. Marks & Spencer's was trawled that late afternoon, its half price sell-by section zoomed past.

Anton brimmed his basket with best bubbly (judged by cost €44.50), Coopershill venison steaks, artichoke hearts that he had heard of but never bitten into, the costliest of dainty mini puddings. In the wee kitchen that stuck into the garden he sizzled and blanched and drizzled. All of a sudden his helmet headed blue eyed Padraic loomed in in time for *Fair City*.

"Wow. What a smell!"

"Deer dear."

"Bought or snared?" said the usual Hunter and he grab hugged the Cooker from behind and kissed the back flap of Anton's left ear as only a tender west Leinster man can.

All soaps were put on Record - a sure sign of serious matters. They sat, Padraic all a wonder why Monday was such a National Banquet. A row of the next door's could be muffle heard like its own episode of a vulgar soap opera through the thin 1940s cement walls. "Your vuckin mother again. She is a criminal, a vuckin crim" a crash and a bang of a door and silence. 'Gentrification my eye' would smart-alec Padraic usually but not this time.

Anton smiled and waited till the final scooping of artichoke then told Padraic the glad news of his preferment. Padraic ignored the proffered glass of bubbling 2013 Moët that sought the clink and strode round the table and placed his Offaly long arms about his sweetheart's head, pulled it gently backwards like some Alexander technique and kissed him where the Brahminical caste believe the third eye behoves 'stinction.

"My lovely Anton you do us proud. Well done. " As Padraic returned to his chair and clinked flutes he saw a chequered patio stretch half way down, then all the way down the garden with the extra p.c.m. income then in its far corner a repetitive water feature that he could not picture but it would not represent a

Bodhisattva but a Attic Nymph of sorts, her gurgles quite quiet, then he perished the thought.

"Will it mean much extra time ?"

"I'll be well able to delegate," Anton lied. 'Ceptin making sure folk called him Anton, not Anthony, he never gathered the bollox to ask a work colleague to do anything.

"Travel ?"

"The odd conference. Mostly means I'll have to know more, or will have to know how to know more."

"Well you're already the 39 Steps when it comes to recall."

Before Tuesday sex they watched two episodes of THE WASTERS, series three. Colin Farrell got to have sex with Julie Christie's niece. "Flabby arse" said Anton at the wafer-wall 50 inch and they snuggled and giggled.

Both lads were sensitive sexperts and in their clownish cloning, each caringly sought, nay fought out the others g-spot or at the least its suburbs. Clones in that they were both one metre and eighty two. 'Tall seeks Tall for time wasting,' not suspecting full on cravats and tails at CityWest Hotel before you could say 'year 'n' a day.' Clownish in that their skin affectations while sincere were laughable, and they were prone to laugh during orgasm where others await the collapse. As they'd become no longer embarrassed by their sameness and their bonding, then binding - they'd annoyed neither themselves nor others when they hosted 170 guests, 70% of them straight as dyes. Their penetrations were as infrequent in proportion to the frequent public assumption that full on entry was the 'dilection most favoured by those devoted to homosexual diversion. Homefield Road #36 was bought from a widow, Kay Shercock, who died in the house from being 95. The re-possession took a fortnight. Her too many varieties and era of wallpapers were blow torched from the walls as if her spirit might be persisting in their paste. The two did that in the height of Summer and shirtless, ten times more home erotic than their over purposeful, over planned honeymoon in Key West.

Turned out there was no sex that Tuesday night. Sometimes good news just makes it unnecessary. They were not ones for occupying all the acreage of the queen side bed. That night Padraic spooned cum hugged Anton in this ratio 3:1. Anton had the escape side of the bed and gazed back across his awfully perfect husband framed against the fawn sponge-paint dabbed wall. Anton was discarding and planning shelving and without accuracy doing a rough *feng shui* of the once 'Dots' Dingham office. It was going to get a family size block of Jade Sage aromatic to counter the six nation straight-as-feck stench of it. He placed his softish penis against foetal Padraic and entered Nod.

CHAPTER SEVEN

The darkness was some sort of sports sock about the eyes. Lar's loins felt cryogenic; he'd peed himself again and again and each relief warmed him but then froze him. Shuffling he met a metal table leg and managed to snag enough sock to reveal the upside of his left eye which gave some optics. There was definitely a lack of windows, perhaps none but there was some natural light. There was air from somewhere or bad insulation in the person high ceiling. There was a key hole and some air sighed through, poured like liquid on top of his utrified, bound body. There was not much on the visible wall, an NCF calendar. Lar viewed it with his head resting on the pillow of dirty carpet tiles and his eyes made the most of the glimmers from the door. His only focus for hours now on end, unending was a 1999 North Connaught Farmers calendar, stuck on April, a glossy photo of a great array of ugly food and a North Connaught Farmer or possibly a butcher of theirs showing off fare, thankfully clothed: all a big picture ad for every possible way of pudding and slicing a pig and about them three litre plastic vessels of low fat milk and litre tetra vessels of milk, lite, lo, buttery and in front of them Lar peered some plasticated orange cheeses towered over by three old time Irish aluminium churns to associate Nature with the display. The churns themselves small beneath the burly butcher or maybe grocer, a fellah of about fifty five or an actor pretending to be same with his arms outstretched, caring and grinning with all that lactose, porcine cornucopia of protein beneath him and his cheeks real or photoshopped, scarlet as a blushing rose or a lapsed teetotaller making up for lost time. His grin was the grin of a feckless universal higher power in the face of senselessness and would be particularly off putting if one was oneself a pig concluded Lar, a pig along with five hundred other pigs in a dirty Scania en route to a euro-battoir; the tags in your animal ears tweaking. None of this would be visible to the horrid eye but for a light from the beneath of the fake teak of a door, and this too was the source of the cold. Such was Lar's internment.

Lar felt not far from his rumbling, but there was this half sense of missing time, a concussion, perhaps a cocktail of drugs, a plane, a rendering. His hands were as bound as were his ankles; 'such professionality.' Unlikely to be North Connaught Farmer calendars in a safe house abroad. The wind felt Irish too, Connaught even. Before he slept again he peed again and it warmed him enough for sleep to grip before his bollix went *gelato*. His dead ancestor PIOUS sent him a dream - the results of which gave him solace and some thud in it woke him. He could not recall the cast, period nor his role in the scenography of this dream and as he woke the door bolt of his prison ran away from home and he returned to the disbelief of his abduction. Occasionally his esteem blamed his belligerent agnosticism for whatever was happening. Even bound and filthy he could not invoke any deity; nor feign a hero within so he was left with just his *nous*, his heartbeat and some wildfire assumptions.   Lar missed his devout wife, his worn slippers and mostly his maps.

One assumption of why the rumble sent his recall back a couple of years, a July fifth, a shrilling kite high over the west fringe of Knock, over the Ewing B&B. Lar heard its squeal and his pendulum was circling circling above a Fate *Teoranta* prospect off Hook, twenty miles northeast of the ooze of oil that lies suspected off the shorelines of Ardmore and nine leagues south south east of the fat Norman black and white lighthouse on the Hook's nose.   Fate *Teoranta* Ltd, with some truth, to excite their share prices, had put about that there was a touch and go condensate at 'X' number of metres in their who knows if it was Wex or Waterford waters. Lar was a feet and furlongs man, God or not, and he translated their 'X' to 'seventeen fathom depth,' oil more than gas by a small amount, one hundred and sixty dollars a barrel would about justify the extractive efforts factoring overtime; a lot of financial quarters and shareholders grumblings'd pass before its landfall might be achieved,' he'd told his self. That day Lar had taken out again the ordnance Map 69, and its sizeable seascape from the dotty, gannet Saltees, a junction for ole UFOs disturbing angry Viking ghosts, and taking in most of the Deise coast to the south beyond ken of the bungaloidal Devonian cottages of south east Wexford. Lar had an intuit, itself informed by his visit to Fate's website where under NEWS was headlined "Hook Find Triples Fate's Share Price." The kite went quiet, dining on his church mouse. Lar recalled he took his pendulum and hovered over the known find of Folio 69. He had charted these waters years before and had noted finds but not been inclined to measure them precisely; now he would. His memory got interrupted.

The bolt shot across and Lar's prison door opened, extra light streamed in. The sock as he lifted his head fell back about his sight, yet he smelt the priest. A metallic plate was placed on the table in front of him and he could smell his favourite: Tesco pock holed crumpet-lettes and a mug of Milo. Only Flo could know such or only the priest could have extracted said info.

"It is you Op. It is you. Talk to me, you blackguard. Op come back here." The door was growled shut, "and we gave you every courtesy."

An hour past. There was a pointless rain falling on the roof. Lar forgot to revisit Wexford, that coast or its offshore in his head. He dwelt on other facets. The door opens and Lar is pulled from the floor to a seat and one hand is freed to let him eat with his fingers, and grasp the cold mug o'Milo. Some device of metal is at his nape. It is clear he is not to turn around. The sock is made tight round his pounding head. The Milo tasted so, so life endorsing, everything a cold grave or a hearse with a busted alternator isn't.

The Dutch agent starts complaining. "So difficult to get gluten free grub in these parts."

Lar is shaken to the core by the self interest of this ice breaker. This faked up priest is beyond pale. Worst psychos have empathy at least in thimbles. Ryan the dog's nose and gut were mostly right about this hokey prelate, Lar weighed up too late. Feck there was some sleeping draught in the Milo; he could sense altered states.

Op said, "we can get you to better conditions and keep your wife safe, if, this time you cooperate with us?"

"You want what of me exactly?"

"We just want your cooperation. How many thousands of times do I need to ask. Sometimes too often you Irish have called it collaboration. Make earth life concur with some semblance of ease. Life is difficult just plain difficult but it needn't be so. I can fetch you warm Milo."

"Please." Lar wondered how he was to placate this misanthrope and how could he escape or survive. First he should not be too contrarian and do everything to assure Flo's safety. He wondered had he been already non cooperative. His last normal memory was Op returning to his study, opening the door. Perhaps the Dutch cleric had smothered him in ether or its likes but no recall of him refusing.

Op came back and had a Milo mug with steamy Milo in it. This in itself was creepy, very, very premeditated.

"Are you feeling disorientated?" Op who up till now had seemed a reasonable chancer appeared to have slid into an episode of *Captive.*

"I feel my pants need changing."

"Before we get you better circumstances. I need to get some sense of how you work. We don't want fear clamping you up. Your wife is safe but she doesn't necessarily need to stay that way in our terms. We can make her pain your pain. Yes. I just need you to know that. However I need you to be clear headed and steady handed."

"Why are you so sure my talents work? I only found water on a bit of a half acre?" Lar decided best not ever repeat a reference to his wife to the psychopath; the nameless shall keep their health and safety.

"Our mole in Fate."

"My, I have badgered one and every oil company in this land and the only joy is to get rumbled by the likes of you."

"Our chaps at Hilversum were gobsmacked. You were so accurate and likes you were working it all out on, on toilet paper." Op sneezed. "We only intercepted what you sent Fate. Had you tried the bigger guns?"

"I thought to stick with Irish tryers. Sure I thought Fate was a big gun."

"They're about as Oi-rish as a pinta Guinness. Not."

"I sent them info about what was below the find they had made, their first find was not moneywise viable."

"Guess what oil barrel is today. Go on."

"Haven't a bog."

"One hundred and eighty five point six. The Arabian peninsula is up her creek so we need to hurry."

Lar wondered why the greedy always needed to keep greedying. "What is your real name?"

The Dutch removed Lar's pendulum from his own pocket and gave it back to him, folded it into his one free hand, like a grandmother might a rosary beads of her first communicant grandchild. Lar was overcharged. The agent made sure the door was shut and removed the blindfold. Lar looked at an unshaven man, like a wind surfer who should have given up two decades back. He was wearing a navy boiler suit without insignia. He indicated a brown paper bag and told Lar to change into *v*arm clothes and he would be back with a leg of lamb and slippery gravied colcannon; another Lar favourite. While undoing Lar's bounds the spoilt priest described Lar's wife's situation being so pleasant but if he ran away or gave it a go the consequence was far from uncertain. The Dutch can really rigmarole.

The captor returned, after twenty minutes and no car noise, with the promised dish. Lar in the *v*arm clothes trapped in the prefab of a metal box with the NCF fellah with the big gligeen grin proffering all his heart attack victuals, stuck in April 1999. Lar looked deeper into the situation and realised with a "Christ" or two that this was not simply the picture for April 1999 but for the entire year. He'd be stuck with the grinning butcher forever maybe. Op was able to turn on a faint bulb from outside the cabin. Talk of good secret agent/ bad secret agent. Next thing Op was is in the door and it is all camaraderie and practical talk like their night out at the International. Lar ate up his grub.

"Run it by me, not the locating but the measuring."

"I need my log tables."

"I took I imagined everything, from your walls, drawers, the loft, all paperwork."

"There is stuff under the sofa, the floor in a refuse sack; keeps the dust off. There is the outer waters in rolls by folio, up under the fake loft." He scoffs mighty dollops of his grub. "That colcannon is better than Flo's." said like as if he denigrated his wife, perhaps she'd be left alone. "The logs you're after. Easy enough. Under the sofa I have a big shiny poster, an ad for a come to a Mickey Flavin tribute night in Hollymount and on the back of it there are four col-umes, one for depth beneath the seabed, one each for the gas and the oil, then another for volume by the square foot of gas, even for small finds, in the small millions....."

"......I know."

"Some of it is bound up tight like in those orange Calor gas bottles; it takes a sizeable cave of gas just to make a bottle."

"Four hundred and sixty two cubic metres in the EU average gas bottle." Op certains.

"Right. Then I have another col-ume for how many barrels of the crude fellah. I don't do depth of sea above seabed much, not so necessary; it's well known, necessary for knowing of course what legs your rig needs, how long I mean and whether the bother is worth it."

Lar assumed that his wife was being kept elsewhere. He'd heard a helicopter off and on but thought it was part of dream time. Lar reckoned he should entice Op to return to his house under some ruse of the divine and the *Garda* would more likely nab him; 'not so likely.' Perhaps if he could suggest a "conjugal" access and his maps back and him back in his converted garage; he could do his divine job properly. Reminded him how Google create atmospheres to ruse their worker's productivity. Was on *The Business*, yes, added frills that Google give to giddy-up their minions; avocado on toast on tap, psychotherapy every second Wednesday, foot massages mid afternoon: 'Sing from our happy hymn sheet.' After so long that nobody gave a tinker's fiddle for Lar' finds; he wondered were his actions those of a traitor but he couldn't be surely; or not yet.

CHAPTER EIGHT

Anton a Principal Officer, "an E.O. was what I saw in me wildest dreams" was how he broke the promotion news to his needed-to-be-seated ma as they collapsed laughing but both his sisters didn't and his mother just had to get the jovial boot in "and with the least Leaving points since records were 'magined." Not true. Mrs. Fruen couldn't believe he'd a team of four to boss at will, "tables well turned; what !"

Dots Dingham retired civil serpent, had had nothing and left nothing on the wall pertinent to his last job remit, just a 2020 calendar of the Irish Draught Horse Society stuck on June with some hippy looking shires trapped in a sad Laois makeshift paddock, mid far too green a grass against a far too bright, yet grey sky. Only item left in his drawers was a prefect's badge from 1989 from some school called Buckminster; chewing gum bound about its pin to keep it from pricking. A canny heirloom to "forget" Anton detectivated. 'This is like an artist's studio my new office, my new home from home, it faces north.' Anton knew this because his first homo-sensual act was with a painter in a lane off a lane off Ely Place or Terrace. He had been drunk and had not recalled the act of decision. I shall now go home, like to embrace and sleep with A MAN. Till then he had had sportive sex with women whose nakedness and various forms of friction could harden him and his heart. Men were mere conjectures in his fantasy island. That night he came three times, once on to an almost complete canvas in erotic crayon that was later sold to a Smurfette for seventy K. His third was accidental and in dawn light and a grand view over the North Side. The painter was half Corsican, half lay man and he said how the light from the north side is immutable and insubstantial or could be and Anton said "tell us something we don't know." The man about town was a model in looks but possessed no smell, possibly because he was 'the Devil or a sorta vampire,' as his apartment was never again apparent in the light of daylight investigation, never find-able ever again, the building, let alone a doorbell.

Anton had had two coats of magnolia to bring the south office wall to life and then he ordered in a load of ply and it got painted just the one coat of magnolia and these boards got joined together and Tanya Gibbons with a 2B pencil started the faintest outline of the one million square-ish kilometres (give or take a crevasse) of Ireland's territory and territorial waters, each degree of latitude a shoe or so apart height wise. She was size five. The longitudes Anton insisted must taper mildly polar bound, tapering up from precisely forty eight degrees atop the North of France to sixty degrees more or less, a stone's throw off the equivalent of Iceland's Carnsore, its scrags jagging at 60N 16W. The south bauble of the Mull of Kintyre like a glottal cock was to be done out in a basic, possibly Campbell tartan to hint that Scotland was relevant and leant scale to the watery enormity. Below that the flat sands of Morecambe Bay and finally (and Tanya needed a power naplette before commencing) a low tided for now charcoal Ireland, all three thousand one hundred and seventy one kilometres of her bay watches and inlets, her imaginary kelp, her pea screedy beaches, her horse gallops of peopleless sand. Ireland appeared so, so east of middle in the overall wall terms, like a crude platform for a higher power, stretching from left of Anton's door seven metres to the east wall, representative of five degrees west of Greenwich to eighteen degrees west of Greenwich. "That's a lotta, lotta seasick to cross beneath you -

that full stretch of thirteen degrees," said Tanya goin' pale thinking about it. All that grand combustible fortune, which if immolated at once would make the planet's ozone blush russet a degree or more. Anton followed her thinking: 'the grid of blocks that divide Ireland's sea also divide Ireland-of-the-Welcomes land-wise.' Anton in the past would have hinted but he now suggested (he didn't order) Tanya that Ireland be a sickly green wash. Tanya did not like it when he took that tone with her.

"What are we to do with Northern Ireland ?" Anton asked the air.

"Make it a tiny bit differenter green." Tanya was sure and she squished some tangerine into a pallet and got mixing.

"You could be right," he said with doubt as re-unity oil-wise, sea-wise was still a lotta lotta St. Andrews agreements of their own off. Way after going home time, Anton was sticking known light houses hither and thither on points and rosses, wholly unnecessary in yellow. Psychologically Anton reckoned they were beacons and warnings simultaneously - otherwise the Ocean was a morass of wobbling blank. Anton had made it plane to Tanya "don't put the extant prospects on and who owns them till you've done the entire map." Tanya couldn't wait to get to cutting out scarlet serge for the Kinsales and Corrib Errises and all the rigs going active in Dooish, Norwegian mostly. "Be sure our continental shelf is as sharp as...." here Anton stalled, "sharp as razors." Tanya stared beyond Anton out the window at a fixed point sideways of what she knew to be Mars, which next to and nodding at Anton's red curls was like a dot of salmon tinsel flicker. Next morning would be time enough for laying out the stunning array of boxes of Ireland's most likely gazillions, that would be stuck on in their differing depths of peach melba of likely-hoods: what'll come ashore now/ likely what'll come ashore in some decades/ then in almost violet: licences granted in the past seven years, then in burnt siena the has-beens, throwbacks to when Bacarra were enticing their Yes-Sirs, mere dots that even if a barrel of oil were a grand they'd rest in peace. Anton did the broad sweeps but Tanya's steady hand did great justice in charcoal. There was also green zones and black diagonal zones denoting for public knowledge/ for Department Officials' Eyes Only zones. 'G's were put on likely gas hopes, 'O's for oil, 'GO's for the both and 'OG's where the oil was more pertinent - but these were anonymous gamblers' surmises, virgin prospects, unrigged, unpricked. After lunch and this was day three of Anton's promotion, Duhallow rapped and without waiting answer fell in and there was Anton on his knees on the beige linoleum stacking and sifting A5 cards in piles. From some of these he was calling out to Tanya the salient parts. Tanya had a pass geography book in her hand which was possibly from the diligent attention she was giving it, inspiring the continental shelf she was etching on the wall, "not quite the Last Judgement," summarises and chortles Duhallow. Tanya doesn't turn her sand of mousy hair because she's stuck on the Scandinavian look alike droop-alike of the Porcupine. It was hard when one inflated the scale to get the juts and crags right. "I should have bothered to get the loan of the overhead projector in floor five," she says excusing her free hand. Duhallow stands over Anton and adjusts his bifocals to focus on how neat the Olympian type of the surely pre 1980s cards appeared. Tanya scratched on silently, perfectly and Anton went beside her encouraging this swirl for that inlet, "nice zag" for such-and-such a crag. Anton thought it was more professional not to stop their activities boss-presence-wise but to plough on.

"My my the *maitre d*'s on his knees."
Anton rose to his hunkers of a sudden like a Moslem from a prayer bow; 'woops: can give your brain a wee cat purr that can.'

"I'm verifying."

"I see." grandpahs Duhallow.

"It's not all computerised you know." Tanya puts out from her still, live drawing.

"Some fairly forgotten zones by the looks of things."

"Oil is set in its way; it doesn't exactly go anywhere." Tanya vouches and she meant relative to an average human's life time it remains in one place but over plasticine eras of aeons it's as errant and flighty as a basin of water flung out the back door.

"A riot of colours for all the find types. Brilliant. I imagine you've exhausted all the known categories of the rainbow." Duhallow condescended and condescended. His mention of the rainbow was just his un-unconscious having a dig at Anton.

"Not yet. If I had my way I'd even have a category for rumours." Anton actually did have such a category and wasn't at ease or disposed to air the idea until he could decide what precise shade of grey the rumours would be, given the gigantic grey anyway Atlantic. 'Come the Conference 2023 at St. Helen's would be time enough' and Duhallow concluded his ludicrous thought: 'he'd also need to weigh up the frequency of the rumour, over time, multiplied by the numbers of pints taken to get some derek-grunt to squeal that they reckon drill attempt 'X' was a gush when it was demarcated 'useless,' 'Y' was barren or vice versa.'

"Here's something very not a gray coloured rumour; I've had the Norwegians on to me." Duhallow quartermasters.

"Oh God." says Tanya to imply, though new, that that means trouble or might mean trouble.

"I think they are mooting a.n.other application, possibly without the Brits and Dutch and more than likely for the bloody same zones."

"Yes. Well I gave them everything or most of everything."

"I reckon the Dutch and Brits are not letting them in on the next applic...."

"They usually pass each other info to some degree...."

"When there's billions in it - the Angly Dutch will quietly shaft," and Duhallow imitates the fisting of a prone Viking. Anton is taken aback and Duhallow swings about to Tanya and remarks.

"Tanya, I thought you were defacing the wall but now I can see how precise you are ?"

Tanya stands back, shows off the just completed and drying greening of Ireland. "I thought won't bother giving the sick counties a border. What do you think? And I have this off green for them." She aims latter at Anton. Tanya can't even see power when it is so elephantine and room filling - so she not even tactically talks round it, just talks through it, like how mortals neglect spirits.

"Looks as if Ireland is still gleaming like after a shower." says Anton dreamily to the elvine Tanya.

She dawdles as she finds curves hard to curve when they had to also keep precise. So she moves east and taking the charcoal from Anton's hand in bold sweeps makes the clefts, south off the Nymph Tray, more deft aerial-wise. Duhallow saw the cut of the book in Tanya's hand:

"Tanya, not even honours."

Anton rose to his height and her defence: "it's a process Jarlath, when it is coloured in and defined more in acrylic come back and judge."

Tanya defends her book. "This book has the sharpest contours and the only and best definition I seen yet of the Gardiner principle." Tanya uses her rubber and rubs out three kilometres of subsea head. "Tanya," she says to herself, "Get it right," and then "this underwater peninsula has a gorgeous name like what you'd get for your ma for Mother's Day."

Anton answers too and they jinx the both of them at Duhallow: "Nymph's Tray."

"Tanya you were right we could've wasted less time if you had overhead projected it on to the wall." vexes Duhallow.

"Not true. Our wall is too long for that....." Tanya practickles.

"But you can use them in panorama segment by segment and then join the dots," Anton recalls.

"Oh yeh. Hadn't thought of that......" Tanya is ventriloquising blame to promotion Man his self in a tone that says 'if I'd a real boss I'd have proper guidelines guidelinin' me mixed with not a little 'as if we'd be bleedin' bothered.'

Jarlath chortled again his Bilderberg Michelin star doubled chin chortle, which made no sense to the two young uns, not realising when they were passive-aggressive harassed in their workplace ? They wondered wrong. The chortle was Duhallow's inward recall that Dots had been so right about promoting Anton was the best way to keep him from meddling. His ascent to power had given him fabulously time wasting notions of import connected to things of no importance.

".... and not half the fun." delay answered bisexual Tanya spending her flippance ha'pence worth.

"Mr. Jarlath Secretary. What about the S.A.C.s " asked Anton. This got asked cause Tanya pointed at one and then pointed at Secretary Duhallow's turning back toward the door.

"What about 'em, Anthony?" Jarlath Duhallow's paled with conjecture.

"Anton ! Should we update them, granted there is so many of them these days ? That will take time."

"This map is for whose benefit."

"Well it is on six 8 x 4 ply sheets MDF stuff so if it is worthy we can use it at 2023 Expo like you encouraged; if you'll give it the ole thumbs up."

"Yes. Load it up with Special Areas of Conservation but don't go into detail much about their logic."

"There' hardly any detail anyway. Any ole plaice gets an S.A.C."

"Nice one Anton. Plaice. Place. Yeh. Looks like they been mating like rabbits." says Tanya. "We'll keep them pale coloured boss; then nobody'll notice much."

Anton had this line in his head since his promotion with regard to S.A.C s and he was darned if he wasn't going to utter it before Duhallow could leave: "Year on year; threefold increase in S.A.C.s."

Tanya took the immediate mickey: "Dolphins must've gotten a lobby group."

"Or they're up to something." says Anton to ally some with Tanya in front of Boss Man, not wanting to seem he'd gone all Management, like Oreo's white insides-outside-wise.

The supremely cautious Duhallow for two decades, possibly more, told half of everything that went on at work to his wife, Blonid, who was a daughter's worth in age difference to him and an half cocked spy. She'd not married JayDu to spy on him but the odd snippet of divulge kept her underused mind adrenalined and meant she was out of hock at The Kildare Village brand outlet emporia. Her style of spying suddenly one day kicked off after her lounging in her lime negligee and her postcoital Secretary-in-Chief had veered interesting from the bed. Doing her puff pall of powderings and dabbling herself with high end profumos about her nose and nape respectably she heard something that switched on her percolator: "there'd be many another who'd pay to know that," the hubby'd nonchalanted. That started a domino of wonders, escape routes in a grand spread of seasons and episodes that her disparate house-wifery really, really craved: 'ideally,' thought she, 'tall narrow, bit wasted and handsome, some gorge with feck all sense of humour,' light-bulbed the trainee adulteress. 'I'm sick to the eyeballs with just sense of humour.' The particular item hubby was ponderosing was that ole turtle: S.A.C.s, Special Areas of Conservation or as Mrs. Duhallow with Gilbeys taken'd put it "Spatial Arias of Consternation." She had caught her high powered husband say that some so-and-so had been suggesting SACs to be made much, much, more plentiful than subsea critters needs-bees and that this somebody person or body or entity was not themselves/ itself known to Jarlath - was beyond his reach, remit or clearance but the gist after some subtle soundings of her seeking clarification, casual like as if only filling the air with chat rather than post sex Sweet Afton and hubby answered her first idle sounding enquiry with "these Special Areas of Conservation are a means or should we say a ruse to keep undesirables away from key prospects, keeping them out of sight and mind into some vague decades into the future." Mrs. Duhallows first act of Mata Hari took place as early as the late naughties and early menopause like a matter of time bomb Jihadist within her. It was a start; some sounder information followed and such-and-such so much national interest got shared in one cycle of Saturn that whenever Jarlath suggested retiring she would rub his favourite spot and persuade him to remain "at the helm" and make him more slices of toasted St. Pierre, a sliced yellowy pan dotten with choco chips, new got from Morton's on Dunville Street. Her first lucky *gigolo* got paid in information and he in turn found that the highest bidder for Mrs. Duhallows cougarine whispers were the Chinese but *en route* East it got further slept with and Brazil then got a fraction of the information, and believed little of it, and what they did believe they didn't care about much, yet placed it in a drawer that was marked with an index card that'd translate as "next to useless" in the offices of *Petoril Santos* in the Province of São Paolo, a creaming semi state entity in charge of sea prospectables beyond the beauties of her own Seas. That *gigolo* and the second cousin who replaced him gained ever greater confidence by faking half falling for Mrs. Duhallow, same made more convincing by refusing payment and showering her with this or that frock of the season and finest shoes that got ever more gracious Kelly each every second Tuesday of a month, compo for ever more precise descries of the high clearances 'n' cleavages 'n' clefts of the Erin subsea. Apart from treachery Mrs. Duhallow had the sallowest shaped legs of all the inverted socialites of Sandyford, Glencairn and to the southern sweep of the parish of Stepaside. The British Ambassador his self had asked her first dance on St. George's day hooly at his residence. Blonid Duhallow'd never be in the Sunday papers gossip columns, not her, she suffered from a wound that even her loftiest *gigoli* could not plug even on long, long chats along her favourite drag, the Bull Pier as far as the Spit Buoy and back, her hand held firmly, handsomely, deliberately, all of her, truly appreciated without feeling a moment's Mrs. Robinson; these walks were an ass's roar more vital than all the gym-khan-ahhhhh of the Queenside bed in Room #33, Freemason Hotel o' Ballsbridge where she registered herself as L. MacPartland, Mizz. Despite all this spying Mrs. Duhallow loved her husband and they had the nicest plot in Attyroe by the Four Masters o' Donegal and fully intended using it. Their death mass would be at Our Lady of the Wayside, a loveable wooden Salem of a Church by Kiltiernan, their immolation at the Cavan crematorium, hardly a google mapping divert off the Attyroe road, itself an M3 paved with good intentions.

CHAPTER NINE

The occasional murderer, an award winning wheel greaser, goes by the name of McGeown, Inny McGeown, onetimes, Bluff Dardis, sometimes more beguiling other names. On this long drawn out assignment he is McGeown and has been for best part of three point five decades on and off consultancy and about the same dead: three outright, one comatose; two speechless. His silencer is ever attached his Mauser. Without age, he might have been attempt 178 on Castro's life; if same ever gets declassified. Today's rain is not Havana's but Irish endless, subspecies WestMayo 165 degrees horizontal.

"Just find the go'darn render-*vous*; driver. Yeh a peat power plant."

McGeown is in some kind of possibly 9 series Beamer, a heavy set navy black girl, vrooming her hybrid 221 reg best on across the yellow serrates of the N59. Out of the bog rose then the dead turf station of Bellacroy, not a John Hinde of its former days powering the forty watt darkness busters of the 50s and faulty PIE radios keeping simple people simpler and abreast of nothing, as nothing with consequences happened till 1988.

The larger than life 'McG' sat in the middle of the back seat, like he is the minister for counter-bulimicks, his butt not much from either doors. In his breast pocket are his seven passports, none of which do justice to his smile. Smiles not allowed on passports these days; no cause for. This particular morning's appointment was pencilled by Jo-anne back in Austin: Fri, November 18th 2022. The memo went 'best mole yet, young, got stubble, attitude and appears sober. Just $s to him, paid thru

Basel, Here's the wests/ norths so don't get too lost. p.s. not the murmuring kind. D.S. file attached.' Murmuring being code for you know what.

Darren Shivnan sat on a dank rusted turbine and the rooks of the roofless station watched his movement by movement toward treachery. Kraw kraw krah. If only Ireland knew rooky there'd've been a lot less gallows ballads and we'd be a lot more Trondelag.

The clanking turbine hall gate clangered the entry of McGeown in fat arse jeans and JCB booties like he is foreman of his unfolding.   He pondered the rooks, the fused rustic dead machinery, mossed, mottled, mediocre.

"What a fakin' mick mess of a place." McGeown trip advised his self.

Darren Shivnan had the wrong channel. He'd foreseen suave clinked-in interface, narrower personality, some middle management of con-fi-dent meritocracy with a bright new age of five star lobby teeth. He knew he'd be driving, hence the zero eight Focus with designee saline rust hid out the back. This gleaming Pavarotti comic looming at him unnerved while yet the zippity zip o' rising digits on his crisp bancohelvetii.ch account's mind's eye cured much. His hand gets scrunched by the salami fingered insinkable half Paddy/ half Texa-coco herald o' fry enterprise.

McGeown had surveyed his own offensiveness and long ago solved it by instant go-on-offensive action-stations: "I like you already," McG releases the former student of I.T. *informatique* general vagueness's thin claw. Direct eyeball to eyeball contact remained as the hands sundered. "Yes I do," which was subliminal hypnotism for 'now we're married.' This intense avuncular instantaneousness McGeown knew could cut through oceanic mistrusts that persist between folk such as murderers, traitors and blackmailers.

"Well, well" is all Shivnan could manage as he fell easier with the toupēed marshmallow and his Ronald MacDonald instagram of a smile wisp.

They walked toward the hidden side of the station where the Focus was and off they drove down the tertiary bog road westward. Where the bog boreen started to grate the Focus' sump they halted in a depression nameless to them: Lahernlathair, the half place of now in Aboriginal. Depressions were the ideal places for dubious chats out of reach of Site Specific Voice Distance Reader Mechanism. It was like a desolation where Fu Man Chu would have his palace shrouded in unexorcisable fog.

"Nice clear day," said Shivnan killing his engine.

"Yeh. I love blue blue blue skies," excited McGeown believably "though, being an Austin-ean I like all the cover-up Ireland gets. Sun, sun, sun, effing melon-nomas-ville."

Shivnan had fancied less cursing from a Lieutenant of the oil magnetry.

"Good ole clouds," as if pathetically awaiting McGeown's muster, a phalanx of cumulus lined up over Ceathru Thaigh stretching their evaporatant inland to shadow Rossport as far as the Port o' the Chief, as McGeown sped spoke the complexities of Shivnan's big gear shift mission to come, six silverine bullet points, with some tangents on tactics, a digression on self protection and motivants, then the white fluffs went back out to sea, keeping the blues. Shivnan was shaken and stirred.

"So you like spying?" said as chit chat sigh. Shivnan thought short and soft before replying. He had got the job with Close I Inc, not cause he'd gotten a first from Gaiety Acting School but simply he was the best hacker in Connaught and his fourth girl friend had dumped his worse side for being not adventurous and he was skint and his moral compass was not directly south, more Spike Island. Shivnan became chief spy in the Anti Refinery

Expansion Camp; chief for sure, the only; not so sure. He had taken to the acting, could manage to look handsome enough in dreadlocks, some Zulu beading keeping their ravelling, could keep even if skunk-drunk some plot to himself even with a whole night's worth o'THCs.

"Full time being a.n.other is dreamboat," said Shivnan as if he were talking to a bunch of the Anti Refine mob; then qualified, "but after this long the company can get tedious."

"Seems to me lookin at you you're still fairly darn Darren?"

Darren imagined that in his mid sixties the current treachery would haunt his less capable self. "I give notice to quit after this task."

"Sure, I understand. Pressure. Nothing in common," the brusque American could Oprah when at full wheedle.

"Boredom. New horizons. Stack of money and nowhere to spend it."

"I will let Austin know." The bulk of McGeown was so extensive, he covered the hand brake. In the wrong mind his being in the middle of not quite bog with a young man might be highly suggestive. McGeown, bar being raped while drunk in the late Autumn of 2005 while in Dubai, was straight as. Some under advisor to the under minister of the Dubai Department of Trade and Trinkets had forgotten to dial-a-broad. He was gee-eyed with cocaine after a successful day getting Sheik Ahmed bin Slithers to meet Ireland's then Minister of Energetic Good Things.

"So being Shiva is no great leap. Figures. SHIVA, SHIVA, now I get it, better cover than Rainbow or River Phoenix."

"Close I's Chief of Strategy had said choose a name close to your own, spacier the better."

"Shiva's some dead Indian; holds a trident ? He destroys stuff or he makes stuff." McGeown makes a violent jerk towards

Shivnan, rocking the car, like Shiva before an Episode, his fist reddening in the grasp of the illusory trifingered fork. "Are those dreads real?"

"Two years but I wash them a LOT, when nobody is about."

"Dirt keeps them clingy like that though ?"

Shivnan stares at the fat man, one of the most out of touch humans he'd ever had to rely on and who had to keep the air ever full with words: "you get much Stockholm syndrome doin' what you do?" Shivnan was exhausted. The spliff which he had gotten more used to revealed his seven egos, all of them more like uncles living in digs in callous suburbs, than any sort of higher self with a future lookout. He felt too old for idealism and spending his life in the Anti Refinery Camp was making a Swiss cheese of his brain cogs: dry toilet, vegan fare, the ps and qs of being all day p.c. His problem was that he could not resolve his in storage Maserati/ his reasonable good lucks and his dull reaction to reality. His great discovery for the past year was using his time to write rap verse of on-the-hop resistance, some of which had become well liked and his *Vindication VI* twenty five verser had virused quarter mill' in spread. It was good cover and some use of grey matter. McGeown sings a recall of a google of it: "*Vindi me vindi you take it from me we'ze the vindicants/ Our diligence is four square the wind giants supplicants....*" Shivnan not likin' much the out-of-con-text cite-back vents, opens his window and the sloping wind howls a reality into them, dilutes McGeown's *Beckham Uomo* 2020 and his outa-touch 'n' his outa-tune.

McGeown can't stay long quiet: "I'm dealing with spy and implants day in day out. The long termers become empats with their placement. Get me? Their *mill-you* is their life. They can forget why they're there. Some o' my guys are an entire generation ratting, Jesus imagine a lifetime rat-a-tat-tat. Quite often the human thing overrides the dollar lids." McG bats his eyes coquettishly and rapidly at Darren Shivnan like he was a Vegas slut machine jacking out. The wind drops an octet and some bird noises lark up high and the heather shivers without cease, without cease and the mind boggles. Darren knows too well the named syndrome. He has never undone an iota of his instructions nor traversed a tee of his Close I contract. He had fallen in love twice, which was advised by management, made his cover eider. Other spy and black ops colleges have whole chapters on faking an enduring love.

" My second girl, Snickerz, I thought she was spying and she knew I thought so. Anyway I am paid well and my info has saved you guys a few million. My small clear actions and dis-info I was told saved a six months delay risk on the refinery, phase four, the hushed up bit."

"Yes of course. I know your file arseways," lied McG, "Shivnan, can you make this new jump from spy to instigator? See me as your fave Uncle Mickey Finn. Talk to me. You'll be the "metaphorical" fuse and you're gonna have to be so sure of your allies in the camp, I mean know your 'apless 'ippies from other mum-feckers like yourself," says Inny M doing his cut of a cockney crusty. "I say so cause the cops and Ministry likely also have a spy or three keeping tabs. Sometimes our purposes cross their purposes, sometimes not."

"The cops do for sure. We call him Crew Cut. His hair is down to his belly button but he is so so Sergeant Promotion dude material. He kinda knows we know but still hangs with us. He is kept from key Disrupt strategy meetings. He is my best cover. Crusties can only handle one bad apple per....."

"We know that the Ministry of Energy does not have a spy. The gob-shysters trust outsourcing to us."

"Yep."

"Is there anything in our plan that you cannot handle?"

"Plenty. When do I get the detail."

"One to four is hunky dory doo? Detail yeh yeh on item five and six. Sure ..... Alligator."

"Sooner I'd prefer. I am sure it is worth the rise. Number six is particularly straying into very new territory and frankly not sure I can stomach it."

"Don't worry you won't have to hurt the fly. We'll send help," and for some reason McGeown places both index fingers to each of his eyes and stretches them into narrow horizons like he was himself Fu Man Chu and world domination round his corner.

They drove back toward Bellacroy by Pollnagoppaleen Lake, keeping the bog desolation to their east. Occasional lines of drying turf, some sprang with now dead ragwort, the whole like a Paul Henry oil bar the lack of a serf's cottage.

"Do the locals still burn this shit?"

"The government forbids or possibly Bruxelles forbids them."

"What a mull-ark-key. They can't suck their own sea oil nor slice their own sponge cake. So what kinda jobs do people have here?"

"Unskilled stuff to do with the refinery. Canteen staff, cooks. It's a divided place. Those with fancy verandas and tarmac took the King's shilling, as they say."

"As they say!!!" McGeown looks Shivnan sideways like the Spy was getting bigger than his supplied boots. "Sure sure. Leave me at that crossroads comin'. "

Darren was confused. There was not a bungalow or tigeen for sight nor sound and there ahead was McGeown's crossroads which had been invisible with hefts of blanket bog fetching hard about it.

"You don't mean here?"

"Yeh, here is fine. We decided to issue you no firearms so you really betta stay lower than the bee beep radar."

The Focus stopped and the large man got out holding his belly unto himself. McGeown waved a pinky cheerio through the unwound down window. "Toodle pip. I'll be fine and you'll be fine" he lip-synched and turned to look out away west and leave the youth square and quandary his Omaha Beach to come.

Darren watched in mirrored hind sight at the bend of the River Ninchy the tinty windowed Beamer swooshed by all ink coloured and kick-sure, coolly, calmly slowed, collected the larger than life smooth Operator.

McGeown didn't speak to the driver until they reached a decisive 'T' in the road.

"Sir?"

"Time to see how big a pikie the Dutchman caught?" and the driver nodded and turned west along the Glenamoy Empty Quarter.

CHAPTER TEN

The Hongqi L5 bullet proof limousine purred south downtown along The Avenue of the People's Revolution till Xi Inning Chi Boulevard junction, bore left and halted its hybrid in front of the might of the former Chong Ding Corporation building reaching to the sky. A dapper gentleman, old guard has the quarter tonne back middle door opened for him and out steps he and regards up the floors and shudders at the anti-swing of the 60s' central floors' art deco columns that'd been thrashed and replaced with fake rock Mount-Rushmore-esque, from the belt upwards half sized rigger caryatids, *faux* positive sexism for its time: three women, three men, Marx of determinations on their six grey brows, aged by the wrinkling o' decades of Peking soot, each impossible human bearing a mining or oil tool or ratchet ahand balanced by a raised fist each. Within, the roof foyer of China's Ministry for Prosperous Explores is mosaiced with stars, planets and outsized dereks, sort of sitting gigantically on the planet as if the Little Prince had sold his prospects to the Seven Sisters for an uplifting marching song.

Chou Chi Shook's role is half Duhallow, half Power of Energy Minister, the almost retiring, not half dapper man had more than usual interest in the morning's dossier; his swan song doubling as an exit strategy. Unlike Duhallow one hundred and twenty six thousand employees depend on his whim. At seventy two years old, he'd been overlooked yet again by Xi Jinping for Party preferment. Shook thought the rest of his days tiger claw powder and *bunga bunga* lite in north eastern enclave of Fu En Lie where the party cadres clustered beyond intrigue. In advance of his retirement every weekly meeting was now being given five star priority but he seemed to be ever shifting his thrown tea leaves. In his mindful eye his swansong was seven star and not something left to the whims of Luck. After he could take to the hammock of delights and acquiesce to the glad touching of whores once he'd sorted what only in his own head he referred to as Operation 'Land of the Setting Sun.' He west-winged through the corridor yammering with Chief of Eurasian Strategies Ms. Xushi. He listened to her council while flicking a skimpy file, jumped to its addendum: *Further information about proposed agent 700 to be sent into the field.* Shook was ushered into the cagey elevator and taken to the upper floor. Xushi talks fairly massive geopolities while Shook continues reading: under Agent 700's 'Hobbies & Worries' was written 'naturism and mind control.' Under Formation: 'Shaolin convent four years to seventeen years beyond the Song Mountains. Win Dow Shin. Shook had heard of the strictures of this far far away hilltop training camp, top Dao, ways away some place beyond peaks in a wetter plateau of Jangxi Province.

In the Great Room of Peoples' Prospects the monstrous teak table would've weighed tonnes were it not that it was teak skinned only. Above it a dazzling ceiling with a story; a god like statist almost finger pointing sistine hand with the blue fabric of the worker's clobber as its sleeve giving spark to Comrade-kind. Shook took middle position in mauve velvetine throneen beneath "Everyman-god." Spacious, curious faces with various arrays and affronts of medals gaped at him expectantly and sensing but not seeing all was Agent 700, sat in a booth sort of an affair like a heretic being quizzed in might sit, its plate glass meant that the sitter could have aspects of the meeting sheltered from her ears. Agent 700 could differentiate resentment from admiration even with her back turned through hand wide plate glass. This bunch of Darwinists she could sense were half half. By the by through foot wide fifty newton concrete she could perceive love or hate. Flighty as a bamboo in the wind, as rooted as a bamboo in itself; she had learnt flawless English during her touring circus days and in balancing scarlet orange bricks on her head while dancing a Sichuan polka she had won hearts through the quiet proof of her supremacy and her disinterest in pain; hers or others. All told she had attracted the attention of the People's Intelligence of External Knowing & Meddling.

The room's five windowed side faced east on Guangchang West Side Road, its west on Guanchang East side road and its North onto Tianemen Square, and beyond the Xing dynasty gate of the Forbidden City's entrance, with massive Mao snap smug-you-like, his third eye wart visible so far. Shook sat, gazed at the table for some silence, that could have been confused for awkward prayer, that was broken by a cough from likely successor Xang Chu, 'a braggart and such a dry unnecessary cough' thought Shook 'if you are not given an accident - you'll become our next Capitalistickle Emperor.' Xang at fifty five still had pencil enough to leaden Beijing's most sought starlettes of opera, both soap and sung without recourse to tiger claw. Shook's wife referred to Xang as 'xiāosǎ ér huálì' (kinda Chinese for 'dashing and gorgeous'). Shook could not grasp how this snake-in-the-straw could be seen as dashing, though he was granted, a Victor Mature in Han terms, where respect and sensuality is visited on the black haired mid fifties man 'o' the world, as opposed to true and vigorous youth.

Comrade Xushi rose at Shook's nod. She pressed her tiny compact and a screen unbound itself from the high ceiling stretched like matinée cinemascope the length of those mentioned five windows, simultaneously the lights dimmed to stars and the entire world blinked on to the screen, as wide as itself, oddly nationless, bordering on desolate. Xian is the Chinese Greenwich maps-wise; after all it is The Middle Kingdom, so China was middling, Ireland was the Far East, Bermuda the Wild West. It was that gaunt world, Peter's Projection sized, Africa seeming to dwarf the lands of all her descendents. Xushi clicked and clicked and clicked again and instant idiot proof icons indicating oil reserves coloured the world, deep purple being lush, the palest lilac indicating sucked dry or feck all. From the South China Seas scant pink polka dots to the sizeable royal purples stretching from Broom to Dili, to Royal Brunei. There seemed a flood of some antique tributary extending the Orinoco endlessly into the aquatic Atlantic, a deep protracted mauve. The middle of Saudi and the resorts of Qatar were delightfully extensive, way into the sea. Sudan's south was a rhododendron before its petals fall and had a serrated edge that looked unsure of herself drifting into Chad. Nigeria seemed Saudi in waiting but its hues paled in comparisons. The shores to the east of the USA not known for prospecting had vast purples but sorely distant from shore - these widened as they went north and what was most startling turning straight east was a massive kingdom of reserves in an Egypt sized zone of waterland off the west coast of what the Chinese call Ire-Lang, four thousand kilometres east of the Beautiful Land. Xushi, huskily explained the past decades actions and intrusions and extractions in the seven key reserve zones. She concluded on the peaceful takeover of key wells in Darfur being a way forward, then she handed over to Ministry Secretary Shook, who lit a Hongtashan 400 blew smoke away and stood. He strolled, stopped, his head haloed by Antarctica, like ice clad mammoth era antlers. His Communist red pointer laser divided the air as a lightsabre 'Made in Guangzhou' might. He threw a few diagonals and his cigarette smoke caught the light magically. Shook was well liked and he made memories. Then he points the laser straight at the third eye, mid forehead of Xang, which caused a gasp among the younger apparatchiks. Then he swung around and pointed his laser at Spanish Point, County Clare, Western Ire-Lang.

"Our great Country's exponential need for hydrocarbons could soon draw us into destructive war. You General Li," and he points his pointer at the well decorated General of Combined Land Forces, "have advocated expansion of our Motherland to Manchu-times sized China, to embrace Mongolia, the Outer, even parts of Buryatia. Part of this noble, if risky opportunism would allow us uncomplicated access to Mongolian coal. That is one part of the *expansionista* argument. I say to you, Mongolia needs our influence but we have no need to invade Mongolia; ninety per cent of its coal will soon cross our border and right now there are great mountains of it stock piled near Xanadu, and to its north, enough for fifteen years but coal is dirty, awkward stuff. Am I right." Last three words were not a question.

Shook then uses the red laser to descry a nonexistent empire, in the vast silk of Central Asia that to all intents and simplifications could be clept Stan-i-stan. "Our Xang and his neighbour, Hawk and Haughty here," and again he brutally stabs the General with his laser, wishes that we simplify our dilemma and move direct west from Kashgar and get ourselves a Stan or two or at least cajole greater control there. That would hasten a third world war with Hollywood and the Bear." (Shook never called the Beautiful Land, America or U.S. or U.S.A. or the States). "Further up; dabbling in the Arctic could mean angering once more both the Russian Bear and Hollywood."

Shook indicated for a short gentleman to rise. "Comrade Yimou, Trade attaché in Kuala Lumpur; his real job running spies in the Malaysian and Brunei oil ministries. Tell us!"

As the in-the-know sniggers stop Yimou rises and bows awk -wardly, "we have every right to tender for wells and zones of exploration within Malaysian waters through artifice companies but tabs are kept on all our movements. The local Chinese community's first loyalty is to their sovereign government, not to us. The Royal House of Brunei has us almost virtually excluded unless we disguise as Western small time prospectors which is of no use when it comes to viable extraction. We have some hopeful front companies operating from East Timor but we have no sizeable access at below market rate to the finds about Timor to North Western Australia, itself the largest gas reserve outside of Qatar. Sir!"

"Thank you Comrade Yimou. Our gains in Sudan and her periphery are well known and we imagine a decade more there. However the reds, whites and blues, all five of them are waking up like they want to make new scrambled, poachy eggs of Africa. They have secured new finds in Libya. Algeria is now a secular western leaning government and in their hands since the orchestrated skirmishes in Niger and Mali surrounded her. We have, since the Peace of Homs, no great favours or deals in the Middle East. We are left with Angola, Venezuela and Ireland, yes Ireland. Brazil is now impossibly red white blue. Venezuela, well, one long Hollywood ball-buster. If we want access to competitively priced oil and gas without a war we have Angola and Ireland, and right now our expert advice," and Shook pays nod service to two bespectacled geophysicist looking types sat rigid at the end of the grand teak of a table, "tells us Ireland's awkwardly deep reserves are three to seven times that of Angola if one goes deep enough into big wavy waters."

Xang interrupts. "They know because of science or from good espionage."

Shook puts Xang to rest. "R.O.V.s Comrade Xang."

"Three to seven times. Big difference." Xang's being could not but opportune some cold water pouring on Shook's parade.

Shook ignores Xang. "Might I ask Xushi to explain further."

The perfectly turned out Xushi takes the floor and walks under the giant map and presses her zapper and Ireland goes zoom zoom, big big, as quick, if not better than SKY News. "Our eyes were opened two years back by a sudden rush of exploration blocks in what we would reckon to be unlikely places: big focus on South of Dunquin and North of Do-wish. Unlikely; by that I mean extremely unlikely. The explorations were in geologically ridiculous points. The Dutch and British lead the charge, and one Norwegian half entity; possibly the Anglo-Dutch faking keeping them on board. The Italians and French appeared in terms of these types of prospects, to be getting the squeeze-out. We don't know why. The Malaysians despite being the only operator with gas coming ashore in the south in their King Sale fields: they have not made any tenders for more prospect acre-age, except here." Xushi points at an area west of Spanish Point, "it is code-named Mack Dara. It is from our investigations next to useless; so the Malaysians are being hung out to dry."

Now she zaps her clicker over her left shoulder without looking at the result; the way the superstitious might chuck salt, or more like how an Irish speaking meteorologist forecasts five days of spells with confidence, without mercy. Huge South Western Scotland pops up as map map and stylishly as it skyfalls the fast as lightning slides go terrain terrain till the outskirts of a wee enough city. "Until 2018," Comrade Xushi continues, "there had been a decade of hectickle construction activity in Ayr in this dull part of Scotland. To all intents it looked to becoming the Aberdeen of the Western, assumedly British Seas. Those who knew their Shetlands could not comprehend why this new builds were so huge. Generally these huge new structures were never limelit and when they were discussed in hydrocarbon journals and oil press; they were for new imagined finds off West Shetland that everyone knew or assumed were on the dwindle. Now in the post Brexit and United Ireland and the first re-entry attempts of Ireland into Common Welt, Ayr begins to appear less like the clearing zone for the last driplets of Scottish oil but the first bounties coming off Ireland.

"How you know this ?" asks Xang

"Scottish West Regions spy 17 oh 7 sir.   All construction at Ayr has stopped.   We were never sure if this construction was 'build and it will flow' mentality or there was longer term view. Now for three years there has been an equivalent and higher build up of holding tanks, liquefiers and pipe junctions at the bulkhead of the huge Atlantic pipe in Sruh Wad Ah Khan Bay. The shift from Ayr to Mayo is a signal of great confidence in relations between once warring Ireland and the United Kingdom.   Our intelligence says that the finds have a half century life and are worth seven point five trillion *yuan* in that fifty year life span. Sixty per cent gas, forty percent oil, in waters that till now were almost entirely impossible. With tensions building in the Arabia, prices spiking. There'll be a lotta lotta happy shareholders in the mansions of leafy Warwickshire," she precised.

"So they are moving what is intended at Ayr to Sruh Wad what you me call it ?" Xang wants to make his mark. "This sounds like a lot bigger than Angola."

Xushi agrees: "Our sources close to the Oil Ministry in Dublin have put about that finds may be gargantuan, much more than our R.O.V. surveillance indicated."

Xang bangs on for clarity. "Ayr is yet important ?"

Xushi soothes: "The ramifications of Brexit's ramifications appear to us to have been a much successful cover so much so that much of their facilities can be at Srud Wad Akonh; no questions asked. Mess, Comrade Xang can be great camouflage."

Xang does not appreciate whimsy generalisations and blows up over nothing: "Ayr still has some function ?" and he left fists the teak.

"To go back to your question, Comrade, Ayr is likely the place to sort your rigs and repair ships, ancillary services and liquefiers will come and go from there. What is being built in phases at Irish landfall is the greatest refinery and oil alpha-artery known to kind human."

Shook puts up his hands like a good Sheriff that must give in to Destiny: "must stop you there Comrade Xushi. How can the Motherland intrude in the distant Land of the Setting Sun?" To his audience, his question is rehearsed and the answer doubly so. "As Minister's Secretary, I Shook say 'No warships, nor missiles ladies and gentlemen, Comrades and no topping "legitimate" governments. Let me introduce you to......" Shook takes the baton of the zapper from Xushi presses it and a picture of Chairman Xi Jinping in Ireland with a newborn calf in County Clare looms. The unfatted calf looks terrified. "This was the then future Irish Minister for Brexitix along with yours truly our Chairman," latter lording with paternal care but with a glint of Abraham having that episode again; Jinping is touching the calf's mane. If this were a Rembrandt the tall Minister, a medium rare Irish Bilderburger with chips 'n' Fanta would be Issac and the calf his stunt double.

"This is our own Chairman's Ire-lang visit in 2012. That is where we begin our *guĭjì* (roughly 'intrigue.') Our orders and blessing come from the top. Our Chairman gave love and fatherly attention to Ire-lang."

Shook presses his zapper and the group can now see inside a little glass box in the centre of the room. The viewee can be heard and seen but the voyeurs are not visible but can be heard by the watched one. "Let me introduce Agent 700."

Xushi endorses her: "She works entirely alone and only engages fully if the task is well beyond normal human reach. Agent 700."

"I know that the strength given by Obedience," here the Agent bows as she stands, "usually lessens the difficulty of things that seem impossible." Half the apparatchiks in their noggins thought *zhème lǎo de màozi* / 'such old hat.'

"Agent 700 has been "ambassador" for the Motherland for......"

"Nine years, Minister Shook." replies the agent, "nine joyous year."

Agent 700 was released from her booth and enters the hall proper, stands with an obedient tilt to the west of the table. She is wearing what in the 1970s were called trouser suits. She has nun's shoes and displays ankle cheek.

Shook explains "You are to make contact within Ireland and or elsewhere that hasten our undisputed access to the bigger proportion of that sea wealth. We are not seeking to steal but control access and double bonus points if we can cream some profits. At our Dublin embassy we have been, since President's Chairman's visit, busy figuring the movers and shakers, the bribable and the honourable members of the Irish *Daw-Ill*, their answer for a People's Congress." Shook raised his hands in a wise old way in the air for no particular reason and waved them toward Agent 700 who as a lay woman was plain Susan Xeng. Shook was rather chuffed by the get-the-job-done just-add-water Frankenstein of her betimes, yet none of her screws loose.

"I've always been curious about our President's visit. He went a decade ago to the two corners of Europe...." Xang squiggles some coded ideograms in his jotting paper.

"Correct, its security in its heel: Turkey, its energy hub: Ireland. The Europeans won't be so dependent on the whims of the Czar anymore. Our worry is that the Bri-tish are making a complete shire of Ireland and the muppets don't even see it coming."

"Hobbits," corrects Xang.

"Our Deep Intelligence have nick named their *Anschluss*: "Shire 101." We have little proof, only hunches from the drunken chit chat of cocktail parties, "the BallsBridge set" our Embassy calls it in Dublin. You get me? We need to move before they fully consolidate and lock us out."

Agent 700 understood. She had read and foto-recalled all three hundred and seventy nine pages of the Ire-lang dossier which she then destroyed in her domestic crucible.

Agent 700, for you *fashionistas*, was wearing yet a gorgeous Spring '21 Xang Xang suit, striped and tucked. She had lotions of almond oil keeping her supple. Those nun shoes of hers were *faux* Prada; better than the real thing, their soles had Olympic grip for long jumps or if you were driven up the wall by a situation.

Dress-casual Susan took the 'A' train east seven stops toward Yangtze Park & Ride station which already mid afternoon was an 'X' shaped clatter of folk moving between work purposes and their smattering o'children, their food, their soft ball soccer, their predilections in Downtown. Agent 700 walked five blocks west to Hoh Hotte Street, two south to Feng La Song Avenue in the 29th Prefecture. There at immediate ground level set into a tasteful garden an elevator that was vertical's answer to the Tianjin bullet train, possibly zoomier. She got azoomed to the 29th floor and the parting metals had her straight into her spartan bling of an apartment, as auspicious as it was spacious. Her body scent set off the projector that shone on to the wall. Best of *Westlife* was still in the system. She had prepared psychically for the morning's meeting. She played it again *I'll Be Home*. Her panes tinted so she divested. 'Fabulous tune,' she thought. The music's syrup swept her inside. As its emotion seared the video helicoptered out and all WestLives were left like yodelling lemmings on the edge of the Cliffs of Moher, sharp suicidal tourist attractions at the edge of the Irish world view. Agent 700 had just commenced the Dao of push ups with one hand clapping when her eye caught the low tide shot as west and west went the camera, the singers dotty now with distance and the big reveal was an exquisite low tide channel complex beneath the cliffs. She completed her exertions went punched on the Chinese version of Bing called Jing and quick as a blink an oblique angled terrain map and sure enough, clear as day if you kept going south this same geological quirk all the way to Loop Head. Agent 700 realised that the reason this part of the coast had been ignored was not simply a safari of seaweed. "It's a Mississippian-Pennsylvanian deep water deltaic basin fill succession." Agent 700 wondered if Minister Shook realised that there were hydrocarbon possibilities much closer to the coast than had been reckoned, the supposed Malaysian red herring feeding ground might not be so red. Agent 700 juiced herself a celery and durian boozeless daiquiri and took her good self to bed and further researched on a bedroom widescreen the coast north till she reached Mayo. She pressed update and got connection to live transmitter from the Long March XVII satellite that overrode Jing once you had the top clearance codes. She watched a live, long suffering Force 8 trouncing the dawn coast north of the Sound. There such and such a nurse going to work in her Astra near Bangor Erris, such and such a guard asleep in his Speed Van but move across to the valley beyond the Empty Quarter of Magheracroy and there was a visual fuzz. Agent 700 had seen permanent distortions like this over parts of for example: Nevada always, over Diego Garcia much of the time. Somebody local or astral was preventing visual feed to any satellite for sure, possibly high flying spy jets passing by. Something was afoot at the refinery .

CHAPTER ELEVEN

Anton aslouch and chlorinated on the dark grey Harvey Norman having the lols and lolls with Mister Pee, his Offaly husband. Both were in their respective sense of PJs. Series 12 of *Homeland* got zappered off as the torture of a Kurdish (Syrio) separatist was becoming a tad *Reservoir Dogs* and it was Mr. Pee who insisted. Padraig liked *Homeland* "a brilliant way to understand geopolicies." They landed on the RTE2 *Late News* and newscaster Blanchard Doolie had been doing her best to enthuse after a fashion a teacher's conference in Marsh Mallow. Next to Mayo and a Mr. Lawrence Ewing in a plaid jacket last seen Friday, a man of sixty five years. Our wild western correspondent has the details. Next seen is an intense woman moving away from a crowd of widowing Knock pilgrims. The shot is stylish as if dollied or possibly a low horizon use of a drone and the entire moment captures with adept happenstance and unthinking continuity the passing by of a handsome tanned priest around the fifty holding a delightful Edwardian monstrance as the looming correspondent with mighty sponge of mic descries the mystery. The priest in the circumstance winks to camera or may have. The said Ewing was last seen driving his Passat along the Kilkelly bypass, little worried, quite late. He works as security at I.W.A. The same woman with suave timing swung to her East and there was a giant of a Sergeant at the ready: "we are following as certain inquiry line and ask the public to come forward with any story they'd've that'd help whereabout......"

"Thank you Sergeant," and with that wild western correspondent Eyelash Knee Gullet continued that Ewing was childless, a house-bound, prone to humours, invested in his job, had a love of fishing, of the divine, and this guff edited with howls of wind and visible a dripping shot of St. Dervla's B&B sign swinging in the rain (meaning not Ewing's place at all) and then cut like she is St. Dervla herself, the real Mrs. Ewing stood up and viewed through her genuine squinting windows being wary and warier of some flash photography - pull back to bird house, sad carping pond and her lawn pocked with wodges of rotting sycamore leaves.

Anton placed his hand on Padraic's lower lumber and pinched his vertebrae with play vehemence. Padraic winces and writhes with athletic baratones, while in-digesting the TV info, "like zap and he's gone," says Anton stopping the feck acting.

"Who's gone?" asks Padraic balancing his giggles.

"That man in Mayo there." Anton sits back down and his long arms hold his chin.   "Do you imagine he got fed up and vamoosed."

"We neither know the hour or the minute." Padraic if he'd not become a gym instructor for the handicapped and if he'd been transported to the Ireland of the fifties would have made the ideal big girl's blouse of an Oblate or Reformed Norbertine.

The weather forecaster in her leather skirt had a blockbuster swirl heading Ireland ways and warned plain and inexpert people to keep from the coasts. Valery was her name, the Storm, not the prophetess.

The self same warning was being listened to by 1.92 million so-and-soes nationwide, as if Nature plus all the grand sires of geopolity at once and for all were about to swallow in one mighty sausage the five farrows of *Fodladh*, which means to scoff Ireland and her hegemonies in one rude oink of a bite.

Two among them were at once the attracted and acted on sat in affront of the thirty two inch Sanyo flat screen: Mrs. Ewing and the self styled Fr. Van Der Op. Mrs. Ewing is mortified by her winter garden in national display, but her worry is kept to herself and said to her companion only after she had poured a dash of low fat tepid Oranmore to prolong the Dutch Father's organic cocoa.

"It is so important that you stayed. I would be in bigger bits."
"No big deal, Mrs. Ewing. Really. What are we for ?" and he drops the hand, displays the full Versace of his cleric black cloth.

"It's like you're my witness; force me to be upright. I'd collapse on my own. The Travellers above Charlestown, they'd take a child I heard but I'd never imagine a grown fellah of Lar's type."
"Would the gypsies do that?" Fr. Op nonplussed.

"They're not strictly Gypsies race-wise though they beg on bridges since Cromwell pushed us all West and those that found no solid ground, even rushy acres took to the bohareens as roaming and feck-free as Gypsies."

"I hear they have their own language."

"Yarra, nonsense, feck this and 'f' word the next."

Then the phone rang dring dring dring likes a phantom from the Lynch era.

"Philo." Mrs. Ewing smiled her first smile since the seventy two hours of ordeal kicked off its pain and uncertainty.

"Flo. Your Shaw's curtains are fading fast."

"They didn't fetch well. You're right. It is the colours in their TV camera didn't catch it right."

"Did they search at his brother's?"

"Which?"

"The one as is gone in on himself."

"Yeh, Josey. They've been in the barns and out sheds of every cousin. Their policy is to check on suspecting lakes after seventy two hours. *Garda* divers if you get me."

"It's hard, very hard Flo."

"I have the priest from Holland here still. He went but then he saw me cryin' on telly his heart, he says, wept out for me and...... yeh....... he came back about tea, this evening" and she regarded him with a mild twinkle then covered the phone mouth. "I'll take it in the upstairs."

"No. No. I'll go *deaudeau*" and dredging his Green & Black hot chocolate Op hoofed out the door of what in his mind was a way too overlit living room. Dutch rooms are twilit as if in ever readiness for amour and net curtains are abhorred as from the pavement every house is an interpretive centre unto itself. He didn't bother to pick up the phone to have a listen but went for a slink in Lar's study. As he searched the room AGAIN, all the while through the floor above he was hearing the cribby tones cut with grief, with occasional giddy intake of Mrs. Ewing's breaths. His psychopathic triggers he was trying to stop viraling out of control between the listening and the not so successful rifling. Lar had possibly lied that he had all the marine maps of the whole State just to delay his death. He found some ordnance maps under a sofa but they looked like for hill walkers trapped in some fog from the forties. Op thought 'I will hit the hay now, rendition could be trying, half botched rendition doubly tiresome.' Then he noticed that the off cut carpet had an uplift and he pulls its tacks and there's a catch inlaid in the floor beneath it. It is a trap door beneath and inside dusty black refuse bags tied with twine. He feels the bags and it is rolled up sheets of paper. "*Grace a Jubilon*" says Op to himself but aloud. He has his own continental mumbo jumbo belief system after a fashion. Jubilon is best known as the Minotaur like entity at the innermost hewn maze of Masonic highest of hi degrees. Op has gotten so busy what between work and gym that the threshold of the Lodge at Hilversum gets hardly his darkening but its purview still informs. He opens the bags and they are coast hugging sailor's maps with

Oxfam price stickers on each map: €0.50 on each, National Geographic maps of Ocean currents, the 'East Atlantic,' raggedy from so much opening and bad refolding. They are scrawled across with grids in pencil and squiggles of numbers all over. 'All in one scoop,' thinks Op in Dutch, 'a top of his game secret agent could wish for nothing better so long as sense could be made of this *bordeel'* (Dutch for 'mess,' with the assumption that brothels are messy work situations).

Flo Ewing was entering that age, one decade after menopause where stories already known to another can be freely reconstituted, much as twenty four hour news is on a twenty seven minute loop of very-similitude, and re-jargoned spokes-person-speak.

She is on third repeat yakking with Philo "He was definitely out of sorts and I told Garda Nangle same and he just does more cross examining me like I'd the paraclete put in his porridge and buried him under the sadfoils. Lar's mother said once she'd lost him in Moon's on Shopping Street but he was five. They'd got parted by the crowds and there he sat unbothered out wet on the street watching a squeeze box man."

"Like Jesus in the Temple," added Philo.

"I know but he was only five."

"And not finding the car, now that's odd and all his posters off the wall. You hear of far younger men who do that kind of disappearance and next things someone's spotted them in Rotherham or Darlington and they've already a near grown up family."

"I know but it is not the same."

"But you have your faith as always."

"It's shaken. It's shaky."

"Taking a battering."

I'll take you and your priest over a marble cake."

"You're a dote. God in heaven it is not like we didn't have a priest in the house before; in case that hunted Lar. All that holy cloth must've sent him packing."

"Why don't you dig up one of his divining friends. Shouldn't they be able to help each other out; 'diviner find yourselves' and such. They can find poor lost pets."

"Lar's thing was water and submarine..... I can't find his notebook that would have all the numbers. Remote views. Yes Philo."

"Garda Nangle will help you. I'll be over about nine."

"Philo, quick question. Was it an agency or an order who put Fr. Op our way?"

"Just himself rang and said he'd no number for you, nor the wherewithal...... It was the garden view he liked, or your interest in flowers he liked. Something along those lines, Flo. See you at nine. Try some rest."

Rain fell like the clappers all night. Flo kept the radio low and turned it up on the hour as if that was where she would find first news. Teachers strike pending still first news. Pro-democracy, muslin or silk revolution something in Riyadh. Rubber and real bullets. No fly zones possibly. Lar was down to third item and by 6am news he was not there at all. The light doesn't bother people till 7:50am that time o'year.

Op waved goodbye to Flo. He was going to drive to Shannon and return to his Parishioners in the LowLands. She had finally figured out his coeliac and found some Holland & Barrett farley-rusks for him to dunk in his dippy egg with. He told her he was so glad that her sister from Akron was coming that day. A lie; she was sisterless. She'd be a great consolation. Flo waved genuinely while yet taking note of his reg plate and the car was a silver hatchback, no an estate, bit much for his wants. A car dislodged from parking opposite and followed the silver car as it made its way to the N17, Op heading North, not South, his tail following.

CHAPTER TWELVE

Meanwhile 20th January 1996, BAE ZE700 landed in a right Mayo of a fog. It had been but an hour and ten from Northolt to NOC. The British Embassy in Dublin sent a spotless gorgeous Jag to Knock Airport to protect the arrival, with a gorgeous driver and not bad security detail plus a girl who had never met a Prince before. His Royal Highness got stuck in the rear with her.

The Minister for Trad 'n' Tourism, himself a Mayo man, a Mister Kenny shunned umbrellas and got saturated talking pleasantries with the youthful Prince Edward till they got themselves from the sort of royal when necessary plane to the bit of an airport term-i-nal. The Prince was entranced by the fabulous memory of Mister Kenny, how he knew his Coat of Arms, that he loved tennis and was an out and out thesp like himself. Mister Kenny was touched that the Prince admired the statue of Christ the King that is just for and against the said term-i-nal and that he didn't seem to give a shite about the shite weather. The Prince was by then, the twenty ninth person to be aware of Operation 'Fat One,' itself in its eighth year, two years ahead of schedule, so long as the Ceasefire held. His Palace <u>Day in Mayo Dossier</u>, 3 x A4s of schedule, tips and phrases concluded with a wee summary: 'vouch landfall location suitability and 'humanise' the local polity and be a recognition of Peace in Our Coming 'Good Times.' Act Noble yet Normal!'

Lawrence Ewing, a dapper thirty nine year young security man formed part of a reluctant guard of honour supposed to salute but compromised to not slouching as Prince Edward, then fourth, some said sixth in line to the throne of the Great Britons sauntered along the couth staff of Knock Regional Airport, a guard of honour to all intents. A mere thirty two, every bit a Dickie Mountbatten-alike and a Cheshire stroke Burmese grin beguiling and reductive, the Prince had in his own head landed in some class of an Orkney, just with a lot more understated reluctance and it only one year and one half since the Ulster War seemingly ended. Anyway he could be in and out of the foggy dew and back in Surrey for slippers and cup-hands Complan in time for *Top of the Pops*, so long as he didn't get 'Robert-Kennedied,' or so he had said to his man servant over more dippy egg. He had intended to spend time on the plane writing scene six of *Edward on Edward*, a documentary he was shooting on his Grand Uncle, abdicant King Edward VIII, a scene where he introduces, then meets the New York jeweller where the Yorks in exile spent their notes on some stylish carat 'n' rocks. Edward had turned to documentary film making as an expression of his own divine rectitude and in particular had zoned in on his namesake, his dapperest grand uncle who "history had grossly mistreated." His mission summary of the Palace Day in Mayo, versus the more jaunty Embassy one's goals proved a tad too interesting in their glaring differences; agenda-wise an East Atlantic ocean apart. The more he read the more he felt at the hub of a great moment, like King Henry II arriving in sackcloth after the siege of Dublin.

The Prince was whisked to Castlebar where he gave out Duke of Edinburgh awards which in Erse are called *Gaisces*, medals for daring youth, to keep girls as much as boys diverted in gruelling activities and not fomenting rebellion. Silver medals for basic hike about Mount Nephin say and knowing North from South on a compass. Gold medals for Navajo style vision quests, how to dispel fog, how and where to drink from a mountain stream, how to allow solitude breakthrough higher selves. The Prince had insightful thoughts for each medallist. He did an interview with Community Radio Castlebar where he was told by a youthful girl that she would not kiss him lest he become a frog. 'Thankfully she's at the end of a phone line,' prince bubble thought.

His eldest brother, Prince Charles had been to Mayo the previous May, taking full advantage of Peaceful surroundings. The chance just to see the ocean from the top of Mount Mweelrea was giddy for the Crown Prince. He, unlike his younger brother, knew the full extents of Operation 'Fat One,' its name derived from the Erse fabliau of a rather splendid imaginary place referred to as *Tir fa Tonn*, 'Land Beneath the Waves.' Charles told Mummy his excitement when he returned to Buckingham Palace, that he could see and see the endless Ukraine (because that was about the size of it) of it all and "oddly Mummy, suddenly London felt jolly well east of Eden." On this second public royal 'reconnaissance' sending young, sweet Prince Edward out was easier especially now as it was the eighteenth month of Cease-your-fire in the Fourth Green Field and Prince Edward could move about without too much paparazzmatazz. How and ever the local media were all about the Prince Edward at Castlebar but were kept at bay for the remainder of the day. Lunch was trout and caper at *The Connaught Inn*, Spencer Street. The waitress, an Aoife, told the Prince that Princess Diana saved her mother's life.

"I'm delighted."

When she arrived with the largest Macedonia ever made from Mayo grown fruit he had to ask: "how exactly ?"

"The CAT scan at the General caught her stroke before it could strike," says she as she outpoured a heart attack of Bird's best custard atop and about the bowl.

"I'm really delighted."

"Her Highness Diana paid for it; just earlier this year."

"Entirely ?" said the Prince surprised plus double surprised that 'Background Summaries' were a tad too summary sometimes.

It was put about that the handsome prince was doing some eel fishing or something for the afternoon. He did not eel fish; he did an almost four hour detour to the coast. Prince within Jag departed discreetly via Spencer Close. He told the gorgeous driver he wanted "to see something special." Secure Detail and Driver gave each other knowing eyes. 'Dockland Doris' sat in the back, saw nothing and relaxed; the cruellest of nicknames picked up when he worked for showbizz. Princess Doris de Docklands had done time in the theatre and had achieved some wilde somnambulating between the taverns of Soho and the 'Laundries' about Shoreditch but those days were now numbering.

The tinted *Tuath* sped by: Trianlár gave way to Newport and on they went. Imagine he imagined 'in the past you needed to conquer in chain mail, sat ahorse and it could lame, even if the mare was white. Then out of an unsuspecting thicket might leap a Sirhan Sirhan savage slinging outrageous poisoned arrows at one as one added some Bally, Carrick or Insha to your Angevin ones Hesse your Hanover House.' Doris'd been put well to bed and now he was eager to see the ancestral home of his girlfriend, Sophie. He reminded the more and more gorgeous driver with each mirror flirt to turn at the sign for Rossport. He pointed out to the embassy's driver that this off the record visit was to take a few snaps to show Sophie what expanse of clearances her ancestral thaneens had had. "I believe in Ahland they're called *Tawnistes*," he told the two disinterested beefs up front. The future Countess of Wessex's Great Grandmama he identified as a Mrs. Bournes. The Erse speakers about these Errises styled her *Maisteras Ruadh,* and with her kirtle length *gruach* of strawberry locks she could clip some cupla fuckles at the natives to chastise, jape betimes admonster them." Perhaps he was telling too much but they'd both sworn secrets' acts. "When Lady, well sort of Lady Bourne, Bournes died an obliging *banshee* was paid a groat a shriek." The two smirked for him. He was in the middle of the back seat, leaning into their frontage. What he said was all true: *banshees* were mostly for the Ladies of that house and demise-eve they'd shrike the airways; enough to vix the boreenless wuthering, kinda how a milestone would puncture a clutch of decades. By dint of a parchment The Bournes were the Masters of all the eye-ken thereabout the North and East extents of the Bay of Sruth Fada Con (from the Aboriginal that meant 'long current of the hound ').

Princely hadn't wanted the Dublin Embassy to get too fussed up about his detour so he had to nonchalant his otherwise enthusiastickles. They drove beyond the turn at Muingabo and took the next west and zoomed off ways away over blankets of bog till just to remains of what, he could hardly read the dossier, yes, the old relic of the once decent Greannaigh Chapel. "Bingo; we're getting hot." The Prince popped up and beheld his Olympus OM10. He downed the Jag's back tint left baywatch. "There that's it; the ruins of the Hice o' Rossport." He had all the shine of the back seat to himself.

Necessary tangenteen two. Go back one month and a week to the day after the Garter and Thistle became one, June 1707, when Queen Anne clunk glasses with delight at Team GB's birthday, England & Scotland one happy isle "at lang laste" she japed. Said News likely took that long to arrive to The-Land-That-Time-Forgot that is Erris. As that 'hear yee, hear yee' was being belled by the lame village-crier the Bournes were on their way to an awfully important appointment. The Bournes Family on the tenth of June, 1707 had a rather large tract of land granted them by a Sir Arthur Shine. Apart from the generosity of the hectarage there was a long list of what the family had rights to on that land and how far into the future their among-other-things, their ground rents'd stretch, one year short of the Thousand. There was also a delight of wee details: 'on sealing hereof it is agreed that the within named Thomas Bourne shall have the Liberty of taking seaweed for manuring the lands of Kilgallen and a lease on all salmon fisheries abutting the cartrons of Kilcommon to LeeNoMore.' The Vicar of Kilcommon, the Reverend Josiah Toilet was their witness. Over decades the succeeding Bourneses got more and more hundreds, upon hundreds of snipish bogland till in that and their happy year of 1847 they ultimately went lived in their Squirage and built a house for themselves. There were no roads to speak about so they were borne by piggyback by the local Irishry, like something you'd see in the Carleton, along hare ways and half wild goat tracks.

Just the night before the royal excursion a certain Pender Jones, some Mi5 sort of chap, the Prince Edward believed, had come over specially to show his Principe-ship aerials and satellite obliques and now in te the delight o'day the happy Prince could make sense of them in realty and clickedy booh with his OM10. He was discreet so only whispered "there that's *Gort na hAscaile*" (from the meant Aboriginal; 'Fields of the Arm'), "there the long forgotten homestead of the Bournes," self-defiled Lairds of Rossport and their outstretched lands. Sophie Bournes Rhys-Jones, his soon to be fiancée, the simple seeming daughter of a tyre salesman was the direct descendent of these sort of *Tawnistahs*. The house and extensive lands of Sophie's ancestor, 'the Master Bournes' were on a lease renewable as good as FOREVER made on that overcast attempt of a June day, 1707, same lands extend their ground rent into Modernity to that grand pine forest that comes right to the edge of Sruwadacan Bay. 'Ceptin the salmon rights all was intact. Seaweed manure pah !

Roll on Galveston/ Stavanger, what an excellent spot for a spot of refining,' the Prince weighed 'and a dial 9-9-9 of a lease: there'd be hardly a drop of the black stuff left chaffing in th'East Atlantic's depths by June 9th, 2706 AD.' As he surveyed the innocent sod he chuckled with the bemuse how the modern Irish think ole hooey to grind rents; 'read the small print of yore.'

The Prince took some snaps of the ruins of Rossport House; with a longer lens, shots along the bay. Then 'feck it' he opened the door and gestured the detail to stay put. He went towards the sea and decided to earth. He removed his St. Hilliers and his creamyish socks and for more yards than he cared to count entertained the acupuncture of the crushed bonndals, periwinkleens and sloak underfoot, such a freezing sea, salty, yet non Saxon. The handsome bodyguard did both a buzz kill and an enticing seaside silhouette, hands in his pockets doing God knows. He wasn't in the way as Edward took snaps of bay and west but was when he pointed his lense eastish inland where a Dunsinane of Christmas trees were busy growing and unusually they reached to the ever angrier sea-waters. 'In a decade they'll be as high as Norwegian trees for Trafalgar Christmas and be ready and able to hide our future's mighty bounty and that big stout Pipe they've planned entering the ever-enlarge-able, modular terminal and the biggest effing refinery ever.' Enough geomancy and he went to imagining making Sophie honourable 'in bridal white, Her Royal Highness The Princess Edward, Countess of Wessex, Dame Grand Cross of the Royal Victorian Order, Dame of Justice of the Most Venerable Order of the Hospital of St John of Jerusalem and most, most importantly Mistress Bournes. Double imagine a *HELLO* mag cover of him and her paddling right here. Not likely.' He plashes brine north with a little kick. 'FOREVER!!! If it were Gilbert 'n' Sullivan the chorus'd be *well tickle me title deeds* ! Well not for-ever forever but nine hundred nice plus ninety years on nine years; how speedy can that be? Even in regal eagle terms it is long but it does go by.'

Edward was only too delighted to do his part for the Family but was worried the body guardian, making towards him, might make umbrage: red royal feet and more. This was before ankles were welcome fetish and as for his calves. So without proper drying them he resocked and reshod.

After that prince and driver and detail made off in the smoothest car then and there in all North Connaught towards Bangor. At the Burmah garage they picked up the scheduling girl and went west to Our Lady's School Belmullet-on-Sea, many of whose students would become employees of the way-in-the-future refinery, putting their chemistry to practical use foil wrapping breakfast baps for 'finery workers but for now Prince Edward got trapped in the lower corridor and the smell of girl and got his snap taken with the best purchase of a gligeen of a smile mid the clatter and mob of milling teenage girls in navy blue uniforms and goose pimpled legs fancying him so rotten, that just a cheeky peck at him, might liberate his reptile, if he were so inclined.

CHAPTER THIRTEEN

Duhallow had already asked Anton and Tanya to transfer their map to Eamon Ceannt, Conference Room 6, a floor above, "put it high on the brightest wall." He left them to it and by threeses he wanted to go surprise them with a tray of tea and Marietta lathered with Flora.

Duhallow bursts in on them both: "shocking brilliant, love it; there be stratagems." He gaped at the outlines of their mighty map, leaves down the tray and fake hobbles his Captain Hook leg. He stops his piracy and normalises: "we can make easy reference back to your wall map once applications start to arrive for block this or that; brilliant, up they'll go on your map. The info is digital but your big visible map; so much easier. Brilliant Tanya; the makings of a war room hey. Anton; I am really, really impressed," Duhallow wasn't really able to do the exhaustion of under-35s-positivism'll-move-mountains, but this was his best go at same.

The new map was being done up on a magnolia coloured ply that while stuck to the solid wall with industrial grade blue tack, could yet be prised off. All this process was another fine waste of days in Duhallow's head and would be "what dimensions all told ?" The both of them knew but Tanya with her short legs measured out thirteen metres along in seventeen tight jean-strides. At the door jam she leapt, more pogoed and hollered out: "three metres high, Boss." "Imagine" Anton imagined but also said "'thirty nine square metres.'"

"What are the 39 steps ? What are the 39 steps ?" Duhallow antiquates.

Anton had gotten a compassionate day off, just that yesterday so that let Tanya hold her own, passionate leave cause Padraic had had an accident and was still in St. James's but the concussion was mild. He had been getting the hump of Rialto canal bridge when thump, bump, sigh not a thing could be remembered and his left leg was gashed radically. Thank the Great-War-answering-the-Redmondite-call-cock-oh-hay-and-the-cold-milk-tea-face-now-in-flounder-trench-of-him'd   been preserved but track pants; no protection. Anton had bought an arnica salve that he loved anointing twice a day the worst bits. He'd go visit before work and afters. Tanya Electra Gibbons had been able to keep motoring on with the map but, though fastidious for her years (4 x cycles of Saturnine returns), she was not so Mizz Diligent as Anton von Colour-themes, but top notch on peninsulae curves, specially the deep dippers. After threezies Anton sends a text to Padraic: 'ill be delay at work. the blinkin map. kisses. flowers. RUB-A-DUB.' He can text and take two steps down a stairs at a time.

Then it's almost five Duhallow enters this time Anton's office as he was eager to learn something new to keep his late afternoon right brain taxed, "wards off the de-ments" but he also needed to pre-empt press questions around the new extended continental shelf plus at the coming "Oil Slithers 2023" Conference legal arguments might trump shelf technical pernickities specially over Fursy and MacDara block zones and policy beyond the Gollum Crest so "I'd best be at top bamboozle." This was Anton's third attempt at sinking in the sub-marine detail for Duhallow: "The legal Continental Shelf consists of the shelf, slope and rise and extends two hundred nautical miles from the coast line, or further if the shelf naturally extends beyond that limit. It's that simple."

"That's what be-fucking-fuddles."

Anton got a little jolt from the tetragrammaton infixed. Late in the day Duhallow's fuse got cursory.

"Show me again on your gorgeous map." They went upstairs. The Doctor at Law, shoddy Hibernia's Secretary of General NRG was not wasting time this time; he just figured that since he himself could not understand the definition then Anton could not possibly understand, but as it turned out descrying Continental Shelves was so much jelly and pink custard to Anton.

"This map is ever more stunning," opined Duhallow yet again with as Oxbridge an ed-uke as he could genuine and he furthered, while fathering Tanya's shoulders from behind, "talk of wow factor," he modernised for the second time that day. For Tanya this was coming from a place of realish marvel. "The dirty teal of the carpet tiles seems to make it jump at one," Tanya said imitating posh, her Harasstown loosening from his dubious patrickle grip. Landmass Ireland had finally gotten over her sicky and gone become an Aer Lingus green blue. The nerdy exactitude of longitude and latitude lines really animated all thirty nine square metres; the eensy widths of red ribbon threads for the downs, thin as paper cuts on a teenager's wrist plus the wiliest exactitude for curvature for the world, 1mm per something metres. Mauve thread for the acrosses, thirty blocks per each degree latitude and longitude, five by sixwise. All this gridlock made a cage effect, and Ireland the young prisoner, albeit gilded in spartan parts. Duhallow spoke his thoughts "Dots Dingham used call this room the 'Can't-Stand-Losin' Room'" but he didn't explain why. Anton wondered if this was the chambre of some of the inner deepest circular treachery; 'in this very place the former freckled public servant'd purvey and deny licence contracts and likely cream damn fine percentage fixer fees for himself and those he served; whoever they were.'

"Anton; the Shelf; once more from your breaches! Don't tell; show me."

Anton aims his lecture at Tanya first, but she'll go accuse him of mansplaining so he diverts to the boss. Tanya doesn't care about continental shelves anyhow; her chosen subject is micro caverns of oil condensate and how uptodate and agile is the technology in relation to how to suck 'em dry.

Thus TEDs off Anton - Continental Shelf, this, that, how many thousands of kilometres it is likely to be wigglewise. He shows the outer outer parts of it and ratios them in relation to Ireland's coastal circumference. He is way out of his depth beyond the glowiest sunsets o'Mordar. He explains how the Shelf grows a per cent per year as its declivities become better charted. Then Duhallow switches off from the words and goes has a sort of road-to-Damascus moment. The sheer wonder. He has never seen the parts for the whole ever. He is grasping the full whack of the MAP. He sees what Anton always sees. The dells and parishes of the under milk foam. He sees beyond the crude yet accurate 5,140 block grids all there presented, sized so they'd fit a gold leaf sized paper perfectly, real gold. Anton had over spent buying the leaf at Daintree's for the extant gushers, then silver for everything currently at market value worth bringing ashore via pipe. All the other taken blocks were coloured according to company with reference to the years left in their exploration licence. Anton places lovingly a sheet of gold leaf over Block 1916, one block east of Corrib Erris and no longer virgin, 75 illusory klicks off Maya. She'd been drilled, was brim with gases but the round-tabulists, top Department, had kept that mum for now. Duhallow ponders as Anton fusses with the gold: 'if he only knew the fifth of it.' Then once more, Cynic's given shore leave and Duhallow's inner Disney Mermaid gets virgilled about, to and through the sanctimost clefts of the deep saline Nirvana.

Usually for Sec. Duhallow Irish waters equalled what; The Grey Sea, that one thousand Jason Paddy Dans could hooker over, gather biteens o'their wrack, glimpse a whale a whileen then drown be the drag o'their bawneens; essentially 50 shades of fleeceless bollock-shrinkage but today Duhallow heard the Sirens shout 'LOOK AT ME I have my own boundless Glen-Vays, Malures, Aherlows in perfect dilsk.' Anton concludes his lecture on self continence and goes to decrinkling some gold leaf then precise places it with a camp sigh that ryles Duhallow back from his mesmer; in a flicker boss man's back persecuting Christians once more.

"Anton, have you ever had folk ringing you up about shifts in Gardiner's Continental Shelf whatnots?"

Not with gold, but with what looks to be Woodbine's pack-a-twenty foil, Anton flattens more Longford sized stormy whale lanes but he's using real silver paper. Red was the usual colour in the oil industry to illustrate hopeful fields. Anton could be quite the rococo and these silvers were in his mind for areas of hope. Tanya the brutalist compos for Anton's away-with-the-fairies moment. "He has," says she, dead giving away that Anton told her most everything.

"Sort of." says Anton reconnecting.

"Rattle that noggin-the-nog. Yes or No answer."

"Actually round Halloween. I remember last time......"

"Tricky treatin.'" says Tanya.

"Go on." Duhallow wishes he'd waited till he'd gotten Anton alone.

"I go to the phone. Answer it. A guy with a Latin sorta voice asks if the Gardiner's model's been implemented....."

".......sounds like you remember it word for perfect word." that's Tanya just actin' the Columbo maggit. "And what did he say?" Tanya steps in for Duhallow.

"Well I said, I believed as much and the rude fellow hung up without name or tanks."

"I see." Duhallow senses a conclude.

"What I do get more calls about is these fellows." Anton hops about the map on wall pointing to blocks that have photocopied wee pale postcards of what Anton thought were twin dolphins, their necks entwined. Each block gets the twinky dauphin love card. They are in reality killer whales not dolphin silhouettes. "These lads. In one particular zone there are four of these nature blocks all clustered in one area. He marionettes with a flick of his arm to way way off Loop Head, then drops down and it is well west south west beyond the Dingle Peninsula.

"Special Areas of Con-serve-ation." says Duhallow chomping his bits.

"A lot of questions, often I would say from the same source."

"Meaning...?"

"Zero zero five, five prefix. Always slipped my mind to write down the entire number."

"What happy place is that?"

"Brazil. Sir." With that Anton's iphone made its sex appetite app ping ding in his pocket. Any gay man between twink and red sports car crisis would recognise its exhilaration.

"What sorts of questions ?

"Don't go opaque on uz now Anton," guns Tanya.

"I imagine they are trying to figure how fussy we are in defining these special areas of conversation."

"Tell them it is not our field nor the Department's. We accept whatever we are told defines an S.A.C. at a given time."

"Get you. I say to dem go talk to Institute *Namara* place."

"Proper procedure. Nought to do with uz."

"And I warn them that that ground can be shifty. One year it's kelpies, the next stony coloured corals, not much cleverer than mud or a mating rock o' gannets."

"Easy on the t.m.f.i." suggests Tanya.

"I agree."

"And they get consternated likes I've invented the rules and I recall they asked once or twice does one speck of an S.A.C. negate a whole block from being explored or even analysed let alone drilled and I replied 'as far as I am aware,' so I did."

By six he said to Tanya, "let's call it a day." Tanya said "break, me arse; not now Anto" said 'cause she was mid the swirls of the contours of the bank about Eriador, eight hundred metres beneath the known world. Anton was determined for a Twirl. There was only Flakes. He input one euro and a fifty cent coin and the Vector Vendor dropped one. He decided to eat it by the canal on his favourite bench. Picnic Bar was midweek treat. Twirl each second Wednesday. He noted that the top floor of the mystery building on Herberton Terrace had a window open. 'That's a terrace.' If he could find a suitable fire escape after dark at the back lane...... 'but sure it is dark.'

Anton's ECCE app signalled again that joyous bing, twice as mindful in its ding as whatsapp. 3 x messages in his message box. How wanted is that? For a man who'd over the past two days poked, hearted and favourite-d a score of guys it was slow going. Lack of a penis shot possibly. There was no close up pic either of Rigger's (Anton's ECCE tag name) shapely fingers therefore no clue to the white gold band of trust; costed the earth his wedding ring. Anton's main ECCE picky was from his 33rd year in white vest, his tan glowering health, his teeth like the David's, his peptides like the Goliath with full mammoth bone a-swing but no coy smile, as no face. He didn't need Padraic or a Squealer stumbling on his cybernetic sexy flirt-life. The bing and ping of his phone one'd imagine could give the game away but as a bookie's has no windows, same with *l'addiction d'*Anton; it was done in unnatural lite. Look his arsewise pic pure Abercrumble with randy butter melting 'tween his cheeklettes. He had no penis picture out of fear of cognition and a modesty common to Dublin West. The first msg. was from an insomniac '52 year young non feminate sout tipp farmer,' sent at zero four nineteen a.m. with a picture of d'unbelievable beer belly: *Into rubber. Into wellies.* Delete *sans lire* so he does. 'God you'd wish these guys could at least have the *nous* to lie a little,' thinks Anton between his ears. Then delight a msg. from a handsome goatee who speaks seven languages, is Hispanic stroke Other, his penis is set back, its length undefined, working in I.T. in Dublin. 'Likely Google bitch.' Anton presumed yet saved the message on the basis of mystery, and the tad of virility implied by sideburns. That his body was described as average was not a negative. There were no supportive pics of this average body. Irish averages equalled beer bellies, a Paddy slim could be a Japanese stocky. Hispanic averages were likely Trojan Hectors say after a Christmas overdoing it. Anton never consummated in 3D any of these dalliances. The pings and bings were his Canal Turns, his Beecher's Brook, his photo fin..... Padraic had his own hobby: gay bored games club each bi Tuesday.

The final message had no picture and Anton ignored it, some fellah called CERETIC. A female duck quacked at him from the canal; paddle boating, she was keeping her distance from the mother-of-pearl vanity of some bloke ducks. 'Me2,' figured Anton of the animal kingdom then all of a sudden bottle city, up he stands. 'My spy plan,' like phone Apps had been sapping his resolver-aero; if not a proper spy he'd have the go at being the quack spy. Off he traipses, eastish, meets Callows Lane, enters a car park by bending under a scarlet 'n' cream car check point.

Beyond is really dark. 'Hah there is a fire escape' but it only works from above so he leaps up like a Moldovan bronze medallist and catches it and it clangs down to him; so up he clombers, up four floors of it. He keeps to the backs of the buildings, Dick-Van-Dykes about the chimneys and eaves till he reaches the one he assumed was #26 and double 'Hah'; the window is yet open and the only such, a sort of a garret of a window, grubby as. In he sleuths, lands him in a box room with ageing files. Their kind is familiar to him. Only then big dawn: where's the ole comfort zone gone 'n' gotten to ? 'Am I a law breaker technically ?' The door is not locked. There is some light from dodgy fluros and a sense of nobody about the open top floor space with many, many top of the range filing cabinets dominating an undone up office, like nobody'd shown it a jot of t.l.c. since 1991. There is a p.c. at a corner desk humming but dark. He approaches it and presses 'B' and it awakens with a fairly old fashioned hullabaloo. On screen, being recently worked on with yesterday's date is a letter in Energy Department format, addressed to a familiar name in Stately Oil. It is a list of blocks that they'd been interested in and a list as long as your arm as to why they were out of bounds in the coming bonanza, all kinds of strong to weak excuses, including recently designated S.A.C.s. Stately Oil'd already been doing great explorations in Dooish district and were in terms of admin and honesty second to some, so 'what was this reluctance ?' He scrolled to see who was signing off on such work. Duhallow's electronic signature, possibly not likely really him, Anton imagined, then hoped.

More mouse and single finger types and Anton is so far out of his comfort zone that he can hardly register his steps, moving deeper through the snarls and lianas, to ticker thickets, into deepest primeval uncomfort without even the weeniest crumbles of Flake to Hansel & Gretel his way back to Normalcy. He pressed Desktop, then Documents, then scanned the Titles of Folders: HISTORY was one of eleven headings and he clicked it and it had five subcategories: GolfBall Pollytomish/ Knock Airport Runway/ Securitisation Gal-Mayo / Pipe's Connectors/ Fat One latest Timeli... He screenshot with his i9 the contents and the content's content. He clicked back to DOCUMENTS with eleven sub buttons, second from the bottom was a category heading; ANG.IE. Anton wondered in particular about the GolfBall so he back clicked and clickedy clack more and speedy enough up come gorgeous PDF pages and diagrams of radio signals and o'er his head post Cold War stratagems. GolfBall appeared to equal some sort of a RADAR as he found diagrams and a picture of a giant white ball. Over the photo of the golf ball atop its mountain is headlined **North West Mayo** in Rockitt Extra Bold. Anton squints to see if there are cars parked by the ball building; he needed clarity on scale. A Focus and a Fluence indicated that the ball was the half size of a not modest planetarium. Likely manned; it appeared to be a fancy enough radar station specially constructed across the late nineties. The facility was "dedicated to the East Atlantic area." Where precisely? The picture said underneath itself that it was *Hill above Pollatomish, Rossport.* Overlooking the entrance to Shrew Wodcan Bay. Anton knew nothing about radionix but he sped read that hilltop watch had top o'the range span of radar - massive scan-ability and its nearest neighbour - a similar giant golf ball on the Shetlands and oh another in the place called the Schull in the county of Cork. Like Martello towers thought Anton 'but what's their Napoleon? How scoundrel and what genus o' bogey man are they keepin' sketch for ?' Then the driest wispeen of metaphorical straw that breaks backs broke Anton's. He read words, sort of items that once seen, can't be unseen. In plain 12 font Times New Roman he read that this Mayo golf ball plus its sister radars, casual as you please, were "high energy monitor's whose job was to control rigs and shipping without recourse to national meteorology nor to normal (native) aviation." (their underlining). There was some cross referencing to orders from Ayr. Anton knows Ayr is in Scotland as he'd met a lovely Scot called Scott once in the sauna before his marriage, before even clapping eyes on salt-of-his-awfully-ert. They'd had half an afternoon's worth of the yang-yin of 69s then some dozy 96s, even shared the sun tanning facility, ten minutes each: back front/ front back, so five minutes this way and that and Scott yammering on about tan-lines this and that. Using his big purposely limp hand, Scott had indicated what south inclined droop of Scotland Ayr sat on 'cause that was his hailfrom.

Just as Anton clicks on ANG.IE file his ECCE's zen-like bing ping bad-times a ding ting; new message. Anton scrambles it to silence but his sex drive grabs the info straight off. That CERETIC once more. Logline: HERETIC FOR FUN NOW. These tantalising apps, their vibrations and pings were near instant gratification yet contained steps of 'courtship.' First a 'Hi,' then send a face pic, or a 'WHAT U INTO?' Orientals favoured long winded explanations of self that nobody reads unless anonymous, incurable rice queens. Anton hears a creaking and two voices in a room at the back. No, it is a single voice on a telephone. He looks to his iphone: Ceretic speaks English and Spanish, while his Profession stated 'Hardware,' his cock was XL, his inclination top/versatile could mean he was prone after a bloody mary or three to a jolly good chakring . There was a picture of an adorable waxed chest. Anton starts to move back towards the way he came in. As Anton was a paid up annual ECCE Platinum he could see in picture four and more inflated in five a clear view of this Ceretic's soft bedevilling sausage, set in a mash of pubic manicure. It looked oddly familiar. Anton is back in the open air; he can see the edge of the canal below between a gap in the buildings and normal people heading home from their nine to fives without any crevasses opening.

The next   msg was 'Hi.'   and then, without his replying, a second msg boldly stated 'CAT BURGLAR?'   Anton stopped in his tracks on the rooftop. 'What the feck!!!'   Next vibrate and it has a pic attached and he opens it. A shot of a bruised leg, a strong unmistakeable calf. 'OMG it's like Padraic, from his hospital bed ?'   Then another pic of a sock jutting above cyclo pro's trainers, more ad than enticement. 'It is Padraic in his hospital bed and they've gone 'n' waxed him ?!'

The self styled Ceretic had no face so Anton asked for it, still wish-filling that this is normal app seduction. Ceretic claimed he was based in Dublin 32; wherever that lies. Anton sent a simple fifteen character msg. from the top of the fire escape. 'Face pic please'. He needed to understand.   He needed a hug of understanding. Get better my husband. His bladder longed for a toilet. Ceretic's swift reply said simply *Oy Rigger; meet me @ LemonCello in 1hour, enclosed close up recent pic as requested, jajaja, C.* There was one picture attachment. It made Anton wretch a vomit on the lane below; only the flakiest chocolate. There was this picture of Padraic in the most awful Pieta of suffering on the roadway, his bike the Virgin, him an Offaly Christ, conked out, as good as dead to the world and a knife, a Stanley (all purpose) held to his ear by a hand with a genuine Tag Heuer. Ding, another message:

'Want Pee on Life-Support? Keep mum alive ! Keep our *rendezvu* mum. No snoopers. No snipers. LOL.'

Anton arrived in the Italian Quarter early and went to the magazine area of Centra (*'for the way we live today')*. His planking was offset some by solace in the form of a butch Togolese man secure and bouncering the west Centra entrance with a name tag that said 'Admire' which might be an order but it was his name.   Anton could see that Admire was alert to movements 'like a mother rhino must after calving.' Admire possibly an Adventist trapped in the evil city. He didn't just perceive the magazine gawpers but the street walkers and it was easy to see into Lemoncello's bright world. If a shoplifter pocketed a brie he could look forward to both a manhandle and a moral approbation from a rare gift of righteousness or a heroin adept would have her shrift and loud mouth shortened if she got lippy with the likes of Admire. Anton didn't feel abductable if he was within the ken of this broadly African. The footfall about and into Lemoncello in and about 18:30 was straight acting. One woman that could have been his Aunt went in and then went out again, off put.   He could yet ring his cousin who was married to a detective in Store Street Garda station and get backup or at least a wise-up. He went as far as googling their confidential number ? At least he wouldn't be shot and this mystery could stop cliffhanging about him. He felt that whatever black op was about him, i or u or any phones were easy peasy access-wise - NSA or the blinkin' Kremlin.

The Lemoncello staff were really nice considering. They floated mallow dice in his mug of fair play hot chocolate and insisted he have the fabulous day, though the night was all about. There were twelve innocents in the shining place, mostly homosexual pretending at things, adjusting their butts on the extreme yellow plastic.

The only fellow who could be Ceretic was already in the space, though Anton'd not seen him arrive. He was about 43 and half ish and not creepy looking in the slightest. He did that smile that only English can dare pull off, a sort of smirk, then turned out not to be *Sasanach* in the slightest. He proffered the emptiness opposite himself so Anton sat there in front of the murderous

131

eyes. His accent when he said things was Irish gone to America and back, creative industries pulled-pork Williamsburg but no more than a decade away. He was saying things to Anton and Anton grasped only parts, one was about Hydrocarbon distillate, another was "a good find left in the ground is money in the bank." He was sure that is what the fellow said. Anton blocked his need to shit and said straight to the man "listen you nut job; don't murder my boyfriend, in fact my husband?" That's a hard statement to whisper in a barby coffee joint. His blurt came though he hadn't heard anything yet pertinent to blackmail, threats to his family life and the assassin maybe didn't heed what he had just said and maybe Anton's gone sat with the wrong fellow but then the stranger went and said:

"We need you alive," the guy sat there as if he could live in Moyne Road D6 or D4 without a bother with a *Room-To-Improve* kitchen extended into a garden likely. He could have two kids in Michaels he was so flippin' upper middle normal, sort of fellow you'd see in a window graphicing or architecting the next snazz in the way of the city at some fancy design apparatus that could only deal with minimalism and temporary-ism.

"Our need of you will become clear inside next some weeks. Till then enjoy your free time. You actually have nothing to worry about. We need your help with something. Also we need you to stop being a cat."

"Pardon you, sorry me."

"Curiousity?"

"Why me. I'm a...."

"Quit snooping. The threat to your mother's life is what we hope will persuade you most but for now we choose your 'husband's' welfare. Should you go to police, Store Street, or any Garda station or journalist. If you persist like being cat-Robin we will have accidents to first him, Mr. Pee as you say, then your mother, then your sister, then your estranged father. Sometimes they, we do niece and nephew injuries, just to be clear from the start. Not killed though but we have no time for that now. Accidents include heart attacks, a very paralysing stroke. Bikes obviously. Electrical fault fires. At the first sign of not cooperating we will kill Mrs. Fruen nee Cloherty. Do you understand me? You are not dealing with a criminal. This is not curable or quantifiable. The *Garda* Ombudsman's scope enquiry won't even know we exist. We are a household name doing corporate diligence. We are a corporation that is sometimes a country or more than one." The blackguard takes a last appreciating gasp of his rosehip and fennel tea. "Bribery oddly can backfire. Primal fear works the wonders," he says putting on a post inner city Dublin accent as if that will 'gratiate Anton. He goes silent, face droops this sorta lilt of certitude like to cover his own ass and moral tracks and says he: "I have my own hands tied. Don't imagine you're the only one living a nightmare, even on this island where nothing happens or appears to happen."

"You saw me on the rooftop?"

"This is a small city. If you might simply be going down Wicklow Street and see me. Do not under any circumstances acknowledge me. I will contact you through ECCE, not always Ceretic. Ceretic for now. He'll do."

"I have no cause to go next nor near Wicklah street, mister."

" When you hear the ping - I always intro 'what you into?' then you'll know soon enough that our Operation is moving to full mobilisation and most importantly our need of you. Ultimately the turn around'll be swift and the demand on you moderate to medium. Any hint of straying like if you thought to confide to your shrink, should you need one, your mate, Cyril, whoever, especially Store Street," and Ceretic points at Anton's iphone with a chiding grimace that implied 'yih big eejit yih for googling the cops.' "This will be all over very soon, a short nightmare and you know if you play your part - you might even get a few bonbons for Xmas bonus."

Anton hadn't touched his not hot chocolate. The Ceretic, was clearly not even bisexual and clearly had emerged out of a reality that must be at least four dimensions away. The threatener got up and walked out the door, passed Centra and nodded to Admire and Admire nodded back, out of politeness, one hopes. 'God if there were in some Clayton Hotel a Butchest Security of the Year Award (category: Small Stores), no prizes for guessin' who'd win !' Anton diverts his right brain a moment then back to his moving horror. ECCE, "Jesus;" there was no Ceretic, no messages, all was swiped clean away. Last taken snaps were his mum at the Marina in Donabate holding her hat in the wind. The screen shots from the alternate Department of Double Dealing be the canal in the attic had all gone.

CHAPTER FOURTEEN

In the reception of The Sound Hotel Agent 700, Susan Zeng, was receiving one hundred thousand welcomes and a thanks-a-million for choosing pre Christmas offer: Dinner + B&B all in €49.99. The receptionist, tagged Laura said "Mrs. Zeng, welcome to the windiest spot in Ireland." Laura looked back at her guest's looking back and wondered if 'spot' was not in her vocab. Laura gave her her room card and explained how to use it, as if her developing world required such upgrading.

After saying her version of prayers Ms. Zeng drove west o'er the causeway, then careered south. On a screen in the coastal fringes of Tianjin, 'Shire 101' team operatives on a wall screen could track Agent 700's motoring slow as a drunk along the eastern road down Belmullet peninsula - the street view version showed her pass the frontier from the English speaking north to the southern Belles who speak the cleanest Aboriginal, Zeng sped up, a sign indicating the border's language border says simply and to the point 'ON GAEL TALK.'

Zeng arrives at the gravel entrance of St. Derbhladh's Chapel and parks her Accord beside a ramshackle Focus. Nobody paid heed to the bit of a seventh century starless chapel except on Pattern Day Sunday. TripAdvisor were still seeking a comment on it. Zeng leapt the stile and entered the roofless bit of a temple. She looked skywards; God's speed was in the form of lily white yet impatient clouds. A youngish man with hair of ropes peered in the wee qitab of an early medieval window and coughed mildly. It was not a cough for attention but of a few too many Old Holburns. Zeng went to the window and the youth was gone, so as she waited she read the Office of Public Works sign that told the legend of Derbhladh and her eyes issue. She'd plucked them both out. Seems Derbhladh, the daughter of a Chieftain had two offending eyes, Zeng was not sure if they were enchanting others to lust her ways or were the vehicles for her own wishful thinking. Anyway out they came like delicacies.

The young man approached the Chinese lady. The latter piped up "that's a drizzle and a half," though the sun, if meagre, was persistent.

"Down for the day."

Susan Zeng, that is Agent 700 regarded the young man questioningly, sensing a lack.

"Oh yeh. Mark my words. Down for the day."

Zeng had to correct the native speaker: "Down for the day. Mark my wuds."

"Oh yeh. Yeh." the young spy toes the pea gravel with his shoddy red Penney's runners.

"Mr. Shivnan, I am assumed."

"Yes 700."

"Zeng, Susan Zeng. We'll be working close together."

"Delighted." Darren Shivnan smiled like he'd never imagined to be in a Cormanesque B-remake of a Derek Flint prequel.

Close I, a security agency affiliated to S.N.A.K. Oil came across Darren Shivnan who'd been working in Galway mid to late 2020, doing programming that was countering hacks. Best learning was to hack by night and day job, unravel. He was no Essange but had hacked the Diocese of Elphin for practice; vocations page and replaced it with an ad for a Shamanic Coven and he had hacked an unnameable Milk Coop and inset large human woman breasts on their ABOUT page. Childish yet gifted stuff. That was when Close I realised they may have found their man, a seeming contrarian who yet dug reliability, had half an inkling to a Celbridge like life, his rebel self was just touching but not higher than a mean 20% in Close I's Dept of Psyche's version of enneagram character types. They delved his bank accounts, saw he was renting half a house in Knocknacarra (St. Jude's) with dreadful mould in its bathroom. Close I, formerly BlackGuard arranged for Shivnan's main contract at work to fall through and then the sly approach. In the *Roisin Dubh* bar one late October Thursday when the fogs were heavy about the Corrib and tens of thousands of ghosts were bating their breaths at the coming of Veil-thinning. Essentially a dangerous time for making life changes. In the bar was a line of eager stout fans shaking their tenners at the bar man and one among them was Shivnan and persistent beside him was a woman acting drunk enough, the sort that prefers a nerd to the centre forward. Even her jouncing against Shivnan had been planned, that it would appear not of her volition, but of the melee. Shivnan must also be alone; not difficult. The lovely go-between got in ahead of Shivnan and did her Gaiety Acting School best slur: "Boru 'n' pie-napple," and as she swung out of the mayhem klept eyes at Shivnan, did the teensiest destiny's child co-twinkling and then whoops-ied off to find the only plonk spot - by Shivnan's fawn anorak. She sipped and bided. Shivnan returns with Beamish dashed with black currant. All as natural as an expanding universe, like there was no other space for the voluptriste to park her buns 'n' bits. The plan was keep stumb and she did but it took some dregs before Shivnan turned south more or less and proffered his slippery pale left hand at an high indefatigable angle and said "Darren."

She couldn't but duplicate and lefted him as if they were doing a "Peace Be With You" at the half eleven at St. Dominix. Skip the hour and forty minutes of chick flex and lads-u-like and she with perfect dexter planted the seed:

"White boy. Did you ever surf?" she hoodwinked.

"I don't like cold."

"With a 5mm rubber you don't feel a thing."

The fifth pint for many humans has them mildly miasmic, especially the skinny and dinnerless. Then started the tilting inwardly at one another and outwardly awkwardly. Once Shivnan leant a stagger that got a satellite of cleavage. His disequilibrium study was a success and he says to her "zip, zip."

The Close I operative whose past four vodkas were fake whispered a protracted slurry of fantasy into the troubled hacker cum desktop flop's right ear. All he could recall of what she said was "surf-ragettes annual outing weekend after next." "Where," he asks. "Up Mayo!" says she. "If you've the wheels" code for 'if you've the bollocks, come along.' "I have the wherewithal" and snap she rose and did that Jesus parting the crowd of blind tax collectors exit, like her will drew her to the air. She did a brilliant job. Her acting'd gotten better as Shivnan got drunker. Next morning in his knee ripped Boss Jeans he found a card with her name and for double trouble one in his wallet. So began his career break, a half decade of secrets, treasons and fancy goods: poor bantam waiting soul.

Now he was face to face with the People's Republic of China's fifth greatest killing machine, not by body count but stealth-wise.

"Can you swim?" asks Shivnan. Zeng bows without saying a word. "O.K. would you be worried about drowning?"

"I never worry."

"Well if you were, well, if you wanted not to drown: the old wife's tale goes if you can shimmy your way through that narrow window," and he points at the bit of a qitab of a slim goth of a window of antique chapel, "you'll never drown. St Derbhladh'll look out for you; as much as she can." 700 half gets it and leaps up to try. Her bosom is above average but could make it through but her bubble butt was too taut, long years of Shaolin training: bamboo thwacks, pails of ice water, birch thwacks. Breakfast of millet, thimbles of soya and sprigs of aspen after. If her butt and bust were not on a vertical she could do it. Shivnan horizontal snaking through the window was not on; no luck from that.

"We'll stick to the land." Zeng 700 moved closer toward and about Shivnan, closer yet and touched his dreadlocks, not able to hide her potent disgust.

"They're real ?"

"You'd expected hair extensions?"

"You've been growing them two, no two and half years."

"Spot on."

"You've been embedded that long. No sign of suspicion." Zeng was a statements woman.

"Almost. Sometimes I had to go on the dole cause at the camp they couldn't figure how I was that flush?"

"Flush. So how long dole?"

"I sign on every week at Pollatomish post office. The post mistress who was dead against us at the start - now she loves us, says she'd be closed only for us and we buy most of our emergency grub from her Mace. Mushy peas. She now stocks black eyed beans and lentils on the back of us."

Agent 700 went behind Shivnan and uttered nothing. Shivnan unnerved swung about and Zeng had her eyes closed, was making pre-ordained sighs like she was channelling the forecast.

"Can I help?"

"For now embed me in your camp. When I arrive do not recognise me. Our action must be happening oh one hundred, day after my arrival."

"My own updated information is that my, our insurgency plan has one or two, too many moles anyway and that is a big reason for moving earlier."

"Talk to your people. Lay clear ground" Agent 700 stalls for her first time. "All the top dogs will be in Dublin some big oil gas expo, like how the British were at Fairyhouse during your Putsch of 1916 but what we do will be low key, small potato, a slight awkwardness but enough to wake up, shake up. Our gesture is symbolic, stop flow."

To kill time Darren explained to Agent Susan the antecedents of the camp. He was talking to the person who knew and had memorised the volumetrix of the pipe, had glimpsed and stored 29 pages of political background had memorised as she said herself all the threads of all of Siggin's guidebook ONCE UPON A TIME IN THE WEST but she humoured the mole. He explained how the opposition to the Rossport pipe began, a fat pipe sat atop the sea bed, reaching to the initial find on Block 2016, seventy four kilometres of gorgeous metal, easy money for those in charge of the flow-o-metre. "Lexi, villas in the Med, Daimlers, choppers, Le Broquets if not quite Monets come from it." He forgot to mention Death and Envy. Zeng reckoned Agent Shivnan a tad emotive for a reliable spy and gave him a glower but on he went. He was so over-used to being method stoned that he could not exit his part. "There's about as much luck out of that type of a pipe as what Mesopotamians get from theirs."

"Yes Fire Worship," simply says Zeng putting a lid on his ideation.

It was a rite of passage for many the idealist to spend some time at the anti-pipe camp which had gone under several times from troughs of crushed-by-the-machine syndrome, or simply the tent canvases got sundered by gales, mixed with crushed-by-the-machine syndrome. Leadership, purpose, effectiveness, purposelessness, horizontal deluges all played their parts. The first camp in 2004 overlooked the gap surge entrance to Sruwadacan Bay; it had a glorious aspect, and was sat back like how an 18th century fort does at bay entrance and instead of cannon it had prayer flags, instead of ordnance it had young heads full of caprice for Atlantic-Home-care-free forms of reality.

Zeng to ground Shivnan asked how the camp began. She could sense what a high level of needing to be needed he vibrated.

"This protest was 90% about the safety issue of raw gas moving at such high bar; only 10% wondered who owned the flamin' stuff." Darren incited away at the unsmiling, knowing Chinese lady. "When the pipe finally got to have full intercource with the refinery via a tunnel under the shifting terrain of the bay, the camp was no more." He was right; how quick human endeavour vanishes; just pale rectangles, blotchlettes in the sodding field like North West Mayo was no Wiltshire when it came to grand spirograph in the Summer crops UFO-eyeview-wise.

"Now that the pipe was flowing, the refinery expansion became our new beef and after a gap of years the camp set up closer to the Refinery entrance in the Field of the German, Gurtan-gyarmawnig," she thought she heard him say.

This she weighed was not a camp made for a night before a war. 'It has no bugles, no berserkers keeping watch, fear is low and conspiracy rife, specially about the open fire in dead winter. Shivnan interrupted her fancy train: "there are, see, the full on macro conspiracies (spread by rough as guts skunk mostly), sometimes by a bored spy like me self. Real macros would be like S.N.A.K. are, I don't know stage-managed, by the Annunaki. Then there's the localised conspiracy like anyone with a car younger than 2015 is likely commanded by a collaborator. Any munificence shown by the oil company toward the local community is hypocritical. Take, like the G.A.A., the Gaelic Athlete's 'Sociation," he qualifies for the foreign spy.

"They're the guys who can take briar thorn from feet without stopping."

"Definitely not. They got this amazing new complex. You really should see the spanking new showers, feckin' made with brass, some inclined gold, *faux-cettes*, each with a five minute burst of negatively ionised water. I met the guy who installed them. Crazy but true. Each family with a recent conservatory or weedless tarmac new and steaming; yep they must've pocketed the King's shilling. Get me ?"

"I get it totally. Negatively ionised water can deliver a huge charge. They would be readier for battle."

D.S. explained to Susan/700 more and other local nuances. She leant against the wall and did her own thing. He told her how the refinery was built in stages and she imagined how Sruwadacan Bay must've appeared empty to the first gas pioneers who sailed into the roaring waters first day of April, Year of Our Lord Nineteen Hundred and Eighty Nine. The Chinese know-it-all however didn't know all of it. She didn't know that this Botany Bay grand entrance was scarce months after Their distant Majesties had clinked their pact in The Dam Palace, a cheers to the recovery or discovery of another subcontinent *mar yah*. 700 was, as we know, an 'A' plus at geography; she mused and chewed the cudd of musing that 'this bit of Mayo is the nearest landfall that's not sheer but neat-as, manageable beach, nearest solid matter to the nearest point of Continental Shelf, 75 km off; there their Imperialist pipe can furcate north and south, stretch hundreds of kilometres further up and down the coast but clever enough to have just have this one massive come-ashore-fellow here. They struck luck, handy enough, the nearest piece of shelf offered so much, before the true depths of ocean reveal their Precious.' Her mind got carried ways away awhile and Shivnan yet describing rituals involving brown envelopes.

In the meanderin' of her Mandarin she pieced clews to hunches. In summary she grasped those incontinent clefts held such oozing, treasure fart enough for a gazillion barrels o' laughs-to-the-bank. They found so much and told so few, those wildcat first Pioneers had no ken, more like no care to the existence of the Fomorians who clung to their plots about the long winded name of a bay. Along the shore from Ceathru Thadhg are the wee-est homesteads where real people had no awareness that their Prefecture was in some London futures office or a design bureau in The Hag zoned Basra-Bahrain to stretch its gain across the twenty first century and way inland and mighty refineries fit for a Kuwait or a Qatar gleam on gleam. Her reckoning got the better of her so she breathed in the Shaolin of the stoic-of-the-one-thousand-breaths-in-one and in the concluding exhale got asked by sidling Darren, wedging into her precious space new smudged with her out-breath "what is your real name ?" and she answered cool, yet tinged with amicable "700, just call me 700" talk-to-the-hand for I told you big eejit-of-a-stoner my real name and you've gone forgotten it all ready.

The next evening Darren Shivnan's name was up on the frittered, flapping camp rota to do wash-up. The policy was use extremely hot water with a squidge of vinegar and lemon juice to degrease the chipped plates. Jemima, a barefoot girl did the drying. There was really no drying cause the plates were dry already from the hot water, more she had to nail off a stuck dot of food. She smelt of stale spliff, had ample breasts and suffered fools gladly. She asked Darren:

"We've a late arrival. Is there remainders?"

"By the hob."

Some eaters were still at the trestles and a capricious wind grappled the tent's tarpaulins. More marquis than tent. Shivnan gathered stray mugs and returned to his washing up and watched low esteemed cloud invade the bay for the fortieth pathetic time that day. The camp had no shelter from the Atlantic's worst. He swung about to ask Jem..... then saw a rare woolly technicoloured lady take her food from the hob and go sit sideways to him, eating her dahl and pickles with bare brown hands. The lady had long hair and unnecessary shades, was labradorless and had sandaled feet. Shivnan watched more. When the lady'd eaten all and licked her plate with such a wide of tongue, Shivnan went to collect it. The rough enough oriental goes "Tishi-dih-lig" which is Tibetan for 'Thank You' pronounced properly.

"I'm Darren."

"I'm Wendywee."

"Wendyway or wee ?"

"Wendy like wendy house and wee like Scotch gallic 'eensy.' Eejit."

The camp of twenty three souls,four dogs and newborn kitten were all out of sight but sound. The Tibetan-alike removed her dude round shades and Shivnan gasped . If there were an Oscar for cover-up, she'd win. The seeming Tibetan grabbed Shivnan's wrist like she was the black hatted villain of a 'B' wild western.

"Can I take dessert now?" and there wasn't a hint of possible cotton balls about her mouth nor cheeks. 'What brilliant deformity; how feral,' astounded the half baked hacker bit of a spy.

CHAPTER FIFTEEN

Anton'd been told Padraic was moved to St. Dominix ward from Treezaha's ward cause he'd gone in for that evening's visiting time and not seen Padraic as was normal, sang-idged between a Mrs. G. Delahunty with the wheeze and Mr. G. O'Something with the glad eye. G. Delahunty had an oxygen tank the size of an atom bomb keeping G. Reaper some more fortnights at bay. In St. Dominitricks there are just four beds, a set up that appeared privater and visitors were fewer and less ebullient. There was only one by an empty bed staring at a documentary with Joanna Lumley (she must be eighty if a day) in Yucatan or such a place and she making risky fun of needless human sacrifices in the ruinations of tacky pyramids.

Anton was like a new man for some forgetful seconds, life endorsing. For those moments his step was fresh and the pallor returning to his darling's eye atwinkle from the door gave him some born-a-gain. Life was not elsewhere, but here in the septic flowery perfection with the whiff of meatloaf and cabbage still comforting the air. Nothing like death threat to make life zing. "Health Insurance?" says Anton to Padraic indicating the snazzier modern surround. Padraic responds with a whispered kinda lip-synch of the chorus of Mercury's WHO WANTS TO LIVE FOREVER and they have the laugh. Padraic can't understand why Anton cannot lol-along longer. Anton has slipped again into his plight and an half. How and ever Padraic gets kissed on his left cheek, then turns the other but halfways gets a moist Clondalkin special on his tender Shannon-side lips, slow to medium smacky. Anton takes out the arnica mixed with E45 and puts it on the locker, goes to draw the blue curtain (last changed April 22nd 2021). As he is drawing the curtain, the man in the bed adjacent strikes him as being extremely unsick looking. He looks across the room and there is another person of indeterminate sex living off a drip, then the empty bed. With the curtain shut without chit chat he frees up his husband's body from beneath the immaculate white bedspread. Off with the sheet and there is the perfect leg and the scourged leg. Anton starts at the Achilles heel in tender circles, along the calf, slow as he pleases and to the knee. He adores that back of Padraic's knee, so biddable but the injuries are about the cap and he swirls gentle anticlockwise, clockwise, so slowly about the precious drumlin. On up the thigh. He closes his eyes to better perform, that touch can conquer agenda and ducks and dives with the faintest subtlety clockywise such so many, then about turns willy nilly. Anton looks up and sees a dozing husband and a might of penis tent-poling the sheet. Anton is glad of the sleeping and hides the engorgement with the bedspread and has a chance to weep without questions. It is a protracted grief. Padraic is not really sleeping, just anticipating. When he sees Anton crying, he fakes sleep and is touched by his husband's soft heart. He takes a glimpse after some minutes; Anton is himself again and crushes his hand in his. Anton smiles but then without a word leaves the ward, goes to the nurse's station and asks that he can leave his phone with them as he is afraid it might interrupt the delicate life support systems. The nurses amused agree. Anton goes has a leak in the ward's Jaded toilet. He returns to Padraic's bed and is very quiet. They watch some Joanna Lumley - her presence in the room makes them braver and they hold hands with the curtain open. The adjacent has his back to them and makes sleepy gruntlettes. Anton checks round the bed in a casual way for bugs or hidden cameras. There is a centralised camera in the ceiling like a supermarket's. He jokes with Padraic that it's for wankers, while yet trying to study its angle and wonders its ability to be hacked from without. Perhaps he could slip a paper to Padraic. Padraic keeps going in and out of bursts of guffaws of laughing at the in-secure wanker-cam idea. Anton suggests that he can take time off work and nurse Padraic at home. "Safer. I mean homelier." Padraic won't hear of it. Anton departs and kisses his husband so, so tenderly about his forehead. He turns quickly; Padraic's neighbour had been faking low snores, his left eye half wide shut.

"Morning." Terrence on security tilts his head sideways and notes "bit pale aren't we. Wan or what in the new day sun ?"

"Man flu Terrence. Man flu *in extreme-is*." Anton goes to his office. He is clear. He is going to do nothing and pretend nothing is happening, stop snooping. Keep colouring in his and Tanya's map. Turn off all his apps. No. Possibly keep ECCE. Yes. No. Why ? If these enemies of the State are so super powered they can darn well catch him on extension 256 like always, like anybody else. He deletes ECCE and seven minutes later Padraic's mobile phone texts him WHAT YOU INTO? He re-instigates ECCE without answering the text.

He spends all the morning stacking the applications for licences for 2023 on shelves according to blocks sought. There is an inordinate interest in this year's round because every last one of Ireland's blocks bar those currently under licence is ripe for prospecting, from within ken of the Isle of Man to the deepest shelves well nye the thousand kilometres to the west. Many companies are efficient and send applications in early; don't wait for deadline day. Duhallow had said to not order the applications according to company name but to check first which blocks were sought and in what order of preference and to file them "by block popularity" or cynical Anton by coffee break thought 'file by black op-r-tunism' but he kept calm and by high noon he has great piles on such and such a prospect or another, which he then scribbled in pencil the companies name onto the wall map block. In such wise some blocks had multiple applications. 'Seems there's a lot of new, small companies seeking prospects near SACs,' from minnows he'd never heard of before. He treats lunch as elevenses and has his Kellogs Yoghurt bar (vanilla). His appetite has left him and the bar'll do. On his return he sees patterns; 'so many this year have a penchant not for the nosey droop of the Porcupine or thereabouts but for not so beyond Looper's Head and less near enough of her.' More than half have second choices all about Dooish, south of Rockal and as always some gamblers anonymous have set sites and sea-wagons on the furthest west-i-est, windiest outposts beyond even where neither Saints Barrind or Brandon had even sailed in their holy corracles, within chant 'n' yodel o' the Isengard Ridge. Such wildcat chancer-your-arms Duhallow'd suggest be filed under "schemes planned on napkins after liquid luncheons in the bay window o' the Shelbourne Hotel."

Anton decides to go visit Duhallow mostly as he just needs some grandpa-ing, no intention bar a psychic cuddle but with the excuse of seeing baffling patterns in the first applications - many, new unheard of companies seeking licences in ridiculous districts. Anton shuffles towards the lift, goes up in the world and comes out and strays to the window that looks over at the suspect building. It has lights in every room and six or seven humans or their silhouettes being busy stand-ups and gad-abouts. Anton thinks 'den of thieves squared.' He'd never seen the place so bright and bustly. Duhallow's secretary Yollande was not back from her lunch. He can hear Duhallow raging. He goes to open the door.

"I can't do anymore. Do your worst. Do your fucking worst." Anton leaves off turning the door knob. He goes away from the door and re-approaches after a delay, raps, raps twice, thrice even. No answer but a deep sigh.

"Jarlath. Sir."

Anton opens the door. Duhallow is a sallow heap of tweed. His King's Inns have no rooms, sat sideways positioned looking at the wall, at a 3D map, ever so marine and yachty; *Latitude Kinsale* makes them. It is a version of Donegal Bay. Jarlath's inner child is staring at it. He cannot see home.

"Jarlath. If I open my mouth to you, Sir, will it save my nearests......?"

"Anton. Don't tell me anything. The walls are ear-ed." and for a tick he is old self, pulling big boozy ears upwards like he is Dumbo then gives Anton the saddest eyes imagined. "So sorry, Anthony. So, deep deep sorry. You're a lovely fellow. We are in a very phoney war, without sirens, with no shelter. I never ever suspected you could be drawn in. Do as you are told by me, by them, by who-the-fuck-ever. It will be over soon and they claim we'll be blameless. Fat chance I imagine. Fat bloody one."

Anton hovers by the side of the great desk of powers. Jarlath isn't thick, picks up on his need. He has been grandad long enough to get it. He rises and his seat creaks its swivel. "You need one big one." Anton lanky in the arm-maul enjoys the *Kölnwasser 911;* such comfort. As he is released from the forty second hug he says "back to business, I suppose, Mister Duhallow. May I be sit......?"

"Yes. Anth..... and the walls have...." the boss strings up his jumbos with his fingertips and eyes sideways, both ways, like a *fin de siecle* belly dancer might.

".....bugs," says Anton fed up with com-promises. Oddly the only living entity right then listening to them is a low level operative of Peeking Dept of Internet Scuppers 61098; through the webcam. The Shadow Energy Ministry across have the pair on record. They'll listen back when Hand-over is done *for training & quality purposes* without doubt.

"I assume all the terms is the same as 2022's ?" Anton sits.

"This year, as every year, the lucky winner who strikes yee black gold has our jolly favourable ZERO royalties arrangement. The Doyle you recall just in time for this round has voted to ride back on an old Green Party awkward tax amendment so from 1 Jan it's back to 25% tax on profits from even the big, big finds. As we know profits are a rather moveable feast."

"25% hhmmmm; that changes not a lot, just changes it back to pre 2007 ways of doin' things."

"And they can right off all techy developments elsewhere that could be put to use in Irish waters. Like if they invented a deep sea something in the say Gulf of Mex....."

"No. Grand; I get it. Tanya, you know mega tech head. Factoid this that...." Anton makes rabbiting muppet of his left hand to left ear, indicating a lorra, lorra womansplainin.' ".....she could give you a right unasked for extra mural on non-trad rig extraction advances." Tanya loved particularly new breakthroughs in hydrocarbon *succubi.*

"Who is showing interest in what this year, Anthony ?"

"Are we on air ? Real answer or makey-uppy answer ?"

"Both at once."

Anton was not sure if Jarlath gave a shite what he answered so he told it as it was. "Far more than before there's multiple applications for the same block, same blocks."

"Bin all accept these companies - don't need to go into nitty gritty of logic for rejections. You can say 'not top of the range prospecting from our experts view of your proposed prospectus etc. etc., *Mise Lemass* etc. etc. ' As he spoke he scribbled names some Dutch, some English companies and some spanking new agent companies. He hands the scrap to Anton. "You know the routine."

"Actually boss, I don't. You're not havin' face time with Mister Dignam now. Do you get me?"

"Bin as said. Shred thoroughly if you feel like it. Endorse these. Welcome these." He whisper lip-synches "Uck" for U.K. "plus these Paddy minnows which are the U.K. and their admirers' *agents provocateurs*."

"Don't push me."

Jarlath eyeballs Anton and adds no words but scribbles so quick it comes out like a Doctor's prescription for incontinence. Anton right-side-ups it and squints a long while.

"Ah O.K Get you." Anton conciliates.

'I need to be saying what I'm saying. Don't take it to..... HEART EMOJI,' says the fine ink.

"Anton. Between now and the end of the Conference. Could you manage a few white lies. Half our S.A.C.s are not quite what they say on the tin but our allies are going to get licences for blocks in reasonable proximity to them, some on them or a siphon's spit from same. Blame me later. Would you do that for me ?"

"Sure. Whatever."

"To avoid too many undesirables vying for our preferred spots; don't outright tell them to go 'f.' themselves. Lead them on. No let them lead themselves along. Should they say, say what hopes between Loop and the Shelf. Drag out a big 'weellllllllllll' and dot dot dot tell them you will favour them with early access to some nineties 2D analysis; like WOW it up."

"What for ?"

"Distract.   You could sweeten it and say specially extended licence lengths for companies willing to go get extra wet for the sake of new invaluable size-micky 3D...."

".....on useless spots?"

"On *Terra-incognitas*."

"Can we just be more clear with the wool-pulling. I get hidin' good finds .I don't get sending the bad guys, sorry d'unsuspectin' guys down a swanny."

"Anton to be blunt and excuse uz Oh Listening Bugs but soon enough blocks and their locations and all that mullarkey won't matter hardly a legal fig."

"You're going to part the seas ?"

"The rigs in the near future won't be so visible. None of our present *modi operandi* will matter much. Things'll be a bit below the belt from here on and a lot more scifi. For the sake o'reasonable continuity in the interim..."

"....below the belt."

"Below the belt is right."

"Beneath the surface."

"Just so, Anton."

Anton rises and by the oaken door about turns: "Jarlath won't all what we are doing now look very, very rigged. If the finds are huge; the world will know ?"

"Wait till that horse has bolted."

"Get you; but mighty odd that it was a handful of companies from the same so to speak stable."

"Not much of a worry versus the continuance of your nearests and dearests."

"For the record," and Anton nods at the walls' assumed bugs, "I am very worried about my husband's wellbeing."

Duhallow grimaces that idea away and changes tack: "Our chaps, our friends in Galway who determine you know the yay and nay of what S.A.C. is no longer teaming with whatever beast or oppositely 'Oh Look we've just found a new species' or 'Oh look new oyster hatchings.' We take or leave whatever info they supply. Sometimes we or our "agents" supply them with false but of course "peer reviewed" porpoise information or whatever; just so you know; pertinent places that our "interests" want to stake their claim on get staked that way." Jarlath winks at Anton.

"Everything's in hand by the sounds of things." Anton is beyond hurt at his boss's bhatherous deflection of his darling's plight. 'Feck bugs and their listening weasels,' curses Anton.

"Whatever shenanigan needs doing will get done. Good day Anton."

CHAPTER SIXTEEN

The animal testing laboratory closed 'cause of Deh Downturn. It sits shy of the corner for Glenamoy, before the turn for Rossport, hidden like most of the science fiction of that district behind spruces or rhododendron, their purple blossom and year round foliage thick as thieves, perfect p.r. for commoner garden regular Joe-industry.   It wasn't like every *Gaeltacht* requires a primate-Dachau of its own, more that cosmetics needs be smeared on humans and some brunt has to be bewildered for it and likely die in the cause. Demand supplies hence the Aughoose Animal TestLab re-opened for business first sign of Upturn without fuss and notice; some noticed; one thousand Bodhisattvas were peeked, one thousand more alerted; how could they cleanse both the collective if evitable animal agony and the numb plod of their obeying-orders human keepsakes.   The damaged beasts die by the dozen in that barbed zone doing their darndest for the cosmetics industry.   Their dystopic Butlins of a zoo abutted the ever expanding oil 'n' gas refinery.   Mid all that squawk and gossip and with so many outbuildings - it was a fabulous location also for some relaxing rendition and the airport at Knock was but a spin and a bit away.   Dutch secret service just needed to invoice the A.A.T. for use of a small mizzen: low season €85 per 24 hours + 9% V.A.T.   The capuchin racket'd smother even a twenty decibel human cry of pain, for help.

A male capuchin, who had been in the first whiles of concentration the clown of the lab had now become slow and surly.   This capuchin, let's call him X-case, had had it.   A diet of night and day debased looking *Ready Brek*, the earful bandwidth of a racket that is ManTalk, yakkidying moans, barking orders, then the terror of the scope of his smearing, indiffered by some eejit of an intern who possibly dreamt he was the next Mengele. He could at least still swing; slow as he pleased in the small "airside" cage taking the chill Erris air on a rope of knots.

He stops his swing, clings, regards lecky gates opened. His eyes widened, bloodshot and short sighted from his evening job, contact lens liquid trials, but enough pixels to see the top of the range blue or black or blue black Beamer enter and disappear behind this swing zone he and his fellows had. X-case climbed a fake tree and there was some bars that looked directly west. He saw this enormous *Homo Sapien* in a suit exit the car, gape about himself. The *homo sapien* was greeted by a second taller, less wide *homo sapien*. A magpie flew above them and the capuchin wondered why the larger humankind flicked his podgy fingers towards the bird, once, twice, three times. Collectively capuchins are fairly religious but don't get superstition.

Lar Ewing, if confused, had never felt so appreciated; winter holliers, Madagascar, if that is where the capuchins centre their origin. Their refusing hullabaloo at dawn really was refreshing for him. He'd been moved from his shed, cross a yard but he could never see the critters. Op had said he was on some class of an estate. Lar imagined some old hand-me-down Laird and his Bar'ness had penchant for saving these type of little monkeys. He could hear sometimes the roar of the Ocean and smelt pines - that was hard to square with Anglo demesnes territory who loved the dull innards of sea shy counties and crow roosterages of evening mid dreary everlasting buildings and the requisite shell folly like they wished it could be Halloween every blinking day. There was also the home comfort of burnt gas in the air day and night; 'inefficient pile-heating system likely.'

Those posters for socials, Lar had made use of one, a big shiny one, where you write the bar where a band or a singer'll sing at: "*Mickey Flavin Tribute Night Slatt's Bar, Roundfort.*"   On the back of it Lar'd with blue thick-enough marker had free hand drawn three lines, thus four col-umes, each filled with numbers: depth beneath the sea surface at average neap tide, depth beneath the seabed, volume of the cubed feet of gas per find and lastly a volume of the barrells of the crude fellah numeral.

Lar told Op "I don't write in depth of sea above seabed."

"I see that; I noticed those blanks.   You don't think it important?" Op asked as if they were pals again.

"In terms of the longs and lats I am so spot on; like the position is the position and my pendulum swing has never lied. I feel it is my job to supply the known unknowns. Any Joe Bathymetry will know her depths from a sonar."

"It is surely useful and necessary for knowing what length of legs your rig." Op spoon-fed, "you know how long I mean the rig's legs need to be. That is jolly important when you're talking deep Atlantic, when you are deciding: Commercial find/ Not Commercial find."

"My gift is for the things that cannot be seen. I've proved my pudding for volumes of the black stuff and the gas stuff beneath and hidden. I am definitely rusty on sea depth cause no mystery there."

"Leave that to the real world experts." Op puts out lamely.

"Spot on, good fellow" said Lar to keep Op thinking he didn't think him Charles Van Manson. He looked at the Dutch man with his own rigs for legs and wondered if all Dutch were so, so tall so as searise wouldn't wet nor drown them, thumb or no thumb in the dyke.

Lar with Op's assistance set up a workshop with blank walls galore and he has all his marine maps up, some from the 1930s, inland duns for marshes and ordnance lime greens for elfless forests. He moves about the Goldilocks sized mizen hut with a shackle on his left leg but the grub is second to none, the heating twenty four seven and he can play his 78s. Nelson Eddy helps the plumb swing. He just wishes he could tell Flo all is good. He sends her good intentions but she never picks up. Telepathy can be awfully one-sided and he is not lucid enough in the nights to inveigle via the abstractions of her dream time and it is not easy as his hut is windowless.

The two homo sapiens that the four limbed X-case'd been checking out were none other than larger than life McGeown and Dutch Agent X98/ so-stylish Fr. Van Der Op. Op had stepped out of the mizzen hut to greet McGeown's arrival. "Lar is in his element Mister Mack Gyone, by that I mean things are moving along jolly nicely." McGeown sees a magpie fly over and flushes it away with three waves of his hand. "Fucking bad luck buzzard asses." Op in the short walk to the hut suggests McGeown act the Oil Baron, that the entire rumble was predicated on seeing Lar at work, seeing his worth. Op fills in McGeown more: "He gets twice daily an injection of Kelyn XtP 9 that keeps this seventh son of a seventh son pliant without ruining his incredible talents." McGeown had rocked up expecting serious Lar reluctance and all that that necessitates, had hyped up his over strained adrenals for some 'C' grade cruelty, mostly alpha-show to impress the Dutch operative, 'cause McGeown lives in the solid world not the vapours of pendule swinging makey-uppy-believe so he goes asks Op "you fig pikie wizard Ewing in there is the real ma-ho-ney then ?" yet unsays 'he's a friggin' figment of Dutch flatness, that's what Lawrence Ewing is.' For McGeown, Lar's just some 'white puddin' bait for the way bigger pictura.'

The two scoundrels enter the overheated hut and Lar is on his hunkers crouched over an old expanse of Nat Geo marine map,

North East Atlantic, gloriously impractical scale-wise but that does not deter Lar. If he gets a hunch from a macro map he can scale down later. Lar knelt like a child, with his *mar yah* of a yoyo dangling from his fingers, is close to the abyss of the Isengard Ridge. He doesn't greet his visitors till he has gotten a sound clockwise vortex of a YES swing east of the Ridge.

"Afternoon." Lar says to the two men.

"Lar. This is an executive from Austin. An oil man. Do you mind if I *au-fait* him about you and Fate?"

"Fire ahead." Lar is so caught up with doing pendulum over his maps and with a small pencil writing in his findings: "Half an hour ago found at an awkward depth a fine sized oil deposit on Edoras Bank, block 4329. Quite the shocker."

"How big ?" inquires Op.

"'t'd put the Brents to shame." This is the Kelyn XtP 9 talking, not his usual cautious country man reserves. "Working my way up Isengaard now."

"When you say awkward depth how awkward ?" asks Inny McGeown with a hokey if idyllic left of centre smarm. He has littler sense that this Lar-is-Uri-Geller-idea has traction now that he sees a grown man playing psychic spirograph in a mess of papers. He believes it is diverting time and gung-ho from the complex steps of the false flag, itself hard enough to keep dominos on in the brewery of his left brain.

Op continues prattling like a pyramid sales broker to McGeown, loud enough so that deaf enough Lar can appreciate. "Fate, you see, had a field off Ireland's South West and it was not so promising. Our genius here, " and he nods to Lar, "tells them there is a huge reservoir of oil beneath the upper one. So get this, the upper find is a five million barrels of oil. But Lar says go straight beneath it. It takes them a year to come back but they do and they say yes Mr. Ewing, we note that a substantial and economically viable find close to your 2,300 <u>feet</u> depth below our find from 2019, with an almost an 'OLD MAN' underlining of the feet. But; get this. Next he goes sends them another one of his divining reckonings and they go follow it up and get this, get this he is saying there is point two five trillion cubic feet of gas, well worth a terminal in I don't know Dingle or BallinSkelligs or dredge up Sneem bay and get those liquifier tanks liquifying. So Lar writes up his findings on July 6th that year posts them to Ragnal Suite, Maxwell House D2, HQ of Fate. For one year and one month there's not a whisper and Lar's phoning and phoning, always fobbed at reception.   Am I right?"

"Yes you are." says Lar.

"Then bingo after more wait he gets on Fate's letterhead......"

"....their logo is a rig sitting kind of lop sided on a whale of an island, punctuating her blubber, blows fire out her mouth, inspired to be presumed by the AGIP dog with the five legs." qualifies Lar.

"Yeh yeh some mythology stuff. Go on." McGeown wants Op to get to some point.

Op's worried he has given too much of what in the business is referred to as "Calpol" to Lar who is spacing out; possibly might impede his findings. To keep tabs on his ability Op has been giving him Angola and Orinoco knowns to gauge his drugged gifts.

Lar out of kilter with the chat says from his kneeling "3,200 feet.   I found it two years before them and it was 3,200 below, not 2,300 like you said. Fate thanked me for my findings but made no song and dance...."

Op cuts him off "......they stated that his estimates were proven true by Fate's own thorough 3D seismic of an eight square kilometre area, all in waters quite a distance from land they, I believe, code or file named 'The Kingdom;' some oil industry injoke we imagine. The prospect I have checked it. Point, give or take a jot or two, point two six ish trillion cubic feet of gas, hundred and eighty five million barrels of oil." Op hunkers down to Lar's eyelevel, like you might to a child before an egg 'n' spoon race, to adulterate them with courage. "Lar here reckons these vast numbers by gliding his pendulum along a scale he has drawn up in these boxes with coloured pencils. He usually writes up finds like say 70:30, gas to oil in these ratios. I had him do some new finds that we know but are not public knowledge in the Mayombe ridge off Angola and he is accurate on location by a factor of 97%. He knows his gas to oil ratios too, and I reckon he is 85% right from what our boys have as predicted volume."

"It's a moveable *fiesta*. Get you." McGeown pansies about the room listening, not believing, butting his head almost against these way out of date maps of Ireland's far horizons thumb tacked to the prefab wall. He adjusts his bifocals to see headlands and way beyonds. His brow perspires - gets some hanky panky.

"What Fate did not pass on to Mr. Ewing here is that the impetus that inspired that 3D reassessment of the not so promising area had been Lar's initial letter. Their response was polite but ungrateful. They were not going to come clean that his voodoo had found them a side chapel of El Dorado, albeit in an impossible area in terms of known tech......"

McGeown twinkles at Op like 'top prize for buttering-up Mr. Yoyo Voodoo bogman here' but he still does not believe based on this hocum story. He fidgets his Mauser in his breast pocket. He moves over to behind where Lar is doing his dingle dangle over a body of water. Inny sees Lar has a kid's attention span; he is fed up with Munster and is off ae cleft that falls into the Maury Channel, a spit or so south of Iceland. He pushes his bifocals back up to his squinters, then they nearly fall off him. Lar, five horizontal columns up from his last input, has just written 2.18

billion barrels of oil beside Isengard Ridge block 4532 (Department of NRG 'real world' block divisions have been written in as a thin fifth column by Op to clarify Lar's imprecision). McGeown almost collapses onto Lar. 'Lar knows his black stuff.'

Op is still rambling on: "Lar only picked up on the success of his prediction in relation to Fate's operations but not on their tone of distance."

"Huh."

"In terms of their off hand response to him.   Fate had discovered a shocking volume of oil and gas in the precise ratio Lar had informed them. Granted there is no easy getting it ashore but it is money in the bank and worth a landfall at some stage."

"How did you Clogs get to know?" McGeown just checked a fact on his iphone. "Shit. This numbty Pikie is spot on."
"We have a mole in Fate. We passed our information to S.N.A.K. who we are intimate with."

"I bet you did. You holy moly." McGeown every time gets the 'A' plus for decisiveness, swings round, Mauser already silenced and he klops Op in the forehead bbbyuuuff. Lar can hear the cranium crack. Blood spurts across his 1976 map, makes scarlet contours about the Goban Spur.

Inny McG unnecessarily blows away nonexistent smoke from the barrel of the gun, turns to Lar. "Mister Lawrence Ewing. You are the Golden Child. Glad we shut up that Enemy of the People."

CHAPTER SEVENTEEN

The ant-i-Refinery Camp's unCEO's name was Fang (inspired
from Fagan), a bright 1:1 and the incitefullest PhD in
retrotroscopy from his Bristol year, born in Gorey, with that
shared Leinster brag, Parnellesque beard and flippant clothing
range. He could have been the head hunted actuary but he'd
pinned his skywalk to this skellig of a promontory, had become a
real asset to the protest camp through time in tents and
purposeless and in the end was made Anarch-in-Chief by *de
facto* default. Darren Shivnan, remember the mole-een, and he
had once masturbated together on the beach by some rocks
roughly for quarter hour on one of those July days that are
windless and reach 29 degrees every seven years; very
impromptu, unexplained and never after mentioned. They got to,
not touching just each appreciating the sand, the shroomed
wave-u-*lette*s of ocean and their beautiful losses, just a skinny dip
that went 'wry really and pent hormones. On RTE *News* Fang
could drive home points without coming across all Forest of
Dean - a touch of *The Pogues* in ribaldry mixed with the learnt hi
rhetoric of under-dog, sorta Justice-will-Triumph that English
persist upon and pull off better than average Paddy, even though
he is an average Paddy from a County Wexford version of 'burbs.
Fang's face was normal Irish too, exceeding sincere and red from
the wind. Red ears were hidden in his wide mass o' black curls.
He was not great at keeping a sweetheart but had at his whim a
Louth girl, Jemima, not much liberty short of his sex slave, first
for fun then the S.M. of it lost its borders despite the Me2 part of
his right brain calling order, in that cortical where Earnest lodges.

Today's "ninja Camp Cabinet" was to hand-wave or not a breach of the perimetre fence of the by now one hundred and twenty three hectare refinery. This twenty foot fence had just a fortnight earlier gotten rural electrification: not massive, 110V. Shivnan, as a spy, was aware that this could be doubled in Yellow Orangish Alerts. On the Monday past a plump for the time of year fawn had been found at the base of the current fence between Gate H12 and G19, stunned, dead, fresh, 220V testing, testing, was spot on. After a tempestuous hand waving meeting they had spit roasted Bambi and the camp vegans went to Ballina for the evening in disgust. Hand waving, both in the air at once, and flapped, was a way of yaying a new rule, action, suggestion, amendment to the rota or what have you. 'Rather late noughties,' griped Shivnan.

In anticipation of this key decision meeting Shivnan had managed to bundle all his dreads into an Easter-egg shaped big bun for the first time ever. Jemima had helped him, her breasts confronting his nose. Tied about themselves, he felt taller and doubly at ease, so it was not difficult for him to request that his best new chum 'Wendywee' could join in first the meeting and all going well get her on to one of the breach teams. Fang and the others looked from Shivnan to Wendywee, every bit the lady agent of the People's Republic, spy Zeng, THE 700, standing in the tent threshold flap and the sun calling it golden quits without. As the camp central command sussed and assessed Wendywee née Susan Zeng - she entered the tent in slowmo cause a flashback was ahold of her: her last impersonation cum mission on behalf of the People's China Republic; togged out as a convincing Huigur black-currency exchange hoodlum high on the Tibetan plateau. Her mission on that occasion was to foment trouble among the Tibetans against the Han administrators who were constructing a branch rail line south of the Taklimakan off the Golmud-Lhasa mainline, ahead of the Tibetans being trouble themselves. Her trouble-making was a means to fast track and she flushed and she flushed till she'd flushed out each and every anti-statist Tibetan and third born fomenting about those yak-lanes in a minority report pre-crime way. Before Tibet, back in 2019 she was sent on a mission to test her mingling metal; she also mastered her three favourite Karluk Uigarian languages: Äynu, Lop, Ili Turki. She had gotten high commendation for 'ability to embed,' loved method acting and in this Wild West China mission she had the challenge and wit to be a dumb prisoner for six hungry months. Month five she was leading a failed prison break for adult pupils at this re-education camp for non Han scoundrels in maximum Lopnur Perfecture, Xingiang Waste. Her mission was to seek and incriminate the impossibly Moslem. She had free will how-to from Beijing HQ. The offending women really trusted this recent prisoner. Her silence became mystic, they made her their hope. Self-styled Dummy became a visionic leader, became 'the Dumb One.' She lead "the Great Escape" hundreds gashed their way through and beneath three barby fences, at the far end of which what became almost one thousand of them were apprehended, arrested in long files, smacked across their faces if they spoke and were given a choice of execution or work in Jeans factory near Lanjou till their menopauses put manners at them, possibly about them - the desolate Uighur women's smattering of Hannisch did them no favours. In some wise the present operation in perfect Mayo had similarities more to 700's Tibet mission: much wind, cow pats, an inappropriate disguise and an underuse of her talents, so far.

Wendywee née Agent 700 needed to win trust: "Mr. Fang. My name is Wendywee. I am from Xiahe high, high up where the Yellow River melts it way east but my parents are nomads from Kham District." Shivnan was impressed what an eejit the

Chinese spy could conjure but worried that she might be so good a fool that Fang might prevent her from the planned breach mission.

"Tibetan. Nice." Fang said in all vagueness. Canny that Camp Cabinet meetings were in the round, in a chucked out glamping tent, a convincing *ger* with its open fire coping upwards to a bold hole, and the starry Bolivarian night getting dottier and dottier in the firmament. Fang dawdled.

"Fang. I think we should bring our operation forward." Shivnan's usual was stout "n' blackcurrant 'n' delayed actions. He was paid to delay or reduce the impact of actions - so odd tonight it was reverse.

"How so? How long far?" Fang throws out.

"Tonight we must strike. Perfect weather and no moon."

"The veil is thin tonight. That's foregone. Are we, all of us, up to orienteering in that thick fir wood and no torches?" Fang asks semi rhetorically. Fang believes he is Ralph to the Jack of Shivnan but any observer of Alpha male combat might mistakenly reverse that lairdship o'flies.

In the flickery light, in the shadowy round, the commandos committee-wave like politically incorrect black and white minstrels their show of hands in favour of Shivnan's suggestion. Fang accepts like democracy is important to him "I think we can do it. Yep. Some star light for sure but if we wear black clothes." Shivnan had planted much of the suggestion in Fang's head, enough days ago that he could let him lay claim to the plan.

Fang walked about with his arms behind his back as General Montgomery did before El Alamein. "if we have enough waders we can enter the refinery zone via the marsh. Have we?"

Lou says there are six pairs of waders. Lou is slight; if she were leader she'd've have wiped the refinery off the map by now. She has a neat belief that paradise is possible on earth even in places with shite climates but first all normalcies need to be ceased: radio news broadcasts that feed on emotion, terms and conditions applying ads, bungalows or whatever had taken over from them, each with their Tara/Pascal nuclear families and their lazy reliance from the first scream of their first child of either sex on Hurling stroke Kamogee, a decrepit Church, the two failing, gaelic Fiannas. Her paradises were zones of permaculture spreading out and among well coppiced woods of birch, rowan and alder, had hens mucking about unslaughtered and where possible oak-sheltered spinnies allowed abundant fruit trees and beneath their dew-glinting canopy frogs hopped and hares ate unstartled. That sorta Saxo-crusty pastoral which she on one level yearned at sat uneasily with her 'fuck-em-all' frontal Mick-lobe and she was well prone to minds-eying the refinery going up bboooooomb; feck the carbon imprint and all the collateral pines that could've been biocharred. "There are only six pairs of waders," she says. With the right handler Lou could be Joan of Arc but she was well stuck in the male-strom, on every side begrudging lesser i.q.s ball-and-chaining her every move.

"Well that means we are going to have to reduce our incursion teams." says Fang.

"Really? Can we not just send the others another way." Shivnan needs to get Wendywee over the line.

"I can," and all eyes turn to Wendywee. "I am happy to go bare legs."

Fang stares at the artificial nomad of Kham and strategizes. "We shall go in in two groups. The faster one, 'A' team will go north and execute and the second group, 'B' team will assure a split of their security if chase is given."

"From the Rossport side?" asked Lou

"Yes and downwind of the dogs." Shivnan adds.

"Which way is the wind from tonight?" Lou is the quare one for realistic questions.

Fang didn't know so to sidestep ignorance he had the group cluster round an Apple and clicks off a slide show: here a forest clearing to keep to, then south past some mizzen huts near the Glenamoy turn that hid nobody knew what type of chimpanzees but what squawks, then Bing terrain map, right a bit, then a bit left, a path of a track west, and bingo pipe point where it was vulnerable for four metres and stauncher faucet 14B out of range of the main building complexes, vision-wise. Bing *Terrain* for clearings colour-wise has the loveliest Green Tara sheen. With an August Spring tide, the lark high Bing map-view has bogs of ruddy bounce o' moss to lie a late Summer's doze on but in reality are shockin' rheumatic spongiforms. "There see that sorta pillar box and disused cement circular thingummy right here, that is where we can prepare out of sight. See." They obey Fang's certainty and see. "We will split the resin and epoxy between our bags and on say that tree we can attach the webcam so the public can get a few laughs. We are legally, technically not destroying anything." Fang is adamant. Lou goes out by the glamorous tent flap with her thumb in her mouth like a baby, points it skywards, revolves. "The wind is from Crossmolina, easterly."

"So if we are caught; it's trespass." Shivnan says and removed the webcam from its packaging and showed it to Wendywee who checked out its menu and was surprised by its weight for what it was. "Made in China," sneers Wendywee and she spits a boyish milky toward but not at the object and steps into the dark.

Glinting across the bay not far by sea from the camp is the Erris Bar, with its first 'r' long gone in a gale away. This is Ceathru Thadgh's only legal portering hole, nineteen klicks by road from the anti-refinement camp. Weekends start early in the *Gaeltacht*, a Thursday is perfect cover then for unusual night movements.

The assault teams needed a cover to be over that ways for their breach. Four obvious and three hidden insurgents went by zero four Octavia Estate. Four went into the E_ris bar and had their nice pints apiece then ordered a bottle of Boru vodka, a Tullamore Dew, a Gilbeys and twenty four Bavarias to take away for later wastage or so it should appear. The other three stayed cranky and hid in the boot. In the pub, locals Micheál Shine and his wife Caitlín were having a hot port apiece, a Thursday evening ritual before the later trad'd score the night air.

Lou figured it'd be courtesy to introduce the 'Tibetan' to the most respected couple about the inlet. The old couple liked new blood in the bay. Lou had been inspired to come to Rossport 'cause of this pair.

Lou chummy-drags Wendywee by the Parka sleeve.

"Micheál and Caitlín Uí Sheighin; let me introduce you to this wonder woman, Wendywee, from the province of Calm. Have I got it correct?"

"More or less." says Wendywee.

"Tibet anyhow."

"Ethnically Tibet but not in the Autonomous Region *per se*," clarifies Wendywee.

The seated Shines smiled at the florid *per se.*

"Well I am Me-Hall and this is my wife Ban Uí Moon-shine," over emphasises the former Secondary Head Teacher.

The old lady slaps the back of his hand. "My name is Caitlín. Don't listen to my addled husband. There was some old bit of a spy a time ago gave me that nickname," and she nods at a Goretex covered man high stooling it up at the bar, warming his Bass in his big hand.

Lou explains low to Wendywee how a local *Sasanach* and she nods back at the base relief called to the bar of a spy "his grandparents were from here-abouts he claimed. He'd mastered

Irish, so he thought and wanted to take the respected lady down a peg or more hence," and she nods Caitlín-wards, "Bean Uí Moonshine."

"They believe we are the last dregs of the Firbolgs." says Caitlín a.k.a Ban Uí MoonShine.

"So Caitlín. Why that knicked name?" asks Wendywee, all care-in-the-community.

"Ah any ole thing to make an ass of you. The *Sasanach*s imagine we are skuttered punch day and night" says Micheál Shine for her with the wheezeen of a former fan of Players #6.

"I get the picture." says Wendywee grabbing a short stool to settle in. She enjoys the wisdom of Elders but eyes the not-so-atomic clock of an advert for Harp. Darren bangs on his watchless wrist to hurry the sweet talkin.' Lou sits too, to equalise. There is no chance of a moon so what'd be the hurry and there the Shines sipping their lukewarm cloven ports. Mr. Shine allows the quiet hover; old people with all the time of their remaining world views.

"Micheál was in prison for his objection to the pipe. He was the local head master of the *Árd* Skull; weren't you?" as if Lou didn't know.

By his Christ-like silence he agrees that he was. "He also, might I say it, will go to his grave with the greatest knowledge of what is goin' on out there in the Atlantic. No journo has the suss he has." Mrs. Shine gleams at Lou's words. She basks on her husband's modest behalf and Lou beams along with her at her old hero.

To add fuel to further praise Lou relates how Micheál the year past "early April a Standing Rock Lakota delegation came to visit. They go about the world honouring those who have given most honour to saving our world. They gave him an honorary name......."

"Rain-in-your-face - so *voila* Me-Hall Rain-in-Your-Face Shine."

Wendywee despite her innate respect for Elders can't abide this goodwill twaddle and somewhat abruptly asks Micheál "How you know what you know?" and so saying strays, not a little, from her recent half wit.

"So you want to know what is really afoot about here?" Micheál twinkles at the say-it-as-it-is Oriental and nods west to the quiet roar of th'Atlantic without door.

"Not what I asked. Just how do you know?"

"I keep abreast of who is selling what to whom."

"Oil rigs.....?"

".....more possibilities and licences that are running out - AGIP sells to Exxon, then Exxon sell a third share to the French who ask S.N.A.K. for a half hand at some prospect or advice on getting the stuff ashore."

"I get."

"..... and I have a list of tall rumours about what is going on from this or that off the record so-and-so as long as your arm."

"Off the record."

"Not willing to go public," explains Lou: "chicken shits."

"I'll tell you some story." Nobody'd sought such entertainment but the old man continues anyhow and a touching grasp on the foreign lady's elbow waylays any opportunity for impatience like Darren plus now Fang coughing attentions but nobody takes heed of them.

"One blustery November and the rains like that, along comes one of my Rumours." Micheál mimes the awful horizontal of the wet buffets towards his worn face, his fingers swimming at him like ghastly sperms. There was an intense rapping on our door." He includes his wife by gesture. "Herself goes answers and came back with a wet looking Continental." At this Caitlín blushes thinking the term might be racist in present company. "She takes his trench coat and he thanks her politely. I ask him to step into my study, he does. I sit him down and wait for him to explain why he is about in the wet and dark like that."

"I must tell somebody."

"Okay. What might that be that you must tell?"

"He gazed about the room as if we might have bugs in the wainscot."

Lou sees that Wendywee doesn't grasp but wants the story to flow. She loves this story and has heard it nineteen, if not twenty times; the delay factors and details always that bit changed. Darren coughs toward Wendywee who veers on him. 'Respect the Elder Lemon' says her frown.

"I call out to Caitlín to get a nice Roy Bosch for the perished fellow. He thanks me and not a little forwardly says two sugars, no milk."

"I detest milk in mine." interrupts Caitlín.

"Well anyway, says I: 'take your time.' The man does, takes a deep breath then starts telling me about his being in a private jet just a month before. His company - I never got to know who they were - wanted him in Qatar in a hurry on a job, I imagine. So the fellow is sat in this speedy *gonsalez* of a plane. I asked him how many seats and he was able to answer an odd nine and that he was sat alone on the front right and the conversation he overhears is two seats back. They had some drink taken and as the man, my informant, was small, possibly the two having their natter clear forgot his presence. Drink; you know loosens the tongue and they couldn't see him." he zones this last information close into Wendywee's face.

Shivnan needs to shift the assault team's asses and blunts: "we are way late."

Micheál eyes the youth's disrespect of his ancient marinating "What precisely is the hurry Rapunzel?"

Shivnan detests disparages of his dreads as he hates them himself. He just imagines that anyone willing to abuse their tresses so could never be suspected of being an agent of the E-lite Machine.

"A party down at Bungalow Villy's......" says Shivnan looking for Fang to back him up.

"Where precisely ?" asked the barman winking at the obvious fisherman-me-bollix   cum year-round-tourist-bit-of-a-spy-in-himself mentioned already, a clot from Irthlingborough, North Hants with the lukewarm Bass and those hands.

"Bungalow Villllll-y," said Fang.

"*Oh go hiontach ar fad*," said the barman in Aboriginal, translated as 'Jolly Good' by the twelve year old level of Irish o' the bit of a spy.

"Oh the Bungalow." says Micheál. "Oh Gaud, you'd not want to be late for that Social...."

Lou "so then what"

"Then what....." reconnects Mr. Shine. "The two *mar yah* oil magnates were talking about our own prospect out there. Corrib Erris. It is as far out in the sea west, as say Dowra or so is east of us. Imagine Dowra love." The old man teasily guffaws, all Irish-eyes-are-smiling, goodnatured mock on mock at Wendywee but he could never have known that she takes it in DOW-RAH and does RE-CALL in her head: '1959; most hopeful land derek of all the late 50s Madonna oil tries, best of nine tries' but she says not a thing just gawps back her windswept tent dwelling Kham-as-you-please.

"So my, I don't know what to call him, my 'informant' says his fellow frequent flyers are drowning the Don Perigg-nonn like there is no tomorrow. Aw they were backslappin' and I suppose you could say congratulatin' each other on the fact that their prospect, that was publicly put about as worth $15 billion or €s, was really three times that figure. The Irish State took what these so-and-soes said as gospel; that sizeable yet smaller figure. Can you credit it? English sorts he said they were. Or English fellah with a Dutch sort who can act the *Sasanach* when they're put to it."

"Woh !" says Wendywee, "eejits of a high order." She either thought the story warranted such an answer or that she needed to lay on more of the gobshite.

"And sure he was just a bloke at the door - it could have been all ole guff made up out of his head, him on his fancy plane this high off the ground. It is not quite the info that parades as big and bauld headlines in a Tuesday's *Indo*, now is it? 'Mayo-of-the-Sorrows €45 billion Bonanza.' In what? Her hungry fields ? Christ no, in an ole hole in her sea bed or likely three or more of them; in her deepest self, down there deep with the barracudas."

Lou was peeved that the tale'd been foreshortened but was glad the gorgeous skulduggery of the rumour had been spread that bit further and the hidden depths of what was truly afoot be it on the flash planes or in the wave jounced rigs - surely'd the Old Man's fable'd put pepp in their step for this coming night's dent in the armour of the Greater Bad.

"Tell me something," and Micheál's imperative takes in all four of assault Team A, "who among you have actually seen a picture of the rig or rigs out there in Corrib Erris?" and expecting the usual negative sits back in the scuffed upholstery to rest his cases.

Wendywee had to stop herself putting up her hand.

It is Caitlín who continues the strain of thought: "What should be a national pride is not in any newspaper, no news item shows the rigs. We don't know their shapes. Nothing."

"Taller than the tallest Dutch giant, huge legs on 'em" gags Micheál to dent the serious.

"No interviews with the riggers, nor chief whoever engineer. It is not like they are so far out that our fishermen'd tip over the edge o' the world to find them. Our trawler men can take selfies of them from a distance, wobbly. But honestly after all went on here twelve years back nobody wants getting too near them." Caitlín holds her bag like the Queen to hold her peace.

Micheál rallies: "what kind of a country takes no pride in such resource and engineering? Gives it away to foreigners." His three point five unit limit has been reached.

Wendywee had seen every last winter, every night blinking summer satellite view of these rigs. She'd even seen the Bing 'n' Google out-of-bounds ones. She knew the rig makes, their capacities, their shelf life. She knew that the worth they were drawing on in just the known zone was more or less spot on the old man's not so tall story. She knew there were ample fields to their East and had cursory grasp of other finds up, about long-winded Dooish, near shore Loops, the not verified portents about the Hook and Saltees. 700 sighs and smarts inwardly: 'Pretending to be thick: my speciality these days.' Peeking's Ministry of Espionistics knew deeper depths than their Agent; she'd gotten the top secrets, not the toppest tops before her departure for the Land-of-the-Setting-Sun The Slippery Ministry insisted she should view a dossier entitled *Knowledge Subterfuge*: item seven was their 2019 report re. the 2016 crash of Rescue 116. Chopper 116'd been flying east at dark then wallop, hits a non existent big enough skelligeen *darbh ainm* Black Rock off Belmullet. 'Not pilot error,' says the Report. Three dead cause the radar said the self-styled rock had no existence. In this day and age how can a creepy upcrop just a.w.o.l. his self. 'Some kind of Keep-Jo-Paddy-Mick-fathomless policy,' assumed Zeng. 'A not so much where's me woods from me trees, as me sea wrack from me carrigeen.......?' Susan 700 weighed that if there were forces that could remove solid islands off radars and maps, what other jokerage could they up to ? Reading above and below redacted parts of same report there was a strong odour of an Anglican-Lowland alliance that could control navigations, *Eire*'s instruments. 'Much of the marine-mapping of a half sovereign of a Notion was likely in alien hands. If they can vamoose a rock that can be easily trip-advised from land, what might they do with the clefts 'n' dales of that vast Seaworld to its wild west.' 700's surmises were 85% spot on.

Between those in the boot and the seated four in the Octavia an argument had broke out. Shivnan was defending Wendywee's ability to run and keep up with 'A' team. The rusty NCTless Skoda veered off the mainish road and wound back east along the wee coastal 'L' of a road. A car's lights did the same after them, though the bockety boreen so lonesome. They past the old bit of a demesnes of the Master Bourneses that used sit proud of the coast and came to the alcoholic's bungalow, Liam Fall-Upon-the-Parish Paroisteen, better known as Bungalow Villy's. The one story had one bare bulb in the curtainless living room, grass in meadowlettes all about the drive and a nineties child's swing creaking in its own reverence of an American wake. As the four loaded in the booze, sure enough, Irthlingborough motors by making damn sure Paddy was being Paddy. Inside Shivnan turns up the stereo to 29, and it fair blasts the district. Fang turns it down in case "migratory guillemots might be pissed off." The music is on shuffle and Liam Fall-Upon-the-Parish Paroisteen is given a tidy amount of Dew to keep the party going single-handedly. In the kitchen rucksacks are prepared, weights equalled out, compasses checked, spectacles wiped clean, bright parts of clothing tucked.

Fang turns the music lower again and says to Wendywee, the unsuspected Agent o'the Middle Kingdom. "This is really really dangerous. As a non E.U. you risk deportation. I'd really advise you return to camp." Wendysee looks at Fang, and using Hypnotix Technique 2B basic, mesmers the Westerner and simply says "I can see in the dark."

'Valid answer. Jacquiline Chan here is possibly a talisman,' thinks Fang, 'and her legs are something else.'

The night is dun, the waders reached to some groins and despite fears, the murk of the bit of an estuary was not quick and their advance fast. The dirty clutch of Eagles-Dare-Yihs gain the foreshore of the subtownland of Mucknishish, scored by the fading FINAL COUNTDOWN ooh-booming over the broad of bay from the open Bungalow Villy windows. Shivnan had lashed the music volume back up on exit and Wendywee'd opened the 70s windows. They co-winked at one another and joined Team 'A.' Fang, Shivnan, Wendywee and the visionary Lou makes four. They set out ten minutes after team 'B.' 'B' can be caught. No need for their names: they will soon be dead. Liam Fall-Upon-the-Parish Paroisteen has lashed the volume up further just when ALL NIGHT LONG came on random. Some jaded moore hens in a wide bulrush gully just settling in thank you very much and dozy with reruns of brook side are pretty pissed off: 'call that music' their bird-brains vex and they squeak and squeak discontent in their shifty nests.

Tom bo li de say de moi ya/ Yeah jambo jumbo/ Way to parti' we goin'/ Oh jambali/ Tom bo li de say de moi ya/ Yeah jumbo jumbo.

'A' Team cross the bit of a stream at Gortacragher then prepare their balance for the Kwai-wide Bunowna of the mossy stones. In they wade. While crossing Wendywee asked Fang if he spoke Irish and Fang ignores the question but whispers to Wendywee the gist of the sabotage, like loud thinking: "Spencer's Epoxy Resin Superset, fascinating innovation, once set, the more it's bashed, vibrated whatever, the more it sets and sets. Vibrations make it kickass newton, yet tensile."

"Tensile Newton," repeats Wendywee like she recalls some Tulku's holy name yet undiscovered ways up in some *pluaish* of a cave above and beyond Amdo Province. Susan Zeng aka Wendywee repeats aloud alien terms and words, a note taking for later *baidu*-translating. "After sixty or more years, like concrete the whatever sort of compound it is crumbles, but in damp climates that'd stretch another twenty, twenty five years." Wendywee is praying, not listening much. She is summoning the smell of the dark water which is drawing the blood to the skin of her bare muscular legs, her grey Umbros are rolled up about her thighs and because every thing she does is perfect they stay dry. Fang tells her that his Irish is shite, all he knows is 'hi' 'blackberries' 'sandwiches' and 'nice enough day.' One day he will get some more Irish some place.

Shivnan is trailing a little. He realises there is a pin prick of a hole in his wader and water trickling in. Wendywee could give him a crash course in many things, like how to make the cold one's ally.

Both teams are now across the wide of river, on the wrong side of the self-styled law and treading on the moss and mush of the western extent of the old Master Bournes Estate, its inimaginable nine hundred and ninety nine years of tithe 'n' hold in dry parchment deed in the safe cleavage of the so called Countess of Wessex, wife o' Prince Edward, son of Queen Elsbeth Two, Her

Self, in a stylish line of 'nointed World Leaders reaching back to Solomon.

Meanwhile on nano cue seventeen point six two kilometres away a seeming pleasure skiff rounds the head by the Port o' the Chief where sea stacks shaped like Vulcans' ears guard Killgalligan Head from the worst sprites of the endless caprice of ocean. Two navy engineers and ten soldiers, by the Spartan loyal look of them, not mercenaries, for in the dark twinkling in their Far Eastern eyes peering from synthetic Balaclavas is the pure zing of patriotic purpose, not the zang of the pay-cheque. The mouth of Sruwadacan bay is to their lee and gaining, the tide is rising so they'll be able to reach deep about the bends of the bay almost to the tidal point where Bunowna's sweetness turns brackish then salty; that is where their landfall coordinates are set to land them. The music, as planned, blaring from a one story house on the north side of the bay but safety first; dull those engines, lights off, seabed quarter fathom and gaining. The propeller is a smidgen above the dredge. This boat can go so shallow and drifts in the wind half a knot, a quarter knot.

Fang has stopped to check why Wendywee is sniffing yet again. She simply repeats a line she'd learnt on the CityJet from CDG "couldn't give a monkeys." Fang accepts the *non sequitur.* They are by the fence. The capuchin test lab is a sniff by wind away.

"You go do first shimmy." Fang play-orders Wendywee/ 700.

She bolts down and hugs her arms to herself like a mad wan in a county home. She wriggles in her parka strait jacket beneath the 110 volt razor wire. She's not heard the roast fawn story and recalls her Xinjiang great escape, when she lead and delivered the thousand brave Moslem ladies to their death or destiny. She lends courage to the other three who go-to some serious earth-Ypres where the wire crosses a eensiest depression. They've gone and caught up with Team 'B' as they'd been so slow figuring how not to be shocked be the fence. Adults don't get much genuine chance to be ten again but Fang does: "Split up again. Youz that way. Uz four this way." Imagine if he knew he was ordering a high not so delicate agent of the People's Public China with strictest to the second orders from the Forbidden City or a stone's throw from.

In the guard house of Refinery Sector West, the Station of choice is Ocean FM, broadcasting from way east in Collooney. After 21 hundred news each weekday requests for the dead are put out and an apt song gets played. Fran Yalloway of Bangor Erris is eating chicken *bhajee*s, and pork s*amosa*s helped by Lukasz Wasilenko. They are both tall and calm, ambitious yet cautious, in equal measure phlegmatic and self-justifying (tendency of security personnel), both have sorts of Leaving Certificates and both at that moment are listening to FOUR ROADS TO GLENAMADDY, a Brendan Shine classic from 1981. Flo Ewing is listening to the same song and wondering when she in her turn'd leave Ocean's answer phone details of funeral times. 'What song might she play for Lar ? Sure *Let It Be* would do his likes, hymn enough 'n' ag-gnostic enough.' On screen the two able bodied refined security men noted seven trespassers but grunted agreement to complete their delicious truffles and triangles in their rectilinear foil box brought the nine miles from Belmullet before apprehension and cold wind. They saw the seven split: become four and three as silver heat sought dots on a black to grey background. A faintest percept of waving pines could be glimpsed too, the tory tops of them. The screens, of a sudden, not so much blank as go not so nanoparticular so the two secure men could not wherewithal were those dots of life just sheep or a pack of straying wild dogs or badgers heading to a social. Ahh they're back defined again, definite 'surgent wood-

kernes, their seven heated movements had that aforethought
associated with contrarian humans who believe in better worlds.
Yalloway and Wasilenko could not guess the next tech error, Xian
Xi satellite 432 orbiting North East Atlantic had just popped the
microns of Hilversum V satellite. All seventeen channels linking
Glenamoy to twenty three miles high and 250kg of
Dutch-English cleverness went a.w.o.l. for a planned half hour.
The intruders were 47 seconds late and were now known knowns.
Blame a butterfly; Lou's respect for the elderly; that tall story of
Shine and his nervous rapper at his rainy door and the story of the
rigged estimates was, though shortened yet those few seconds too
long.

Wendywee had thought she could set the pace. 'Crusties trump
my fake yak-herd for doziness,' she peeved in Mandarin. The
amateurs tended to look for ways round ruts and wet places -
she'd jump straight in and wade, her skin glinting promisingly.
Then in a clearing, Venus lit their dare, along where fence-post
thick pines had been felled and the slimed lengths of pools made
by felling trucks' mighty tyres got small reflections of said
planet's Advent glow. Come roughly Valentine's these long pools
become frog-orgy conurbations, reptilian sex parties, threes and
fivesomes not uncommon, croaks, groans and joys loudening as
to tropic the fooled ear. Spragged about this Sitka clearing,
deciduous try their best: here an acorn trying to be a sprout, here
a badger hazel, there a hurling ash's trunk, no thicker than a biro,
even a crabby apple that'd blown from the Ford of the Scuffle and
other less robotic conifers: a shapely holly bush pushing ahead, a
Scots pine in its hole cursing the damp of its roots, now a bonsai
of a yew that'd clung into a hump of muck. The yew has the last
laugh. After all the hominids battles for lazy fuel the yew is so
patient, pastoral, outlives rusting terminals, gets to check in for

and out the fourth millennium and all the Crown Heads of Europe so much HELLO mulch.

Fran Halloway took up a hotline phone to the satellite operatives at Hilversum but reached an answering machine that says "hotline - leave your issue after *de bleeb*" says Dutch woman machine. "Screens are down at Glenamoy. All of them. Incursion in zone 'G.' So NOT human error. Repeat not human error." Before one could say Mary Robinson, the phone rings back.

"Joop Van der Walk, here. Who am I speaking with?"

"Mr. Francis Yalloway, County Mayo."

"As it could take time to resolve. Best seek and apprehend intrusion. I believe we've been compromised. Hacked." The Dutch cannot help speak the truth.

Fran cradled the receiver and repeated to colleague Wasilenko "they've been compromised" and winked the pants down *Kompromat* of it but Wasilenko could only answer literally cause he'd been never taught double meanings at either his English course in Castlebar nor from pints at *The Detri-ment*, Belmullet, and offered toward the receiver: "Well hurry the screens back up - I don't want wandering about chasing cold goose."

All this banter and confusion meant the two posses of the woods got closer then closer and closer yet to the tangle of chrome and aluminium that was the point where the vain Atlantic pipe enters the mainland and after a furlong divides to refinery sectors East and West. Group 'B' "insurgents" were moving west of west in a semi arc that made it look they were heading towards the Refinery canteen ultimately: laxative in the builder's tea; enema in the coleslaw? Group 'A' threw down their heavy sacks, Shivnan pointed at the giant horizontal valve of the truly humongous pipe. He and Fang removed chunks of flat wood and assembled them, clipped them round the pipe valve, checked it for size and stability. A big box got formed, modest hutch sized, about the valve. Then all four of them jemmied and heaved and managed to turn off the gaspipe's massive valve. They could hear the comforting guzzle of the gazillion slowly discomfiting itself then stop and the shiny landside side of the pipe had the echo of emptiness of a sudden. It took seven five litre cans of resin to fill the box mould which was wired onto the pipe to steady it. The horizontal of the valve was midway positioned in this mould. The epoxy, tubes and tubes of it were squirted in to stiffen the mix, that started to harden within the timber cuboid cauldron and Lou turned the gloop with a robust spruce stick, more and more hard it got till a famine stir about consistency, more stirs and it was a tougher gloop, then a fetid jelly like gloop for a sick giant, then in the night air as hard as a kola cube for a better giant, that boiled sweet consistency, then as the team mustered to leave, Lou stopped as it was hey presto tough as a rough ashlar. As they walked away. Shivnan sat on a trunk and removed his wader to sluice his water out. "I'll catch up."

Fang said don't forget the webcam. 'Dauh!' Shivnan eye widens at Fang. Latter can't grasp such facials in that gloom. Shivnan removed from his satchel a little pouch and the webcam, a basic one he'd got from the fat man, got half price PC World, Castlebar, or so he said. Wait and see. After some tests and foosters he placed the webcam device two point seven three metres from the spanner-in-the-works box appendage about the pipe. Shivan as he rejoined the group assured the group it was pointing the correct way and he'd pressed 'ON.'

The agreed route was make tracks back the way they came to the Bunowna. Wendywee and Shivnan now make to gain the lead and keep moving across clearings and more clearings till they are no longer heading toward the ocean's anger and froth.

They are bringing Group 'A' inland, the saline air is less and the trees hold their own quiet. Oddly from out the silence faint primate sounds chirrup.

"Miss Wendywee. Shivnan; you got early onset Alzheimer's? This is not the route." Lou shush shouts from the rear.

"We'll go closer to the main road and avoid crossing the widest part of the river." Shivnan says, his confidence bolstered by eye contact with Wendywee. Fang and Lou, rare allies are quizzical each to each.

Security Fran Yalloway is being dragged through the briars and fern stumps by his two best mutts; Snoop and Snipe. Yalloway lets the beasts loose. Careering through the sprucelettes till a clearing and Venus glimmering in a frog pool's bog dark water. Their master's whistle stops their chase. They have gotten medals for their noses: wet from sniffling out the sweat o' idealites. Fran listens to his treasures' yelpering and yelpering and sees the three insurgents, possibly four giddy shadows aways away. The two bull mastiffs are triply unimpressed and vocal with the rank hash reek of them at half a furlong. Yalloway follows procedure and unclips his Motorola Walky Talky "625, 625, 625 are you reading me?"

"Yes 625. Over." says Wasilenko, resting his stockinged feet upon a monitor, watching Lublin thrash Woodge. He is a persuasive Slav. He promised Yalloway next time he'd go apprehend in the cold and Reason Two somebody had to keep in touch with Hilversum to keep track of the screens coming back and that was essential for any court hearing that the evidence showed how many insurgents and where they headed and what were they doing in there for themselves. He rambled on into the walky talky as Woodge took a vital corner: "all them crusty feckers wants is to graffiti naff mythology on the effin pipe, don smiley smart-ass Gay-Falkes-Anonymous masks and upload their selfie-selves and think that makes them the top red-eyed black panthers in the woods." Reason Three he had the start of what might be manFlu H2N5. Lublin's goaly dressed in orange and black gets the ball and boots it way way way up and beyont.

"Three 'surgents in Quadrant C." He hears from a disjointed British voice in his roger over and out system; possibly an interrupting channel. "Wasilenko, You reading. Backup is on its way." He wasn't sure if it actually was the case but the voice said to the general compound on a series of megaphones. "Close I team have been mustered."

"Am proceeding to apprehend." says Yalloway in the field, for the record and to keep his job.

"If you say so; over." says Wasilenko conscious that the match would conclude soon and disturbances were good for over time. The screens pinged on again, the hums of drives rebooting comforted the security man with ongoing Normalcy. On the screen Wasilenko could see the heat of Yalloway, the two obvious dog shapes, brighter yet, three sweaty insurgents skirting the pipe and really bright a separate four beams of heat skirting by the fence of the Aughoose Animal Laboratory place, then, hold on, a further ten like a Roman army booting up from the banks of that wider river, ten in military formation, making for, making for what. Wasilenko leaps up. Heading for Aughoose? Then six split toward the refinery or are possibly circling to close in on Aughoose from another angle.

Snoop and Snipe with their fabulous muscles throwing shapes in the owl-light gained their quarry of three for sure and Yalloway saw the unending battle the woodkernes, too few, each unending century, who can never risk to confront in open battle the amassed colonial enemy but skirmish in the dense but spiritless furrowed forests o' Glenamoy, Crone, Slish, Ballandreeeee, Thomond, Sherwood. Wherever. Clout thrashes dare, and dare, legs ajig, swings on the cross roads gallows for the *nth* time.

CHAPTER EIGHTEEN
"O petróleo é nosso"

Take a break from bleak, early Connaught winter 2022. Mean-our-whiles back to that terrific day, March 20th 2001 and Petrobras 36 lolling in early afternoon, bobbing its boast, being the largest floating oil platform in the world; then it goes *kabbooommm*, then boom. It listed and listed till at sixteen degrees of listing, after one hundred and twenty hours, the platform sank deep into the South Atlantic; three gringo thousand, nine hundred and forty oldie worldly feet above the slippery oil reserves called *Roncador 3*, two hundred kill-o-metric clicks east of Rio de Janeiro. Imperious operative, Texas McGeown, a mere fifteen stone at the time, five and one quarter pounds for every year on this particular Earth that some Slippery-as-Feck-God had granted him or planted him.

Bit of bi-ogg on Mr. Insider-Trad-McGeown. He kept Dick le Cheney in on some of the loops regarding what got coded Operation *Gaivota/* 'Seagull' and he did half day per week consultancy on assessing ripple effects of 911 '01. Though not in his remit he'd actually dated the 'Twinky' Towers, McGeown's proudest ever, drunker suggestion. After first hearing of that most complex o'falsiest flag, tequila-clever-sunshine-in-flat-plimsolls and tank-top that he was, McGeown urged the supra-famous emergency response number for the day of that particular catalyst: "I can see it in BOLD," he enthusiastickled "get them 3D specks on, that NINE just wants to frig that skinny legged ELEVEN." Le Cheney had run it by his closest, nearest, dearest Neoconmen and they lapped it up, saw its perfect tie-a-yellow-ribbon sincerity about the vomitous oak; what genius on the bottle, and McGeown's huge-i-tudy-ness got loved into even smaller bits by that small coterie within a coterie within a mob.

The earlier unexplained Brazilian booms on Petrobras Platform 36 were mostly McGeown's brainchild, first shots of short to medium term 'Operation *Gaivotta*.' He had suggested a clutch of extraneous brown ops (smaller sabotage) that could up the price of oil and this was the third of five; idea being keep lefty developing world wannabes from entering the real world once 911 had done its eff-feck-tive butterfly. (As it turned out 911 had eleven out of thirteen other good reasons for being a perfect Pearl Harbour for both the Mesopotamian and Central Asian oil heists. 2002's Martin Luther King Day had been the runner up for working title 'Operation Twin Tower Topple' OTTT - but even the cynics thought that too cynical and boots were due on the ground anyway before first snowfall Oh One for a yet again Afghan Year Zero.

Eleven died on Petrobras-36 and the first conclusion was the enormous platform's explosions were unexplained, then they became explained, albeit in an unexplained way. McGeown made a speech to top gas-hawks know-hows in Galveston late normal year Zero Zero. The Über-logic of the destruction of 36 he flummoxed was to delay Brazil getting her own *nous*, suss and means of financing her own explorations, particularly in such deep, deep water. Brazil was getting far too ahead of the possy in the way of depths. *Roncador* was in four prospects, the gain of sector one would finance ever cleverer auto-*mechanismoes* for *os extracaos* from the other three and the Bra-zil-aeros were now the mintiest in the world at plumbing underworld prospects even in the most un-obtainium of depths.

McGeown had top three piece Dallases and five star generalised in civvies snacking his geo-putty: "Knock Brazil's mojo out of the picture for a decade or more sideways. PrivatiZe their expertiZe or go bribe/ threat 'em over." What he could not, did not mention was that Platform 36's destruction logic was to make clowns o' the *Petrobrassieroes*, underlining 'you need our likes,' then under his bad breath during luncheon he added in the right wings of the most vital ears: "you guys go shock the be-doc-trine outa I-raq, fuck over Trip-ly and make sure the pipeline through Afghan-stan gets some snake bite to it - quickass - and I'll deal with the Lazy-lay-roes." In the so-and-so's so many words at the afternoon plenary oh-tee-tee-total-arian totterin' McGeown bullet pointed that Brazil be kept in Cameroon-land till Gringonia could come up with best meritocracy. The hatch by hatch of the plan was in no big hurry. "Oil has waited hundreds of big-ones-of-years in its dark and can wait fifteen more for its appreciation."

The Mack is doing a lot of texting. Something's afoot. Lula and lovely legged Dhilma are herstory. Time for cocky take-over cum make-over. McGeown does his part; execks the required op actions from Rio; he hates Brasilia and the tall bustle of SP. He calculates over croissants at *The Four Seasons* "we've not had an improper dictatorship in thirty three tropical yearoids. It's 2016; *coup-ette* time."

Stage 1: spotify one ripe 32 grade Mason, just gagging to be a 33rd grade Mason, with all its perks & eternals. His name was Temer and he'd read all those trashy books on FreeMasons, just wanted that last *eureka*: "Jemmy open that acacia cedar of a pandora box," would wonder Count Temerous, "what shape is that five hooved *entitaje* at the core o' the Lodgings; what's the holy of its sacred name: crouched Jubilon or coiled Baal there at the dead centre of the maze?" Talk of elevation from two bit

Grandish Poobah of Lebanon Chapter of Divinopolis to full on Soloman of all the *Ordem e Progresso* you could throw a silver stick at. Tremor, fresh from signing his soul on the dotty bloodline, was now every bit the thirty three degrees bidable OverWretch o'er all that is delicious & thievable of close to a brazilian square kilometres of great forests and all that troves beneath vast seas stretching half ways to Africa. Lyre-listening Tremor was but the skimpy *vorspeisse*, a foreshock before the great *terramoto* to come; roll on, roll up the antiMessias, the Jair slouch, borne on the Autumn Equinox, year of auspicions, 1955 and from that invert caul begat the proper dick-ratatatatat-or-ship.

This descent into fasces was abhorred by those 20% within the Energies Sector of Brazil who suffer from idealism; they were numb with the national stupidity of voting in your very own prison walls. 20% of that 20% statist cohort, among them top dollar hydro-*carbonisti* sorts had to really hide their left leans; if their poor-option intentions were known, they'd be target practice for the coming death squads. (In 2007 it was worked out that 80% of hominids are continuationists and 20% are libertarian/ *cambio-mondistis* - this brain state is genetical, not astrological). That means this wee coterie was 4% (20% of 20%) of high end techies and econo-strategists. They 'go underground,' to foment and foment, a mixed bag of post Gramsci-ist Maoists, pre-air-conditioned Trotskyites but all good old plonking Statists. As the fledgeling dick-ship hated broads, queers 'n' anybody a shadow derner than *maronne* there were more women, *viados* and the 'tar-brushed' in this cell than would operate normally in top *positiones* of the average *Bord na* Burnables *Brasilaeriano*: Subsection Techy-nerdix. Many women despite their nestling stereotypificty prefer justice to status. Among them was one Lucineide, second to none when it came to depth analysis of condensate reservoirs and top quiver 'n' flex of *jujitsu* three years running. She didn't forget to have babies; more "the tots already 'carnate should be fostered until the era of perspicacity had dawned." (Google translate)

March 2001 on that oil platform 36 at *Roncador 3* her father who she loved to bits died in segments. He was himself semi Angolan, four sixteenths drawn from Iberia, the maternal nan from the Mawayana quarter of Manaus, the paternal a *cochina* seller from the Ambiente District overlooking Todos os Santos Bay, just north of the Nose, where Salvador City snoots th'Atlantic in a most unGlenamoy way. Lucineide was pure Public University. She was the glue of this lofty group, gave it its insuspicious name: HydroCarbonBrasil. Their first meets were on Thor-defended conference calls that while not infiltrated were quite likely suspected by the what she termed "the root-vegetables at dipshit intelligence," the worst wing o' the tayto-ship. Then the brightest and prettiest among the *ideal-mundistis*, Lucineide of the *jujitsu* and no babies had the bright spark of an idea that their Red Armani Faction meet every half year in the real on-land Roncador, a nonplussed town of the Interior, a place so hot, not a net curtain got twitched after elevenses. So the left over visionaries for their first long week-end went faked their names and flew zig ways and zag ways across Brazil to fool those who might suspect their existence. They could not have imagined this was the start of an incanny path that would require them in a different hemisphere, a Wild Atlantic Way different to their own.

On-land Roncador is full of bugs, mostly flying, not so much listening. It is the remote of all remotes of the state of Mato Grosso which translates as 'Humongous Jungle.' Lucineide's father, Dr. Nouson de Gamba, had much of his infancy in Roncador. His Mawayana grandma told him fables of one legged humanoids. The Sea Prospects that he had overseen the discovery of, for less than occult reasons, got the name Roncador and he dreamed of creating rigs that were not four legged. His passion for life spilt quickly into his personal life; at 18 he had Lucineide.

The twice yearly meetings at Roncador were held at the Cardeq Hotel, a dilapidation of a clifftop retirement home for spiders the size of golf balls and sash windows coloured orange with time and again. The group disguised as Spiritists in December 2019 met for a second time: the minutes of Saturday Morning session had a majority agree to shorten their name to HyBrasil. Second item was a minute's silence for the eleven who'd died on Petrobras 36 at   Roncador-on-sea, a remarkable show of respect and grief for the passing of native ability and self empowerment - that not every cleverer thing costing over a billion big ones needs a *gringo* impresario-ing it into existence and barking orders from under their often, highly unnecessary hard yellow hats - for all those objects that ever fail to fall on them? Item Three in the light of failed efforts to ally with PDVSA (Venezuela's version of Stately Oil) was a show of hands to not continue nurturing their help and know-how as said body was not quite as folksy as what they claimed on the Bolivarian tin.   Item Four; why were overtures made to Evo Morales of Bolivia now stalled ?   Evo they suspected suspected the oil *idealisti* were just a sweetie pie front for the Dick-trap to reclaim Brasil gas prospects that he had barred them from when Petrobras got upset with his 82% 'you wish' royalties.

A long weekend of "séances" was a fine ruse for keeping the curious at bay. The group's cover was to wool-pull curious hotel staff. The dozy Roncadores just thought 'here comes the freak show townies again.' The immense double doors to the hotel's marble banquet hall were guarded by a lovely tall man, much more than a bouncer, he was a so carefully groomed ABIN operative, Brasilia's excuse for a CIA. He'd become the group's eyes, ear and cock, and was well over-qualified for the job description. The group had become a settled twelve and on this outing they'd grown comfortable with one another and could talk freely almost like they were not so much a sort of Government-in-exile but at least the Energize Ministry: Subsection Practical Geekatonicks in internal exile. Cross their hearts, touch the termite gnawed wood but none had yet gotten disappeared in the night from their normal beds and bet till they revealed their apostles creed and whereabouts.

So around comes Sunday's "séance." That tall desirable man in tuxedo at the door is Clivenden, ABIN's top dollar and boy does he turn heads as much as he himself has been turned. ABIN'd gotten too bloody 'n' blinkered; the growing mounds of fingernails meant that secret service had gotten an awful distance wrong of right, already so, so east of the average right of centre. The flutter of jaded netting on the windows keeps out the larger stinging flyers. Air condition was not installed so for the best part of an hour Cliveneden'd been doing the metal bug sweep, with windows open wide and the jungle mid morning quiet and not a sweat drop on him. At his nod he opens the doors and the twelve enter and seat themselves about the *Dom Pedro II* table. Lucineide gets a text buzz. Clivenden. She reads "I think there is a hotel staff or somebody ..... up about the mezzanine. Act the part. Clive." Lucineide cannot see anybody but she hears some creeps and errs caution. She crinkles her forehead. The others get it and purse lips to various sizes of understanding. She starts pretending to be a Medium and god hardly has she swayed and swooned much but she is touched; a spirit called simply "JUST.....IN," says she. It will be seen that JUSTIN was not too long discarnate and his Portuguese Beginner's and incapable of the least melody. The others could hardly contain their lols at Lucineide's authenticity.

Some soft to mid thinking Brasilians whose souls tend atheist can have a soft spot for Spiritism; it pertains to being scientific. Lucineide had never had such truck with Spiritism. However she was waiting in the acupuncturist's the May before and saw an ad for *Spiritism in the Forest* and she said 'isn't that a great way to gather and not rouse suspects.' She told the group she'd "chanced" on Spiritism; as if the Multiverse is an interaction of a 'zillion chancers! The others reckoned it the best of ruses and the Cardeq Hotel was chosen as it had no reviews nor stars nor wifi or any 'G whatsoever but also of course the name. What Marx is to Social Climbing, what Darwin is to beggar-thy-neighbour is Frenchman, Alain Cardeq to the Spirit lay-overs; Le Cardeq was the fifth Evangelist when it came to inkling and inking the ghasty *hwihhohohoo*-zone. Cardeq not so much founded Spiritism as Spirits found him out and for a few decades mid nineteenth century they had him day and night logging their channels. After the group settled on the wooh-wooh ruse Lucineide was googling about and found by CHANCE the Cardeq Hotel, by CHANCE close to her father's ancestral patch. The Cardeq Hotel was founded by Laurent Cardeq who was a fourth cousin of the man who'd gone written the equi-valent to the DAS KAPITAL of the movers 'n' shakers of NextWorldFare. The first meeting at Hotel Cardeq was talk about prospects, not possessions and they agreed to shorten their name to HyBrasil. They also worked out funding streams and secrecy means and divvied out tech roles. This second outing however took a heeby-jeeby turn for betterment: what's in a name ?

"JUSTIN seems dead decent." Lucineide mutters with her eyes closed and her convictions as to what disincarnate hominids did or didn't do or influence after they'd ditched their sack of skin doing a proverbial 180 degrees. Lucineide seeks strength, beckoning tighter holds of hands with her nearests and then enjoins the others about the oval table to link.

"We are here for you." said a sandy haired hydrologist from Piaui, tightening with her medium build hand Lucineide's hand smiling play-along but then she also gets a jolt: "what was that ?"

"The energy. Minister from Energy, of...." Lucineide says by way of her mouth moving and her voice goes from being sultry North East's answer to the *garrotta* of Ipanema typique to an oldish male. "I am of the Depths."

"Lucineide; your voice is so deep ?" says the geophysics noddy guarding the end of the table, her black auburns framing her bright brown face and her long earrings acting the part. She is in transition from man to woman.

"I am of the sweet but dark Depths." says the self styled spirit lip-synching the unshuddering Lucineide.

Clivenden looks down at the proceedings from the upper mezzanine excuse for a walkway of a library of crumbling words of a place. His hands crossed, gird his gut in that classic bouncer mode, resting between his outie and his willy. He cares then for Lucineide.

"I am from that island."

"God, is that Spanish ?" asks another.

"I think he is thinking he is speaking Portuguese." Trans weighs.

"Why have you come among us ?" asks Miss Piaui 2017.

" The Spirit of the Depths has conquered my Arrogance and sent me back to Time."

"Lucy. You definitely do a great man." says a.n.other on our right.

"In the Depths my innards were devoured but now......"

"But now what....."

"I can hint at you; that's all."

"Please do and then we can get down to business," says a most doubting Tomaso from what once was clept Departing of Rig Adjustments, now part of consolidated one stop-shop: Oil Power Absolutely Corps.

"36. Eleven did not die for no reason. 36." Spirits are permitted double negatives; as is Portuguese.

"Are you one of those dead ?"

"No. I've had their council since."

"Where do you come from ?" asked one Euvertson of Leme: an hydrocarbon econo-class-warfairy.

"Find the real HyBrasil. Be slick." and then he quit the lodgings of Lucineide's mouth and with the weensiest pufflette of wind he may have gone.

Lucineide is back proper and first thing she looks up and sees for her benefit, Clivenden doing something like as if everybody understands Deaf-Sign these days. Taking a moment to de-trance she realises the coast is clear, possibly was always clear. Now however she is faced with her eleven colleagues, all national resources types as long as they are prospected for the benefice of the plain people and she has just gone and done an *Exorcist III* on them.

Most dreams get forgotten like so much drying sex-dripping on a chucked away cum-rag. Lucineide had dreamt of her dead father before but her underused un-un-conscious did not process it into Normalcy sunlight. The night after JUSTIN's channel one, this featureless left side of her "father's" or stand-in face of her father appeared with a chalice because it had import but was way planer, more like a handle-less mug, like what Bruegel peasants would have a knees-up with, jouncing them together on their Holiday on Ice Special. Inside the mug there is this molasses gloop. It is like the father character is looking on at a hope that

Lucineide will partake of the cup or take solace or prophet from the vagueness of the set up.

"Dreams are such veiled bollocks," she murmured into her morning bowl of chia and pia seed grams.

"Spiritist Convention" Day 3's morning was for reflection. Reconvening after lunch for concluding plenary indulgences: *kashasha* with plans and diagrams. Clivenden was knocking back the Black Princess beers, forty two degrees celcius and the jungle'd gone 'n' changed hertz to 432. Alone he is upon the pavilion balcony that dangles over the River Ilikuuueueue. Lucineide sees his drinking problem and is drawn to Clivenden; out she comes through squared doors half cracked. She adores the tiniest of slopes and the security detail of his eyes. She feels a third lucky marriage in her drifts. She is without child but is Brazil welter-women's champion *jujitsu* black belt. A gesture of his clears that she is welcome.

Lucineide sips her *kashasa* dregs and eyes the forest: "we can only persist in the rat-holes of theory, of subterfuge, the more the Bolsonoristi grasp, grab 'n' backhand the more our belove-able-ly Brazil is each day more poverty cute...." (again defer to Google Translate)

"....a suzerain of Gringonia," Clivenden agrees for agreeing sake. He is not had his afternoon's sex and is counting odds while timing his mindful breaths to heave of passionate heave of Lucineide's freedom-loving bosom. This is the first weekend he has met her.

"Our faction's problem is how little we can do in the three dimensional world, society's layers have gotten so, so monitor-able." Lucineide has non masonic degrees in Organic Feasibles within Physics, *Universidade de* Belo Horizonte. She watches a condor descending and moving off toward the River Ilikueuuuueue. She sips some more booze and notes that her ice is water. She turns to Clivenden and prods his shoulder and speaks her vision: "Hmmmm. My idea is out there........" and to delay her impact she lets the condor become one with the forest eyesight-wise. "I'm thinking of a monster." She scans Mother Nature for a name: "A much, much improved 36...... let's call her the, *The HyBrasil, HyBrasil 2525.* She'll dive fathoms of leagues and rise without the bends. She can take oil, inhale gas even in the tiniest, deepest nooks. With the profits we can alter reality."

After scant courtship, a nod, hardly a wink, a short stroll Lucineide and Clivenden made love in Lucineide's room; awesome sweatin' n' slithering without precautions nor preconceptions and almost broke the Mato Grosso record for slowness, more like how strictly familiars might dent an afternoon. 43 degrees and 44 minutes later said the mercury, said the LED clock and them there spent and smokin.'

Most of Brasil is an hour late. So at 4pm they reconvened. All doors were locked from the inside. Lucineide hair natty coughs politely. The group continue to brag and gossip. She biros the glass tumbler and the mindfulness silences them.

"I'm going to suggest to the group we resurrect P-36. Let's do it and reconnect its tentacles, create a Brazilian Man-o-war orders and orders of magnitude, twenty thousand leagues, no, greater...."

Clivenden, this time at the table, knows certain women love the drone of facts: "......in her heyday P-36 was considered the world's biggest semi-submersible."

"Yes," agrees Lucineide steadying her butt on the termitic seat below her 'carnate perfectoids.

Clivenden goes into prattle overdrive like he'd swallowed some terrabit o' Wikipedia since the love making: "36 produced 84,000 bbl/d and 1.3 MMcm/d of gas, with the world's first drill pipe riser, subsea tree and early production riser rated for a max of 2,000 metres."

Tomaso butts in: "I thought you were security. Now you are Mister Universe of Aggregate and Depths.

"I am well rounded."

"How can we trust anybody who at some dumb stage in their career thought to join ABIN ?" asks the leftiest of the beards among them.

"Lula." answered Clivenden. "I was the youngest then operative oh five; picked out from Santos police academy. Lula presented hope. I got it."

"Can we trust his sincerity ?"

"Yes you can," and Lucineide managed just about not to give away the cosy satience of his recent channelling. What a weekend.

Abridge two-and-a-half-ish dedicated years; the Socialites said goodbye to their families went and located P-36 on the feast of St. Anthony 2020. To do this they hacked and jammed the satellites of the west to mid South Atlantic consecutively till they'd gotten P-36 lifted to just below the sea surface, then secreted her enough east and more east into African waters, so she could be dragged proud of the depths under no eye; especially not any subsidiary of Close I. She saw daylight and like a well behaved saint appeared, miraculously preserved bar some rusty rivets and soaked living quarters. Two of P-36's pneumatic float feet were replaced so she could float again with a hardly noticeable wobble. Eighteen years since she died; she was well due a generous make-overhaul.

Lucineide said "make her invisible. This girl needs to be shy......." dramatic pause, "..... to radar, sonar, satellite, eye and ear. Get it? Let's make her magnificent: a real sucker." They chose a spot and went at best practice tinkering, welding, riveting and more riveting, extensions, diamond studded the drills, extended their voluptuary, upped the bar of the suck pipes, extended storage, empowered blow-out and blow-back facilities. For god knows how many months the blow-ins with local help and expertise dreamt and did in impossibly measures.

Then one day presto: FIN. We're talking top industry grade Chitty Chitty Bang Bang. Unveil and test day, Harvest Moon again, Southern Hemisphere 2020. We're just out of mind and sight of the north west coast of Mayombe. There's definitely something 'neath the wave, a child's dream of a device. Intents and purposes wise; this Thing sucks diesel potential; albeit literally. TEST 1: her lungs in extraordinary depths at known positions off that vaguer part of Angola, that strip well west of munificent Kitina prospect, out of eyeline of that coast where the proud Mayombe vex the disputable Republic of Cabinda. "Ticks perfect up to 21,000 leagues more or less." says the mostly doubting Tomaso. Lucineide captain-blighs: "Surface her" The rhime of natives' drums scored that celebration, carried on rare easterlies mixed with the PROGRESSive after-din of the cut and throotle of the state-of-the-science sucu-busy octopussy days and nights without cease, no breaks for the earnest. What extra-ordinary finds in tight wedges, a barracuda's house could be explored unwarranted and even a half barrel of crude couldn't be left unsucked from her back parlour. They offloaded the oil finds on to tanker after blessed tanker that got took to irregular ports to avoid accumulating suspicion.

HyBrasil N4P invested half the oil wealth in making the People of Mayombe less blind, more yellow-hatted and they replaced mine shattered limbs all over the Republic of Cabinda and their right hands didn't recognise the kindness of their leftovers. HyBrasil 2525 and her exploits was becoming ever more difficult to hide and they wanted to also make her bigger and more beautiful so they went North apiece to a pirate's cove of a shipyard in the lee of Enclave Bay, one push over 'n' heave ho from Fernando Po. Here the Angolan not-so-profits left after do-gooding were reinvested in re jigging HyBrasil 2525's rigging and her computer skills were given the fetac ten, always with a view that she and they'd return soon to Brazil, once the dicktattyship with a small 'd' had its phallic tower un-Sarumanned and the profits could build Primary Care Centres in the each and every Favella *d'uma Nova Brasil*. Spring 2022 meant, election time; the 'garchs get their 94% approval. God Bless Whataspp plus Evangelican preachcraft plus the invisibility of electronic voting; so press button. What a length of whiles they've whiled without home then Lucineide remembered something JUSTIN'd dreamt at her, oddly on the self same day that Pender Jones Junior was shown the first satellite images of unusual machinations in the waters about Enclave Bay. GCHQ UK sniffed not only a vacuum but a "ruddy great chordless, Sir, have a look at this. Have you ever seen its likes: a giant sea-Dyson." There were a queue of Qs eager to cock a snoop at the Future when said image was blown up on a Dr. Strangelove size screen. Elder Q advises "Let's scout that baby out." Pender Jones arms akimbo furthers and concludes: "We might just make those cheps an offer they can't refuse."

Lucineide's dream arrived fully formed; much informed by the look of the end of Star Wars Episode VII. JUSTIN who she'd not put a face to before is dressed in monk's garb of an elderly Luke SkyWalker pointing his dull stave towards a point southish from his bit of a pointed skelligeen. He turns to Lucineide's inner-eye says "thy Kingdom come," bit rich for a well rounded agnostic.

CHAPTER NINETEEN

The wind in the willows along the canal again and Anton's sat on the very seat where his feline curiousity snatched him off into an unspecified episode of his very own uninvited box set. In one hand he has a L.UA.S. ticket in his other hand a red biro. From its top he thought it was blue, but it's red. He doesn't cycle anymore much, likes the comfort of strangers though he keeps to the front of the tram to be near the driver and where talking on phones is out of bounds. It is a gorgeous day and the first chemtrails are gridding the south Dublin skies as if Spring had arrived, and skipped Advent such was the earth warming snow dropsy. He watches the chemtrails' pooofy lengths of exhaustion spread out till stagecraft sized liniments o' "clouds" have been begotten across the half morning, long skinny fingered at first then web out from the terminus of Bull Wall, the breadth of the city, a cage well bound by the time farthest ganglands about Ronanstown are reached, all a delightful sedative of ethylene dibromide, mixed with cheery nano-particulates of aluminium and barium for taking the breath away; the self styled cumulation glint on glint equaled a way too open a skies policy, like the bad yerk of a cheap, vast muslin plat unravelled. Anton just saw them; he didn't know what they do. 'They sure'd make gorgeous pink orange at sunset.'

By the time the wind had whishted some of its soughing, Anton has written six names on the still useable tram ticket: Mum, Padraic, his half brother Finton, step sister Nigella, his dad if still living (out of courtesy), and his ex ex. He'd forced himself to reduce his vital family and loyalty to as small a number as possible. It turned out easier than expected, as a year or more before he made exactly same list based on a sorta fancy of whose grave or crematorium service was he likely to cry at. No first and not a hint of a second cousins. Friends he just had to leave out and they tended to change every half decade or quicker by their own free will, or according to the sorrow and troubles of losing your mobile ever and anon or it falling down a jax at *Adonnoyed.* Just then he wondered if weeping for half bro Finton would be courtesy or expectation but he was sure if Nigella was bawling, snivelling, his ducts'd yawn tears too, crying is that affectacious. The number 666 8100 was in his head non stop, ring it, ring it. Ring it from a payphone. Do they exist? 666 8100 is the confidential number for Store Street, *Garda* Station. It struck him as a bit thick to have the Devil's favourite numbers for folk who were building up the bottle to grass. Ring from a mate's phone. Ring from a Nigerian Wells Fargo joint. 'This super-grass is feckin' steppe sized.' If he could keep well behaved like Duhallow said, all the Edward Snowdonia that is non whisper to whisper human yacking could simply be ignored. Just do nothing reckless, make normal calls, texts, 'Hi Mum, how's your day, hi Padraic how's your repercussions ?' Stick to his irrelevant map, grids, grads, degradations, be a know-it-all that obeys the ole order. Then a penny dropped and with the remaining quarter hour of L.U.A.S. ticket he hopped aboard a not so jammers tram at Charlemont, got off at Westmoreland and passed the Waxworks and saw his affliction in its window tint, yellow hoodied warrior with his curls sticking out. He was sang-idged between Hannibal Lector and a transitioning Grainne Whale. He braced himself, crosses O'Connell bridge and a westerly at his loins and ears. He wests his self down Abbey street and pops into *Govinda's* restaurant. He ordered medium mixed platter, took his aluminium cup of de-chlorinated Vartry water and sat way at the back, looking inward but could see 'flections of the door in a tapestry behind glass of Lord Krishna dispensing syrup to warriors, and in gratitude they gave Him a mighty Mexican wave with their braceletted arms akimbo, hundreds of them, big grins 'n' taches on them, like earth life was one fab dance sequence. He had divvied the Kailash sized mound of grub into defined food sector types; now half way through his chickpeas with relief the tall man came in and ordered a man size version of Anton's platter but splashed out on mango lhasi and fudge balls for dessert. 'Detectives with three kids get plenty of over time,' noted Anton.

"Me own *segosha*." exclaims the man, just from the back lit of the halfways sideburns of Anton and sits down opposite him. "Are you become a Harry, Anton, hah ?" asks the big jowls of a man from Temple Tuohy, as was obvious from the thrusts 'n' clicks of his Tipp tongue. He lashes into the food and dabs his mouth with his orange pink napkin after every few hoofs of nourishment.

"That was a feck off wedding, wasn't it."

"Good yeh." answers Anton, "God yeh."

"You and Pat; ye're the right laugh when ye're plastered."

"Jasper. Have you a phone on you?"

"Of course. Fire away." D.I. Jasper Dwyer hands over his ever so 2015 looking phone.

"It can do fuck all." Some of the serving staff frown at table eleven. Anton turns the phone off. It looks too old to be an NSA portal to a Langley or a GCHQ. Jasper frowns but smirks along.

"Jasper. I am in a pickle."

"What you done? I can't arrest you for infidelity these days."

Anton shakes his head and Jasper sees Anton's had to grow up since their shared cousin-in-law's wedding an August before.

Jasper tries to see the spark in Anton's eyes but he can only see the wee-est harrow ruts of growing pains.

"Trouble at mill!" he hoofs more food in, then slows his pace, realising. "You came here specially; didn't you now ?" Anton nods. "The only Vegan guard in the Metropolitan Constabulary........ Queer bashers?"

"No. Work related. You're going to think I've gone bipolar." "Always thought you were on some spectrum," and he winks at Anton and chucks a sugar fudge of a bollock looking thing into his great mouth, though he is yet dealing with savoury.

"Tell me Anton. Have you killt someone or are you planning same?"

"I'm surrounded." His eyes are welling garden cities, with no law enforcement.

"Jesus Anto. It's writ all over you: *'I'm in trouble deep'* or what."

"You know my job. I got promotion."

" Well wear. Actually Anton, I did know that. Better half said."

"Oil."

"I've the right to remain silent and you...... shoot." Jasper, to indicate full attention folds his arms despite the choice dainties yet to be wolved and leans the chair back and rocks it.

"There is a plot going on or is afoot for long time I would say. I know. A lot of what would appear to be normal boring inquiries for our energy are getting side tracked, getting no answers."

"I don't get the picture."

"Our department has a mirror department that is probably running the show, and it may have been operating for thirty, no more, or more years. It is in an opposite building."

"Anton. Picture's gone fuzzy." Jasper picks up his turned off phone, points it at Anton, like he is going to up the volume or change channel with his imagined remote zapping.

"They do a certain amount with the help of us inside the normal in inverted commas department, either by way of bribes, threats or hoping we think like planks. Please Jasper put that down and please I beg you do not, do not turn it on."

Jasper takes in deeper the look of Anton, he is bloodshot, sleep deprived maybe. He actually reaches out and taps Anton's hand. "It's okay. Listen I remember when I was promoted. I went from beat to plain clothes and my god I had to learn in a big hurry. Anton, you are an outsider. You're the boys-in-blue. You're just shocked by the antics of public school brats who never seen a queer, let alone a Dub of one. They are just being normal, corrupt as the latest gravy train, first class cunts. That's all."

Jasper recommences eating. Anton sighs and asks if he can have one of Jasper's fudge bollocks. As he savours it - he looks Jasper in the eye with a deep Spaghetti Western look of life and death, he knows any words, and lack of any proof of his predicament make him simply nuts. This transmission is short and he tries to upload facts into the glare, this man to man gaze, but he is not an alien from the fifth millennium which becomes obvious as Jasper says: "Anton. Haven't you possibly time in *lieu* owing?"

"Jasper. I am going to tell you the bare facts. I don't care how nuts you take me for. I am exploding. Since three days. Yeh it started last Friday. I had a hunch and the hunches have multiplied."

"Right so."

"There's some sort of scam going on to make sure certainly us Paddies, possibly others don't know what is being sought or dug or got ashore out there." Anton points dead west towards a big garish picture of Monkey God Hanuman but means the Atlantic. "I am talking mostly gas but in some way oil too. I don't see a pattern. I half hunch it is English Netherlands are at it. Really I have no idea what they are at. Whoever THEY are, they have huge control. I was being the dumb, over curious, get yourself killed cat-fellow......."

".... and ....."

"........ well; I was actually in at least some small part of their mirror department. Grubby place by the canal, busy some o' the time, then no people much but possibly recently more busy somehow. I fiddled with one of their p.c.s."

"Jesus. Seriously," Jasper was in some episode of Netflix Series Four, Episode Two, meaning the Jesus wasn't genuine.

"At this stage I imagine all that hullabaloo about that pipe in Rossport twenty less years ago was total herring, code red, big time. I saw references to funny goings-on all around there, satellite control mechanisms, even Knock Airport being capable of landing herculeses. It is like Ireland is an irrelevance, to be deadly honest an inconvenience or a platform for taking over our bit of Atlantic."

"And we have loads of it; you been blue in the face tellin' me."

"It is so secretive. All the stuff'll come in through Mayo but much of heavy lifting is dealt with from Ayr."

"No Aberdeen for Mayo then," understands Jasper.

"Seems that way." Jasper nods along with Anton like they are both rare ole mates slipping into double figures of stout at the Patriot Inn, then the lhasi kicks in: "Describe the enemy."

"Normal as normal can be."

"God similar to fundamental Moslems. Never the damned obvious fellow with the Abe Lincoln frantic beard - always the skater dude; 'Boom boom boom - I gotcha in me room.' Or the cheesy grin geek."

"This normal guy of normal appearance; oh shuddering creeps, he gives me the shivers yet, he is threatening not me, but Josie."

"Your mum's Josie."

"Correct."

"Threaten means kill."

"So he says. My Padraic they caused an accident to."

"I heard, by the way how......"

"They told me not to contact anybody, Store Street *Garda*, nobody."

"Anton. It's like Sandra Bullock in a mov....."

"How can I make this not seem all in me noggin?"

"Evidence helps loads."

"I iphoned a screenshot of that p.c. up in the their makeshift department but it got de-leer-ed......"

"Sorry."

"Remotely of course. Anything pert-nent to this...... ORDEAL is vanished. There was files, names like 'Fat One,' 'Angie,' 'History.'"

Jasper gulped the entire lhasi, typical thirsty for something, turned teetotal Pisces. "Anton I like you. I am going to humour you and pretend to believe your every last word. That means; keep going." Jasper chucks the last fudge bollock into his healthy mouth. For Anton at least this was like cheap therapy if not a judicial remedy. He got seven minutes and forty seven seconds of further attention and none of his two and twos added up to anything even close to a strategy; Jasper fell pensive with each word, and turn of them. Lemoncello and the Ecce man who hadn't a hint of bi about him, his dubious promotion, fudged Malaysians, unticked boxes, giant filing stacks, fairly time wasting cartography, his turned boss, a mature blackmail, husky voices from zero zero five five calling out quarae. All the time nodding Jasper. He did jot some notes. Anton went on and concluded with the privatised Dots being maybe the crime boss.

Jasper took it in then slid across the table to look Anton straight in the eye: "I sometimes suspect that the 'all is not as it seems' is likely worse than even one's worst assumption; if you get me. You suspect things are wobbly but they're way, way worse. You know, take for example Tone-ure run our Intel for uz. God knows how they got let the gig. They sift half at least of our I.T. at Store Street and from what I know more than, over at HQ on Harcourt Street. Where does all that info sit, how many penalty points has Anton Fruen, how often does he ring his mother. All stored in Nevada, U-tah-very-much."

Anton stared at Jasper, reminded of some of the worst aspects of his closer friends when you go confide: one fraughts, outpours - the response: me, far, low, me me me me me.

Jasper pondered the scowl of somebody he likes in his heart and rebalances just as Anton remonstrates: "this is not a chat. This is me risking lives by even sitting here."

"An entire Department compromised for maybe a generation." ponders aloud Jasper. "That boss of yours, he'd be in the *Indo* sometimes. He has a fairly hardcore wife."

Anton makes the international hand gesture for ample breasts in agreement without even an upturn of a smile then hurries to say: "Duhallow, born as he's always saying between the Anywater and Oily rivers. He's always saying goofy things. He is in on it but he's trapped in it. He's no help. Likely he needs help. Maybe the invisible force put a price on his wife."

"Epic. Well if it helps Anton, me own boss swore allegiance to the British monarch once upon a time."

"Yesterday I was in *Easons* and in an alcove where I thought there was no CCTV, I flicked through a book on conspiracies;

this thick and some mad big pictures. They'll go to all lengths. There was a chapter that had Mi5 or 6, I never remember which what does. They invented a religion for the Saudis to keep them in order. Wannabee-ists. Meanwhile suck you dry. Foist some Joe or Ahmed What-to-be on them, saying give up this and that. Meanwhile derek derek the devils dry. It's appalling."

"Sure MI5 had a campaign to make it out the Rah were all at black masses every other week. During The Troubles, I mean."

"Never heard that."

"Ah the seventies. What's our version then of the Saudi means of doing things in your view?"

"I don't know. Gah and which county hurled best at who, lads, ladsiness. Six effin' Nations. Drink. Confirmation. Rosary. Anything to keep us lookin' at our belly buttons at all costs." Anton went red in case he'd overstretched his straight bashin.'
"Yeh. The internet is up to here with con-spires." Jasper deflected and showed that such rich imaginings on the internet did not persist above his own large nostrils.

"But I don't want them to even know that I am trying to figure it out. I won't even try a booth at the Chinese net cafe. Most invisible one is on Parnell Street actually. I.P. address or not I don't dare." Then Anton cried from like nowhere. He felt his hand touched, and was grateful and then more salts and toxins streamed his cheeks gently, yet plentifully.

"I see what I can do even though I believe you this much." Jasper measured his hands a certain harmonium wide, and Anton had the autis-ticity to measure the generosity at 30% *credo* which was enough to slow snuffles and taking up his Hare Krishna orange pink napkin dabbed his eye pads dry and rallied. At least he'd shared. Padraic, the big brick, was advising that all the time. Don't bottle it. Share and share alike.

CHAPTER TWENTY

Ministry of Defence - Porton Down: Early Afternoon, Early Summer 1998
Dramatis Personae:
Charles, Prince of Wales
Philip, Prince of the U.K.
Garth Pender-Jones Snr, S.A.S., Y Squadron
Ruth Coppinger, Chief Inspector of Mi7, B-wing, Arts, Culture & the Islands
Sir Naseby Harbinger, Chief Secretary of their Department of Energy.

A large American gentleman aged anything from forty to fifty five years old. His security clearance clearly says **MCGEOWN**.

ALL ARE SEATED
"No need to minute." Prince Charles breaks ice nervily, "keep it up here." and he taps with his disloyal wedding finger his left brain like an easily knackered woodpecker.

"No sonny. This ain't one for the Anglo Saxon Chronicle," slightly double negatives Prince Philip back slapping his first born; to *chi* up his *chutzpah.*

The chuckling group hunker into their seats in the high windowless triangular room, so sound proof that supersonic jets taking off and landing without, are gliders. A slide pops up on the yellowing of the least wide wall of the darkening room, a 10 foot by 8 foot image. Two o' the company rise and their silhouettes bob about mid the projected light. Standing legs apart and regarding the slide is the sleek, muscular lady's man, Pender

Jones Snr and to his left the large American. The former, ex Captain of a Goose Green battalion back in the last battle for the oils; South Atlantic '82. Sixteen years on his point five shorn side fronds are the taddiest grey. He frowns back at the black and white slide that's just popped up, ignores it and with the honey-est Llanbrynmair of a Welsh Eton introduces the favourite fixer of all the oil barons of the slippery flipperty world. McGeown is introduced by Pender Jones. Bar Philip the rest haven't had the pleasure of him before.

"This is Ignatius McGeown, of Texas." The audience regard the width of him.

"Inny'll do." says Inny McGeown.

He looks fun in a poopy cushion sorta way. McGeown makes his stand: "this meeting sure ain't no Tuesday meeting o' The Porton Diner's Butterfly Net Collectin' Society. This is the unminuted, unspoken day and place when our operation gets properly name called.

"*Fa Ton.*" Prince Charles jumps the large man's gun. He pronounces like he is Emeritus Don of pre-ancient P 'n' Q-it Keltickle tongues.

"Thank you highness." McGeown ignored the royal protocol detail: small 'h's, no bows, touching, no backward moonwalking; all that pep claptrap Pender Jones had insisted on. Pender Jones, a pillar, the pillar, remains standing and swaying with practised interest as McGeown explains: "'Fat One' starts now," McGeown fairly spits the words out; Self-deprecation not being his confirmation name. Then he turns serious-ish conducting with a teacherly pointer cane at the cinemascope of the silent slide behind him. "Best of Mates, Best of mates" he repeats, reminds and draws the raggle taggle group minds towards the illuminated slide on screen. The gathered secret seven are looking at a sepia old snap of a big crowd of people greeting some important fellow. McGeown plot points and points out: "This here slide shows a King, here, a queen here, some, a lot of rookies, some recent knights, some long in the tooth knights, a lotta lotta pawns. Pawns. Pawns. Pawns." McGeown points with his cane at almost indecipherable, people, dotty bystanders: "even the Pawns, these wee pixeleenies, clearly are extremely well dressed. Look again the focal front of the picture two bishops greeting the King, not just bishops but red hat, full on claudia-card-holding card-i-nalez."

Pender Jones steadies the ship for those not used to Cross-pond: "this snap is the visit of King George V to Maynooth, greeted by Ahland's Primates. Maynooth is in the County of Kildare, this snap is sharpish oh 315pm, a Wednesday, July twelfth."

" Of all days," chips in Philip dapper and erect despite being a dozen years after retirement, all the sevens, seventy seven.

"King George has come to do some pat-the-back." Pender Jones continues. "This a Seminary, an establishment for fledgling Men o' the Cloth, a lot less in funding than a full on standing army. It's 1911."

McGeown cuts in: "Centre snap their Graces: Cardinal Rogue trying outdoing Cardinal D'Alton with the wide flap of their wide-ass bonnets on their holy-ass heads. The hats are a telling black and when they're doffed for the English Czar double they make much warm wind. Sophia Loren would been well put in the shade by these hats' likes. Sophia loves her hats."

"Mind your mouth, that's my Great Gramp !" Prince Charles cuts in and looks around to the others to show he is quipping, not being insulted.

"Your Gramps was a Cardinal?" McGeown jests.

"Of course He wasn't - He was the Emperor of India and .... Ahland to boot."

Pender Jones cuts in: "Note the date. 1911. The apogee of British power on that ahland, our neighbour. It never was nor got better on that outsized Orkney."

McGeown gets extra microscopic, squints up at the picture: "I imagine these Excellencies can do one feck off doff of those hats. We don't have that snap sadly. Big poufs of warmth issue from such movements, one imagines. This is their biggest month of Sundays ever, dollied up 'n' rolled up to one big, big heyday. If only their mums were above ground to share, their chaste sons bowing to the Emperor of all them Pink Places. After the niceties, cucumber sandwiches, the upper crustless-iest ever, with the crunchiest tastiest cucumbers of all the walled secret gardens of all the county of bridal Kildare." McGeown swings back towards his audience. "No time for further conjecture. This black and white picture literally speaks one big one of words, at least, and I ain't adding any."

Pender Jones nods to Prince Philip who speaks *ex cathedra*; "In our line of business there are funny little rules. A not too obscure, but not too obvious royal rule but a very important rule is a British Monarch must visit the sectors of Their dominions one time per century. If then Her Present Majesty or Her Dad, and/ or Her/ our Little Treasure Charlie here didn't tread on say Cheshire one time across the past hundred years; those Cheese dips could up and leave Our United Queen-dome and they'd be right; they'd have the right."

Pender Jones takes up "This was the last day of His then Majesty's visit to Ireland. He stayed at Dublin Castle, to secure His person. The Viceregal Lodge being a tad too open to wood kerne Feen-yen types."

McGeown can't resist: "Don't want a Molotov through your window. This is five years before their Easter bunny thingummy, their 1916."

Pender Jones lets his metaphorical hair down, waves his hands above his ears, the imitation of a Punch cartoon of an Irish rabbit caught in English headlights and all have a bonding chortle. P.J. then re-engages with the slide: "This image. We are agreed it was our high point. Some would say Queen Victoria's visit to Ireland was. I believe 1911 is our *Pax Britannica* fulcrum. 'The Titanic' was getting her last rivets. Every last doily was dainty, and bleachy in the better homes of the Second City of the Empire. The trams and their ads of Bovril ran their tracks. Workers knew their shillings from their thruppences."

"Jones, I imagine is trying to say we never stood in better favour as that year." enjoinders the Prince of Wales, himself getting it.

"1911, " muses Coppinger. She is the head of essentially Cultural Manipulation which can be anything from facilitating Man United shop franchises to overseeing foreign policy trends in relation to all new Bond movie scripts to promoting Robbie Williams concerts or advising how Oasis's first tour of The Gulf could leverage gas prospect concessions if the right Sheikhs could be granted a snort with their Gallagher-ships.

"We have thirteen short years to prepare. Peace is broken out now, what, two months and I guarantee it'll last."

"Prepare for what," asks Coppinger.

Philip does his key point frogless cough, then drops the clanger: "the return of the Monarch...... If Her Present majesty is alive we're talking latest late Spring 2011. She will visit the Republic and if Her clogs are popped wee C-PAG here." Nobody needs to extrapolate. The point is got and the royal dad play flicks the apparent heir on his bigger ear.

Pender Jones cuts through the awkward silence. "Our meeting today has ticked its first box," and he nods to Philip to acknowledge the accepted elephant in the room, albeit she is wearing a natty sash that says *Ms. Anschluss 2011* about her massive grey tummy. "Next item; make a choice: establish similar goodwill to our treasured 1911 scenario by we imagine the early 2020s or go for decades long Greater Intention Co-version; ole bit of G.I.C. as we say or a bit of both."

"I'm lost and the GOAL?" enquires Coppinger.

"Ahh. Mummsy. Mum is the word, is the word, is the word. We need to capture this." Pender Jones clicks along quickly some slides, leaving unexplained aerial shots of the Treaty Ports, the Bog of Allen, and one time Erse President, Eamon De Valera in Indian headdress. He settles on this large, square shaped slide, a snazzy graphic, that marks every undulant of the Atlantic seabed, shot 70mm Grand Canyon style and to its east a wee Ireland draped be a matt, flat shameless, yet complete, Union Jack, 3D wrinkled.

"WOW. There is nothing like mentalising a conquest to make it manifest. Positive thinking here here. " praises Coppinger.

"Yes. British Isles'll mean what it says on the ruddy tin again." Philip can be quite the dominatrix. "Obviously not quite so brash as our present graphic," he continues nodding at the screen.

Coppinger is flabbergasted though loving the daring do. "How many *Ark Royals* we fixing to send......?"

"Zero. Hypnotism. Sleight of the proverbial." Pender Jones raises his hand in a 'So Help Me God' way then waves it queenly. "Simple, slow moving, soothing. No need for military intention or a big flap of union jacks on every building."

Coppinger's stout body shades the slide as she's gotten up from her seat to get a closer look at the terrifyingly detailed contour map of the East Atlantic about Ireland.

"Over-Commander Coppinger. We have almost every gloaming, ben and boulder 3Ded to a 'T.' Each year we know more and more, the Irish, for sure and many who might be seen as our competitors know less and less." Prince Philip is so proud of the secretest battle plan he has ever connived.

"Don't be silly." puts out Coppinger, "so mesmerised that she disrespects royalty.

"What we mean by more is that they are fed ant-i information of the terrain's uselessness by our operatives." Pender Jones answers her back.

"So what are we here to discuss."   The savvy look at her and, apart from McGeown, do a collective Britannic smirk.   "OK; what the Devil is so beguiling in these glens and bonnies beneath water world ? Seaweed nymphs?"

Prince Philip nods and Pender Jones gets quite excited and with his pointy cane he circles the clefts of Dooish without Tory: "that'd be the take of Brunei across say most or all the 1970s."

Coppinger cannot resist: "Oh P.J. you too adore mastering long haul strategies."

P.J. ignores the flattery comment, knows she is too, too right and with a further swish, another larger than life geopolitical brush stroke effectively rings Corrib Erris, down to Clew Bay out to the deepest *Outre-Meer* beyond the Mayo shelf, "that is Lake Maracaibo on a good decade OR a fairly full fraction of Norway's infamous Snorre-dorado. Gas-wise my team are still estimating its hugeness." Then he twirls, for delay, his cane, like a majorette with tan, tightēd, nylon hips might, before spelling out with his long wand a magic circle off Kerry "and this is the wet dream of the Bedouin, not far off The Kingdom sized. Not 100% clarity but it looks like it may be volumetrically speaking." His circle takes in the full Scandinavian shape of the Porcupine and its Abyssal Plain that propels out from the south and west of the Dingle finger.

"Faisal a-gogo." McGeown who was feeling side lined does a wee dance, his podged fingers doing a slippery flamenco mudra the shape of the accepted international gesture for filthy lucre. "Shake your Money," likes he's the town crier in the pay o' the oil snake entity.

"A big, big oil field, a zone of fields." Pender Jones translates. "Very big."

"Not neatly in its altogether," cautions Philip, "but extremely large pockets, some jolly, jolly deep. It can't be rigs as we know them now. Piper Alpha and that."

"I get it; massive. Co-version policy please ? What is implied." Coppinger is taking notes.

Philip frowns at any hint of paper trail. "Across the decades of Scottish oil we've talked it down by a factor of ten. Managed to do it whether it was the Reds or Tories. Kept the Jox from going off and getting all Norway on us; leaving us even."

Pender Jones takes inspiration: "Since their Independence in 1922, in inverted commas, the Irish have become less and less Irish. Their language has dwindled to a gasp on the outer fingers." Jones smirks inwardly in fluent Welsh as he points out some peninsulae where said dwindling is busy: Dingle, knobbles along South Connemara, Magheraroarty up North or as good as. Prince Philip looks genuinely concerned but is actually doing some math connected to prospect budgets and dividing it by years, then months, then overdoes some averages, then smiles at his conclusion, then pipes up. "It is off these Erse speaking zones that the oil and gas is most bountiful, oil is often under the Aborigine, the Bedouin, the Ogoni; one finds."

"Which has higher priority; regaining Crown Territory or accessing the gases and oil?" Coppinger needs to know.

Philip regards her answerlessly and his quiet, and the raised left eyebrow speak one thousand years' anointments.

Not cowed she gingers: "How many know; are in on this ?"

"Top clearance. Any leak and we're swannied. Twenty three excellent people know our plan, Coppinger. Today that becomes twenty five; yourself and Sir Nosey Naseby here though I imagine he knew something was up......" brims Philip.

Pender Jones checks if Sir Naseby Harbinger can take an insult. Seems his back is pure duck down so on he details: "We decided a twenty year run in. Keep exploring, mapping for sure and when it is safe, some testing, prospecting covertly and possibly overtly-ish across that time. Their navy and surveillance pure piffle and delightfully relies on uz far too much. We employ non Irish, non English speakers if possible in exploration rigs. We cap fruitful tries and mark them as uncommercial or mediocre."

"How goes it at their energy ministry. Surely they keep some tabs," asks Coppinger biting her nib with excitement and wonder.

"Oh ! If we get inspections on declared rigs from their Energy Ministry, we're well versed in best fob practise or failing that usual trinketry: Bottle of Bushmills, hollierz in Grand Cayman for all the family, that kinda thing. Over to you McGeown."

Cue that suave much younger McGeown than the one we met in the bog with that Shivnan fellow best part of a generation later. He clicks another black and white brownie looking slide. "This "campaign" is about who's minding the mint ? The average Paddy is proud but clueless to big stuff. Let's take inspiration from the very genesis of Oil Exploration, Bundy's Republic Hibernia is just out of short pants. Forty long years ago the Pad-wacks are gettin' their high on turf smoke 'n' maybe foggy frankincense." McGeown splutters and coughs and foists off the imagined, sacred cloud. "Up to their oxters in tilths of bog, cuttin' it with crap shlawns cause they're having an economic war with you guys, no fancy steelware from Sheffield. Then along comes this dude, like a phoney phonograph playing all their favourite hymns."

A black and white picture of a group of smiling men in front of *Aras an Uachtarán.* "This is the Republic's presidential palace. That is their President back in '58. He's one Sean T. O'Kelly."

"Humpty numpty as far as I can recall." Philip disdains.

"Recognise anybody else in this picture." The group gawp 'n' squint. Prince Charles guesses first. "That's Lindbergh, Charles Lindbergh or that drawling fellow who plays in the movie of him. What's his real blinking name: Harvey the Rabbit."

McGeown does his James Stewart actor being Lindbergh impersonation: "go way fly..... go away fly." There was a fly in the fictitious version of the first transAtlantic cockpit.

"I knew it. The guy with the giant rabbit on his tail," Charles is excited that he more or less guessed right.

"That your royal high-asses is James Stewart, the actor. Off screen he's as snake oil as the rest of uz. He's the newly incorporated Madonna Oil's man, their show man for the ur-Irish oil heist, back when Ambassador Oil from Austin, Tee-Ex-cess made their sweep on Ireland on and off shore, gallon hatted wolverines in communion girl rigouts."

"Madonna Oil. What the heck?" Charles thought he knew all the dossier for the Irish heist.

"These Texas hoodlum's knew best way of in-grace-effikating with the Holy Jolenes: Sean T, the Prez, their P.M., Sean Le Mass-goer and the rest of 'em. James Stewart was not the white steed o' the Fables, just a lucre lovin' no good Sheriff... fronting a Texas oil holding with a Mother of God cover story, got itself listed, named as said Madonna all stamped and articled and associated in the Dublin Company's Office, I recall 1959."

Charles muses again: "Madonna Oil. If the name is dormant we could possibly resurrect......"

"Look Prince Charles. Credit note where it's due - the Pad-wax not quite so dumb these-a-days. Back on yer saddles. This is how I see it: Stewart and his oil snakes rock up to the Mick-*Elysée*, buy the rights to the whole coast for five hundred guineas. Back then Ireland's seas, its wealth was a dumb hunch. These clever Texan wit-asses thought it might have vie with the big kahunas, the big Figurias o' the Middle East. Bit romantic but..... they have Harvey six foot rabbit Good Sherriff on board aka our Mr. Stewart; he comes to town offering the Wonderful Life, the Paddies buy it. They can't believe they're gettin' pictured with top Hollywood." McGeown points at the big grin on the Irish President's, badly drawn old boyeen-in-top-*segosha*-hat face being seen alongside Sheriff Stewart.

"Had they only an eye for the sea ?" asks Charles.

"I said for five hundred Irish guineas they get the complete sow and a lotta, lotta miles beyonds its seaweed."

"Pure genius," interrupts Coppinger. "We've had our own versions of myth making but nothing that subtle."

"Fairly crude; I'd've thought." pipes Philip.

"Don't get you Coppinger." tutts Charles and his dad replies: "the Irish had an odd fable that a Stewart would rescue them from their serv-i-tu....."

"Pull the other one," says Charles. The Crown Prince is himself a heck load of Stewart on his dad's side and a bigger heck o' Stewart on his Mum's side.

A voice from the side pipes up: "at times of utmost desperation a people dream up impossibly romantic rescue packages. Think Sioux and the Ghost Dance. Their civilisation was on the ropes." All stare about like they'd forgotten his presence, Sir Naseby Harbinger, longest in the tooth civil servant, sixty four and losing no hair. He has a cottage in the Isle of Wight where he paints windmills in primary acrylics. His face is unimaginable. "The

Sioux dreamt they could don special shirts that would withstand the White Man's bullets."

"Poor blinking fools." Philip had suggested Naseby for O.B.E. but disliked him teetotally but felt people with such want of imagination tended to be impeccable secret keepers. Philip turns back to strategy: "Coppinger. Coppinger; you and your team we don't expect you can convince Jo Paddy that the British Monarchy is some sort of........ cavalry. That'd be a task too far....." and Pender Jones completes the thought:

"No. The Crown is not the cavalry. We don't expect royal visits to be panda item on their New-*acht*s."

Coppinger says " we can do it, we've done worse, well better but I get where you're going that need to cultivate an us running things feeling, should become as normal in Ireland as it'd be in Huddersfield, say."

Prince Philip eyeballs the only woman in the room: "Coppinger; you and your team over in Manipulation Whatnot have made excellent strides already, I've heard."

"Why thank you your highness. Admittedly we didn't know the grandeur of the goal. This is a lot more than High Street brands." She'd love the plaid of a baronetcy to round her career or failing that be Vicerine of a Virgin Island.

Charles is frowning juggling King James Stewart and actor James Stewart so Coppinger pots some history: "The Irish in 1601 believed the newly acceding James Stewart would be their rescue, after the Tudor plantations and laying wastes. Boy were they wrong. Your great, great, great, great, great, great.........."

"Why the snail's pace ?" Charles inquires, not interested in pursuing history know-more.

"This is big brush stroke, son."

McGeown regains dominance, cane points their eyes back to the screen: "James-Harvey-the-Rabbit-Stewart and his Devil's

Hole gang set up Madonna Oil and get the whole Potato signed over; all six and score counties of it. The Irish only use the sea for to paddle their ugly feet in when it hits 72 degrees and then only up to here." McGeown whacks his plump left calf with his cane. "The Texans wanted low fruit, easy pickings. Their first excitement is not in the sea at all they hit Leitrim." McGeown clicks a slide. "This is a shambles of a rig in Dowra, County Leitrim in 1959; might be sixty. Great sex to be had their by the way. Good porter too. Lots of."

Philip winced at McGeown's rawness. He'd crossed paths with him at a Bilderberger meeting mid late seventies at The Swanson Hotel, Stockholm. He was an aid to an Axxon vital, not a direct guest but Philip was struck even pre-Amstrad by his computer memory and his ability to be ten faced to adversity. He recalled Prince Bernhard of the Netherlands taking an interest in him too, late in the evening as the three skuttered their antique brandies. Bernhard was so, so impressed by his derek to door knowledge and he asided to Philip in low German: "He's the proper Dirty Harry at getting a job done" and McGeown had winked all knowingly from behind his blotto and said: "watch your princely asses; I speak Nazi too."

Prince Philip has huge enough hands and their fingers he spreads wide and touches and decrees and stands and dominates the others: "We have already gotten the Irish government on side. Trinkets, trinkets. We have established a schema second only to The Cameroon in pro-industry favour. We need to be in different forms the winners in all bounties sought. We cannot avoid open market competitiveness but we can control central command in Dublin, thereby control information and thereby keep best finds for our side of the tracks; companies like S.N.A.K., B.L.I.P. You get me. The Norwegians we cannot trust in our plan."

"Too bloody nice." Charles loudens, chances.

"Yes. Poor earnest Lutherans in marooned monopoly houses. We hive off medium finds to them and say AGIP, if they are singing our hymns, possibly the Frogs. With time and confidence we can expand our "cartel."

Charles continues heirily. "Much of this is in place. What is required now is to make ourselves less enem...... less Conquistador and most important is to control the o-metre on incoming pipe or possibly pipes." says he pandering to Dad like he understands all the south and north forks of oil baronies. The very same tweed slax he was wearing now he'd worn two years ago leaning on his one-man-and-his-dog shephardly staff, grasp on quick gasp o' the full climb and there the full on massive Ukraine of it, from his long gaze journey 'cross undulations of th' Atlantic from the height of Mount Mweelrea. There he was a different Prince, the Prince of Whales and all their whalelanes and their wains' wains thanking him for chaining it to their males-to-be.

Pender Jones takes over, as he knows Charles must be exhausted from his say. "Good Friday 'Greement took a lot. Keeping those bloody Paisleyites from flying off the handle. Our Republican chaps really I have to say have been second to none." He clicks a slide that shows twin *Taoisigh* of Northern Ireland McGuinness and Paisley having a genuine hug.

Next is a picture of Jack Charlton and it says JACK CHARLTON above his sort of mug shot. "This man has done more for us; unwittingly, am I right?" Pender Jones nods at the former Republic of Ireland soccer manager.

"Yes. Totally. He is not our man." Harbinger vouches.

"Sorry he is our man." Philip cuts in while still doing math with his fingers. "Coppinger that was a great job. The Irish think Nordy England types, what they call them, Nordies are like us?"
"Jordies."

"Those sorts they reckon are like their own feckless, abstracted selves." Philip comes into his own: "Charlton's remit was double: get the Irish into the World Cup but much more importantly emphasise that they needed English *nous*, albeit plebeian to make that happen. Sure Paddy Granma, Mickelleen Granpah 25% mick but the other 75% hhmmmmm? " Philip rubs his smig to drive home his eugenick. "All those English accents on the Paddy team did its chip, chip. Can Mick build a rig? No. Can Mick prospect in two thousand feet of water in swells size of Big Ben ? Can R oh I beat Italy without us? Not on your nellio !"

Ms. Anschluss 2011 the metaphorical mammoth was still about the room shedding hairs the size of chellos's.

"Next," orders Coppinger. Slides quick clicked show Tesco Mullingar in Spring '96 obvious after the mid nineties' fashions and the daffodils, another slide another Tesco, The-Folly, Waterford City in the skanky tinsel of some mid December, pure unadulterated Grimsby-on-Sea-alike. "Take Tesco; other than making themselves a shed load of poonts, they and their ilk had very important psyche effect from my Department's view, essentially zone-sevening the island of Ahland. So in less than a decade we go from British Home Stores hidden within BMS getting bomb after bomb threat to all our household brand stores creaming 37% of Paddy's high street spend through these outlets," Coppinger reminds.   "By the buy our goal is 67.5% by 2009."

"Zone 9, your Highnesses. South Yorkshire is Tesco zone 7. Zone 9 Ahland." Sir Naseby simply adores detail and any swipe with his misodge-io-gene is a relief to his thyroid. Prince Charles stares at both commoners and can only wince at their dwelling mid the dirty pedestrian linen halls of imagined topshoppery.

"Next," Coppinger exclaims to her slide and as she revolves, her plaid skirt's pleats are the tone of Lucozade in their tartan variations. "Just thought to include this. Simple enough quick shot of a long line of Irish queuing for hours without Manchester United's shop on Westmoreland Street. Looks almost Soviet what with the reds and all the cowed faces.

"Next: this shot champion stuff: F.E., Fake Empowerment. We worked on this with the Tavistock Institute." On view proud-ish looking Irish Ryanair passengers filing past portraits and photos of "Irish" scientists in a gangway tunnel connecting the old to the new Dublin airport '*a celebration of Irish scientific ingenuity*.' "If one were a negative thinker on second sight one might grasp this slide's contents as gawpy people, albeit propelled by a top of the range ambulator are yet having their shoulder chips looked down on by these musty, fusty ole eggheads...."

".......and a token looking spinster. See there is what's her name," says Charles chomping for say.

Spinster Coppinger frowns the heir's way, explains the campaign. "Chaps at The Tav advised that the most subtle form of I.C., Infiltrative Confusion is through appeals to vanity. Look at an average Ryanair passenger." The cane pointer scourges the slide. "They feel WOW look at uz we invented certainly something more than the *shillelagh*. Their left brain however is in a right tangle as its sub and for some their sub subconscious knows........."

".......they were all our chaps really." Prince Charles bombasts. "Tavistock won, Paddy Athletic zilch."

"Coppinger. Genius tactic." Pender Jones doesn't compliment much. "I note the obvious Anglo-I-wish names of these eggen heads. As said all our chaps," and the canny Welsh lilt of him. "I recognise him, the wig chap; that is Boyle's law chap."

"Spot on Pender Jones. Waterford fellow." Coppinger is taking the small mickey out of Pender Jones, "Gas expands under pressure proportionate to whatnot......" she Etonizes at him. "We

did a top nine, note, not a top ten of Opportunity Knocks Irish
Science boffins.   Implication again was even with your Angloid
types can't quite get the ten."

"Inish Boffins my eye." Charles infuses.

Philip   cuts in "Quiet C-PAG.   And who is that suave fellow
with the evening dressed collar?"

"Beaufort   Scale;   a   Navan   man;   like   our   present   Bond   by
coincidence.   To his right are Gregg,   Mallet, Rynd, Kathleen
Yardley-Lonsdale.   To his left are, if I'm not mistaken, Stoney,
Tyndall and Thomson aka Baron 273 below Kelvin himself. A
few are from North of the Border mind."

McGeown has been quiet.   He loves the British when they go
full tilt sneer.   He comes in abullying "Message driven home is;
Corcorans, Shaughnessies don't invent wheels 'n' bulbs.   Don't
hold your breath for Mikey Shenanigan to get the physics prize
for tele-whatyouhavin-portation."

Coppinger   cuts   cross   McGeown.   Though   the   group   are
wearying of her tack she gets nods of curiousity as she proceeds.
She doesn't get much chance to powerpoint in front of top brass
royalty: "our, one's British acceptable-isation policy had another
triumph."   Click all teeth and red carpet, Pierce Brosnan, the
Savoy Cinema on O'Connell Street; premiere of *GoldenEye*.
"The national psyche had a place at our ample, inclusive table.
Sean Connery had the same effect for Scotland, albeit in real life
he's a traitor.   Bond Brosnan's next outing has him, imagine, an
Irish man defending to the death a petroleum pipe of interest to
uz and our friends.   For the life of me I've forgotten what it's
called."

"The World, no *This World is Not Enough*."

"Thank you Sir Naseby. I had our chaps clear the script."

Philip has been doodling and frankly smiling moots: "well
between Holland's Submarine and Gregg's shorthand and the

Stoney chap's electron and Beaufort's knowing when a storm'll hit the rig....."

Pender Jones ".......and Mallet was the father of seismology so they have the full craic team, dead or alive, to find their very own hydrocarbons. That takes some of our biscuit, what!"

Coppinger like all English people of her class know everything about everything: "and Lady Yardley-Lonsdale realised benzene molecularly was flat. That proved jolly useful for ballasting tankers." She swung back to her slide. "Can you handle one more then I will hand you back to PJ. Oh just a note from the Science Boffin showcase at Dublin Airport. It was so successful we kept on that tack and did all we could to facilitate British Telecom becoming the sponsor of the Ahrish Young Scientists of the Year whatnot." Coppinger presses a slide of all of Ireland. She shows its land-naming "Next we had Chris Lomas organise the Postcodes for Ireland. Slow business......"

"....... numeralise their bogs and back passages," says Charles, "though I love to bits some of their tyne-lands: Carrow-no-guilty. You couldn't make it up!"

Coppinger endorses same: "yes a primitive, well nigh aboriginal form of literal land holding. Their obsessive subdivisions of tyne-lands was in their penal time of non ownership a means of having a grasp on their territory. Zip Codes as our good Mr. McGeown would have it are a rather simple way of detaching place from folk. There was also a policy to use Tolkien terms to humanise Ahland's subsea; hydrologists were encouraged to give FUNnames......."

"Yee aulde bog road L549939." Charles tries out.

Philip reckons they've detailed to death and patiences are fraying: "We need to precise certain items today."

He nods at Sir Naseby Harbinger who takes the floor and up pops a slide, an aerial shot like a side shot of a deep throat, except it's geographical. It is obviously Sruwadacan Bay in North West Mayo, ridges of recent forest planting hug where its tonsil might object. "We'll be constructing a modular refinery that will be hid mid dense forestry. It is a mix of us and the Dutch chaps who are bank rolling it. It's mid-landfall island-wise; Mayo is mid way-ish along their coast, though finds might be most plentiful off Kingdom Kerry but we're gambling on having a central landfall to cover the entire Irish East Atlantic. As such a big HQ for oil and gas landfall is a tad hard to hide, despite the trees, which by the by you'll be glad to hear were planted already three years ago; we'll operate usual strategy of O.I....., Opposition Invention."

Pender Jones as the meeting is winding down, feels a knighthood is owing and these might be his last postures till New Year's: "We are planning a protest campaign against our incoming pipe that will connect to the first "trial find," less than fifty English miles off land, bang on the Continental shelf, nearest point to that mighty subsea cliff to the landmass of Ahland. The protest'll be to "delay" this pipe, entirely environmental, keeps their eyes off our balls."

"Excellent." Philip puts out. "My daughter in law's people hail from thereabouts." he says absently.

McGeown shows a boring slide of the exterior of the Irish Department of Energistix, like what a hungover spy would take with a Polaroid from a moving taxi. It reveals some civil servants heading out to lunch, Fall '95 by the look of the fashion statements. "They had a meddlesome first secretary in Energy, the chap was a statist. Gone. So has and was their smug Minister, a Justing Something."

"Justin Keating," says Prince Philip.

"Well he's gone and thankfully the statist first secretary has shuffled himself off, resigned in quiet protest when Longrun Oil bought out what was left of the Madonna gangsters, ten years back for I recall five baubles, two trinkets and a mirror image. Our "shadow" ministry in Dublin, energy-wise is fledgling but we are adding to it year by year." Squint and young Duhallow with bouncing black hair waves is seen leaving the NRG building with his ever so Yazoo suit, top dapper.

Pender Jones seeks to conclude, to be last man standing: "I suggest we meet in say a decade. In the meantime we have a team working on weighing up finds secretisation methods, technology means and another on E.U. scrutiny and envy."

Philip nonchalants, essentially clarifying the last statement: "We may have to do a jump ship from Bruxelles. E.E.C. bye bye, bigger fish to frytex."

"Excuse me." Coppinger and Naseby jinx.

"Updates next meeting." avoids Philip but their scrunched faces demand a tad less left-hanging. "The subtleties of doubling, tripling our land plus sea mass is best done without some *petite-bourge* Brussels Luxembourg buro chap wagging at us. Just must cut our losses with our EEC friends and go about our own Clann-dyking."

"When again ?" asks Coppinger reaching for her diary - she is that shocked not to seek further 'extraps' as she'd say herself.

"Ten years," suggests Pender Jones.

Coppinger seeks clarification of the silent air: "we are leaving the European Union so that....."

"Hhhmmmm. Make it fifteen years. Same time roughly-ish 2013?" suggests Philip.

"Are we agreed?" says Jones, ooozy-ing that last bit of born-leadership certitude-y-ness a photo finish away from that O.B.E. being pinned to his taut breast and all the more for having helped Hiness avoid expanding the heist's most delicate crunch.

   "Yes. We'll have the 100 years Monarchy malarkey sorted by then. Leaving Common Market not so hurry Murray. Early twenties, late teens." Philip stretches his Danish, German, Greek, English limbs in one star anise and a full stop of a yawn dissolves his last words.   Charles needs to punctuate the stale air. He has a question: "And what was it that Tyndall figured out, invented?"

   Sir Naseby Harbinger goose pimples: "he realised why the sky is blue."

CHAPTER TWENTY ONE

Wendywee/Susan/700 Zeng could hear her fellow Chinese, move through the forest; could vouch by its speed and gentilesse it was, as planned, elite force amphibious infantry, XIV battalion special ops not the planned twelve, two less. Twenty feet moving in military boots over a half a foot thick o' pine needles. Wendywee had a *rendezvous*. Shivnan knew nothing of the Chinese incursion. He knew he had to meet the large Texan at the TestLab. Their goal the Aughoose Animal TestLab. Zeng followed her modest nose, the smell of capuchin dung was on the light breeze sighing from Glenamoy. The tread of the oriental feet was hastening that same way and only forty seven seconds behind time.

There is a zone way off Kirkukgeenagh, Kerry where the turmoil of the Conjugate Margin meets the slopes of the Porcupine, an area that Lar Ewing had ignored all his Lord given decades. Five thousand one hundred and forty blocks in Irish waters plus her solid baronies and each pendulum swing of Lar's took some minutes. He has been asked to move across it in swings from the cardinal points; not his usual tactic. If there was a sign of hope from a clockwise yes, then the depth needed also to be known, the volumetric needed to be baubled, the oil to gas ratio always required the nerd of tallying. To what end? To what end ? What the devil was his gift, he more than wondered, now that he was a captive frackshow, a monkey wound-up for freaking gain.

The fat jolly man had had the body of the Dutch gentleman, taken away by two East European looking fellows who were, by their dress and mien, not exactly funereal parlour. A jeep engine had likely been the 'hearse,' muffled by trees in its slow going and a gate was opened mechanically. Lar's front lobe didn't miss a thing and didn't miss Op much but he had never seen a murder or assassination before. He half fancied the fat man must be working with the *Garda* and that offences against his own Lar-person were not going to follow. He thought by now as the kidnapper had been 'put down' that the *Garda Síochána* might have arrived, like how they did with caring blue light and wind-down sirens in *Barnaby Jones*; the cops crack a joke and Flo'd get out of a cop car, her lime cardigan about her shoulders and run to greet 'n' hug him. The large man was an American but he said he had great, grand paternal roots about Tulsk and his mother's people were of the Ballygawley of Tyrone side; great, great, great "and they'd scrammed just after the famine, hungry grass, made for Milwaukee." He said his name was Mister McGeown and with a smirk and a gloat let Lar know too to his being one sixteenth Nativian, Su, he said. Lar nodded approval at that but could not assemble much in the way of a question or sequester. He wanted to know if that gave him the right to attend *pow wows* but he had a flu or a flu jab or something and could not assemble the words in his closing mind. The man had ordered more grub for Lar but didn't know his preferred foods in the way that Op had incite. Lar ate it up with a white plastic spoon that was not a teaspoon, not a dessert spoon but a Goldilocks spoon size-wise. When he'd finished he was encouraged back to work. "Divide each block into small segments, a square mile apiece and dangle your noose 'n' lodestone above the giving given waters and when you hit liquid liquorice we will get you to be even more eeensy weeensy," had play encouraged the mid American accent of him, "thataways we can save a lotta lotta dollar-*osos* when it comes to dwillin,' you get me."

Venus can be extremely brash in winter and she shone and shone onto the clearing about the mizzen huts of the animal lab of a place. Seen through the pine waverings made Her appear moving, as large, shifty and glinty as a Kardashian jewel. Police forces of the world are fat with reports of UFO this shape, or that hovering above the landscape when Venus is big with Herself, such is the caprice of that planet where women come from and the capuchin girl monkeys who had their bits yet intact felt like it was a month of Friday nights all at once, such was their lust unsatisfied and them kept apart from their *beaux* capuchinos. What happens next is not Venus's fault, but more likely Mars entering Taurus. The impatient sky was lit by other stars too but far more gentle in their twinkles. Lar thought he heard McGeown turn from his gawping out the door and say "This is the most important day in the history of this country, most significant 24 hours at the least-i-est and it starts now, in one jiffy." Lar did really hear that said but couldn't comment. He'd been given fourteen sector blocks by the American, they were all S.A.C.s so he was busy. These SACs seem to always give and give, so much so he began to doubt the generous centrifugal of his pendulum swing. Before meal break he had already located as far west from Dingle as Rathlin is north east of her vast oil reserves to equal the likes of Eastern Saudi's Ghawar 2 on two blocks, north of one point two billion barrels in three others and two Ku-weighty gas fields in a further two. The arrogance of calling your parish of a county, 'The Kingdom' had just taken on a wile new kick. Lar was disappointed that the greatest bounty he'd ever found was not about his precious Erris, nor Dooish, nor finds west of Loop but were that right cliff of the Porcupine, in the twilight zone out of ken of the Sleeping Sisters of Doon

Queen. McGeown had shown Lar how to break the hopeful blocks into tinier zones so that he could crack on with prospects. Once the seas and licences had complied with Lar's tally and got drilled and proven then Lar could "go his merry way" which sounded impossibly far in the future. McGeown'd gave himself little kicks for not believing Lar earlier, 'cause then he'd have gotten more time and more hands on info and some extra per cents of billions a bonus. His right-girded shirt oxters are starting to rank the air. To cover his smell he dazzles his eyes at the precious Knock Man. "Gotta highly recommend you for hunkered-Mayo-Man-of-the-Year this year huh !" Lar thought that implied golden hand shake and he continued parsing seas with more vigour, his right hand all veins and blotches, his plumb clockwise, wider, wider, swing, swing.

McGeown shouts at Lar like he's early in the Nursing Home "McGeown and Co. kick ourselves for not finding you much much sooner. You are low- hangin' fruit city." McGeown was a full-on believer and he eye-balled Lar like two estranged brothers might in a once in a lifetime catharsis.

"Sure I love it." says Lar cancelling the gaze and scratching more huge share-soaring facts with his pencil in his bit of a ledger.

"Lawr Ewing. You best to pack up your bits. We are going further a....a...a..afield."

The fat man bent down to even help, scrolled up some sea salt sad old excuses for maps. Lar flattened his papers and folded them in messy four, and placed them in manila envelopes, which he then placed in a hard case. Lar from the action regained some lucidity and looked sideways at the man, the American. 'We're both of an age, one half the girth of the other,' he figured but actually he said. "Tell me Mister I-don't-Know, Mister Question Mark. 'We' must sooner than later work out how to get all this bounty ashore. I often thought of Killybegs, best Aberdeen we have, now I suppose we are Dingle."

"Yeh sure. No. It'll all come through here - after some repairs - if you get me. Easier to defend one patch. It worked in Niger Delta that way. 'Scusie, I just POP to the loo." McGeown goes through a wee door - regards his Tag Heuer and presses the hash key of his HiPhone and the ground rumbles.

Group 'A' could see the fence of the Animal TestLab. Half a click away Yalloway and his trusty Snoop and Snipe had caught up with Group 'B' insurgents in the dark of the tick forest o'pines; the three in stitches of breathlessness surrendered. The yarping dogs, though only two surrounded the three and their barking became gnashing as their canine transferences held the youths in check. They'd just doubled back toward the river, now caught, Death resolved any furtherance 'cause BOOM and in a nano a blindness, sort of orange shaped and bluey, flashed at them and in another half while four humans and two dogs were so much KFC about the ground in charred 'ragments.

Vision, even bounced from earth to satellite and back, still is faster than sound. Woodge had gone one up in overtime to Lublin. Security man Wasilenko was cheering away in stunned Polish but then his eye got caught by the monitor. He saw the enormous flash of heat on his security screen, the sound followed and that did not knock him to the floor nor the concrete stilts from under the security booth, but the secondary burst of a supra-plosion sent his career to the ground and disintegrated the security building as the start of a full 74 km of pipe mawed out herself dragon upon dragon of gas flame, like as if seven million two hundred and forty thousand and seventy one orange Calor gas bottles went kabooom at once upon a time in a forest on the edge of the world, huge, Connaught's child's portion of a Nagasaki.

The blast frazzled the damp off the pines even up to the edge of Aughoose Animal TestLab. The capuchins were as wild as Pagans at the Coliseum, the leps and squawks of them competing with flames that can be noisy when they are over fifty feet high. The really, really angry belch of the Atlantic's Jurassic-era under-mush just kept on giving, gazillions of herself, heating the Mayo air easily.

The Chinese crack troop had entered the compound of the Animal TestLab zone sanctuary under barby bladed fencing and swooped about the mizzen. Lar, their quarry, was alone at its door and taken. His American had gone as soon as the universe changed with the big bang; or so he recoiled. It took him a second to clear his eyelashes of debris and see a black or navy marooned car, a class o' Beamer heading off quiet as an hybrid through the clearing. All his maps and papers were not about him; likely safe with the carefree American gent in that car making out for the night. Two oriental soldiers took a hold of Lar. Despite the war zone close by their captain bowed before Lar (older / wiser) and said in Mandarin and for clarification in broken English that Lar must come to his launch........ at once. Lar dragged away, his Dubarrys dragging on now the gravel, now the pine needles. He turned and saw that his new American friend was definitely gone, and he looked behind him a second and third time. 'Might as well as go along with these fellows; after all the Mandarin asked so politely, and they seemed to be headed away from the flames and the sea smelt near,' measured the seventh of a seventh who'd just four minutes earlier lost his gift. Shock can be awful. If Lar'd understood Mandarin he could have heard a Chinese Lieutenant say to the Captain "what the fuck bad timing - we get our guy - and Krakatoa blasts off. We need to get well the fuck beyond the twelve mile limit on the double." It is not just American soldiers who talk in curses and riddles and smoke Marlboros or their cool 'quivilent. China seals can also speak Kickass.

Group 'A' insurgents were protected from the blast by a ditch and by a distance. They saw some distance away troops of the elite army of People's Republic of China silently milling through the pines. Wendywee who looked unshocked bowed to her three fellow insurgents and ran across five lines of pines and joined the troops. Shivnan, already afraid to his gut, when he saw Wendywee/ Zeng betray to the soldiers he shat small splidgy shitlettes of fear, small bursts in his ineffectual, unappreciated Aussie Bums.

"Where are you heading?" he shouted after Wendywee/ Zeng/ Agent 700.

"I am going with my people. Nice to meet you, Mister Shivnan. Keep moving towards the sea, that fire is moving fast. That fire is not my doing, not part of plan. Believe that of me." Susan Zeng shed Wendywee, turned, bowed for the momentum of this word: "slawn" which felt more aimed at Lou and Fang and off she sprinted, off aways into the dark

Fang and Shivnan and Lou were left in their another-fine-mess-they'd-gotten-into situ. Shivnan regarded his waders, and removed them. His legs were red and plump.

"How, if it was uz, did we do that ?" Fang says to the ground. Lou does not answer for she is enjoying the pound for pounding breasts of her self like she'd never known the planet before. She feels she is on a Jean d'Arc style learning curve in spades. She is beautifully oblivious to consequence at least for these moments. Shivnan plans his need to get his filthy ass to the safety-first version of the Cayman Islands with his early pension but every new imagined island has some extradition clause. He assumes his Karma must have been the flint to the shavings, that gave birth to the boom. He returns the gaze of the flame to his east. He says what is often said in these situations: "Holy Moly." Despite the infernal flames and his amateur eye, it appears to him that the centre of the explosion was close to their epoxy prank.

"I did it," says Shivnan. "I am sure I must." He ponders: 'did 700 do it ? Was it her prank ? She seemed surprised by it though.'

Fang doesn't answer him as he has his own future aspects to dwell on. Fang has an idea then. "There is a nice bit of 5G proximate the terminal. The blast's not got it, the mast ......as yet." He clicks refine.ie on his Blackberry, clicks WEB-STREAM, clicks ARCHIVE. The view from the 'Made in China' webcam they had just left by the pipe, its imaging was activated by motion - just eight minutes into its life and some seconds by its timecode - there is a first commotion: a faint reed-flexing, mildly in Venus light, next minute the red-eye of a pine marten with a candid if slightly yikes look about it scampering along the cold, cold silver pipe, stopping to smell what the humans had done with resin and epoxy. Nothing again till a sough of wind moved fronds again, then a spark set off the camera and it became brighter right at their meddling point, then came an explosion that unrivetted the mighty pipe and melted the webcam presumably - end of that story. "What is that gank made of?" Fang asks Shivnan. Shivnan admitted taking delivery of it and vouched with an old fashioned Christian crossing of his atheist heart that "the cans for sure seemed perfectly normal, like what they say on the tin." He doubted anybody'd tampered with them. "They were delivered next day delivery via Joyce's Hardware & Consumables in Headford via I'd weigh a fairly convincing truck" but the out-of-his-depth informant turned to pondering and pondered this: 'I am a fullon villain. Perhaps and likely the epoxy order'd been intercepted and replaced by Fatman.' "Some kind of DIY semtex," - 'or maybe my Chinese friend. I imagine more it is Fatman.' "That webcam was boobied or a fuse was inside," he calls out to Fang and in consolation to Lou concludes: "I've, we've been duped. We need to get our asses a long long away away from here."

CHAPTER TWENTY TWO

Paul 'Dots' Dingham that is not his real name. It is his name as
soon as he steps on the holy "dung" of Irish soil. His real name
is Garth Pender Jones Junior, ex decorated SAS meets future
Baron Oil of Slithermouth or similar. He is Anton's amanuensis
and as Today is D-day oilwise he is in full Dots mode, M.C.
squared, loving it, loving himself, pure Fiaruci gleamy silk suit
mit Gucci brogeens, centre stage the Still-Organ Ravishing Hotel
for the Hydrocarbon 'XTRAVAganza 2023.' It is Friday, 2nd of
December, 2022, in less than one hundred hours Ireland'll rollator
toward the Hundred, due her €1,500 cheque and a congrats for
perseverance from President MacWilliams.   Imagine a whole
century of the dirty sow of her playing scoff the *bonamh* and her
priesthood   dolled   up   in   nun-yerked   lace,   exporting   her
farroweens like so many bottles of whiskey clinkin' rattlin'
together on the sickening male boats. The purity of the Church
had not gotten devoured in classy warfare but pundits speaking
Reasonableness albeit with flaccid lower lips had taken command
of Good Ship Banba, their Radio Vatican was clept NewsTalk; all
balanced sensible aul gibber celebrated and acknowledged from
one Insomnia to another. This richman's shoeshine of an hotel is
in the suburb of south Dublin called really that, 'Still' plus
'Organ.' It is particularly popular for high end meritocratic conferences for firm albeit nonMasonic hand shakers who like to
park their 222s safely.   It was called St Helen's before Radisson.
St. Helen was the mother of Constantine and found the true cross
in shards all about the shat upon north side of Calvary. She used
a silver tweezers. '*Mors Potior Macula*,' says the building's motto

meaning 'Death rather than infamy.' A coffee afternoon there + a tray o' dainties'd set you back. Be sure order the Edmund-rice-queens' cakes. Before it was a swanky hotel it was the HQ for the Christian Brothers, their starched collars imagined their selves lord and laddy muck swanning about the later four stars *Trump d'oeil* corridors.

The ManyHeaded-Hydrocarbon Sell-off is being held in the reverend Brothers former refectory where the shimmeriest of the ghosts of them air-condition. Meal times in the early years of the State for Christian Brothers were fulminations of silent awkwardnesses (as they were not monks *per se*) listening to the cites of Rice or Aquinas (*Grace Builds on Nature* - his best album) as they masticated turnip and thin indictments of beef *a la rage* dried with skin-busted florid spuds-they-like, invariably the Marist Pipers from their own once tasteful, Angloid secret walled garden. The faceless ghosts, held together by soutains, don't know what to make of now-a-days' swankers.

"Dr. Duhallow will now present his outline plan for the 2023..." "...fire sale..." shouts a wag from the back of the hall. "....for 2023 and the coming decade of exciting Prospects. Dr. Duhallow has headed up the Department for twelve long years, a great, great friend of the industry." This invites the low level clap from the big gathering, and leading the fakery the speaker his self, Dots the Ding, in from the public service cold, minus three without, "global warming me bollix" he'd be the first to say. Anyway there he confidents, back slappers dead decently his old boss up on the stage, and Duhallow takes to the boards in his hokey tweeds with the lama leather patches like he's a gonna get the gong for life time over achieving award for public nest feathering and private sector sideswipes. He looked haggard, like he had pancreatic cancer or a cousin of it coming on. If he died what use then his just the week before reupholstering the Daimler Mark II, 1982, 6.8 of an engine, a hydro*carobonara* yummy of a beast. Dots ran back up on stage to point out where the laser sabre was, how to arrow back and forth. He cracked a joke about aged-ness and former bossy-ness and everyone laughed on cue. The audience were mostly alpha males, a scattering of betas and hungry oily women in their depth and modern styles. A lot of auspicious folk under one roof. <u>Atlantic Bounty</u> said the first slide and a shot of the snot green of him (the North East Atlantic is a fellah). If Polpott got a DeadSea poll done of the throng o' the hall: there'd be 45% Irish Catlick public school and their attendant noises, 15% British public school and their blusterous certitudes, a bicentenary of perfected sneers, 3% U.K. Grammar School and their non-stop proving Darwin spot on: trample this, trample that; some opportuning Brahmins with multiple PhDs in hydro geo this that, out-smarmed and to their right some brown envelopes fresh landed from São Paolo, three *Udarás* Ní Thuighim-Bottoms, some asylum seeking Al Sauds, stray Yanks by the dozen without decibel limits, half Vulture part Seagull, some Chinese pretending to no English, AGiP oil slitherers, a regime changed also I-ran, two former Analytix U've-been-Kipped execks flanking one grandniece of Colonel Gadfly, some Angolans in Cambdian traditional costume with no knickers to add a spot of darkness to the WE ARE THE WORLD - WE ARE THE CHILDREN concluding group-foto. Polpott, 'God's Peace Be Upon Him,' if alive would have had Junior Cup aged soldiery surround the hotel, shout lots of irrational through the triple glazing, rifle butt the elite-lite out the door, force march them through Sandyford Industrial Estate, over to Balally, past the Jedwardian crumbles of Dundrum Shopping Centre up to Lamb Doyles, and night falling, separate them according to smirk, golf club and shoe brand in groups, for forced re-education at some old depot in Glenasmole and the rest to be shot and flung into a grave of their own slow fearsome unearthing. A mere enough child might shout at the bodies, shovelling disolvant over them, one or two yet twitching: "lime for slimeys, lime for blinkin' slimey; no more best practise for u-m8."

Duhallow starts his spiel. He doesn't use teleprompter. He doesn't have any notes. He uses his brain and confidence; that is why he is first rate Secretary of the Department of Energising Lilt and Fanta: "Why are we here?"

"Surely not to live in pain and fear," thought Anton, sitting left of the stage like a priapic eejit in front of his stand of almost Nordic perfect maps and shiny A4 sized pamphlets with a Malay gas rig being thrashed by some freak of an Irish new wave. He's so tired, his days and nights so marred and they'd gone and confiscated Tanya's and his map. His adrenals were so so fecked 'cause he couldn't measure flight from his fight anymore, brought on the slithery intestine. He had a fine hope that Duhallow would suddenly grab the mammoth thistle in the room, do the right Denzel Washington, and spill-the-beanz. 'Go on. Go ON.'

Duhallow does his honesty wins wonder spiel: "There has been so long a devil of a seesaw about what is our oil and gas industry. Have we enormous prospects or is there damn all or plenty but so awkward, deep or far from shore as not worth sweat, cost, effort. Our own department has been somewhat responsible for this doublespeak. Banner headlines TRILLION EUROS of Hydro-carbs, come 'n' get it. Meanwhile our energy ministers, successive ones, have been circumspective....." and Duhallow wise-owls down his half Speck-Savers for effect ".....essentially downplaying, forever vouching the wisdom of our no royalties to the state....."

"No loyalty to the State neither," shouts that voice again, some Mr. B. Laggard with a sorry Mulhuddart accent, in a tight three piece suit, Versack cloth, ways at the back. Hotel Security are at him in a jiffy. Examine his spoofed-up I.D., rip same from him, haul him lobby-wards. Imagine the dignity as two giants shout "Firbolg" after you as you whir into the cold, propelled thru an Otis revolving door.

   Duhallow doesn't blink or note the protest: ".......our generous to industry tax regime is because there have been no substantial finds, a decade's worth off Mayo and of course our reliable profitable four decades long hiss from the Kinsale fields, seems that is it as he nods at the United Kingdoms of Malaysia contingent at their own round table, their black hats as becoming as their eyes, their sense of fun safe 'n' slapstick 'n' booze-free recalls Duhallow with a jittereen. Next to them for the first time ever bothering about Ireland, was the Saudi table. Duhallow scans them: 'Saudi hate Malays extra because of their deferring to them as keepers of Mekah, knowing too well that all they want to do is poppy their oversized cocks into gold clad orifice and relish Allah's merciful aggrandizing.' The Saudis are not listening to the translation and think they are in Scotland and are mostly catching up with some instructive porn on their platinum Apples. The eldest Sheikh Majoob abin Said is planning to stay in Ireland as he's just been texted he is going to be de-headed should he return home. He feels he is at another auction in some city a lot less pretty than Edinburgh. Yesterday he bought a Chagall at London Sotheby's, for a song. He did so as he acts the maxim: 'One's Security is best preserved in one third real estate, one third bonds or papyrus money and one third fine art 'n' antiques.' Some French sounding Rothschild told this to the left ear of Sheikh Majoob not once, but thrice over a Davos quince strudel 'n' pink custard laced with furmity no doubt. The .75 metre square art work had a guy in purple floating above French chimneys. Only fifteen million starlings knocked him back.

Duhallow had the attention of half the audience. "this afternoon you had a fascinating talk on the advances in submersibles, horizontal seabed rigs and their pipes 'n' tentacles. Vast meccano that I never dreamed could exist, that can operate invisibly and calmly at great, great depths. I believe these stupendous technological leaps will delay peak oil in global terms for close on three decades. They will also help fund our new energies to help our transition. In our Celtic nook here, about our island, ladies and gentlemen we are on the edge of one mighty Klondike."

Next ambient slide simply has an old Guinness barrel with its attendant well-endowed beak-wise toucan sat atop of the oldy worldy portar-barrell and right of same an equals sign, right of that is €178.43 in bold. "The black stuff was the proverbial shilling a pint when I was born." The Irish public school elderhood laughed dead decently at this with their penises like aneroid bar-o-meters depressing and expending in their shiny tight enough suits of clothes.

"Back in May 2011 our Department put about a very, very expansive tender for blocks in our Atlantic, a magic twelve Chinese years later compared to then we now have so much more data open to all. Now with our supreme technology the barrels cannot hide. This year the criteria is a little changed. If a prospect is not explored within eighteen months it is forfeited. On the other hand any one company can apply for whatever number of blocks that they choose. The furthest out, and to encourage you all to take a punt at the deeper prospects we offer a piffling ten per cent tax on profits, I'm talking really far, out there beyond the Isengaard Ridge." And as Duhallow gestured wrongly towards the Muglins the audience gave rise to harrumphs of wonder and the Saudis even quit stereotyping to prick up their ears. Then their attention spans withered as more slides popped up showing bathymetries beyond Macdara, the swell crests of Gollum, below Iceland and in the vortices south o' Rockall - all more than scary for sand-lubbers. They would have their minnows figure out what it meant - so long as investments won a 27.5% dividend, as Amarco and Oil Ministry insists for international concelebration.

Anton's iPhone was on silent but it lit up and moved across his desk. He recognised St. James's generic main switch number with its unlucky gang of twos. He pressed TALK and whispered. "I am in a bored meeting" he said to a female voice. He got up and walked towards the hotel's restaurant entrance. The female voice hadn't got the whisht gist and started speaking so sweetly anyhow though she did ask if he was standing, "better sit." He went through the flap of characterless double doors and the flap of more characterless doors and had not got the phone to his ear when she'd said "better sit" a third time and there he stands looking out over the faint sense of Dublin Bay in this large empty restaurant and a Mount Merrion's answer to if Susan Sontag were a harpist is tuning her harp way off on a podium; she is practicing the *digestif* for the coming dinner with her BLACK IS THE COLOUR OF MY TRUE LOVE'S HAIR air. The sweet female voice on the phone like he's won the Sweeps says "are you seated?" and he wasn't and didn't and his split person hardly needed to ken more and instead of sitting he collapsed on to the top of the range carpet tiles, so clean despite the treads and hopes of hundreds upon hundreds of weddings and conferences and convolutions, their weft that strong. A gorgeous waiter from Tocantins who had been placing dunce hat napkins at possibly one thousand of places saw Anton in mid fall, rushed to him but it was too late, his heart's ventrickles had cracked in three bleedin' places. Clive, the waitering man's name tag said, a likely homosexual type fellow, was Anton's last thought then. The foreigner held Anton in a firm, not so medical Pieta for Pieta's sake and could see his self's own reflection in the tiniest tint of the virgin floor to ceiling glass, thankfully netcurtainless. Anton's eyes were open but as if dead in or to life. His mind registered the lovely weighter but his sight was nowhere. Anton wondered why God made humans so devilishly perfect facewise and he recalled a moment that an article in GCN postulated that Homosexuals were an integral part of human Hominid evolution with the double function of keeping society frisky and soda yet also held families together. He became demidisconscious and the faint waffle of Duhallow could be heard through the doors. "..... am in a position to categorically state that late, sorry last tender process submissions close after noon tomorrow. Over the next hours you're welcome to second thoughts but no questions asked, nor'll be answered apart from courtesy ones; our beautiful assistant Anton over there will do all he can......" Here the PhD in Confidence falters. "We await your tenderness, your tenders with curiousity and enthus......."

Next it seems to be lunch and Anton is sat and kinda self-propped up staring at a Carrot & Coriander coloured pool in a bowl. Some Norwegian opposite keeps offering him butter or salt or natty bread rolls and is telling him about how drizzlier Dublin is than Stavanger/ why oil is sweeter north of the Bode line/ how his mother decided to become a plumber in her mid fifties. The only responsorial that Anton managed was "late in life lesbian" said into his orange laden super bowl. He should've stayed collapsed but the ECCE ping on his me-me-phone had alarmed him back to Hell in the Heaven of the Arms of the Man who Anton still couldn't figure was he naff or batting for team. This is how the ECCE message went. '*Sorry for Your Troubles. You stay at your work as hearse already on M6 + limo for yr kin. Massey's have all Funeral Arrangement. Here is suggested*

TEXT for rip.ie "Padraic, dearly msd by doty husband Anton, mother Eileen, sisters Monica, Cait-Anne, brothers Liam Óg and baby Risteard (illegitimate) passed away after a short rare illness. Removal to Mother of God, Ballycommon, County Offal. Lots and lots and lots of Flowers please. Reposing at Dempsey Household, Craggity tonight BYOB, Mass 11am Friday 2nd December. Donations please to Arrrahan RC GAA club. Up the Casements!

Then the curtains of the temple were not rent but drawn across the faint virgin tint of the floor to ceiling windows for darkness fell out of the Dublin air. Anton slurped some broth and stared thru the perfect merits of the ageless Nor-dick disturbance opposite. On and on went the dinner. Back slappers from every Continent came over to make their quintessence known to the grief aching Principle whose rack of lamb sat in its cooling gravy. Clive of Tocantins made a point of checking Anton was managing. All he knew was what petered out Anton when in his ample arms had whispered at a low timbre into his small ear "I am at a loss. My loss is secret. It is more heavy than can be ever ever said like I can't tell a soul or that'll equal more loss." "Helax, helax," and Clive'd stroked the grievances of Anton's left sideburn, "you've told me; helax, helax." Now Clive removed the uneaten lamb-me-arse, actually Muine Bheag mutton from in front of Anton. Anton said he'd have the Pecan & *Maracuja fluffette*. He had no intention of eating same but wanted to keep up experiences. He couldn't figure why this live Clive guy was waitering these 1000 oaves when he should be making a Lagerfeld of his self on a Milanese catwalk.

The harpist, up close not so Susan Sontag, just Monto Twink via Terenure West, dressed without shame or blush in a Clonakilty widow shawl. She is pinkling her giant harp while Ireland burns. As said BLACK IS THE COLOUR OF MY

TRUE LOVE'S HAIR got its airing. She knows it perfectly and THE CLIFFS OF DOONEEN and to jizz up the just desserts ĒISTIGĪ ĒISTIGĪ; then she loops and alters them twice and ĒISTIGĪ ĒISTIGĪ she actually sings on its third outing and none cares a toss but Anton though he wished the harps of Heaven more twinkling and varied for the love-of-his-life's arrival gave the instrumentalist a slow clap, started the slow clap. Double jobbing Dots saw how Anton clapped then, saw a possible impossible, loose cannon.

Dots was at the head table on his mobile, sat beside the eligible blonde spinster Minster Ní Something or Other. Not long in the job and gloriously at sea with some capable sharks about her floating her pleasure-boat. Dots was bathing in gloat, the very groom o'Lucifer, when up he pops on his clovens as if to make the nuptial speech, moves to the podium surely, bends the mic up to his six foot three and says "aaaahhymn."

The thousand keep to their slobbering and hootching. Dots taps the mic three times. "People. Have some news." As he speaks on cue a screen unscrolls from the ceiling. 'More waffles' wonders much of the crowd, now keener for shift 'n' sozzle than more posturing and oil slick promotion. "There has been a big incident. Please Charlotte. Knock on RTE 24 will you. Thanks." There is a gorgeous shot of spikie trees and bursts and bursts of methanic and sulphuric belching flames. "This is Mayo now." RTE TV 24 western correspondent is flying over the forest and sea and she is roaring over the blades. Below there is the zonal squares of forest and billows and billows of gapeous orange ignites of fumes. The Saudis ignore as they've had weeks of billowing wells but as they look closer they see it's not theirs, know that Sitka Spruces are not of the desert. "There has been an explosion at our main refinery, our only." Western Correspondent Eyelash Knee Gullet is no longer in her broadcast chopper but on

the Rossport to Glenamoy road and she warns that all roads
leading to the refinery have been cordoned off. "What was first
seen as human error might yet not be." Eyelash with her big
Sesame Street sponge-bob is relating and head turning. Some
Garda smirk at her. "You can see the height of the flames,
Brian." She is talking to the Dublin anchor. "The explosion
happened 2140 local time. The conflagration is spreading. "Can
you confirm numbers of injured or dead?" "Nothing as yet; too
early." A lame fire brigade comes careering down from
Belmullet in the background effect, its sirens like from the time
of Boyzone. Its presence is Matchbox in relation to the Infernal
region stretching its way across the rainy forest towards the
heedless width of sky. Hilversum Satellite V measures it as
already 12.54 hectares of hell realm. RTE 24 cut a shot of same
gratis of Dutch Intelligence. Eyelash looks from her monitor to
the camera and adjusts her earwig: "there has been some talk I am
hearing of mercenaries or messianic, sorry of Asian appearing.
We await confirmation. Twelve apprehended making for their
means of escape. A rib that was shot out of the water. All
assailants arrested bar <u>one drowned, assumed drowned, definitely
dead.</u>"

Duhallow sidles awkwardly on stage. "We are here to support
one another at this horrific moment of, for our industry. Mr.
Dingham thanks for bringing this to our attentions. We anticipate
updates from what is going on about our coast off Mayo.
Sketchy is the word. Both Irish and British helicopters, aircorps,
have been scrambled I am aware."

The harpist commences again to play. She plays *BUACHAIL
OWN EIREANN* badly followed by the *ONLY HER RIVERS
RUN FREE* which she sings well, so long as it's the chorus. She
wants to get home. She sings martial then mellow and some of
the delegates dab their crocodiles. Her lilts help calm the

bewildered. Many are on phones reassessing investments and commitments in the light of the debacle in greater Glenamoy-without-Rossport. Dots proud as punch texts his team to multiply to the outlets clearer proofs of China's involvement and outside help being vital etc etc.

CHAPTER TWENTY THREE

Mother of God (mog.ie) is at the nether end of the hamlet of
Ballycommon, Ballyteigue, County Offaly. Padraic's send-off
morning was gleaming wintry, a modest grid of Scot's flags,
Andrew's 'X' marks of yon chemtrails caged the central bog zone
from the Hill of Allen to Clonfert, from Ardara to within ken o'
the Devil's Bit. By the time the *cortege* made the triangular
church-pillars the grid had merged into a gauze of iffy cumulus,
insofar as the the deep blue'd gone fuzzy baby in the chem fusion.

Mrs. Eileen Dempsey was dressed to oppress, a vehement
white. She sat a tad squeezed, middle back seat, Limo 1. She
disliked black so much that she shelled out ready cash for all
night over time for the operatives at Autoparts, Clara Road, Birr
to spray paint an old hearse, a Granada Ghia 1991, twin shaft, a
grass grass green of home, 111,000 miles on the clock. It became
her son, and the flowers, to spite Winter, were so thick his basket
casket affair could hardly be seen. 'What a send off vehicle,'
averred quite the number of onlookers. The grim €170,000 plus
Massey hearse'd been sent back to Dublin with itself. Hearses if
not properly vented can trap morsels of souls in their main body
and their isotropic colouring doesn't help one bit. The mourner's
nine person limo was white anyway; crying-central by the time
they arrived at "the black carpet" of the church entrance. As said
before, crying, while not as contagious as yawning, W.H.O.
reckons, is a keen second.

Mrs. Dempsey's white was forgiven by the mostly
post*FineGael* congregation. She had Anton clutched to her and
his number was a retro first inauguration Obama presidential two

piece spliced by a slimcea black tie affair; leather mind. He had to be man-full to balance bewildered Mother Dempsey, who was staggering grief left and right. She disengaged from him a moment and went and in the bright morning saw her cracked mother-widowing face 'flected in the florid hearse glass and saw herself do three 'promtu signs of the offer-tree to ward aways away any idle demonia sidling about.

NEARER MY GOD THEE as an opening hymn, a bit unusual, was like precoital-catharsis mourning-wise. Anton was dazed in a seating position next Mother Dempsey front left, like he was the chief son of the Mother. As the *Confiteor* was being rumbled by the over sixties, Anton had a lovely embedded memory of Padraic taking his turn as Kling-on, could be three, could be four in the morning and his sallow penis a friendly gluttonous caterpillar moving up along Anton's thigh in its own wild life, girthing in ex-ponents. The sallow was from the Mother, Eileen Dempsey née Rynn, a Clare woman, an impressive breed of a Spanish Pointer, a nineteen times grand daughter of a coin laden Cadizzy sailor afloat ashore on a plank of *La Pinta Something* way back in the mean-whileens of 1588.

Despite his Mother's wariness, the final remnants of Padraic, fifty two times grand nephew of the most sorted King of Uisneach are to be laid to rest in an *a la mode* Yew-Tube, a ewer affair of a vessel with a yew cone placed above the crown chakra of the dis-incarnate. The top of the tall ewer will peek a foot above the ground, looking west across the Shannon about Clonmacnoise. The avid GAA self-centre-half will become an evergreen for a long long time. Around this theme Anton fancied to weave his eulogy. Padraic's sister had offered to do the eulogy if Anton fell into further pieces but Anton in his new found adroitness could see, Pee's wee sis Cait-Anne was half a ghost to her usual girly-camogey-sticks. She'd managed best of the siblings to de-bogger her midland showband.

The Mother of God's mourning congregation (and their admirers) were bemused that the old time speaker system made Anton's Clondalkin talkin' even commoner, big time. Anton only heard boom boom and was trying to autocue his own brain and not dwell on whata scanger he came across to those that can't fathom or at the least strain to comprehend folk who are not them themselves.

"Padraic was a great lad. Padraic was strong. Padraic was a patriot, this high of him. I think I can say he was old fashioned; like he'd belonged in the seventies. I don't think he had any enemies. He teased me about Dublin losing to Offaly - I didn't care but it was a lovely way of him including, embracing me. He liked me to wear Boys in Blue kit. He couldn't have had enemies. I have felt loved by his family and in some ways, though he is my main next king, I feel awkward speaking about him in front of yiz. I will try to say what any of you might say." Anton indicates left-handedly the front right row of blubberers. Some of the local women further back might have good reason to have envy issues for 'n' gainst Anton; as they remember the timbre of Padraic's mildly Dangan brogue in their not so righteous ears in the slow sets at 'The Duo,' Birr, but then he crossed the trackies, got mesmerised by the smell 'n' swagger of his own sex. The bulk of the older tillage farmers are enjoying the complete weirdness of a gay funeral; its suddenness and extreme sadness extra custard on their dearth of tales.

"Padraic was my future, the foundation of all my years to come. We were more and more in love each week, each day. He really thought me that being myself, my gay self was a, a no brainer, meaning completely yourself, complete yourself. Kind of odd that the city fellah learnt that from the Culchie" and he softens the

C-word with limp grief stricken movements of the inverted commas of his fingers' puppets.

"Mrs. Dempsey, Eileen, only a two years back we were celebrating imagine, our marriage. You were a marvel, as was my own mother." Anton catches the not wet eye of his own Mother who is wan. Anton can clearly see all the good people whose funerals he'd cry at all on the left side of the aisle, even the estranged look of the one being called his Father, his sideburns and tache like some daft town to town brush salesman, his attempts at mourning dress, a tad Motorhead. 'That's Anton's father in the dark nut shell brown,' Anton 'magined if an in-law asked, another'd say. The man's name is full and long Christopher Francy Fruen and he'd not been to the wedding, the bloody fuel pump o' the Megan'd gone 'n' seized south of Gorey he'd texted. He'd punch the lights o' the man who'd call him Christy and most of his adult life he went by Francy - at 'The Brooklyn Bar,' West Gorey he'd the nickname St. Francis d'Iageo in honour of his love of pints of Guinness with a drop of Malibu. No human knew it but Francy had lost ambition and a few marbles not from alcohol, not for being uprooted, a bomb shocker tot when his family, part of the Rationalist Community of West Belfast had put all their worldlies and lack of beliefs into a borrowed Humber Interceptor and went south and found solace in Dublin 12; no his "barking" was from layers of the particularates of aluminium bromide that had been falling from the sky since 2004 'round North Slob, County Wexford, that had weakened his resolve and withered his kale. Anton's dad had moved into a prefab mid the pripet marshes o'the Barony o' Shelmalier when Mrs. Fruen flung him out. Mr. C. F. Fruen's ability to handle reality on a given day was 'versely linked to how low down, how dense the chem trails were on a day. Chem-trails themselves he'd not even heard of, nor did he know how much they weaken empathy. FRUEN RULES he still scrawled in toilet cubicles, countrywide. His affection for his son was about as intense as what you'd feel for a first cousin gone ten years some place along like the Gold Coast.

"This is my family." Anton took in his immediates with a wall of cousins beyond them, propped with their spouses and wannabe spouses and all sorts of different sizes 'n' hues o' children. Anton hoped his father was hiding his grief but the bowed head was more likely texting. "These are my dearests. I am so grateful you are all here. I am so so worried though. Yesterday was the first salvo of a war. All that bombing in Mayo is just the Sarajevo, the blink, the blinkin' spark. Padraic was the first unknown soldier to die in this war. Padraic is dead because of me."

Father Haggard who was examining the podge of his fingers looked up. He was wearing an out of season purple Lenten number, with a natty rib of wheat along its midriff. Day after tomorrow'd be the second Sunday of Advent. He rose, swished to the altar and flicked on the mic with a keeeeek.

"So so considered your words, Anton. So loving." Best actor for under-pressure, Father Dennis Haggard belts into the I/WE BELIEVE and nodded to Anton's sister to collect her crumbling brother from the altar. Five foot two Lee-Anne stilettoed towards the altar on her orange legs zag zig zag zig clack clack on the tiling like as if Umpa Lumpas had an eighth dwarf called Recalcitrant. The priest and his congregation'd hardly done with "the all things seen and unseen" when Anton with very soft authority interrupted.

"Padraic was murdered. Padraic had a small accident yes, yet in hospital was killed because I crossed a line. Lee-Anne I know you love to record things. Record this." His sister stops in her tracks and rummages in her bag for her silent Huawei. "Actually come to think of it; don't." The priest's caution gets overrode by his curiousity and he doesn't develop further 'all things seen and unseen.'

"I am going to ask for a leap of faith." Anton continues. "Because in my job I handle a lot of big prospects. There is some plot or other to take over our minerals and resources and I went and found out. I was told to keep quiet after stumbling across whatever it is. I sort of did keep quiet but then Padraic was knocked over. It looked like a freak accident; even though we all know he is Mr. Care-on-Legs. After he was knocked over and in hospital I sought the advice of Jasper, me cousin by marriage 'cause he is Detective, *Garda*. I did this stupid move even though I was told directly if I said a word - my immediate family was in jeopardy."

Jasper stands up five rows back on the east side as if he'd got a mention on the *Late Late Show*. "Anton. It is best you come down now. We can.... "

Mrs. Fruen turns round at Jasper and he gets the devils' big eyes look as she swerves round at her young fellah. "Go on son."

"Thanks ma." The Offaly crowd are glee on legs and reckon this is the proof that the entertainment industry is pure Jackeens.

"Why Jasper are you trying to shut me up?"

Jasper who has sat down starts to cry. He is bawling and takes soakage and solace in his wife's padded shoulder. "Because you are, you are. Oh fucking Christ; the horror. You are right. I was told if I helped you my lovely Beatrice and my three daughters would have a drowning. They even told me which pier. Skerries. Seeming suicide. The fuckers love details. They even predicted the *Evening Herald's* headline: '*Garda*'s Depression Drives Wife to Desperate Act: 4 Dead.'"

Anton has stood back from the mic but leans forward to say numbly, "I embroiled you. I am so sorry. I did it as safely as I could. Mrs. Dempsey, they have such control, are that cynical that Massey's say the hearse was reserved before even Padraic was......"

"We are cctved each and every fucking moment." Jasper cracks up again and his words are muffled into his wife's moist Kildare Village Superdry number. RRP €235. She'd gotten it for a quarter of that.

"Father Haggard; does that camera work? Do those cameras work?" Anton nods up to the roof.

"Not a bit of it. All show. Haven't been operational since twenty oh seven. I really....."

The four hundred strong odd congregation gape about at the different camera angles.

"Can you all please turn off your phones," Anton suggests.

"You'd need to throw them away." Jasper pulls the expert out of his self. "Turning them off is ineffectual."

Anton at full tilt at the altar. "I realise this is not usual behaviours for a funeral. I apologise Mrs. Dempsey. Fr. Haddock."

"Why did he die?" Mrs. Dempsey bewilders.

"He died to help keep their plot secret. This is now a national incident. At least......"

"And we are now all implicatees." chides Father Haggard, more enjoying, finally, than judging. "Now we all sorta know. My Church is your Sanctuary. This is our Church. We can help......" and his holy high brows arch.

Anton stops him short "I suggest we bury my beloved and then all those who are yet in danger shall have to come up with a plan." Anton counts, and then counts again to be sure. "Christ ten, Jesus eleven," picks up the mic and Anton pointing at himself. "Father Hadd...., Haggard if you wouldn't mind fast track." Anton gets beckoned by Father Haggard. He steps away from the pulpit and goes over gets whispered at and then behind his cupped hand into the left ear of the anointed he whispers back his agreement. The priest nods pleased but flustered then grabs back Anton whispers last bones of some plan.

True to form ten minutes later everyone is being fed Christ. Father Haggard is not only saying "body of Christ" but whispering some long winded condolences into the ears of certain key mourners, entirely on the Fruen side. Everybody is bonding through housling, even the agnostics present tongues and right hands; the tabernacle is opened to keep up with demand, a silver family size Dealz looking Ardagh of a chalice. There is a pin drop quiet post Communion. Fr. Haggard has the repose of reflection but is texting furiously neath his chasuble. A solo girl sings the TOTUS TUUS and there is a strong feeling of what the first Christians had to handle. There is such sense of group bonding in a way that only people of the Interior can tender. The quiet is disrupted as final perfunctories are enacted. There's much fumes, out of which Father Haggard is seen to circle thrice the wicken coffin, sallies plucked with low sounds by Lough Derg - the Greater, the soaked faggots plaited by the blind. He invokes away in Latin. An Altar girl refills the thurible's charcoal and the unspoilt priest smiles at her and a matching altar boy has a teaspoon of frankincense ready and the gorgeous blue movie of a fog spreads west along the church with them. The priest nods angrily at the lad to keep the thurible fed that the smoke be as dense as *Thriller* but sure the boy is clueless. Without waiting for the smoke to settle Jasper's misses and their kids, Mrs Fruen and her daughters hide in the blue smoke. Jasper and Anton nod at his dad to help and up gets St Francy d'Iageo and two able lads from the Casements and two cousins of deceased and Massey's funeral man gives the nod and uppsy daisy; the dead, hefty homosexual is moving his last horizontal nave-wards, no better score: HOW GREAT THOU ART till they gained the Saul-facing door. The

Bally-commoners revolve their necks at the departed, are left to their insider knowledge and Fr. Haggard vehe-ment-ly indicates the hamlet folk stay seated, no going following the process to the porch, nor wave the hearse, nor the limo nor be blessing at themselves as the few other spruced up cars, mostly young and Japanese wend their ways away. The village collaborators sit in their teak pews like as if they were readying their sitting-duck-arses for an occupying Nazi reprisal while the cortege makes for the Shannon. When its flooding flow is heard, nine thousand six hundred and three starlings murmurate in a flypast that swerves, bulges, circumvents, makes three ovular Rodins that bulge, thin, scatter, rebulge. Francy Fruen sees an auspicious shamrock in their play-acting. Father Haggard's purple number is flouncing in the gusts, one time even wrapping his empathetic face and him in mid splish. The holy water from his joystick drenches the Yew-Tube that has been placed upright in the ground. The narrow pear shape hole of the ground receives the sally coffin; it slides down at a fifteen degree angle, then one lift and a click and bolts upright. Therefore out over the Old River Padraic's short life can regard, his kinda green eyes west. Jasper takes Anton apart.

"Anton I know this is the worst time of your life."

"An high low point."

"We have no time to make wrong moves. I have been trying to figure why they are so over zealous about you. What do they need you to do that requires such ridiculous threatening."

"Boring stuff."

"Excuse me."

"I think I did most of their bidding yesterday. Would have done it anyway at the blink of an eye if told to. Obedient Anton."

"What did you do?"

"I got a lot of sleazy men to sign dotted lines."

"That's it."

"After the explosion at Glenamoy and the bomb scare at the conference hotel interest in our special offers went serious south like the entire group's mind lost interest but a lot of fly-by-night minnows were suddenly signing up at my desk for this that and the other prospect in absolutely unimagined zones, areas considered unsurveyed, in depths the size of I don't know, the Matterhorn. They are I assume one and all fronts for Mi7, 8 or 9 or whatever gang we can't escape from. The mess in Mayo. Oil prices. I was told simply to accept whatever submissions came to me from certain quarters and lock down the deadline - not go extending it in the extenuated circumstances."

"Yes but that is uncomplicated. My hunch is they fear you know more than you know."

"But I obviously don't."

"Once I was threatened I managed to get through to an old colleague who used guard, might I say spy on the UK Embassy at Merrion Road."

Anton looked back to the mourners and felt this was not the time.

"You told me there was a file called 'Fat One.'"

"Surely."

"Yes and you said, another one."

"Angie."

"How was that spelt?"

"Ang.ie."

"Angie is pure mad. Possibly easiest to call it a decades long seduction."

"To what end."

"To nudge Ireland into a re-United Kingdom, to all intents but name, re-Brit the isles in a sort of lite, hardly noticed sorta kinda

Scandinavian way; no need for brash Jackeens waving from the tops courthouses nor post houses."

"I'd never......."

"..... those flags of theirs."

"So cobblers to our United Ireland."

"Think South Africa BLACK where every or most every *knyick* of economic thing of consequence is WHITE as chalk." It goes back to Italia '90. Our British friends while nurturing a united Ireland have been placing key operatives in top jobs in Ireland: Bank of this that, the *Garda*. Jesus, even for a while our A&E, the HSE!"

"Long while. Big plan."

"They think you opened the file. They think you know what Ang.ie is all about."

"They started with football they finish with what."

"Brexit was their most complicated and the riskiest bit. Our signing up to the Commonwealth was their last straw; the big Tick. Next item Ireland as oil rig. The whole country is just one effin' platform to drain our seabeds of every last drop of juice; our land-beds likely too." Jasper gives the free-flowing Shannon the most envious O'Donovan Rossa of a glareen.

"Jasper let me say my last goodbye." Anton moves back to the Yew-Tube and hunkers down so we can see roughly what Padraic sees. He sees the Esker Riada petering out as it meets the wide of river. He sees the half drunk Naomh Ciarán's chapel, doing its squat Tower of Pisa on the near, quiet end of Clonmacnoise. Anton places some earth from about the ewer in his pocket. He gathers his "nearest and dearest," beckons Jasper and his family and they go to the shore and he collects everybody's phones, one by one, then chucks them all into the River, a once-off, feck-off techy potlatch that'll befuddle archaeologists to come, if and when the Shannon parches her liberties.

The chauffeur of the Limo, a Shinrown of a man through and true nods and winks at the chief mourners plus some extra mourners as they gain the warmth and sanctuary of his limo and they make for the nearest bridge that can gain the other side. Hilversum VII satellite adjusts by .00017 of a degree of a minute accordingly, an aul relic of metallic decency from 1998.

CHAPTER TWENTY FOUR

For the first time since Devalera got the three vital Irish ports
back from Churchill, there is an obvious body of His Serene
Majesty's Ships within Irish waters.   They were not so to
truthspeak invited nor was their crossing, first a fishy 200 km
boundary protested, nor even a slight outrage or awareness when
they came within ken of Nephin's holy-ish peak. The royal ships
are skulking about the almost as good as Common-wealthy
waters of hydrocarbon blocks 1916 and 2016, fifty or less
imperious miles from the BlackSod.   They are full with spank-
ingly uniformed hello-sailors and lorded over by the very fellow
who blew the whistle on 'Conks,' literally *kehppeeeeeep* and S48
HMS *Conqueror* snuck up to and went and sank *ARA General
Belgrano* in the second last great oil war of th'Atlantic that the
British inflamed, about the Falkland Islands forty years 'ere.
Once Officer, now Admiral Roderick G. Filch scans see-throughs
of the juts and crags and landfalls from Achill all the ways to a
wee pier at a townland called Gibraltar on the south edge of
Ballysadare Bay, which gives out to Sligo Bay, an expanse of
calmish brine and home to lazy, shagging seals.   It behoves
Admiral Filch to avoid reckless all out invasion of the Sound of
Belmullet but he wants to remind himself where landing craft
could venture at low tide should the order come - or to second
guess the make believe enemy. For now he must keep astride an
eddy facing south to the right side of the U.N. Law of the Sea.
He awaits further politic excuses, multiplied or implied, and
bemuses that the dread of sheep fields that shape this two
hundred naughty miles of coastline are the same rushy nothing

that the Falklands had herself clad in. 'In the broader decades to
come,' Filch mind-ventured how mad maybe Bellemullet'll get. 'I
see lamb cutlets ate by oil magnates and fatty kebab for the semi
refined techies in the cramped but shining two ups two downs.
Voilà Mulletop-less. "La Belle," the hardened roughnecks'll refer
to her rundown Strumpton sector as. Fortnight old shank for the
make do-ers and their trickle-downed-tos get sheep-tripe and the
Gaelic gleaners get drips of lamb's blood fallen from a once
gleaming monorail, dripping onto the alleys of the eastern 'burbs.
She rust-belts-up after a half a century of infernal extraction; only
stumbling Slavs, drunk Gael-versioned Chavs limpin' 'bout once
opulent   'Opolis,   once   dinky   Riyadh-by-the-Sea   turned
Gorbells-by-Toxteth, just a.n.other dissed O'pec a place.'

Filch turns on SKY BREAKFAST while eating his Frosties.
The forecast herself was for shite weather, five days of it. SKY
Weather had promoted from her start that the British Isles were
in the same psyche zone, indivisible, Ireland Rep. got as near
generous a forecast as Britain or Orphan-Ulster might. Their
prophecies were all inclusive and didn't stop at Belcoo like a
Truman Show vitrine. The Black Lion was as important to them
as a spot like Ullapool; same care and detail for the fate of
'Astings as for Oola. The late Queen herself saw The Pretanic
Isles as a *Cruitheann* of a Trinity, and as mystery prone:
HiBlighty was white bearded God the *Vater*, practical, paternal,
naked with dividers when not dragging his barge like Gull'ver
forever through the locks 'n' grins o' Cheshire quantifying antique
mark-ups. Ireland wasn't Aisling in the slightest but more Jesus,
reckless, jagged, good with the words and the ladies and as
outspoken as they come about the satin millers opposite. That
left the I'll-of-Man as the Holy Spirit, a Manifestation of all the
Liquid wetting of the nearby landmasses. Manxia, so flighty and

unseen from the Father, not surprising it was there that Arthur went at Death, Arthur, the 3rd son of King Aedh MacGabhrain, Ulster via Dal Riada. The dead Queen Elizabeth II was thirty rough generations drop for drop from King Aedh and therefore a Niece chip-off the Legend, even on Her Dad's side. She held a fraction of the once-and-future-of-him in her rhesus positive and passed same to His serene for serene sake, King William V. Through Aedh, Elizabeth was partial to Paddy and part Paddy. Nobody ever weighed how much Queen Elizabeth II cared for her Tree. In the quiet of her auto-traum-attic brain, She was the Tree. The odd fulminations of Her Aryan hubby was Her rock, Her operating claw, Her second thought. Poor Prince Pippins's of the UK, his long life'd been so busy inviting Mi7 in for a chat while Mi8 are in some counter chambre getting a mixed message a moment later. Juggle, giggle, jiggle.

The mixed messages got cross purposed betimes, worst of all when Louis Battenberg II got his kingdom's-uppance in Mullagh-more, not Philip's fault *per se* but a ramification of a domino of badly filed ramifications. The germ of the oil heist, the farrago that is gazillion, the vision of the true extent of the vacuum that granted had to, once known, be filled essentially stems from Louis not handling retirement. Known to the Commoners as Dicky Mountbatten he first trod "Con-naught's most gorgeous" headland two months before the whistle blew for World War Two. It made little impression compared to the vast pink suntan o' countries he had in his foreplay as self-styled Emperor-of-a-thousand-many-coloured-costumes that he was or was waiting for. However his fancied Universe 'cross decades got the con-tractions. He mislaid India, Africa got uppity. Flaccid upper lips became the rage. As his world got the crumbles he found about this Sligo headland an ant-i-torpor; the *faux* battlements were particularly good for sun gazing on clear setting evenings and the glow o'Mordor wild west of Malin Beg bull cloth red.

He had arranged Elizabeth II-in-waiting's marriage to his dashing nephew Philip; he'd noted Edward VIII was never going to have monarchs with Mrs. Simpson (and weren't likely to adopt). Louis wanted to create a House called Battenburg and then British Isles'd could jollywell go back to their four squares. Louis was just done being a twink when the cheek of the Irish had gone and ate their quarter in his imaginary cake. He wanted the full bite of the dual islands sitting proud as Pilate washing their joint hands with the Atlantrickles. The Sligo surf Louis used declaim contained "dreams so likely wrought" and his ample hair for his age billowing when he'd ken its without-end waves from the keep of his highly classified bawn. Philip listened and in his nephine turn Charles listened on Louis's knee: "dreams so likely wrought," there he said it a-gain. Uncle Louis clept that barbaric sea the 'Atlantick-tock-ticktock.' "Beneath its mattress, damnably slippery bullion, albeit deep-as," Louis told Charles-the-Tot sat astride his knee "enough fumes down there for an hundred thousand Burmahs, hissedy hiss out there 'n' beyont, 'neath Erin's soup o'grey," then he'd play-whisper in case a valet's ear was cocked, "Ahland must be taken in; a gain." They all got the ear-full. The Queen hardly needed Persuasion. She adored ticking off boxes of new cash sources but it was doubly a marvel when they jelled with the ancient wood of the heathery leathery past of the pasty nations. She, like Cousin Dicky, loved the shape of the British Isles, neater than Scandinavia and the RNLI protecting all the four corners' of the paddlers' cloth hankies from the noon sun. The Queen, though she wouldn't allow Dicky daughter marry Her crown prince She did rubber stamp his hunchéd dream, the hydrocarbon prrrrr-loin, and one safish gamble later and that fair amount of work that was Philip's

U-Kleave, that got better known as Brexit - then bingo Captain
Filch de Pugwash at yer service station.

   There is a photo of King William V above the Admiral Felch.
Ermine really suits Him and the crown is steady and topped by
the newly glued Eye o'the Celtic Tiger.   In the not black and
white version of this 10 x 8 there is a modestest hint of emerald
from the finely tuned jewel that like the Mona Lisa appears to
take you in no matter where it looks at you. The Frosties make
such a racket in the Admiral's mouth he can hardly hear the
words of the Sky Newscaster. "Suspected bomber, Anton John
Froon (mad assassins always have two Christian names), a key
figure in the plot to destroy Glen Moy's Refinery is on the run.
(Sky'd banned the R-word a decade now. No Rossports.) Froon
is considered ruthless, exceptionally dangerous. It is not known
if he is armed but likelihood is, is likely.   He may have
accomplices."   A picture of Anton on his holidays in Tunisia,
actually the ruins of Carthage is the giveaway, 'cause the
Phoenicians' battle axes can just be seen ahind him on a stunned
early Dido royal old arch. Anton with fetching tan emphasised
by cream Fitch vest-ette looks like he left his empathy back in the
hotel room, the gomb look about him. A second picture, also
Tunisian has bearded Arab sorts behind him, innocent bystanders
or preamble for a not so silken revolution with a sure reluctance
to west-life be the stubble. Mi7 had uploaded the first picture for
News Agencies because the "Dublin Civil Servant of working
class background" looked so guilty before innocent in an highly
unfair Tallaght-goes -sorta-Malaga-crim way.   Scrolling along
under the holiday snaps on the SKY is separate news that the
price of oil's barrels is through the roof. The next thought the
Admiral has is to switch off his ships idling diesel like on the
double; 'five quid a gallon, best part of' then barks down the

intercom to his 2nd Commodore. "Let us go within site of the Erris rigs. Pull four degrees to starboard. Ready torpedo7."

Belmullet was Basra meets Lockerbie that Thursday morning. Journoux and CNN and Turkish telly, Al Jazz Era, the Taiwans, (the Chinese Telly'd been turned back at Knock Airport). The Irish'd had enough of their Han-acting the bollocks. Adam Curtis had gotten demoted by the BBC back to the present, remit rural crime correspondent, no more look back in wonder from hindsight a generation on at shady goings-on. There he stands drenched mid the decorations o'the Century of Self celebrations that spiced up the wintry streetscape of Belmullet's cowboy saloon of a main street, tumbleweed aside. The green, white and orange bunting was being trounced by Storm William. Compared to William, Valery'd been a yellowy doddle in a cocoa mug. Winds, one moment from Azores, the next from Iceland. Batter batter. Batter burger. The black smoke of the still billowy refinery was flattened eastwards by tempest William, billowing for blasting billowy. The Irish Army were loving the phoney war. They had roadblocks for folk coming from Bangor, from Killala, from Crossmolina: 'show me your papers, show us in yer boot, show us your underbellies.' They had devices like for giant dentists that could see chassises. Their barracks was makeshift in the old Belacroy Turf station, their green canvas tents got shelter in the roofless old building. The Bellemuleteers were loving the unending Tora, Tora, Tora of 'the Rupture' and hated the dreary politicians on 24 hour TV saying what a BLOW to the area it was. The area was all blow anyway, not an upright tree till you were that bit east of Dromore West. BLOW to tourism. Tourists love disasters. BLOW to jobs, less whoring. BLOW to morale. Play a reel for those Moral Stancers be the CrossRoads! Everybody adores a hinteen of World - As - We - Know - It - End - Times. Even those who were weighed down with the

King's shillings were top of the world with excitement in their Lexi, Jags, Merclettes. Take high noon choices for example they had 'b' sides of Ronan Collins showbands on RTE Radio 1 in quadrophenia for Christ's Sake or Ciara Kelly on Newstalk discussing Ireland's relationship with self-respect. So not all Normalcy had fecked off. Scale-wise, Storm William was Orange. Telly had so much trouble trying to get grumblers that they hired some actors: that way they got five "devastated" people and twelve different demographics saying life would go on as normal - when everybody hoped the fuck it wouldn't.

The Mayo New's page three had pictures of the Refinery Camp "crusties" (on TG4's *Nuacht* they were referred to as "*na crostaithe*") who were deemed Ace Terrorists in the Pay of Communist China. There was a shot of Fang looking spiteful and Lou looking like an unredeemed shoplifter when she'd never had that look, like they'd gone extracted a devil from the saint of Bernadette on her. *The Sun's* headline was lazy: *No Mao Oil* and a pic of handcuffed Shivnan walking into the court in Belmullet like an eejit; yet as good as simultaneously *The Irish Mirror* (of Reality) managed to nab the same Shivnan a nano tick later and they caught that Charles Manson moment alike - like Shivnan'd had Sharon Tate rasher sarnies for breakfast by the pent up unrepentance of his eyes. He'd said to the interrogating officer, *Garda* Ciaran Snide, that he had a reasonable if windswept recording of his chat in the car with a McGeown just a fortnight before (who he claimed had turned him) to prove he'd been set up but when the Garda Snide handed him back his he-phone and goaded him to prove his alibi: there was divil a yank, scarce or fat, in the audio files. His mother, Mrs. Shivnan could go to her grave with that Son-of-Sam *Mirror* image. *The Irish Male* had taken one seriously disrespectful facepic in the Castlebar morgue, puffed up Zeng. ST. DERBHLADH in the clobber of an eddy took her. 700's lungs had filled with Bunowna. In a nondescript purge zone now and for a limit of aeon her earthly meritocracy gets a really big slap be the emblazened gaze of one thousand HUIGUR WOMEN.

Security analyst Declan Power was sleep deprived with the volume of reporters seeking his smarty pants on what did this mean for Ireland's neutrality this, what kind of security can the United Ireland put about in the face of an army of five million Chinamen soldiers the other, all sorts of over-the-tops, un-thought-thru certainties were put upon him and he was more than Trilateral in his alpha-malleable sound bitten retorts. The death toll in the refinery Conflagration wasn't too bad: just seventeen but for obvious reasons News-anchorites were for always sifting their papers and eyeing the camera and promising the joy of updates that might multiply Death. The obvious reasons being they are toupéed Vampires that need the *chi* of much suffering to persist on their four point fifth dimension.

There was mixed messages as to where the apprehended Chinese soldiers had gotten to, after "they'd blown up the better half of the refinery." Some said they'd been taken by convoy to Portlaoise Prison, some "Finner Army Camp in Site Donegal"9 and then mid morning turned out they were still about Mayo but where. The 24 hour News couldn't believe their luck with the lack o' need o' repetition. One breakthrough tumbled the next and all the while (not so Saudi) Arabia was competing for bandwidth. The Yemenis were besieging Mecca with the cahoots of some S'melly pirate slingers plus Persian finger pointers, the motes finally dropped from their glad eyes like thorned tears. The house of Saud were reputed to be extending their ski holz in Le Coppet, all 634 of them. The fattening *Banque de Suisse* couldn't believe their zeroes; role on that refugee crisis. "The end simply seems nye down there in County

Mayo be the looks of things," said presenter Marian Finucane on her second last ever *Show*.

Our Ladies Island in Wexford has a statue of Our Lady on a big pole and she could have wept then for Ireland, be she Free, Partitioned or Semi Private; she knew that some new fangled hammy Stewarding was on the go, some Plantation was afoot anew. Her russet lips were sealed and if her eyes were moving she'd glimpse the L.E. Enright only at best chugging out past Dungannon beyont the gannet dark Saltees, dragging herself South for West, toward a coordinate beyond her depth, beyond the Shelf of Nymphe (itself oleous) to have a steely go at being a grey presence mid the fracas about Mayo. Meanwhile the second engine of the crafty carrier L.E. Francis McManus docked at Queen's Quay in Galway City was spluttering. The first engine had some gank all over it that made her throttles motionless. Sabotage should be suspected but wasn't. It'd been due to be a centre piece for Galway's shindig, the first gun for the Century of Self celebration meant for and practiced for the coming Tuesday morning, just a small pop from her Potemkin. It had been ordered the evening before to Belmullet area to "search and deploy" but had "gotten herself broke down" said the continual Republican elements about Galway, about Rahoon with nods to heaven and the fingers doing the inverted commas. McManus versus Invincible - what are the odds?

That left *Asgaard III*, the Irish navy's flagship sailing ship as the *Brendan Behan* and *Edna O'Brien* were both helping rescue mostly Jedi in the Red Sea from their top gear inflatables. The mayhem of the Arabs making for Egypt was over familiar 24/7 telly wise. The *Assguard* was a day south of the Isengaard Ridge, in line with La Rochelle, in nobody's waters. That morning she heard the request to come home and tooted her pitch perfect bugle and altered course seven even degrees East North East.

Seven strapping sailors hoisted sail in matching Edwardian clobber, such was the vessel's authenticity.

The Western People got the initial scoop on Lar's whereabouts. Niall, a fresh out of Templemore *Garda*, a Nangle of Nobber, for a bribe of hollierz in Orlando told the paper most of the details. This is how it went and the *The Western People* headlined what should have been the second greatest story ever told: "Mysterious Diviner Found Uninjured." There had been ole talk of Chinamen in the forest from shortly after the grand explosion - but iffy to sketchy in the reliables. Micilín, nephew to Fall-Upon-The-Parish (male) had been lamping for otters and got a squint of their likes fording the Feck-knit. 'The Orientalists had made an emergency litter put together from their belts and long pine stave affairs to carry a Caucasian, I think, an oldish man, who was either dead, asleep or sick. The brains of them appeared to be a woman.' Micilin told *The People* 'She was definitely wearing the trousers but she got into trouble.' That alone got the half million In-sty-graham hits; and lampers for otters could never be but laughed at ever 'gain. On page seven on a gossip column, further ole talk that the Chinese, or a faction of them had gone by submersible out to the main Corrib Erris sea rig and isolated its immense pipework so the gas flow kept on giving and fed the land based dragon and that is why the Conflagration was that angry and long winded. There were as yet no visible photo shots of same. There was no further information and S.N.A.K. and Stately Oil and SoTrom, the operators on the rig were being coy in their extremes. Thirty nine hours after the kaboom, the rig managed to shut off connection. This seemed inordinate. Some wondered if there might not be terrorists or so-and-soes ahold of the rig. There was a no fly zone all the way from Mweelrae to Slieve League so no nosey media to cock a snoop. The rig's operatives had to or appeared to be playing stumb and stumber.

Oleos experts from Exeter to Galveston to Bahrain were two a penny about the telly saying how such a rig ticked and marvellous cartoon time of oil and its ghost, gas, careering through pipes and all the spurts and 'jaculations of fire and wrath 'picted for to lower the ignorance of the glued-be-telly. Virgin One Irish News went to extremes and showed still as you please cartoons of the rumoured Chinese Ninja look alikes climbing the cage like legs of an imaginary Corrib. Next appearance on the 11am version the smallest rig, Stately Oil's, so called, possible so-named King HaKong Rig on block 2016 and next slide a close up cartoon still life: balaclavan slutty-eyed looking this way and that and then a roundup of the rig's roughnecks in their fetching jumpsuits, at gunpoint to the assumed Han captivators. The Broadcast Authority could get complained at for wicket stereo-type-face. The entire item completely liberally made up from the weakest of ole talk. "This is how it could have happened" says the gligeen of a vampire anchor in lisping Templeogue. Lap lap lap go the sofa-spuds, another slice of inactive *Dominus Pizzerium* if you please and the scary spice of chem-trail dew diligents their burboid garden bugs the day long.

As much as the British have their Sci-Ops for disintegrating nations, a sideshow of Mi8, the Chinese have their rather unCommunist fascination with what best can be translated as Department Outlandish: Subsection Spiritry - itself a sub section of United Front Work Department. The Han Communists are so rhino-skinned they can boldly rig a jig the election of say the Panchen Lama, not once but thrice. So when Iwishman, "oil specialist" Mister Lah 'Wing first became some sheaves thick in the People's Department of Oil and Black Things' files and further surveillance proved Ewing legit, meaning his voodoo bore fruit, BlackStuff needed him co-opted and so Spiritry were buzzed on Channel Purple. Anything supranatural required their stamps of approval. Their Spring 2020 survey and eventual findings required trailing Lar, opening his old fashioned hand written letters on bogroll like airmail, not quite A4 and lined. Intercepts of Dutch Intelligence had also discovered that Lar had unusual D.N.A.. His towel was taken from its hook at the 15 metre swimming pool at The East Mayo Hotel, Kilmovee that he infrequented; put back once swabbed. Then Chinese Operation 'Setting Sun' got choreographed but they hadn't banked on being used as dupes when their own operation was uncovered by an Mi7 operative working in Hong Kong, from Dutch tip offs through an Irish registered, Brazilian gigolo. Once Operation 'Fat One's' high command knew that the Chinese were greedy for Lar's gift they had their best ruse and the perfectest baddies (just add water), far more SkyNews-moralisable airtime-wise and balls-wise than the iffy planned splinter of a splinter of a schism of some Continuity IRATE army faction, yuck, too much bad breath o'farls 'n' rollies.

So the media clamoured and they clamoured: 'who had Lar it exactly two weeks since his rumble?' Did he ascend to or merge with his unbelieved-in Maker on that Chinese litter *en route* to their launch. NO. Lar is in a round room, tower three, floor four, might as well be the Rapunzel suite, Ashford Castle. Pre Christmas specials hadn't had a big take up so Operation 'Fat One' had booked the entire hotel till Christmas under the guise of an ungooglable Ornithology World Conference. Birds don't attract hacks, much less Conspiracy admirers. His door is locked but he can to and fro to the dining area with four armed guards. Once his medical needs had been put to rest Flo was allowed her first visit. They'd forgotten how in love they were. Flo did have to sign the Official Secrets Act (an ole Republic of Irish version), and initial particularly subsection 12G, Point ii for in perpetuity *doon do vale*, Erse for 'keep that trap of yours shut lady OR......'

In the VIP, Quiet Man Lounge, they both had organic avocado, with Roonagh lamb liver (pulled - in both directions) doused with a strife of dill seeds. Flo was on Venus with the surroundings and had wondered if her husband might have been all along a Continuous IRA Man what with all the recent enough regged Escorts or he'd become Mr. Whistler Spill-the-beans. 'You'd go Stockholm-over-heels in love with your captors in this like a place,' she prefigured.

Lar had gotten so matter of fact and calm, pacing his grub like an old timer, lever the slither of avocado and sandwich gentleman relish betwixt it and the liver, raise like there was a tomorrow, so slow, an half gaze on Lough Corrib without, then cave it. Flo'd never seen his tongue so healthy, such royal health.

"You are a terror."

Lar drones the plate to see what combo he'll assay this assault. "I am ?"

"Unholy."

"Why on earth did they catch hold of you?"

"They needed some divining done."

"And what's with you that you can't now?"

"They're saying the explosion kind of skewed the nerves that make the pendulum do whatever bidding I have or I had."

"Sure all that divining never got you anywhere." Flo noticed that the four guardsmen were all foreign, their teeth not wanting. "Half the country were praying for finding your, your whereabouts. Your own workplace had a special mass in the Airport oratory. You became a National thing, like biggest thing since Madeleine McCann, even Shergar." Mass true but the rest not; he'd dropped to item five by day two News-wise. She put upon the Nation her own turmoil and concern. Every word they spoke, every mood they made, every vow she might break was being watched from audio, vision and pulse system, dainty hid in the tiffany overhang lamp.

"How's Philo ?" Lar never much did courtesy.

"She's finished their extension but there is a crack in the wall, or its damp, one or both or the other."

"She is in a damp spot."

Two of the four guardsmen altered between Napoleon impersonations (one armed bandits) and exercising their fingers likes you might before you'd garrotte the dispensed-with.

"They've got me doing a course, to keep the gray matter throbbin'," whispers Lar.

"Ah good. Do you get to do a round of the gardens?"

"It is called kin-easy-ology."

"Family tree studies, no? I give up."

"Of all things, finger movements and straight out arm movements." Lar does a wee mudra of placing thumb and ring finger together making an ovaline circle. He then looks at his wife through same monocle and grins at her. She smiles back.

"I know but you could be better faster with more robust physio. Don't you like a swim ? The likes of here'd've a damn fancy pool and their gardens are ex-quis-ite, second to none, it says in their leaflets. On the way over, even in Winter, gorgeous and the lake in the backdrop." Flo pats her napkin. She doesn't like the ear-pieces in the four horsemens' ears. "They can hear our every words."

"Who told you I couldn't do me divining any.....?"

"The high command. They gave me a low down on what had gone with you and they suggested I not dig deep, in case of aftershocks. They said to possibly say something soothing to get ole Lar back."

Lar mashes the avocado with his fork like an impatient child. "The kin-easy-ology is I think their way of replacing my pendulum. But God it feels makey-uppy and hasn't cut the mustard.... yet."

"If you're useless they'll have you home soon." If guardsmen have floor managers, then the eldest who could lip read Lar in case of electric or radio interference failure gave Flo heebie jeebies in buckets but she braved herself "It wouldn't be too soon to have you home, love." She placed her hand on his. "You need a package of Pfizer. THEN.... you'd get mojo back."

The dig stops Lar in his mash mash. He looks at her. "You are such a sweet one. I am so sorry for being such a crotchety bollocks all these years."

"You were never, a bit. You might have been."

The guardsmen look edgy like they are eager for their late elevenses: crumpet and espressos no doubt. Flo has a sudden urge to collaborate. "Lar I really, really hope the kinology regime works out. Be a good boy and do whatever exercises they tell you to, daily, whatever. I will be back tomorrow."

She gets up and kisses her love, her husband on the manly brow furrows and walks out the door on him. Lar sees her lilac frock enter the dark of the early Edwardian corridor, every bit as oakie as it was groovy.

CHAPTER TWENTY FIVE

Imagine this Dutch radio operative who'd retired but'd been redrafted in on the double to monitor the melee of Ireland. He is there having his afternoon tad crumblier Netherlands version o' Arrowroot and his remit just goes stops half way 'cross the Shannon, a white limo with its fugitive plus mourners and driven by a short fused driver. The Dutchman is in charge of a hefty five satellites at once and Hilversum VII has just gotten through the cloud cover in time to see Liam 'Barrack' Clifford of Shinrone, profession, chauffeur getting out of the white stretch vehicle in the midst of the 'Bridge of the Bulls,' that yokes Connaught and WestMeath. The driver is typique Irish Middle-lands in micky-t-sleeved, white buttoned shirt, pants size 52 keeping a feck off Smithwick Shandy of a belly to itself despite his twenty seven years. Barrack's his confirmation name. This man has a wide tie, undone black and he is barking into a sellotaped Blackberry. He has that life contentment that goes with girth as he leans his fatted arse onto the motorway bridge railing and whatever are his arguments they're giddy, involve much weathervanes of the hands and surely the height of disrespect to the funeral party waiting in the sad limo. Dutch's handover notes tell him to keep all eyes and audials on that Limo and its swaggers: eleven mourners plus driver entered it nineteen minutes, two seconds previous. There is an awful breeze jostling the Shannon so he can't hear an ounce of the chat. He gets patched through to Tesco-Ireland-089 number and MP3s the chat, some row over using rhubarb instead of apple in a pie. "Krist. Irish worse than Italians, raise their voices over nothing." He scans previous files in case rhubarb's a pattern, might be that rhubarb is code for something. It wasn't and he was too Dutch to know that 'Rhubarb Rhubarb' and versions of it was just any ole hooey o' chat.

Anton is dying for a leak and he really doesn't want to be taking his todger out in front of the policeman/ 2nd cousin-in-law. Jasper and he are stood on the third pilaster beneath the M6 motorway bridge, the Athlone crossing of the Shannon, Junction 14 that way, Junction 15 sunset-way, a wee wedge, a foot above the free flow o'Shannon. Anton goes about the pilaster so as to face North, eying up the dregs of Lough Ree and widdles away. That relief itself puts him in humour enough to see his predicament as bearable, though he has just endangered 2% of the population of Offaly and the better part of his family. The bridge manhole they'd gotten down while the clouds were thickest; they'd managed to just reclose with the chauffeur nonsensing away on his phonio before the satellite got through the cumulus. Anton zipped his Armani and shivered. Jasper stared at him, less Butch than Sundance. They stood in silence and harrumphed.

"That's a rare priest. Talk of thinkin' on the feet." Jasper says it east looking.

"Strategy or what."

" He must have a bro in the Office of Public Works.

"Or the NRA."

"Here's to Fr. Haggard and his manhole."

To their south a snazz cruiser; as it nears Anton can read her, *Crystal Star V* chugging full tilt 'n' throttle up from the beauty of Athlone Town to their south. It comes to span 3 of the bridge and cuts its engine, drifts. It was there so sudden they'd hardly the chance to fear it.

"All aboard," shouts a diffident man with that wee half quaver of differ that makes him not a Connaught citizen, but an

Athloner of the east of the Shannon, not therefore RoscommonMan but West-meat. The fugitives on their wee pilaster are too surprised to query or quarrel the boat's arrival. Jasper leaps first, then Anton like's if they'd übered a vaporetto to take them from the bridge of sighs.

"Not a bad day now." says the boat Cap'n and the after fart of Storm William adding a lock of knots to their northbound. Anton wasn't in the humour for rustic yammer and went below deck.

"Rain was promised to follow. Who deployed you?" polites Jasper

"That's it now," said the Cap'n, "word came from the priest."

It was a classy cruiser below, the real Foxrock, gleaming and everything appropriate except the "help," the cleaner or the Cap'n's mistress or the stowaway, Anton notes this long leggy woman spread bent about the L-sofa, her shoes trun to the floor. She knew she'd company, and paced a fine disinterest. She was wearing silks of the royalist yellow. Her butt'd make the priciest pillow would've crossed the captain's mind but Anton had the *déja*-view that he'd clepped her before. He put it down to sleep deprivation plus grief.

"Are you hungry?" she says not looking up from her book whose title was "*A Exploração de petróleo e gás em águas muito profundas e turbulentas.*"

"God, I am. I was at a funeral, a very, very important funeral. The mother of the lovely, love; of the dead person had planned a really big spread at the Royal....."

"I know."

"Strange."

She dog eared her page, a thick tome and shut it. Anton could smell the books' fresh pages from the distance and noted that the woman was not wearing perfumes. The woman was tall when she stood. She turned back to Anton and shook his hand softly for his sake.

"I am Lucineide."

"Replaces lost energy quickly."

"No, you gay boy. Lucy Nay Dee. Not Lucozade." and went to the kitchenette and took a cooking mufflette glove, went got her casserole pot and her returning expressive eyes quietly indicated the glass, oval, dining table ready with choice doilies and unlit candles and a bottle of Moche 1987 in the ice bucket that was likely EPNS silver, not solid.

"You shouldn't have," says Anton.

"My God. I should have. Of course. For you. Genuine you. Sit down Mister Fruen." She lights the candles with a long Habitat taper.

When they were sat, Lucineide with a small wee grin, after a fake humble bow, with joined hands said "Grace," then she said "tuck in," then she said "we are surprised you're not dead."

"Lovely grub," Anton had hardly picked up what she was saying. "Serious delish."

He'd wolfed a lot of it down, scoop, scoop and was profoundly impressed by the saline slippery effect. Then his fork hit a hard something and he dregs it up to inspect, prods it, raises it and it's like a purple child's fist sized grizzling thing.

"Crubeens, beans and rice." Lucineide says. "Shaw's crubeens and the rest's from ALDI."

"Where you from?"

"Belo Horizonte." This was said with such a minto Aero that she may as well been born mid the high barley in a barley field on Krypton; it was that Outlandish.

"That's your company?"

"Gorgeous Horizon. That is its meaning. Where's that Mister Hero?"

"Haven't the foggiest." Anton excuses his finger uses and gnaws the pigs' trotters (Saxon for crubeens).

"Organic pork; on special offer." Lucineide is sucking the gristlelettes from the knuckles of her own crubeen.

"Florida, Cuba, Bahamas. The bank place: Caymans?"

"Hotter. Hotter."

"Key West."

"Nope."

"What you famous for?" Anton scoops his kidney beans. "What's your country famous for?"

"For creating this poor man's grub. *Fay-juah-dah*." Lucineide indicates her plate. "We excel at a certain team sport."

"Hurling things ?"

"Futebol."

"Futebol."

"Wow. So well said."

"I think you're Brazilian. I've heard yizz in 'The George.' Exactly that sound you have."

"Bingo Boy." She quits smiling and points her fork towards her guest, its prongs blunted with kidney beans. ALDI doesn't stock black beans. "Anton. I need to update you. The Royal Navy have entered Irish waters at three points, Dooish, Porcupine and most heavily directly west of Belmullet. The refinery fire has stopped."

"I knew the last bit. The invasion not. I think you might think I am somebody I' m not."

"We had some not conclusive intelligence of the Chinese operation but were never clear what their goal was. They had made efforts to contact us or appeared to; pretending to uz to loop uz in. We are 95% certain they, that is the Chinese became false flag dupes ."

"Really fluent." Anton needs less information.

"There is massive propaganda going on to concrete the case to the Irish public to bring the British in, with Dutch help less obvious - not to land - but to monitor the seas, out there and nobody knows this so well as yourself, nobody sees anything out there."

"Lucy. I think our island's finished?" Lucineide doesn't answer so Anton says "question" and interrogates the air with the dagger of his zorro-ing finger.

"Your United Ireland was a fabulous fatted red herring. Your century of indy-pendence was like, I don't want to say it, but just a long holiday."

"Don't talk to me." and Anton meant it - he was loving the *feijoada* and preferred to lick the plate clean than to figure out all this chessy messy geo-impolity; even yaying and nodding in agreement took efforts.

He ladled seconds on to his plate and for politeness: "I know too much but there is one thing I don't know. I do know you are a great cook but I don't know who's side you on? Let me rephrase the chestnut: who you workin' for?"

"HyBrasil."

"A travel company?"

"Well it's involved travel; gotten me about the world."

"Lucky you."

"Anton. We are involved with oil and gas exploration."

"Same here."

"But with the rewards for the people."

"Right. Like People Before Profit."

"Certain people."

"You're selective."

"What connects you to all this?"

"We were half duped into something."

"Into what in particular?"

"We thought we had gotten a friend; a guy who claimed to be creating a non motherfucker version of OPEC."

"He'd've his work cut out."

"He also believed that the profits of hydrocarbons could finance conversion to green energy stuff."

"So what'd he con you into?"

"Co-opting what we're best at; he found out or he got wind of our mother of all extractor submersibles. We got persuaded to cooperate. I won't bore you with the micro details of the dupe but we ended very much not the captains of our own destiny in the calm of some "false" doldrums off Kerry, very very beneath the ocean."

"I do like details. Might you recall the coordinates?"

""Fifty two degrees, zero nine four two five three two minutes north. Thirteen degrees, thirteen, twelve, sixty nine minutes west."

Anton thinks while chewing. "Yes, gotcha. Who was this fellow?" Lucineide is not willing to answer so Anton moves on his thinking and rattles off: "Blocks or their crosshair, at that coordinate more or less 2078, 2079, 3005, 3.... SAC I'm fairly sure; grey coral mounds"

"Or makey-uppy coral mounds!"

"You can't make up coral mounds except over millennia."

".....there were two contacts: a suave Whales fellow?"

"What?"

"Whales, Whelsh fellow."

"Welsh you mean."

"He made those Oxbridge noises and an extremely fat fellow, loud and American."

"Jesus. Dots. The fat one, not sure."

"Fat One. Why you say that?"

"Well you said he was fat."

"The Chinese said they suspected some long term op was afoot, of which they knew nothing; just it's code name was likely 'Fat One.' We imagine the hullabaloo over in Mayo is the start of that, hoping fully that."

"Funny name for an Operation. Liposuction jumps to mind." In the past he'd've laughed at his lame effort o'wit but now his quip hung about the badly ventilated cruiser.

"Our research correlated '*Fa Tone,*' likely mirrors the Old Gaeilge for 'beneath the wave.'" Lucineide is not used to professionals being not cognisant of intelligent things.

"Operation Beneath deh Wave." Anton is pretty twinkled by the name.

Lucineide exasperates and takes a break to regard without the window but....... "Why are we heading towards them reeds?"

"Dose reeds....." and Anton leaps from his seat, legs it up on deck. "Nobody at the helm. Holy Christ."

Neither Jasper nor the Cap'n. He looks to port; two bodily sort of dots bobbedy bob in the cold cola of eddies a furlong and a bit back. He grabs the shiny wheel and spins 'n' spins moving back Leinster direction. FULL what looks like might be THROTTLE. In a blink they starboard alongside the bodies, puffer jackets keeping the dead from sinking but both gonners, hardly a pallor between them.

"Lucy, Lucy, fetch quick that hooky thingummy." Anton's trying to master Death.

Lucineide unhooks the docking thingummy, sort of barge pole distance device. She manages to snag Jasper and drags him toward stern. The Cap'n then goes sinks on them, his puffer was that saturated and a cloud of blood is his byebye. Lucyneide and Anton bond a tad, hefting Jasper aboard, some Ree lough trickling unbecoming down his chin to the immaculate deck; the poor detective has loosed his sweet soul, his animations are has-beens, his pale of ambitions, all seven, forestalled.

"Anton. Your friend is dead."

"Shite." Anton points out the silent bullet hole in his in-law's lumbar region.

"Sorry for your, really sorry for ...."

"........ me troubles."

Anton stares at his ally of sorts, dead and gone. "Really. Shite. Shite. Sweet fuckin' mother. This is completely screwy." Anton takes the beach towel sized Irish flag off the stern pole, and with freezing solemnity covers his second cousin-in-law's head with it, the white of peace squished about his face, the green and orange framing.

"He died for Ireland."

"He did." Lucineide takes a quick gooh at their lack of time on her shePhone.

"Whoever did this could get capital punishment for this."

Lucineide is not getting the drift, so Anton mimes self lynchment.

"In Ireland; seriously?"

"For *Garda*. For Presidents." Anton squints toward the darkening of Longford as if the enemy is lurking. "He is a Guard, top brass detective. Fairly top. Sorry. Was."

"Your security detail?"

"Not officially."

Lucineide uses her eyes. She'd gotten the laser eye surgery late 2020 and Clivenden'd remarked that her vision was 'bionic' but the operation had dulled the infathomable of her eye line. "Whoever did this is over on that *crannóg*." Lucineide is Tomb Raider in pumps thinks Anton and then remembered what's a *crannóg* from Junior Cert history. Fake islands made up on choppy waters with lops of trees, a way to be safe from mammoths and smart Danes possibly snuck up the Shannon from Limerick. "How do you know your *crannóg*s?"

"Our initial briefing included preHistory."

"Are *crannóg*s not real history?"

Lucineide doesn't answer. She is busy undoing the cylinder of a barrel shaped snazzy sort of Norwegian coloured inflatable. She untoggles it and it bursts to being a fancy dinghy and as soon as she's chucked it overboard it gets pocked be bullets, heavy gauge enough as they almost like explode as much as puncture. If the shy enemy destroyed the Cruiser proper; the insurance'd be phenomenal thought Anton as he boots the floor and Lucineide cries, "make for Connaught" but Anton can see the shots are coming outa the west. "Hell no" and he heads east, as now there is some enemy craft coming from the North, "oh cripes" says he and now one from the South, looks like a *Garda* boat or in this present climate, a fake one or who knows what. They are closing, closing is the main thing. "What the feck." Anton makes the vessel a rocket and super-machs his way into some dense ducky everglades to the East. The boat is so up to speed that it is chewing roots while getting ahead. The not forever glades give on to a short patch of open water and their way is blocked by another enemy vessel, a wooden one.

"Go girl," shouts Lucineide and Anton blasts their port with *grand vitesse* and cleaves their twains behind and the shouts of the injured and the mouth-fillers mixes with vexed duck. Anton's never hurt a fly but he has just killed three Mi7 types, their gore tex, their high level training, their i.d. s, their 'Made in Switzerland' balaclavas not now too relevant as they thresh to hold boat shards yet sink. The cruiser appears to have lost assailants and Anton makes for the last light of a feeder river, neat as a canal might be. "Feck that lough." Hardly out of open water there is a bridge ahead; it is humpy and mid 18th century, its granite keystone has a shallow name *Domhlann* Bridge. They just squeeze 'neath it. "Longford. Lucineide." He sees her hairdo shaking, coming up from below deck, like calm as she pleased at the close of a typical day's work: fleeing, conjecturing, manslaughtering or its encouragement. "Nice. We are in Longford. That lake was doing uz no favours." As twilight hastens he slows east through the wastes of Longford. "God Lucineide. You look fantastic." She was in black leathers and had her diver dagger and a another for gutting monkfish. She sported a sort of bomber jacket, with a collar of *caipou* fur. The Irish "hero" cricked his neck south and a notch west, where Clonfert's likely ways away and there the sun set, a teasing close of day special; scarlet dot glow 'neath lead cloud, zingin' red 'cross the turflands. The sky blushed and Storm William was gone.

Chug a chug chug. Chug, a chug chug. Out of the dark the navigable river seemed to have a glower. Some kind of big signage rainbow shaped across the river, some klicks east. Lucineide trained her squids on it.

"What's ahead Lucy?"

"I think, I think it says Central Park. Actually it says 'Centre Park Ireland.'"

With that they could hear the roar of the boat of the remaining enemy with full super troupers finding them; all haste and gain, all haste and gain.

CHAPTER TWENTY SIX

Flo was as good as prevented leaving the Castle. 'Fat One's brawn were wary some compromising info could be passed between her and her husband, possibly, their English being so at odds, Traveller's-Can't maybe or KnickKnock or their own code; Flo could well twitch. Also at handover one operative admitted he'd sneezed and his eyes were shut for 1.6 seconds. 'Fat One' passed same on by way of the afternoon handover minutes and under SUGGESTIONS said they were 'cool to leave Mrs. Florence Ewing back home' but Mi7B really betimes overdo paranoia; they had over read Flo's Republicanism, her cunning Continuity Party voting, a South Roscommon/ East Mayo candidate - a loser every time and a third cousin. 'Fat One' were also beginning to come to terms with the possible loss of their golden goose; Lar's intuits were wilted. They should hardly miss what'd so recently become them but Impatience & Disappointment race to find ideal minds. It would never've been on the cards to "accident" Flo once she'd left the Ashford compound, on her slow drive back to Knock via the black ice-lanes in the hills beyond Cong. Some kind of eternal Saga Holiday was getting planned and drawn up; that Lar and Flo could be golden yeared in an unending Pure Land Bognor Regis cum Trabolgan manner born kind of gaol-way; all the while dreaming up every stratagem for Lar to regain his pendulum swing. The positive thinking was that with the correct therapies Lar could get into his stride predicting again gazillions; rock stadia the size of oil would become clear as day, barrel prices'd skyrocket and the quids of the shareholders' lids would flicker yachts, Mayfair lily pads, a window seat on a Mars-bound Tesla should CO_2 thicken its veil. Granted FAT ONE and Mi7B were thinking on their hooves. For now it was enough graft to consolidate the ocean and wool-pull the Irish out of their state of independence, let alone be being able to have your main cherry behave on brittle icing.

"Wakey wakey. Day 2 Ashford Castle 'Prison.'" Flo is loving the confinement." They are given the weak excuse that a Chinese helicopter gun ship might land out of the air and try nab Lar twice. "It is for your own protection. At least for now."

Lar stretches his four limbs to the cardinal points, bends his ankles as back towards himself as he can and releases lymph and tension. With that there is a wrap at the door and a natty foreign room servitor presents his tall self at the door. He has a Sandringham sized silverine dish cover that has their breakfast 'neath it. He places the grub on a lovely table in the roundel of the casement and what a postcard of Lough Corrib rossy dawn to view he politely proffers, securing back the shutters .

"Very nice entirely," Flo polites at the man whose name tackle says 'Enden.' Simply. "I wish it could be this Christmas every day or what." As Enden exits, Lar says "Slade'd not be on his radar" and nods at the grub and Flo with the use of both hands manages to lift the silver ovular dome.

Lar doesn't look but smells. "Our own canteen in a turret. What!"

"Exact. Get over here and up or it'll get cold."

They are on second coffee when there is a brusque wrap and a rude entry by a fat man.

"Ah it's you," says Lar. "I think I might be right that bad luck follies you about, like I don't know, like a half pointer."

"McGeown, Inny McGeown. So good to meet you Mrs. Ewing." He is plum as jam to the middle ages woman. McGeown eyes her Pioneering pin and the plum jam.

"Ewing, née Lawless, Flo," says herself full of the clout and rascal of her surroundings, not realising that the Vice Govnor o'their Gaol had just crashed their breakfast. Flo was less than impressed when this black belted size 62 waister went for her plate, took some uninvited nibbleeens of her slim whole wheat soldiers, even dipping them into the half dumpty of an opened free range, possibly organic egg.

"Do you mind." she even said.

"Yumm-ah-rooney. How is our Lar Wing?"

"My eminence is fine."

"He needs more rest," answers Flo for him proper. "He needs more air."

McGeown pours coffee from the pourer and makes a black pond in a saucer and has a slurp at it. "I gonna have to make you an offer."

Lar looks worried.

"If somehow we can get you back to working order. We want to set up you guys, up for life. The draw back is you cannot return to your old ways. No more Knock-a-doodle. Do you get me? You are too precious and the enemy knows you now. Possibly even new ones: Venezuelans, Angolans, Al-jerry-annes, Turk, many. You can stay here in the grounds maybe or some place else. If it must be Ireland fine. If you can do your magic elsewhere too. We can arrange suites, pools, takeaways....."

"That is kind but I think my gift has left me. We have tried. There is some fray of the wits. The hand can't message the finds." Lar wobbles his hands over the coffee pot like a priest with level two Parkinson's might over his chalice. Flo frowns.

"Lar, dear man. I was in the first Gulf War. Stormy Desert. Schwarzkopf got me co-opted. I was helping Red Adair put manners on some profligate Kuwaity fire ball wells." McGeown is doing his "I've been there" lie-a-thon for the zillionth and a halfth time. "I was blasted by a failed oil stopper from here to the lake, almost. Seriously almost." Flo regards the comparison without the window and a swan family handling snags of wept willow by the low sounds. She interjects, "Red Adare was dead by then." He wasn't but she wanted to dent the clear lies, call some bluff though she would find it darned difficult to cut short her current holiday in this kinda Purgatory for goody-two-shoeses. To amend her smart ass, she just went touched the fat man's right elbow and grinned her when-required gligeen grin that translated as 'between you and me and the round wall, what matters if the facts land how they will, aren't we the slut in the piggy-bank on its back and lovin' it. We'll cooperate entirely.'

JUSTIN, Lucineide's erstwhile spirit guide then entered the room like a warm sigh, like Santa Claws via the wide draught of chimney. He had been summoned by the third wit of the very servitor who'd just brought the breakfast; 'Enden.'

"Money no object." says McGeown first over reading Flo's fake holy rosaries, overriding same and piercing through to an assumed wanton East Mayo hunger.

"Money no object," repeats Flo to the brilliant starch and devilish be-DAZzles of the scarlet yulesque tablecloth.

McGeown zones again on Lar and priest like grabs for his elbow. He doesn't care if neither believe his story, he needs to fill the air with *spiel* to tick off this task o' the mornin;' the one called on his yellow stick-on-memo in his imaginary back office: 'Blag the ole pikey into doing perpetual oil voodoo.'

"Christ the 'Raq. I got so shocked, couldn't talk for two months, actually, a month, it was. Yeh a month." McGeown looks to Flo with semi shocked eyes that are meant to be bad actor for empathise with me.

"What sort of money are we talking?" Flo asks back at the affront.

"A percentage of finds. Zero point one of a per cent per."

"That sounds feck all."

"That is on royalties on each and every gal-oh-nay or gazillion coming through that feck off pipe; same pipe as when is repaired will be twice as fat." 'Operation Fat One has more than triple meanings in the East Atlantic parlance,' daydreams McGeown, as his wide privilege shuffles and prevails about the casement, darkening the breakfasteers.

"I know but zero point......"

"Your government currently gets zilch-a-rooney." McGeown looks Lar in the eyes like he is going to hypnotise him. When you eyeball Lar that way you tend to get a reverse psyche. Lar hypnotises unwittingly the watcher; as McGeown goes under dreamily he manages to ask his intended question but it comes out all dreamy slur "How goes the kinny-ology?"

Flo tries to interrupt the mesmer: "Lar was useless explaining it. It might be good if you could give me the gist of it so I can help, help, help........ reprogramme him."

McGeown and Lar ignore Flo. They are becoming lost in the uncandlelit bromantic moment. McGeown has gone under. The 7th son of a 7th son of a 7th is beaming the astral's equivalent of binaries at him. Lar himself has succumbed part of his self to Spirit JUSTIN who is then a lukewarm presence ghost-wise. (An odd 5G broadband ripple effect in the national roll-out is that antennae extenuate veil-thinning-nodes and through them, with them, in them a higher frequency unity 'tween spirtry and the

Terra Cognita. Same can ill or well inform on a case by case basis. This Channel 4 of JUSTIN; Lar's never felt its likes and it is so momentary he hardly notices but his mouth says: "the kinesiology is *hocum*. The only chance I have to get back my old self is an apprentice. I need to pass it on; my, my, cure; my douse." Latter'd never crossed his mind ever.

"Cure!" rebuffs his lady wife who looks from pillar to post of a what class of a séance..... "That is a long shot." McGeown mid mesmer has ditched all sneer. "If the position were on jobs.ie what would we write?"

"Required - a sea douser ?" Lar was usually so uninterested in ethereal realms that he didn't even bother his whole joking about them.

"Yes when you are desperate, when you are at the end of your tether then St. Anthony finds and rescues." says Flo. McGeown had enough St. Austin's Austin schooling to know the remits of saints.

Lar doesn't answer and that Spirit Guide known simply as JUSTIN leaves off; his rippling of the yarn succint yet effective.

"Just in time." McGeown looks at his watch. "I need to ring Hill-Billy." McGeown returns to his customary whirring devilish.

CHAPTER TWENTY SEVEN

Lucineide and Anton's handcuffs were removed when they were gaoled. It was off peak and Centre Park's young attractions were grizzling, hibernating. An ignoramus roller coaster, all cables, troughs 'n' drops called DAGDA was not far off a sound sculpture, daunting the turf lands with the last haarpic sighs of Storm William swirling toward royal Meath. The ill-defined enemy were mad with Anton for killing their comrades. They seemed like *East Ender* extras to Anton and he didn't feel a tingerine of guilt about it. "They had it coming" he'd even said while being dragged out of the beach slapped cruiser, *Crystal V*. Lucineide got a bit concussed in the grounding thud that concluded the five mile boat chase but was otherwise grand and could walk a straight line. Anton was so grateful for the grub Lucineide'd prepared earlier as these so-and-soes offered nothing, "not even jellied eel" and then he had to pretend to Lucineide that he knew how jellied eel was prepared, when he hadn't a bog but it was a way of keeping each other entertained, their fates being a bit blurry. They'd been pushed and dragged through an half built Asterix looking village about the North edge of Centre Park, likely a proposed part of the amusement park that hadn't gotten Longford Council's full approval reckoned Anton. Anton told the Brazilian lady'd he'd never wanted to come here but Padraig had said that after Easters it was great value, and oftener than not great weather and there was a package for €199, included half bored, being taken for seven rides including the flagship Dagda. 24 hour access to the water spumes and the pamper spa too. The food was Wetherspoonogue, and delivered that way too. Anton loved Wetherspoon stuffing with feck loads of gravy.

"I'm really sorry about your PawRig." Lucineide piped up.

"I know." Anton is taking in his new surroundings.

"He carried his cross for Ireland," she tilts her head sideways to make clear her eye contacting.

"Yeh. Well said." Anton staunches a weep as the eye-line sunders.

They were banged up in a not at all a silken Thomas of a Norman keep for keep's sake. The walls were fake moist rocks, with fake heavy metal rings at the disturbing height that'd've a skeleton or a heading-that-way skeleton a-dangle for decades from. Lucineide took it all in her stride. The floor she paced was simply poured concrete painted a standard purple, no generosity of rushes yet strewn for the coming season. There was arrow slits in the walls or the appearance of them but they'd simply lengthy, daylightsavingtime sort of bulbs behind them feigning cold light o' day without the plains.

As evening gained Anton was being dead chivalrous. The only soft thing was a sack of dry oak leaves propped in a corner and he let Lucineide sometimes bean bag, sometimes pillow with it. Anton twigged this incarceration seemed to be really fecking with her plans but she did not explicitate but she really appreciated Anton not wanting to sit. He became the pace maker 'cause he was freezing.

"You need to somehow improve your innocence," out of nowhere says she.

Anton was a wee bit thrown by her mistake. His mother, his greatish aunt Melda, not a few of his friends and lovers 'cross years, even decades had made a point of encouraging him to be less of a gobshite is how he saw it; they'd put it like he should be more wary of peoples' motives, less of a gomb to all intents. Right now he felt very non-gomb, very alive, yet vulnerable.

"I would have thought the opposite. Did you mean PROVE?"

"Yes. Bang on. My mistake."

"The only humans gunnin' for me are those poor souls that turned up in the church for my husband's funeral and I'll never say a cross word about the church again; the priest got uz out of a pickle too."

"He knows his manholes among other things," supports Lucineide.

"Every other national eejit at this stage believes the telly version of me. Imagine that."

"Yes I was shocked by the lack of fact checking; just dive in and believe what the Justice or Gwarda or His Majesty's Service view is. Have you ever actually been to China?"

"What a question. No interest."

"Well you really have not been keeping up with the *News* then. They flashed a shot of your being in Beijing entering their sort of Department of Hydro-burnables."

"Monstrous."

"Photoshop. They even said you had suspected links to Huigur Islamists fighting in the oil provinces of Western China or pretending to."

"On me bollocks."

At this Lucineide smiled and a tad o' luxúria (Brasileira for their version of the virtue called Lust) secreted her loins. She thought that Anton could be not always erect but what an ample blood clot behind that zip moment to moment. If Anton could learn poise and straightness he'd be a real lad, no truck mechanic, definitely no Clivenden but something worth seduction, idled the disparate woman.

That night they slept like cat sisters, both using the sack of leaves as a pillow and their bodies tortured by the floor. They spooned each other and in the circumstances Lucineide was well behaved and Anton had never had breasts pushed like that to his spine. Lucineide put her arm around Anton but even in her deep dreams when her Spirit Guide came whispering, yet she never dropped the hand, never below the Irish gentle man's pierced inny. The Spirit Guide, JUSTIN, helped Lucineide sleep, sleep well. The fake keep got woejus cold. The cold would wake Anton and the hard floor would keep him awake, keep him wondering; then sleep would have him again. Anton was no Thatcher, Gorbachev getting by on four hours sleep per night.

At 4 or 6 or 8am there was high commotion. It was dark yet and two Saxons came in; they said they were handlers when Anton asked who they were and what they were up to. Anton needed to leak. They let him do so in a corner and he spotted a poop, and an attempt made at hiding it with leaves.

"Ever heard of the Geneva Convention?" Anton snarls at the Saxons.

"Zip up Mick and get over 'ere. Geneva-facking-in-vention. Right to piss my arse."

Lucineide caught Anton's eye and the message was less found-out about poop; her face said more like: 'what level of eejits of evil have we to contend with here.'

The so called 'surgents were re-handcuffed; together this time. They were blindfolded and led east, Anton reckoned sometimes wrongly, right a bit, left a bit, across a warm calm place, out to driving rain, in a swing door, down a vestibule of soft carpet tiles, across double fire doors. A lock with a six digit code: 801040. A place with lovely smells and cascading sounds like the Botanics in the 90s when Anton was but a chisel stick in his father's eye and the once a fortnight visits. The two captives were forced to kneel. There was marvellous smell of an Irish breakfast and weirdly either sun tan lotion, factor unknown, or coconut or some Malibu of it.

A posher than posh voice asked if they'd slept the sleep of the Just. Anton if he could have kicked himself would've, to recall who this voice was or what celebrity it reminded him of: Male, British, caring, assertive, *faux*-shy-seeming.

"Lads. Tuck in." this time said most likely to the job-well-done deliverers. Sounded like they sat after clicking heels and possibly saluting.

"Don't mind if we do."

"Look at these pair of devils." The voice, this posh voice was changing position, was moving to the captured's left.

"One Amazon, tick. One awfully nosy Mick, and a puff to boot. Tick 'n' KICK." That Voice was now behind and then it was right near them, and Anton felt a wild pain in his backside like he'd not felt since he was ten in Knave Orans yard, lunch time May 6th, a Tuesday, a fifth class knacker. Thirty years on he'd just gotten a size eleven in his backside, a kick so loud that Lucineide screamed on his gay behalf. Now that toffee crisp of a voice was an ounce of breath from their delicate ears. "What the fuck have you two been trying to do with our oil, with my gas. Best kill you both." The two Saxons tucking into their bacons grunted churls of agreement.

Martyr-material Anton's first panic abates, that psycho voice fellow moved away and was next heard some metres away, coffee being poured. If Anton had the *nous* of a James Bond he'd smarm some comment like 'Abyssinian coffee - upland, recently ground strength 5' and got himself another doff in the butt or elsewhere. Anton's chin was resting on the table grappling with the unreal pain in his sphincter region. Then suddenly a hand tugs away his blind man's buff. The reveal, golly, is so peaceful, a long table and five people just eating their breakfast. Behind them a 3D Avatar rainforest and cascade-lettes, like inhouse gushes for toss-yer-tresses *Timotei* ads. Anton looks left and hoodless Lucineide is knelt as he is; she has her squids on the Alpha Toff at the table top. The guy is cutting His cooked tomato in quarters and skewering some tripe and heart. The Man devours and goes to again in that stagey way that Hollywood actors eat in pensive over chomps. There is a middle aged woman to the Bosses right who must be a vegan by her gaunt and plate, opposite her maybe an advisor who has double helping of pork 'n' leek sausages and a nice mound of Effernagh mushrooms. Then there are the two functionaries devouring, those two Saxons. It's odd but Anton was weighing up how to outwit all five by physical force before his brain twigs but can't quite get the words as it is too, too Beyond. He also percolates the death threat that feels more likely now that they don't care his seeing what his unbelieving eyes are seeing. Anton gives the bad eye towards the lot of them as he squints disbelief one more time at the Patriarch, the Padrone, the top Cap-oh-nay at the table head who of a sudden says cool as you please:

"*The Croppy's Lament*; delightful air."

Anton resting his temple on the table, turns it, squints Lucineide.

"Yes; you are not delirious. It's him." says Lucineide to Anton without unclapping her eyes from the famous Toff.

Anton is a bit short in bearings. Still turned to Lucineide he grits through his teeth, says like he is not wanting to be heard: "that's the King's speech, *realisez vous*? We have the livin' King here." Anton's eyes well with pains 'n' aches: "King William the Fift' has just booted me in the hole."

"It would seem so." says Lucineide.

Two breakfast plates arrive and are placed in front of the prisoners. They are given no cutlery. The Saxon deliverers jibe towards the King "wait your Majesty Froon here'll tell us about the Geneva human right to hold cutlery."

"Nice one," says King William "Eat up your English breakfasts; you must be famished," said like's if a Dead Decent entity had gone downloaded thru His Crown chakra, assuming He had one.

"We are in Ireland so they're Irish; they're called brick-fawstahs." Anton stands up and as good as scoops the beans of the dish in his hands and wants to fling them almightily towards the Divine Ritful King, in a long line since Zadoc but Lucineide's arms swing along, cuffed remember. The beans fall mostly short but one lands on His person. The King takes no outward notice.

"None of your effin English beans," shouts Anton with unpracticed H-Block as if in the protection of a magical shatten *blanquette*. Lucineide tugged the Irish separatist's wrist and gave him the Brasileira glare for 'BEHAVE.' No effect.

"Rihanna was right. You are the friggin' AntiChr....." Lucineide gives Anton such a tug he can't quite name the full Messiah-upside-down.

The Sovereign does note by eye the name-call but in continued silence with the one bean on His green sleeve. Scoff for toff scoff and then His plate licked clean. Anton didn't like the cut of His tongue - in Chinese terms wet bellied and lilly-livered. Anton used think some times back before his working life, if he got cornered by a knacker on the 40C he figured he could defend his self; even if it took bites from his charming teeth to survive. Anton had impeccable, but hard won looking teeth. What care he took of his gleamers meant much frequenting of dental waiting areas. He was thereby used to the royal dead and wedlocks of the Crown Heads of Europe, their obscure Hohenzollern side families and Luxembourgeois subsepts of Duchy lines, all ming, bling, coiffed 'n' vazed. Male richness was always about the *bouffant* of the hairdo. Yours Truly was top selling starlet of these HELLOs and VIPs and Anton fairly felt he knew Him, King Hi-5, top of the range hybrid WV, half Nimrod, hemi Yokel when required. Most importantly he was born an hour before Him; so his mother told him at least twice monthly that he was 'The Right Full.' Anton's mother teased that even on a shite day, Anton was more, tons more, gorgeous than his Knobship and if in company Anton'd blush, and that complimented the vermillion of his curls. Talk of Tale of the Prince and the Pen Pusher.

Now Anton's sleep deprivation starts to talk: "You stayin' long?" No reply. "What do I call You?"

The King flips open a laptop beside him and types furies into it, wiggles its external mouse. He doesn't answer.

"I said are You stayin' long......, King?"

The vegan lady does the international gesture for zip yer gob. This flexes Anton further and closing his eyes, he decries inside his head a future portrait of his own dead heroic head, for once a non-selfie and not death-mask-dead more like *An Fearsig*, yes *An bhFhruen* and he glimpses his better side sideways in bronze limited edition in the foyer of the Department of Energy & Enemy Islands, Adelaide Road. ToDieFor-dot-i.e. in that Robert Emmet dock style speechless manner that his actions 'cross Time, will speak louder than. Hang it; he continues to give rope. "King. I said are You stayin' long?"

"Somebody shut Paddy up," edicts King William V.

The two deliverers rise and the heftier slams Anton in his temple, the one that controls reason. Anton liked watching boxing and could never actually imagine what the thuds did, more liked the lycra sheen, the posturing, the dollygirls overdoing holding up the rounds in L.E.D numbers. Anton's temple of instinct was about to get a dig from the other Saxon when the King said:

"I love trashy places. This place is special. Really. I realise this, Our war camp here is temporary but quite, quite special. My mother'd take us, let Me be precise, took Us once to Alton Towers, just once. Dad, the cu..."

"..... You've never experienced Centre Park." completes Anton.

"No. Never experienced Centre Park, any of them." says the King.

"Shame." says Anton really mollifying now, not wanting his person battered more. "So is it proving a good H.Q. all told for whatever You're at here?"

"The most discreet of war camps. A proper *Caster*. Latin for Camp, battyboy." The King puts on an unconvinced Yardy accent. Anton mid after-throbs recalls that the Prince version of William had done a semester in Classics at Saint Andrews. "Granted Our camp is a tad east obviously from the real fray. Batty-spud-boy."

"So what is the plan precisely?"

"Well seeing as you will be dead before lunch I suppose I can let you in." Billy Battenberg, flapped shut His laptop and stood. The rest of the table like-wised.

"In time for your 100 year's celebrations We'll be taking back the keys. We'll be reclaiming Our version of your, the ole fourth green field, our quarter of a jolly tasty Battenburg cake that We can eat and yet have, eat and have without end Ah-men-Ra. My England, My Scotland, Moy Wales and Me lovely lovely Oil-land, back in woyal Hands. If my Gran hadn't come here back when - we were going to lose you cheps to eternity. We're legal sticklers. We do play by the book."

"Excuse me." Anton worries about His gaoler's marbles. The idea of dying because your lord-whimsy Captor was barking multiplied trepidation.

"With this offensive We regain a firm "suzreignty" of your lovely resort of an island. To a certain degree your 32 county whatnot will appear to be running her self, bit like South Africa Oreo-wise."

"Yeh. Lovely resource more like." this from the thicker necked Saxon in delay mode.

"Nice one Vick," says His Liege.

If Anton had to execute an exam in English history and he only had what was in his head and what could be scribbled on his ample forearm: it'd be Boadicea in full Beyoncé from Netflix, sort of a Britvicky answer to an Amazon, 1066 'n' all dat done up as a long hall rug with helmeted soldiers, some bedridden scenes of episodes of *The Tudors* and the feck off Churchill victory smirk; oh and Mrs. Simpson abducting the King just before the War. Otherwise and foremost Diana, Diana, Diana. All those dresses, all those head tilts, and sideswipes of eyes and her gorgeous End *chez la tunnel l'arrondisement premiere.* Fifteen year old spottified Anton nearly cried when he saw the Princes walking behind their Mammy's hearse but he didn't. Later he did, bucketed when the God's eye views showed her hearse going along the car-empty M1 to Althorpe, three lanes wide; the Hominid's Princess being flagged at by miles upon miles of plebs-you-like, waving their little hearts.

"When the Monarch fails to set His royal boot on some fraction of his realm He loses it."

"By same logic Majesty you own Paddy's arse." says Saxon the Second.

"Nice ! Love it Trev."

"You're not serious." says Anton like he understands fully. Lucineide knew even less about English regal history and is being jounced about with her attachment to Anton. "Does that mean say if you didn't visit Yorkshire once a century they could leave you; or you could lose them; or Worst-shire say?"

"Must I repeat Myself for Paddies ? My GrandMother's visit in 2011; She made it by an Heir's breath......."

"Ground rent. When we pay ground rent we pay to a Lord, I don't know, Lord Kimmage some place or Count Argus."

"Bingo, Froon. You're gettin hot." Despite the pains 'n' aches and death waiting; Anton really liked hearing his name said by the King of Great Britain, Lord & Comptroll-General of every mortal from Kent to Kilda.

".... or in your and your deceased's case you were paying King Harold."

"Whah ?"

"Harold's Cross. Gih-dih-dih-ching. So pre Conquest."

'Creepy knowingness or what,' thought Anton who hoped of hopes that King was being prompted by some auto-*AuFait* on His notApple and not from His own batty buggerin' mind. The laptop was silver clad. Perhaps the King was perusing his clinked-in.

Play nice. "I have seen a picture of Queen Victoria visiting Dun Laoghaire." Fruen recalls.

"And most forget; My Great Great Grand Father came in July 1911."

"Was he an Ed or a.... ?"

"*Le George Cinq*. The spit of the Czar chap."

"Did he enjoy himself?" Anton is partly percolating the threat of imminent execution mixed with small curiousity.

"Not so sure. Bit of a grumpy Gramp. I read his diary. He met the Cardinals of Maynooth. They bowed particularly low for him. They had despite the intense heat huge black hats, like Ascots'. Reading between lines I sensed he might've been a bit scared."

"Of some Cardinals? Scared! Really? Whatever for - wasn't he Emperor sure ?" Anton is going so far as to anglicise his self with that mild over curiosity Saxons wont to stir the air about themselves with.   He can't quite conjure "Fantastic" but if he has to he will say it.   On the BBC they say Fantastic every three moments; no matter what is afoot. Yes. Keep some 'Fantastics' up the sleeve.

"I fancy he fancied he'd be blown up by some Gavrillo Fenien chappy. Have a screw bomb flung at him across the hoh hoh. He stayed in the Phoenix Park at the Viceregal Lodge" The other four Saxons still stood and were teetering a tad. William was moving toward His prisoners.

"Where I'm from King, we'd say Dih Pehhhhrk, not Pahk. The Voice Roy liv-id in deh Perk. You got me?" Anton is chewing the cud of the end of hours. He sees a hairpin in Lucineide's hair and smirks. If this were say a swashbuckle like *Never Say Never*, he'd grab that pin in his teeth and in a jiffy he'd have the cuffs off, the Saxons doubled over or head bashed. Heroine and him would be out of this botanical circus joint before you could say 'Billy Feckin' Wind-czar von Sex -Cobra née Bat-buggeree.''

"George Five was a jolly handsome Man. Do you like your looks, Froon?" the King is hind left.

"I never thought to notice. Much." The King had a great way of giving folk unnecessary Willies, just with a tweak of the tone. He had no weapon in His hand and no sharp or hot object within Reach as far as Anton waried.

Lucineide pipes up: "Your Majesty. What's the point in killing us?"

William goes over and pulls at her hair, butch as a Tex Mex villain - then grabs two equal tufts and starts to upbraid them. Lattice, lattice lattice. Tries a pretzel, undoes it then back to simple latticing.

"Kind of obvious isn't it?" says the King dreamily.

"We don't know that much," hastens Lucineide with a smirk.

"Kind of obvious We'd no Sister."

"Yeh; it is kinda Obvious." Anton overcomes his deepest autism to recognise the sociopathic in this Hi-ness. "I am curious. How long have you planned this "take over" ?" Anton had to tone inverted commas as his bound wrist made finger puppets difficult.

"Shortly after Yours Truly's birth" (smirks at His Own-beingness) "my Gran and grump data-gathered and concluded a lotta shocking proof: the North Sea had fifteen years at most. Future oil *quid*s was all in Paddy's pond; awkward, hell of an awkward, fuck off vacuum that needed a good traditional Brit-ish filling." and he does stagie pelvic thrusts to emphasise. "Remember Her Majesty's Government had managed with not great difficulty to talk down the Scottish finds by a factor of ten across the decades of their extraction."

"FANTASTIC........" Anton tries it. No impact so continues: "My boss Duhallow did say something along those lines but I paid him no heed about Scotland. We never thought much in our seas."

"Didn't matter who was in the driver seat at Westminster; Tories who-some, whatever, even that traitor to his Class, Lord Antonio Potato Wedges when he had the Energy 'folio. It was uncannily easy. Those Bravehearts love us so to bits. Jocks get 'roused when we wear their kilts for them. All told not too much skulduggery to keep them blind and stu-pad; a Merc here, a backhand fortnight to Barbados there, a not so veiled threat: we'll get you or yours an accident - or *in extremis* like your present situation outright character dissing cum make earth life hell life or an *aul* murder the better-half." He yanks Lucineide's hair into a strangulation implement. "Kill a naked civil servant's wife or cockamamie; what was Padraic's title precisely ? Concubine ! The Scots are such hag asses all told." The Saxons chortled and the CEO of the Batterburger Empire gestured them to be a-gain seated.

Anton is staring at the Saxon table and says it loud: "Not Fantastic that You said in vain my husband's name." Not so much to cool ire but to divert it, Anton recalls the Junior Cert Irish history book in his dazy starred concussion cum honour death-wish, dog eared pages, biro scribbles, Hitler moustaches, sometimes even on noble women: on Princess (royal) Aoife MacMurrough, on Mary Mother Aikenhead. There is this one image that is far too often reproduced of a lop sided table, the proverbial thousand words image for anything and everything from the Norman invasion to the perspective of the Stewart plantations: goofy Gallows-lasses or Glass-cows, a mass produced lino-like-print with raised goblets and eyebrows, Lairds acting as so-and-soes, seventies taches aplenty, all foreshortened in advance of the Dissolution of the Gael.   Anton looked at the table and thought history's like chickpeas; both repeats.'

King William V who more than many reckoned had had His Father accidented continued: "Ireland was a different kettle. Our war, your own institutions, your priesthood; We had to influence all academia, We had to pull so much wool, enough for a gorgeous balaclava for a really ginormous B.F.G., a really big green one and he's got no eyes......" He stops short so he can do His Anglo sneereen of a smirk to his aides and the Saxons have an inhouse guffaw at the iffy 'RAH-head quip.

Anton stares at the King yet braiding the Brasilian lady's hair. He pipes up, "I cannot believe this. I don't believe You can do all that without somebody seeing the sca...., the shenanigan; a whistle blower for example." Anton worries what the King plans for Lucineide's hair once He has made such chandlery from its silks. "King. I have a 2:3 from Maynooth funnily enough. The geology class teacher was class. We even I remember had some experts in to show how dissimilar our Devonian valleys were from the North Sea, specially how the Norwegian belt is so rich and that our slightly similar was not, that it had vanished before, before the dinosaurs. Can you fool all the people all the time?"

"Global experts. Easy peasy." The King points at His Self and His kind. "Similar to decades of putting blame on fat that should have been on sugar. Exact same. Position the right academics in the right positions. Tweek findings, replace data, misrepresent and misrepresent yet a-gain and do it a-agin till One's achieved delightfully, a false hopelessness. Thanks god my fucking murderous gramps did the donkey work - I, We could've never kept up with the endless Porky Pies. "

Lucineide is not liking one bit having her locks fondled and stroked. The King senses her discomfort and is coarser.

"For God sake. You're the Head of the Church. Can't You leave her hair alone You murdering Thug." says Anton.

"Royalties. I really love that term. So appropriate. Do you recall four years back your Air traffic control kept getting blips."

"I do."

"Unexplained shut downs ho ho ho."

"Shannon and further."

"A salvo."

"Really?"

"You Padds went all like 'Oh gosh where's the hacker ?'"

"You guys ?"

"Heal. Heal dog; more or less. Or more like kneel Mick-Bitches before our Bee-REX-it or we'll shut down your not so tidy towns, your invisible skies; do OUR bidding. When you allow the enemy do your soft and your hardware installs you get the comeback. When you misbehave, get over bromatic with the

Brew-cells we woopsy a virus in there, there, there, wherever necessary. 'Oh Brew-cells HELP HELP John Bull's got us be our bolix again'; gi'Me a break."

"Daylight criminality......." but then Anton sees what he least wanted, a royal Nod, a slight tourette of the *Tête*, some royal sign to the Black 'n' Tan sorts surely to polish him and the nice foreign girl off.

"Royalties for Rex."

"Daylight feckin' robbery."

"Music. Music. How about *The Wind That Shakes the Barley*." The King drops his rapunzelling. "Play it loud so the curious don't hear the reports; I mean the screams. Centre Park...." and he points towards His blue heart with His long fingers "........bids you enjoy your courtesy bog snorkel." With that he pours His Self a tumbler of Middleton twelve year old, every bit the pip that doesn't fall far from its Philip.

As dawn feck-acts the night the two Saxons grasp the prisoners, take them just some yards and it is believed they were placed in a pit beyond their depth, their feet shackled to the ground and a narrow gauge outlet in to it only. Freed yet bound river gushes in along channels, envelops about their persons and the Winter's Tale coloured waters rose to the weakening knees and rose to the loins by elevenses and the Socialite and the Patriot did not scream and it rose to their hearts by Angelus bell electric, heard on a wise wind from Ballymahon and the ballad goes they did not scream. About their throats the martyrs held each other tight and did not scream respectively but looked the part.

"JUSTIN, JUSTIN implores Lucineide o' the astral. JUSTIN is a night owl but these were exceptional circumstances. Some minutes after noon a mobile rings: ringtone GOD SAVE OUR GRACIOUS KING.

"Hi," says the King, "speaking" says the King. "Ahuh. Aha. Could work. No harm. Fine so."

CHAPTER TWENTY EIGHT

King William flew the double wheel chopper himself, hilariously over the homestead and townships of tens of thousands of unsuspecting self styled people, zig this way, zag tudder. Wireless Radio Eireann #1, presenter *darbh ainm* Sean O'Rourke talking about whistles blowing in upper GAA management when not since King John had the entire country been in such danger of being pilfered in the shortest space of time. The gorgeous noise of the whir tickled the King pink, His Roses are brash Red, glow on glow, the cheeks of all England. On He flies over the foglands, till brief clarity over the furzy frames o' the exchequer of cow fields that in a moment gives way to the ruined fosterhalls o'Kincora, the calm waters o'Lough Grrrr, the fairways of Adare, then cloudcover till Camp o' the Maharees. King William left leans His Body and the craft veers south of Brandon Mount wholly visible, leans and veers least this Fuji bermuda the instruments with its *chi*. On over sleeping cow parsley 'n' ole sods, over Mullinagleaming, Gallarus, leaving the Three Sisters doing the dead Navajos to the north, and cleaves then leaves the coast of the landmass o'er the secret island of the lastest yet High King of Ireland, Charles the Horse whose greedy sub-Viziers were high order-lucrists, sold their daughters and daughters' daughters for not a even trinket's gleam but a bent unbitten *pingin rua*; zero royalty me arse and the sky full of Him.

Revolving doorman Dot, no Dots, a man we knew once as an highly capable Irish civil servant, once again, in his leading role: His Majesty's Welsh speaking co-pilot Garth Pender-Jones. (He hadn't actually made use of his chopper pilot's licence since the Erdogan *coup* False Flag). Paul Garth Dingham Dots von Pender Jones Junior half shouts the coordinates to the King again. "five two degrees, zero nine four two five three two north. Lucky for some thirteen degrees, thirteen, twelve, sixty nine minutes west. "Roger" says the King winking. "Roger that." The twenty fourth Monarch since the Rosie War presses AUTO, unbuckles and aft he goes, not without rapping a friendly knuckle rap on Garth Dot's helmet. He goes through the troop holding cabin and gets salutes, salutes and more salutes. Moves through a hatch of a door, not unlike what a *Soyuz* might have. There in this empty zone strapped and gagging for it is Anton and strapped and sleeping is Lucineide, in matching natty boiler cum jumpsuits, a rendition shade of sunkist. They are buckled and duck taped for the duration of the journey. King smiles at them both, and Anton is struck that framed in His helmet that way He can see the ripple o' the caring William, not the Blackguard so-and-so of a spouse-killer that He'd become. The King hunkers down and stares Lucineide in the face, so much that she awakens. He writes on a pad: "I think you're surplus to requirements" and shows it her. She shrugs her shoulders, which the King mistakes for courage when it is that she has no idea what it means.

The King opens the aft door and a whoosh of Dingle Peninsula meeting the start of raw Porcupine storms the senses. He straps himself to a security line and for some moment longs at the Atlantic ocean, that morning, a fluttering U.N. blue. Anton imagines Him imagining rig upon rig, like as if stalks of fracking stools had bred like rabbits and Dryland-beneath-Jellylanes was one Woyal Warren. He further fancies the King can unsee the brine fields, like he, Anton his self can, like how Moses, whooshed away the ocean and there the ravines, the mohers, and if it kept widening there'd be an Upper-Kingdom Egypt expanse, a million square kilometres of mineral Righteousness, milk lakes and honey pots for Pharoah George VII and His ThereAfters to feast and have Their fun with, bankroll Royal Yotty Brittanique II, III too, why not. Anton imagines King William pinning O.B.E. after O.B.E. to CEO after CEO of 'Fat One' or by then and all due normalcies normanised, a subsidiary o'Brent Hydrills for bravery or the Chief Executive of B.L.I.P. for best merging; even as an ole fussing King, pinning the medal to a Sevenoaks sort-it sort, all perfectly decorous, dressed to nines, muttering at one another with their gobs plum with marbles 'n' gulliers, choking in their Saville Row starch top buttoned, not an echo of a boot in the hole anywhere,' nor .007% of the nation's silent cry of "Stop Thieves" nor the promoting of the mismatching of Patriotism for *Comprador*ation. As if King William could read some of Anton's mind, He turns and gives him a sound eyeballing. He retreats to the cockpit and Anton turns to Lucineide and smiles to cheer her. She is starting to come down with a cold and the Head of the Commonwealth and the Church of England, Vicarious of Christ possibly, as if born in a byre leaves the door open, so ignorant and their jump suits ill equipped for the minus twenty nine. The earlier Longford water up to her thyroid and now the Kerry air was making Lucineide onion weather from the outside in. Right before the gush of wind she had been wondering what shape Clivenden was in and whether he was keeping his tackle loyal.

"Where do you imagine we're off to?" Anton shouts.

"The Octo-pussy." says Lucineide.

"'Scuse us?"

"Just an old nickname Clivenden had," and she smiles despite woman flu.

"A ship of some description?"

"A huge octopussy," and she arches her brows and smiles to soften the scare for the quare fellah. "Our Majesty went and stole our "contraption." Just learnt that word Monday a week ago."

It took a dozen minutes to cover a further two ten klicks and then all their estimations began to lower and before long what felt like an alight, not before the Pilot had wrought a circuit of Vanity, of Victory, of downright Venom. Anton imagined their landing on an aircraft carrier likely clept HMS *Just William.* Anton cranes nape, if he wasn't mistaken they were about to land on a metalic atomium of a yoke, gleaming yet lightly, hugely bobbing in the Atlantic. There, as right as rain, right in front of his handsome face, the Future. Lucineide smiled her perfect rattling teeth line up: "the Contraption. Oh, I've missed her. Hope the heat's on."

"Am I dreamin' ?"

"Hybrasil 2525."

"That's a song."

"Poor HyBee," Lucineide little girled, "my lovely *bicha,* kidnappy."

The King once landed got His two best heavies to unbuckle Lucineide, removed her from the vehicle and flung her off the immense round platform. The plane was that noisy that nobody could log if she protested or screamed. Anton couldn't watch and worse was his shock made as the troops as the blades quietened could be heard singing WE ARE THE CHAMPIONS, MY FRIENDS AND I, in a kinda of a sort of a practiced har-mony, quite sweet if the circumstances were less murderous.

The Dubliner was person-handled up a gantry and a brisk enough wind flounced hairdos. 'Waterworld how are yih,' reckoned Anton in his head, looking about at the war-of-the-world's-gone-mad device of a thing in just what was visible above the waves, gleamy knobules so high and far, some golden possibly, some silvery, some brassy, all reached through person sized tubes of chrome and clinky clunking junctures of titanium keeping it tight. Walking was not the easiest as his bottom was throbbing yet and the shock of Lucineide's fling. "That which does not kill yih, makes yih abler," he recalled and mindfulled, then repeated, then disbelieved, then nausea. Another over sized helicopter had just taken off, was heading west south aways from Hybrasil 2525 and ascending. He imagined in hopes that it was to rescue Lucineide, that William sneezed one Whim then countermanded, that He was teaching her some lesson of English. Anton missed her already. She had saved him and he'd hoped they could have become best buddies if and when the War finally ended. Humans mostly believe wars must end; despite their unreliable beginnings and middles.

The newly landed group went down some steps on the giant landing disc of a zone, just a bit west of the industrial sized H for helipad and the sun touching Azores beyond the beyond. They quick stepped across at least a doubles if not triples tennis court of that reconstituted rubber, a circular court, its entire circumference was green, the centre itself was faintly diamond rhombus and its centre centre was dark blue with stars. There was a sash with some words on it but they were approaching it from the wrong way up. Anton wasn't the best at upside down reading and at such speed only sense he could make was it looked like the owners were MEDRO E OSSER CORP. They stood on this round blue part, some yards wide then it just vrrruped downwards, a groovy cylinder elevator sundering from the court. Vyyyyyroom they descended and the Ryanair blue of a sky furthered to a shrinking violet. They were well subsea when the smooth jolt, stopped their infernal passage and vvvvimmmmmh went some metallic doors and they were in the 'Prospect Quarters,' or that is best how to translate the Portuguese on the doors, Anton was no linguist.

This control room as its entry buttons get their punching sound the first *forte tutti* of Handel's *Zadok the Priest*. This is an immense if low ceilinged room with a centre focused about a round boxing ring affair, in terms of size and being roped off. Anton couldn't believe his luck, luck as in fortune, good and bad. "Christ. Yee've gone and fecked me map."

Mootching on his hunkers over the roped off map was to Anton's mind, a dishevelled sort of pensioner; granted he was in the stockinged feet, Primark cream, not shy o' retirement. 'Crikey the awol codger from the telly.' Anton was about to protest the abuse of his map, when the man took a pendulum out of his pocket and dangled it over some place. Anton craned his fair neck and saw that the man was having some class of a douse by the look of it off Hook Head, on some morsel o'prospect off its proud nose of a peninsula.

He says to the old man: "sunny south east, heh! Me dad's from Wexford now."

The seventh son of a seventh of a possible seventh son turns his quick eyes to the Principal Officer. He looks longer than is natural. "Who are you ?"

"I am Fruen, Anton Fruen. Who are you ?" asks Anton like Alice washed ashore on NewWounderland. He'd seen the original once in the Bored Gosh with fiancé; ballet of same. As she slid down her death slide rabbit hole the soon-to-be-married held each others' hands. His dead husband liked very much to caress the life line of Anton's palm, and on this occasion not giving a fig for the Transition Years giving them shocked bogger eyes.

"I'm the cheese who got the cat," and the Mayo sounding man nods towards the King who is being advised aways a bit in front of ometres about stuff and Anton follows the ray o' the nod and sees that Himself has that Charles way of cantilevering His left elbow with His right hand, the entirety propping His full Monty-baton chin with the dintiest bit of Plantagenet about the attempt at a dimple; it really helps Him feign interest in whatever the commoners are wittering about. Granted at this mo He is right interested.

Anton says "do you imagine for a minute He knows how the contraption operates?"

"Like a new toy to him I suppose. What do they call it on Boxing Day ? Please read the manual, Journey-to-the-Centre-of-the-World device."

"You're right. Impatient Wan that King."

"Wants the whole Universe in a gulp. 'About face, submerge and drill.' That's Him all over," says unlikely-lad Lar imitating standardised sergeant major as the King gives the thumbs up to his Deputy charged with complex button pressing. With that there is a shudder then a wheeze. There are then clanks. Hybrasil 2525 is withdrawing its tentacles into herself. Main wall of this *'Zona do Commando'* is all one fuck-off-sized sea & sky wide-screen, split screened, linked to live drone-feeds plus a satellite for a big reveal of the exterior air & marinating world. King W.V. eyes on screen Hybrasil 2525 commence a sink to a new low. The Conqueror, crew, long suffering Angolan prisoners and those Brasilians who preferred collaboration to death in a ratio of 3:7 feel their ears *flllup* as the descent speedens: 500, 1000, 1500, 2000 feet says the man translating the metric to His Imperial Highness.

Meanwhile yards away: "Lar Ewing is, by the way, my name. I work in security in Knock Airport."

"Shite at yer job by the looks of things." Anton indicates the big take over.

Lar smirks "I should've seen it coming. Our own security at the airport got ever so slowly compromised. Security personnel were

Irish, Mayo mostly, then English, them ones like *The Pogues* you know, children of Irish, cursed with those voices. The cursed ones granted have our hearts and our way of seeing no matter what *timbre*. I couldn't imagine the eventual treachery, in one blinking generation so I presumed there was surely some real Brits pretending to be children of Irish. Likely got special training. Then that, all that got blurred and 'they' started to arrive. Take the fellah that monitors the x-ray bags. You'd swear he was genuine newfangled Black 'n' Tan. Then the woman who zaps the bar codes, not an ounce of Mayo in her, pure Kent; what?" Lar had a habit of being over familiar with working class Dubs. He thought you'd have to be. "Home Counties anyway. Then all that was left was the staff o' the breakfasts. Oh fine no problem let the Paudeens feed fat and pig to their own kine but don't let them control the airways. 'Twas like as if we were not capable of ruling ourselves, let alone a regional airport."

This long rawmaish, in the circumstances soothed Anton who was gagging for normalcy. Instead of copping-on the elder to here-n-now realities, he fed the wee pent biles of the man.

"So you had a bit of a hunch."

"There were other subtle hints."

"Such as?"

"Well. In the newspaper section of the airport shop there was a lock of *Daily Telegraphs* getting sold and they don't fool you with Irish supplements. Do you have me?"

Anton didn't so he abandoned the line of questioning and said proudly. "That is my map you are kneeling on. "

"Are you deadly serious? It is very, very...... acc-u-rate. I have to admit I am playing for time." After a wee silence he implores his decrepit drugged eyes at Anton: "don't get me wrong I'm not Anglephobic. I mean *Two Ronnies*. Genius. It's just I, like

Nature, abhor straight lines." Anton felt the old man was recanting as he eyed somebody fearful enter the zone.

Anton cannot believe his eyes; who is it coming through the StarTrek doors but Dots in full military kaboodle. King William's Pender Jones Jnr. is our ole oil privateer of Lady Adelaide Road. He was exceeding dapper. Before Anton recognised the glint eye of the hatted military man he'd been thinking 'Nice' then next nano he realised 'god I just went and almost fancied archy enemy. If only Lucineide was about to share these moments and scares but she is a possible mermaid half a life-time away, spent with the unwelcome first rigours of the late fall.' He really needed to share. 'Crikey.' Dots sidles over on King's nod, Dots aka Garth Pender Jones *le Junior* overdoes click-heels, approaches the blanching Irishman, makes zero reference to their past together bar a straight faced sideswipe and adroits "welcome Mr. de Fruen. I see you've met our Chief Prospect Locations Officer Ewing. We imagine you guys are gonna really jell well. Refreshments are over there. We do 11s and 3s, courtesy Kelloggs bars, all the trimmings." Anton always detested that word 'trimmings.' Right then his loins yearnt to know his own language and what would normally been a thought became a statement: "what's the Irish for trimmings ?" "Not sure," says turn-em-forty-coats but I know the Welsh: "trymmings."

"You bastard," says Anton like he'd heard it a thousandfold from London copper serieses and says it with a real meant sneer.

"Tell him the name of his made over, more like thrashed offices in Dublin," shouts King William at the both of them.

"You tell him," jibes on Pender Jones née Dots.

King William towers up to His fullness. "Don't mind if I do: *Petri-Liam*. Get it? I like to keep things authentic and local," and he swooshes about in his imagined grass skirt, and a coy droop o'the eye, pure Spencer. "Tell 'em to get a move on."

Anton gets told to do such and such and Dotty Garth Should-be-in-Pentonville's, for-now, holstered gun is enough that he does as he gets told, removes his shoes and gets into the "ring" with the elder; treads the map. Anton camply does his own sort of hunkering in his choice wasp stripes o'socks, so dainty, if fairly smelly; well it is almost evening four of the worst of his ordeal. He takes time watching the pendulist and watches more, notes the elder douser's shaking. The two men are hunker paddling off two dimensional Wexford the way Chinese hunker anywhere they please. Anton chooses to ignore the gawp of Pender-Dots about his nape, reaches out as if to feel the old man's pulse with his own fingers. He places his own grasp about the older man's in a wise that stops his shaking left hand. The older man smiles frankly for him, pulls up his pendulum into his tight fist and closes his eyes, imploring, then shakes it out from his grasp and it falls like an anchor diving for surety, nay like a dice, trying luck for the gazillionth time.

It swings a notch over the sea over the baronies of Forth and Bargy, back out to sea above the sealine salty lanes about Bannow Bay, a tad from the Hook herself.

"Hhhmmmmm. I suspected. Same as Carnsore." Lar jots pencilled numerals in his pad with not a jot of celebration for the return of his cure.

Anton says with a wistful eyebrow raising: "how's about closer to home?" Anton whispers some coordinates to Lar Ewing who frowns. "Very close. Hhhmmm. Very, very close."

Lar shuffles across the map, like a man child, crawls ten feet, more, beyond Ballybunion golf course and further then stops at sea, way out, dangles the pendulum in the wide cleavage of the Porcupine, it swings and then swings some more and then the loadstone is like a pole dancer at Crystals, her lengthy tresses outflowing, doing the horizontal. Lar has a right euphoria. He has never doused for oil above the oil. The pendulum is so powerful it swings a horizon plain. His mojo is big time back and or the find is magnificent.

CHAPTER TWENTY NINE

Willem-Alexander by the Grace of God, King of the Netherlands, Prince of Orange-Nassau, Jonkheer van Amsberg, Marquis of Flushing, Burgrave of Antwerp, Count of Spiegelberg and Den Buren flies high as a kite o'er the screech-proof, folkless brine-sway. He has almost clocked up the three thousand hours of flight in the Eurocopter AS 532 U2 Cougar Mark 2. Like his father he doesn't give a fiddlers for throne stuff but loves undressing, undressing his wife, the sex act and precision. Despite and because of same he represents, albeit prefigures most of the needs of his bedyked Low Peoples with panache and due drear. He is every bit not his mother's son: Queen Beatrix the Wise. He does not overdo the biking monarch as mumsy had in her reign and Nan Juliana before her. Wilhemina his great nan wouldn't've been seen dead on a bike. This was Black Peter's Day in Holland; the day your childish sins are weighed. King Wilhem Alexander has never technically killed anyone yet with one switcheen of a green switch he is about to kill thirty seven: seven able seamen, three cooks (one part time) and the most beautiful youth of Ireland from Louth's freckliest, to Foxford's brownest. There's a wee see-thru plastic security flaplette over said switch which is purposely awkwardly pretend jammed, that then he technically has to smash, so his guilt'd be incidental and not warrant his being tried in The Hague. The rest was zip-do-dah on a wee screeneen and then *boynge* the tall Irish sailing ship got its starboard sundered in one whopper bang, from the not bespoken for Anglo-Dutch latest exocet of a thing, the 'quivilence of above one thousand *ye olden* Nassau cannonballs fired at some wee Javan junk o' nutmeg. So that is how Asgaard III got smithered all abouts th'East Atlantic by this De Kooy based chopper.

An hour after the "atrocity" the Irish viewer of RTE1 *News* is being jounced about yet again, what is this, round five, like how much UFC o' shockin' awes can the average votive, tax payer take? RTE, the national parrot pump, put it about that an it's-all-mine-yes-mine, Chinese mine had been placed in the Asgaard III sailing ship's patriotic path - and ou-the-feckin-boom she went, all that future and testy youth so much dolphin grub-u-like, like Ireland's answer to Norway's Brevic Island, the nation's best just mince meat scattered all over the Gollum Crest. Quarter fluthered wild west co-respondent Eyelash Knee-Jerk flew over the planks of debris and just the camera trained on her sad clowning face spoke volumes and volumes before she spoke. She looked aghast the waves like she'd found Bin Laden's grave, his Fu Man Chu gawping at the Normalcies beyonds the hasps of Death's double faceted doors.

The Correspondent couldn't know that Asgaard III's second mate, Euge Halpin had seen the Dutch chopper max-i-mus and imagined it was those red and white ones that do coast guard out of Valentia.... 'it might maybe be,' but as it closed, the largesse was more than creepy, then military threat, alert red: in that Euge's head that is, not in any chart of reason. So not a radio signal or bliperooh before impact and zap, just add water go the best mates of ole Ireland. Euge saw his lives flash fore 'n' aft as gorgeous body parts parted waves, just so much seamens' stains. He left behind one disloyal wife and three ipads, sorry children; some consolation, his cell-bridge to the next Eon.

Niederlaendischer Koning Willem Alexander, Baron of Grave and Breda, all the lands of Cuyk, Ijsselstein, from Crankendonk to the flats of Nozeroy was fully erect despite his 55 years of age;

his regal decisiveness being so rousing. His impact wasn't lost on able co-pilot Gretchen Van Der Movin. When he asked whether due process had been accomplished upon the target - she rogered back in double Dutch that it was so. She technically quoted Christ: "it is finished..... it is finished," which was a sore laugh, given what happens next.

The mighty Netherlands chopper banked back and returned towards where Hybrasil 2525 had been proud abob. It had taken off with love and friendship. There'd been no friction between the Nether People and the Blighty People for two centuries give or take a brawl o'er a sack o'mixed spices. After the execution of the AssGuard the Holland chopper flew for twenty nine minutes, forty seconds on 179 gallons of fuel. This was the end of King Wilhem Alexander. What a move by his a bit removed fifth or seventh Cousin, King Cleverer than Not-So-Clever Clogs, the Long Spenser. King Billy Five o' the Commonweal simply'd done some math of fuel over distance equals death by invisibility for King W.A. von Klaus & Beatrix. How does it sound when you radio De Kooy or Den Haag, 'mayday mayday our mythic purportedly non existent 23rd century oil platform has gone 'n' sunken on us. Yes hey day heydays numbered ! Hear yee ?' 'Half hear yee majesty. Come in your majesty (supposedly cross country skiing in the Ardennes) We can't locate a googling let alone a military slide of what the devil y'er on about your majesty,' referring of course to King W.A. of Flatlandia, Hereditary & Free Lord of Ameland, Lord of Borculo, Hygge-within-Het-Loo and Lord of all carbon-offset Sea-Reclaims about Great Turnhout, Lord of every perfect hamlet from St Maartensdijk to St Vith. All eleven on board Konigs-Kreek chopper were pulverised upon impact on the Porcupine, about that cleft that drops some thousands of feet, Ireland's own wet inconquerable Abyssal Plain, her Marian trench. Their souls will take such and so many gyres before they reach the far shore; each according to their damned meritocracy, each writhing against discarnation, tousled with envy, mocked by the glad snigger of porpoises tucking into main course Hollandaise, their dauphin smirk as glib as an Anonymous mask having the last bloody laugh, at the expense of human wiles.

iLash Ní Jerky hardly done with her eeriest ever reportage about and above the Asgaard III when Mi7c (Factious News Division) fed ever better copy from Vauxhall to Montrose. Inside three minutes RTE Heli-*Diffuseur* II was radioed and given new adventure XYs. 'Charlie Victor that' and the craft banked back east north east and there in the gleam of sun where the shards of the Cougar floated, there a tail fin clearly showing the Dutch flag, in all its illumnati-us prayfrus red, white 'n' blue. iLash reads the feed like it's her very very thoughts like she is Ms. Know-all Van deh Telly: "the Dutch on their manoeuvres in Biscay had gotten word of the Asgaard bing in trouble. They scrambled a helicopter, their specially best rescue helicopter and it's been confirmed, yes downed by a Chinese submarine's torpedo operating in Irish waters; I am assured." The British had really gotten better and better at the old Go-bells maxim: *zeh Bigger zeh Porky Pie - zeh Sicker zeh Believers.* They even provided convincing stutters and doubts in Eyelashes copy.

King William 5 had had Pender Jones Jnr. check the math on the fuel levels. He'd done His own childish napkin math of what extra royalty of hydrocarbons He and His Sort could siphon from the Royal ditched flying Dutch man. Jones did not encourage the regicide and believed in his left brain that was the 'sort of knee jerk action that'd bring on a Shakespearean tragedy jectory-wise.' William counter thought what 'clever cover for Our big black op in case anybody gets wind of Our Nether-Anglo heist stingy op.' William, like his paternal Nan, loved 'cumulations, but not like

Her, He overdid his sums. He reckoned the murder of His name-sake was worth at current and exponential prices £107,109,784,569 over the next three decades to the House of Spencer-Battenburg so long as the CO_2 of it didn't make a Venus of Earth. 'That tad of regicide concludes Our black op and goes not a little way toward gaining the sympathy of the seventeen point five million Dutch folk living in their dim boxes. Blame those slant eyed ones for the death of their anointed one.' He paused wonder, then recomenced and wondered the divine rights-of-way of kings: 'was dead king also of the same crismick line of Zadock as Our Self, matrilineally speaking ? Doubtful; proof being bad retention record the Dutch had when it came to colonies.' With the confirmation of King Wilhem Alexander's death He redid His calculations down. He had not yet figured out the immediate complexities of six o'clock News-itemising the regicide; 'Pender Jones department; he'd spin it for Vauxhall some way and they'd press multisend to their fave News outlets. Outspin Gandhi that fellah could.'

King William V was pleased that His prisoners had calmed to His will. They had a light lunch all together during which he threatened that Lar's Flo'd be strangled and Anton's mother be disembowelled at the low tide by Carn Sore-Point if they didn't cooperate, all said with wild organic salmon quiche melting in His mouth and locally sourced winter kale for veg (Ventry Saturday farmer's market). They hardly needed threatening as they were making great strides together; Lar and Anton had in under two hours mapped much of the the western Porcupine and found massive reserves that would make the Orinoco weep; a volume that'd put serious skates on moody Mother Climate's change-ability. Lar and Anton's makey uppey methods were caught on cameras and sound guns from many an angle. Pender Jones scowled behind his fork o' kale at the King's indiscretion.

Sometimes he wondered if the King wasn't learning Kingcraft from some lost handbook o' Nero's. 'It had taken joules of flattery and pandery to get the douser and his chav aide on side, let alone the years toing and froing to that dreery Second City of the Empire and all the 9 to 5 lie-a-thon so that just when it's all dusted King goes and kings at them.' As the King can read His subjective's thoughts, He nices:

"Pender Jones's whom I've heard was Dots Dingham to you, Mr. Froon, he's been keeping me abreast of you guys and your swing swong this morning. Impressive. This afternoon before tea-break We will have a first go; have an ole prospect. Zzzzzzzh," and He does a bad impression of a dentist while bearing an air drawn Black & Decker drill, cordless, *Man with the Golden Gun* style. "ZZZZZhhhzzzzz," He furthers. "Safety first......"

A tech-flunky in white coat entered, goes to the table, forty fivish, bowed, well, tilted. King taking the piss tilts back at him and in slowmo His head nod'd be about as long as His Granny did at the Garden of Memory in Parnell Square, Dublin 1, Mayday, Mayday 2011.

(Point of Clarification on that fulcrum 2011 Moment. QE2 had been sped-prepped by Merrion Road's third secretary, in the back of the tinted black Rover hying up the peopleless Sackville Street. Her Majesty was 85, all things considered; detail should be the least of Her problems on a day when She had seven appointments: three public, four not so. At Memory Garden She needed to lay a wreath, bow and step back in time. "What's the monument to?" sez She to Gyles FitzRalph or whatever his advising name was. "It's to King Lear Mamm and his children; somehow gone and become swans, can't recall how or why." The Queen rogered the speed-x-planation as She noted the *Phoblacht* Office on 1 Parnell Square. "What is the significance ?" "Like

Yourself Mamm; King Lear was sixty years on the Throne." When the bow in front of the big bronze statue of collapsing birds Moment arrived all the Natives of Ireland were squirming with recognitions, Taurus was in a Tangent to Jupiter and mean-the-while Queen Elsbeth was trying to figure which of the swanherd, who appeared equally beautiful, was the loyalest daughter, Cordelia, the one who loved his majesty, King Lear according to her duty, 'neither more nor less.' She recalled Her delight mixed with horror when She first read about Lear's betrayal by his elder daughters in Lamb's *Shakespeare*; Princess Elizabeth being then but Fourteen. She was Herself of the Brutal line via illegitimate descent of King Lear's loins, 108 generations past. 'We can see why elderly need to lay plans for well laid out HomeCare packages,' She weighed. 'Swan I'd once at Highgrove. No bigger a deal than battery gander; though it is only reserved for the Monarch' and so thinking, Lilith's by anoint-meant Head tilted. It was the first time She had been an unwitting Actor in the Unbeknownst of Her very own Stratagem. There was one mighty cheer at Porton Down that Moment).

"Speak man." The man didn't speak but handed the King a size-able print out. The King looks at it from its right side up to its upside down, to its leftward and rightward ho. He makes a blimey limey look of seeming ignorance and hands the paper to Anton who rights it up and peers intently at it. "Today's target, informed by that man there, your colleague from Knock-Knock-Who-Dares-Wins." says the King nodding at Lar.

"Gorgeous, so gorgeous." Anton wonders at it, thinks for a tick he should've been sleeping with the Enemy yonks ago if this was what they were capable of scale and smart alec wise.

"Make sense of it, man."

"It is sideways."

"Testing, testing." and now the King is pretending to speak into an airdrawn C.B. mic.

"It is a cliff, I'd say a devonian......" Anton is good, real good. The English he imagined loved their shires mentioned.

"Test passed. It is a four dimensional map in the flat." The King has extracted a large lump of wild salmon from its soft burial in the yellow quiche solution and drops it with His fingertips into His mouth.   "We are seeing it sideways."

"Yes. Looks that way."

"We drill sideways.   The first cavern We're after is three hundred feet from that cliff and that cliff is a mile below Our waves."   Already the wall behind their lunch table was parting; some medium sized squids were heading home and a faint wall of cliff is half seen.

King William stands in front of this marine for real Imax: "Royal HyBrasil has massive capabilities of fabrication and installation and most importantly fabulous ten-tackle." So saying He grabs His crotch; so locker room. "She can be connected to seventy eight subsea production wells at a given time and one hundred and five water injection wells."

He takes a breath and beckons over Pender Jones Jnr. and holds him by Him while pointing rudely at the two Irish: "Mother Nature would've way preferred Mick 'n' Paddy' here to have gone gotten lost in the sea-jungle....."

Pender Jones completes "........but no; Stanley met Livingstone and by god we've discovered the Source......"

"Carbon-me-footprint," augurates the King doing his bad Cap'n Sparrow.

Without dropping a gauntlet, nor smashing a *Formula Una* sized bottle o'Krug or fancier, King William the Reddies stomps the floor and low and beheld from bottom screen left a *Guinness Book of Record*'s fattest ever snake oil drill-bit slithers forth into a burst of lighting, revealing the busy dark of water and background, a premier league of a subsea cliff with all kinds of crustaceans and slithers caught short in the first in a lifetime glare.

"The fifteen hundred possible miles of flexible risers and flow-lines can be operated at once and her nine hundred miles of umbilicals and one hundred and twenty five jumpers work like one rather thirsty dragon. We can extract sufficient oil to quench a fleet of tankers in one bloody day, imagine. For now tankers when we are full on operational fatso pipes from south, from west, from north all coming through Shrew Wad-a-money Bay up Mayo way." After such a long winded sales pitch this is where the Villain would usually stroke His pussy and prepare the hero's death, yet no; the susceptible watch as beyond the foot thick window a metallic anaconda of a gleaming mechanism bursts like a party blower outwards, so belligerent, so certain and girthy. It moves, more like, he moves, as if it has a reptilian left brain of its own toward the jaggedy cliff, and without a preamble or dawdle its toothy foreplay drills the basalt of the cliff in such huge chunks that it makes no dust but debris falls off like so much soft coal to the greater depths. The true deep is that dustless. The thereabouts fish, all fangs 'n' whiskers, so deep so dark, a *schlep* of aesthetics short of dainty to say the least, scatter. They've not had their dinners disturbed like this since Atlantis went in on itself.

"Our platform has been operational since late Summer. Since our recent "procuring" we have altered her specs and from today we are confident that she can deliver 200,000 bbl/d peaking to 1,750,000 bbl/d when the right well is pierced. Gas no *objet*. Peak gas production from the test phase was 5.6 MMcm/d. Double me metric. I say double that."

The King's groupies clap along with the royal crescendo, then as if on order there is a gentle alarm; the see-through anaconda has achieved the womb o' cliff, back along its engorgement, a sweet oil bursts "at a pressure of 10.8 bar per square whatnot," maunders on His Highness. Hybrasil 2525 jolts to the right but rights herself right away with the inflow o' the black stuff. Above their heads, one bit of an Irish mile up, like cued and visible from a mix of satellite and drone-cams a tanker the size of Scattery Island, flying bar the oddness of a black arrow to its left, a Swedish coloured Bahammy flag, clanks to her halt. On screen a fatter, less flexible alumo-anaconda of a thing like a wavering vent duct in size exits Hybrasil 2525 and whooshes straight into the brighter underwater and finds easy intercourse with said tanker: *The Queen of Hearts,* her seven tanks equal three Semple stadia apiece. They spew brine ballast out and welcome in this most ancient of oil. Half a jungle of a million year old tropic swamp enters the world class vessel at a rate of one guinea a moment. The King's eyes are pounding and pounding. His Grandparents really had set Him up for Life. When He gets back to Blighty, what a party the 'Fat One' team will deserve. "You've worked tirelessly for past part of 33 years. Some of yee have died. You one and all deserve a cut o' the lucres" and concluding His 'maginary toast, drunkenly concludes "Steady Me notion of shopkeepers," and they'll clink their Middletons and He'd get loved into such iddybrits, a gazillian times smaller than the naked I. Such a party is none too likely that day. Wait for it.

Over the while lanes glides JUSTIN, so dead, so decent. Spirits would get an 'e in geography if they sat pass mocks. HE is some place off Kerry and is liaising with Lucineide's usual GUARDIAN ANGEL. While falling, Lucineide had gotten the inspiration to open her jumpsuit. It had a long stylish zip and thereby *voila* the lovely permanent tan of herself and her breasts flattering 'n' battering in her descent to *terra cognita*. And just before her aerodynamic lep into Dingle Bay *per se*, she just like that, rezipped herself, thus trapping a lock of air unto herself. So she is one lucky floating *Brasilera*. There is a skein of vertex between her and the suit proper and it engenders some warmth. JUSTIN is holding her hand in the Astral, calming her wit and arbitrating. Lucineide floats, must be, feels like hours. Finally a hooker chances the horizon, Sindbad sized and single handed. Lucineide is floating Vitruvian Woman style and looking up at the sky in motion. She whispers in her native kiddish Portuga hypo-thermo-dynamically "JUSTIN, JUSTIN. You again. Is it my time? Is it my time ?" When she finishes her whisper she thinks slowly 'this planet is one messy classroom. Low babies....' Then she hears: "oy, oy, oy." 'Is that JUSTIN,' she thinks. The oy oy oy is not pirate slang but 'hi' in Portuguese. Lucineide knows the voice. 'oh bless his cotton sox; my sex appeal has been answered.' Possibly her brain must be dulling, deluding; her sea sojourn is the world record for a surviving *Brasileira* in cold waters hours-wise.

Next thing she knows she is supping Knorr minestrone soup from a quart flask. Clivenden has his sturdy left hand on the helm o' the hooker. He whets his wedding finger and finds a favourable north easterly coming from Annascaul, sent by the spirits of CASEMENT, ASHE & ASSOCIATES. Given the Emergency; it was high time the Spirit realm got their "hands" dirty.

"Are you sure?" asks Clivenden.

"Of course I am sure as sure can be," says Lucineide who is that leant against his commanding thigh. The lights of Dingle were distancing themselves, even while enticing. Thrills of music were moving over the water in the stilly evening. Cold makes the notes fonder, soothier. "We've worked too long to have Hyby taken away forever and I owe it to Anton."

"If Anton survives they should make him Minister for Persistence."

"For sure." Lucineide sups away like she is an ad in the campgaz light for Knorr cuppas and wearing a tartan rug about her like Peig's great great daughter minus *dudín*. She turns from the coast. "Clivenden. You are a bit off."

"Oh, am I ? I was lost in one thought," he truthes.

"230 degrees and hold course."

He leant his thigh at the helm and made essentially course for Veracruz, cats' eyes the stars of heaven 'flected in the currents. They gained some miles along that heat lane that unLabradors our latitude problem and more leagues by the light of the shivery moon. Lucineide slept in spots but feigned much by him but not against him. The mere testosterone of his presence dissolved much of her melatonin. At one point after a thumpeen in her sleep she jolted up and wondered: "how the feck did you find me?"

Clivenden caressed her ear, her lobe, squeezed it and for the first time she realised there was a hard object in her little ear pouch o'skin, diadem sized.

He smirked at her in the low light and a week grizzle of beard contouring his gorge-in-ossity and she responds: "Crikey. A homing....."

"....... Just some tracker thing from China. Got it online. Cheap as crisps."

"Really."

"I've been out of touch. What state is Ireland?"

"Don't start me."

"A summary."

"Well you can't imagine how ill informed ravage Paddy is. Statist TV RTE News perfect-ly con-trol-éd," and insofar as Clivenden can he 'personates a ro-bot. "Newstalk, usual endless displaced patriotism dressed up as lad's blah. Today FM disco beat thump thump before anybody'd listen on the hour. Irish youth's attention span that shattered, almost like 'the Chinese have taken control of the Mullet Sound *gehhdooooof, gehhhhdooooof* ' house house house music. I'm serious. Everyone's all over the Chinese threat. *The Irish Male* had that the Chinese were fleeing after their I forget, their twin or triple atrocities: '*Sweet 'n' Sour Chicken*' some headline thing, awful or other. The enemy is well normalised; British forces and some Dutch vessels assisting, that kind of jargon. Nobody questioning nothing."

Lucineide gazes south west and Clivenden adds "oh yeh, almost forgot, King of Holland got blown out of the sky by the China lads; pull the other one or what." Lucineide exacerbates with these heard words so Clivenden concludes with a console: "I did hear an interview with a retired plumber from Galway on Mid West Radio, he used work on the rigs in the 90s so knew the shenanigans. The anchor was trying to mince meat him but at least he was allowed float the idea of who precisely in this war footing was controlling rigs and landfall and what given the chaos was going on in the Department of Energy Prospects; and could somebody please ask what had happened to the planned 'Gas-Give-away.'"

"So the tinkering masses know nothing."

"Not a jot."

"The concluding episode of Season 8 of *Hate Love* is more important. Who spiked Joney So-and-So's spritzer that got her kilt."

"Desperate. I think we are going to need to fast track Plan C."

"Not easy but looks so, daunting from this position," and he hams a broad-arm of the gorgeous dark horizon.

"But it is really, really lovely t'be alive, to breathe. Thanks Clivenden. Truly, truly. I would have merged with the Astral by now if you'd....."

"You are more useful on this plane."

"I hope so."

In the dead of night a giant wall of vessel passed them by with weensiest port holes. It was making east lumbering, its wash made a swell the size of the average house perchase. Beyond that in the eerily distant, what could it only be, but mythic Hybrasil rising rising rising again, its twinkles brightening and mesmerising, mirage of all sea-mergers.

CHAPTER THIRTY

The naked civil servant reeks. Not since he departed Harold's Cross some gazillion life lines ago has a flannel seen ankle or oxter. There he is in a power shower and two pass-remarkable security detail have just pointed at his penis like Anton had just landed himself in some life-like Kinsey-report freak-show experiment. He could really empathise then with pink triangulation, how it is to be an unwarranted unwanted minority, like Aha in the Land of Ramstein. He could never have seen it coming the persecution of gay busybodies; final solutions he imagined'd not been fashionable since blue, brown or black shirts.

"Paddy 'ere loves Conspiracies; Nige what caused The GREAT Famine?"

"Pull the uvver one how should I know." Victor, his m8 dumbs to his part.

"Vick you numpty the English went injected mercury in their spuds."

"Fackin Cap'n Fanta-Stick."

"No Vick real as; we'd a lab, was on the 'grinds' of Queen Victoria's I'll've-White pile." Anton stopped listening and presumably he presumed She Victoria wanted Sowshire to go blank, make a Palmerston Park outa the whole place, zebra crossings, World Wildlife Fun but no more nine million Mickileen Bridgets doing the Malthus position in their half quarters.

Wonder & Fear doesn't slink Anton's big prick even as the male shameless gaze of the two lesser British tits conclude their guffaws, oversee his towelling. With what aggression he towelled his self, a form of on the hoof exfoliation.

"Quite the show-er; Mick. In you ?" says Nige - the oink and sweat of him pure darts squaddie, the sort who could break your knee backwards with equal 'motion as he might hazard a wishing bone at table with the Misses in their two up, two down Heartlessshire and the fridge chocker with Iceland.

Anton clad the temple of his body with spare clobber the King was loaning him: Saville Row polo neck *á la* Beckett, black as, leant the forty year old the air of a deep tinker, genuine Reiss socks, slinky as, about the toe postbox red and by appointment Ted Baker undies, royal male flag of St. George ass-wise, sorta joke jackeen cum national affront rally. Anton literally and essentially was King size.

"Feckin' cocksucker Paddy," says Victor, less self-incriminatory than his fellow. Anton for the life of him never understood Cocksucker as a negative, if said, if not nicely, respectfully.

'These are dangerous sorts: these Dels, Trevs brought up on boot- strap 'n' Rod Stewart tributes, these Vicks 'n' Niges, they get bored too easily, especially when their fake *machiasmo*'s been outed; make that a double special of focuslessess on this sort of space station of a sea enemy.' Anton is half afraid that they'd come over all Abu Gharibe with nipple currents or which-dunkin' if he looked at them sideways so he kept his gaze to the newly laid award-winning non-slip floor. He has not been this clean since the morning of Padraic's funeral. As he tucked in the King's garments he wondered how he himself was cuttin'. A full length mirror gave him the response he wanted: 'you'd be mistook for Don Dow Jones himself - look at you - sure you're only gorgeous. Oh mama. Mama. Will she be ever seen again?' "Prayfrus."

There was an endless supply of Kellogg's vanilla bars, wouldn't get through fourteen hour work day without same; paper prospectin' takes its toll. There was also a bowl of complimentary fruit. Despite the time limbo aboard 2525, Lar and Anton are told it is the so-called weekend or so it seems from what's on telly but it may be all just on record. Lar, mile-a-minute puts the younger man to shame: pendulum drop, swing, swing, get the measure of each block, then the find, swing, swing; is it deep, is it worth the dig meaning how expansive is it, then swing swing, how many leagues its landfall. "Prioritise high volume," Pender Dots Jones had been told. In Anton's mind he is not collaborating but biding time. Keep well behaved. Feign, not so much being broken, but 'will o'God acceptin.' Fruen remembers an essay for Junior Cert; Treat for Robert Emmet and some speech he has to give, some words for Irish freedom's brave-heart Sake. He recalled the Britishers wanted to defragment the hero, to consign his character to a blog; I suppose some blog with feck all hits. Anton'd gotten an 'e' for effort.

HyBrasil 2525 had the Brazilian idealists' slogans here and there yet, in tile, socialist hopes in lovely colours, joined up handwriting style for authenticity. Shortly after the English take-over came their thrifty Sealink lookin' makeover. Example; the mess, when the English privateered it it was straight in with the wide screen - mostly SKY PLUS: then a cocktail bar, such a choice of warm ales. For relaxin' the proverbial L-shaped sofas that'd swallow you half-arsed, three life sized snooker tables, gorgeous sorta kinda Dutch low lighting the only halfway feminine thing about the place bar the pastelline Brasil green and yellow theme that came over quite Kerry football colours in uncertain lights and pertinent given present nearest landfall.

Our heroes are taking a break in the fine mess. One indulgence Lar shares with the dry civil servant is they cannot miss *Britain;*

You've Got Talent. The King likes it too and he's been drinking
for different reasons. The two Irish are handcuffed together on an
orange sofa. The head of the Anglican Church and Chief of the
Armed Forces is rather near them and plucking planks from His
commoners' motley eyes, telly-commentary-wise. He jeers on a
naff magician with a poodle, so groomed he is hardly dog. He
never barks or snaps despite his ordeal.

"Look at the state of him; nonce or what!" says King William
the Vth. "Ah worse still his name is Carty. Raving Paddy."

"But he sounds Essex," says Lar.

The wouldbe entertainer looks like a small version of
Emmanuel Macron, with that return-to-the-roaring 20s
flapdoodle dirty strawberry blonde moptop. He places the
robo-poodle in a box the size say of a crash helmet. He shows off
the box that it is dead empty. He has another vessel, seethru,
same size and it is full of water and he pours it in on top of the
dog in the box. The audience intake a shock. Hopeless ! The
young man, he is from Essex, opens two wee slotty doors and the
curly wee diggumses dry paws wave out. The audience amaze.
It is downright silly yet the judges' faces are shocking awed. The
dog survives. Essex's wide curved fingernails remind Anton of
Padraic's professional hands and their compass. Lar not quite
himself elbows Anton to nurture camaraderie but Anton senses
Death: 'how long before he and the ole man get chucked
overboard "live or let die me hearty," so much grub 'n' offal for
the food chain. Some big freezer ship'd come morsel and make
John West of 'em.' That is actually how most heroes world wide
end, their cut price valour is not blogged. It's the flippin comic
victors who control the recounts - be it in New Roman Times or
sing-alongs in ale-yarl-me-a-yarn houses the size o' homestore 'n'
more. Then Anton wondered if humans have tripe in their insides

like cows have that like flippant coral, waves about after mismemberment leagues down.

Saxons love practical jokes, 'aving larfs is their third favourite pastime after vacuum fillin' and believing everything FANTASTIC. The 55 odd million or whatever of them love nothing more than taking the Mick and as their King, William V, loves same extra. "Here yee, here yee, let it be known that Ireland's talentless." When he is drunk his better Althorpe leaves him - he bloats like a hoover bag o' Thetans, vying tit for that tat - hopping evil channels and the eachiest moment, resenting each and everything: "I mean think about it Gilbert O'Sullivan versus Sir Elton. Give Us a break."

The two patriots of the couch stare at His outbursts, at a point where the air itself is stale in front of the royal Lips. "Granted one has real-ish hair but hair apart. Talent. My god. Or Westlife versus I don't know Robbie Williams. You see where I am getting at."

Lar as he is older, dares to answer: "Gilbert O'Sullivan chose to reside in your realm but he's a Waterford man."

"*If ma could see me now, what in the world would she say.......*" talk-sings the King.

"Yes. We can only imagine." Anton whispers. The King ignores the asnide but then can't, "well Who's in the Triumph's driver-seat now ?" He pulls from his jacket inner breast pocket a long legal envelope, flashes His prisoners a gooh at its contents: "'riginal title deeds 1707 for all that Mayo bog place. Rossport refinement bog." The two Irishmen can't fathom This latest gloat. "Uncle Edward got these for Me/Us. Proper homo he is, not like your nonce-ship."

"Sir Elton......" starts Anton.

"......*and Nikita you will never know anything about my home.......* It is just so bloody lovely."

Without consultation the King changes to some GTI race from Denver, Colorado on SKY 750cc PLUS. As the bikes snake their given track He imitates their vrooms, de-accelerations, their crashes in Thunderdrome. 40 is the new 14.

The rally racket is perfect cover for Lucineide who is climbing an inspection ladder of the monopod. She is wearing a tankless snorkel. She is over her cold and has done some heavy duty breath work so her temples are pounding. With each drag up she builds her will to reverse bad odds. She reaches the 490 metre line on the protected, protracted ladder. Twenty more clombers and she is upper hold entry, its combo unchanged since the bousy glordydays. She knows all 2525's rivets, conduits, pings 'n' foibles. She tomb-raiders into a duct that a tot could run in and crouches her way in at an incline. The duct is a circular lung for the score or more rooms that enterprise the vessel's kilometre circumference. Bent double she moves only forward.

William V has his childhood interrupted. A middle aged man has entered the mess in a white coat and dawdles by Him. The two Irish give him half wit.

"Your Majesty. Porcupine 1 is drained." White coat's name tag simply says "Reg."

"Yes. Move the extractor on. Skip to the biggest in sector Y. Ehm. Seven from memory. Go for seven, Reg. Cheers." He dismisses the Reg. His "cheers" was cheerless. The King turns his attention span to the 7th son of a 7th son: "Lar my old fruit. Gotta let you in on this. 7's a gazillion Wemblies. Crazy. When it's empty, 'oil gone,' three to two there'll be a 3.5 richter wobbly jobbly?" He raises His self from the sofa slouch, writhes His arms and then His fists, wiggles Himself entirely. Genuine aftershock doesn't look anything like His royal Mime.

"The odds are about 20:1 chance; quake-wise," says white coat not quite left.

"I'm not a betting man..... King." Lar doesn't disengage eyes from the telly. "Don't you risk sectors, zones; six and eight?"

The telly show has a singing three year old girl in sequins, singing up at her father who responds in Italian. He is tuxed and tubular. Much of the camera caught audience are hand fanning their cheeks beneath the eyes as if there are any real tears left to shed in all the shires o' Blighty.

The King answers too loud: "Not at all - at its thinnest the cavern walls are ab-so-lutely massive. How massive?"

"Two hundred and sixteen feet your Majesty." Reg dawdles by the door in case his Spock is required more.

"Safe as houses." The King was about to offer Lar a drunken O.B.E. but the Mayo man's smarty-pants answer-back de-pre-be-knighted him.

"What did We get from Porky 1 ?"

"Point nine million barrels Your Majesty." Reg staccatoed out.

"Not bad. How much's the ole Brent *Crudités ce soir*?"

"$182.26 the ba......"

"Gloaty glue. Best text Pender Jone's fellow in Riyadh and congratulate him from one mess to a.n.other. Keep those factions schisming. Pass out the scimitars till that pack of Princes and jokers are in a rat hill as high as I don't know, as high as the Gurkin. Reg - we are gonna have Uz some reg-ime change."

"Your Majesty." Reg clicks heels and obeys the vague etch-a-sketch of drink-taken geopolity; agrees even though his remit contract-wise and expertise-3D-wise is volumetricks. Reg Parsons is the volumetrix byword industry-wise.

The King knocks off the telly. This leaves just the chug of the gargle-knots of the massive machine gyring its own hour-orbit noise-wise. 2525 is shaped like a tory top toy generating its own tidal umph from its own centripetals. It would get a Green Award for its carbon neutrality were it not so adding to the demise of the planetosphere with its *succubi*.

The King joins His fingertips like Lesson 1 in key decision making, *Ahar*-vard Busy School. "I have decided. It is a bit early I know. New Year not far though. Anton; what would you say to an ole knighthood. Sir Anthony........ hhhmmmmmmmm? Rise. I mean you've been exemplary, spiffing even......"

"You Majesty. I'm really touched......" As Anton scans his very own left brain for right words he espies Lucineide's gorgeous face framed by wet cold hair gaping through the fire security wire grillade of the escape door. She is eyebrowing him messages that are way too subtle.

"Your Sovereign Maj..... if you had a sword handy, I would bend my knee this moment. The honour is so beyond...... Does it take long, the ceremony? Should I find some garters ?" Anton is buying time: two for twenty. Buying time on whether to prolong life, bite the King's shilling, become the 1st Earl a' Coddle, Barren Froon de Gasyard or die and be terraced, Ronanstown-*sans-drainage* a Close, Anton Fruen Close.

"Bollox." King's gone strayed those 2.75 units of alcohol beyond His moral compass. "Yes I'd fuckin de-Mick you from your head you Sell-out-take cunt if I had a flaming sword." Behind His drunk word-barf the King's better Diana-rama eeks out but It can't get air-time, yet He had imagination enough to conjure right then Anton's childhood home in some East Hammy Unit F burb off a burbo Dublin and lording it over this maquette of a typical royal imagined 90s living room, a big feck-yiz framed photo of military 'tired Michael Collins swaggering to work in his jodhpurs, ordering this or the other English agent's death before he'd reach his desk let alone elevenses; if he had one or other. William's royal Shyness could see the battle of the Ages and His place in the chain male of its sound and fury. King William, divine Authorization stretchin' Rulers back to the parKing, Scoliosis of Tesco, to Canute, to Lear, to Anus de Troye - all given, He assumed, the oily thumbs-up be battered Zadoc. He knew He'd become a Bolox about six months after His crown tickled His Ears. How He wished back His better side. When he was plain ole Bill Mountbatten Windsor he'd land chopchop in the Snowdonias and rescue hypothermic plebs with snapped extremities and chattered lives. His can of Bile, Self-opened once his Nan went back to Heaven. Queen Elizabeth II's death hardly put a rent in the temple's curtain but My God despite Her age She could keep the proverbial can of worm's lid - tight as.

Lucineide had been trying to semaphore Anton that as soon as she burst through the door that he and Lar should grab King William garrott-wise from behind with their handcuffs. Instead she opened the door, quiet as you please. Its combination in her rain-woman ice cream headache: 1.0.3.0. She was three degrees shy of William's eye-ken and damn it with one swagger of her made-for-walking-boots-of-hers and we're not talkin' hill-walkin' she gave the King of England a hurtful up-Purdy to His Patrician nose. Blue blood everywhere. She grabbed His neck in her arm and said totally winner-takes-it-all: "what shall we do now?" Regicide was only a clack and a scrunch away in her ample hold-dot-b.r.. The King tried to heel her calf but she simply upended His tall drunkness. Just as righteous Triumph was scrunching over private grovel the King looked up and sneering said "Crispy Crispinianus" and nothing happened and then He said it right "Crispin Crispianus."

You know those devices that you clap loudly and they find the keys - 'cause your keys are attached to that contraption. Well the King of England's safety net in times of DANGER could even be a whisper, those two words. "Crispin Crispianus" and he whispered them even huskier and all alarms went off and some paramilitary hit squad types could be seen on monitors, click as a jiffy, thronging corridors moving toward the present fine mess. They had stun grenades, tear and laughing gas, sleeping pellets, nets, tazereens, pepper mace, rubber bullets the shape of cones, bayonets as long as is necessary, door smashers, and all sorts of spikes and hatchets. It was all about live capture. A hundred Darth Vader get outs with one intention - "preserve that Monarch."

"Taxidermy would be too slow for the potato-likes of you lot and this, this your jungle bunny call-girl." says the villainous King. William sure hadn't finished finishing school.

Lucineide hiked on His lumber and He did a wight woyal Wince. She, yanking Him to his feet, eyebrowed clearly the exit of her entrance and the four were gone.

Clivenden was scraping recent wee barnacles off the enormous buoyant prong that keeps 2525's giant prospectus abreast of Neptune's sine waves, no matter how swaggering. His hooker, tiny against the girth of the vessel was tied to a ring just below the recently riveted rename: *The Princess Charlotte*. His scraping revealed ..*BRASIL 2525* in Helvetica.

"What took yee so long?" he japed and scraped.

Lucineide answers her excuse for a *beau*: "Just William here was doing some rather unnecessary survival of the fittest. Weren't you not?"

"Weren't you not!" sneers the imagining Emperor of the Never Setting Sun being King-handled into the boat by the two Irish patriots, with the point and nod of the Brazilian oil-Proserpine.

"Shouldn't we get a move on." Lucineide urges Clivenden. Clivenden is like a child who doesn't want the perfect picnic of a day to conclude. He doesn't motion to unrope the hooker till *HY* is public again: scrape, scrape.

"Ballygall ahoy." Clivenen is referring to a windswept ape-shit of a hamlet in a redoubt between hills looking west on the arse end of the Kurka Gheenah peninsula, where Irish is still persisted upon. On they quest eastish and gamey porpoises disposin' and leppin' in the ever dirtier lee of man's proposes.

Clivenden's hooker's yardarm blocks for the most part the enormous scare o'swells from the fugitives and His Majesty, Prisoner. They hye mainlandwards, Inishvickillane, an island, rising and falling in relation to their swelled heads. The swell is so high and so wide that it takes them some time to gather that there is a low flying chopper thing on their tail, gaining. Clivenden is trying to get a signal for his Whatsapp. He gets one on the peak of a trough. It pings a lot with new messages. Then some gunship of a thing departs 2525 and between its imminence and the swell; the meta-farcical swanny is lookin' nye for our anti Royalists.

"Brilliant. Brilliant News."

"What's it?" Lucineide cannot imagine good news when such a Black Hawk of a thing is now blocking the winter moon.

"They have risen in Dublin. Our allies control most of the airwaves or so it says."

The King is puzzled and looks it. Anton is testing his hate level. He has never deeply hated anybody in his life. His Dad he once wished'd die near a sand bank when he was swimming after porter and a sangidge of Denny's ham. Anton was for a thirteen yearling gangly yet golden, watching the grown man doing the waddle stroke. His death-wish was more the glean of funeral drama empathy than wanting his excuse-for-a-father's time done for. Regarding the King of England he felt a dumb sorrow for Him; what an Upbringing? But he really wanted if not two, at least a minute's Hate, out of respect, if for no other reason; for Padraic's sake.

"King. Did you actually order my husband's murder or did You delegate?" Anton's question has extra weight as he simply looks west and does not even deign an eyeline with the King.

The King ignores and scans those same seas King Charles III, as mere Prince had only a generation earlier had the wet dream over, all that Ukrainian-sized possibility; 'Popsickle leaning on his crook on the south coll of Mweelrae. 'Dad you bollocks. Why do I do the dirty work?' is a likely Williamite thought. William saw the gunship clearer nearer. He couldn't be arsed if He died or not in that cold Dangle Bay watch; His Darwin was that sozzled so whether His rescue became a slaughter or one of these plebs stuck the knife in He couldn't give a fiddler's monkey-fanny and His wrestling bashed face said as much and to stir the stew He did what He did best: insulted.

"Sir Anton; what's that you said - couldn't catch what with the wacket?" Anton grabs a really smelly sack made of sack cloth, used for lobster driblets. "Fetching." says he as he puts it over the King, a klan hat of an idea. 'Abu Ghraib digs with the other foot,' Anton thinks as he pulls the King up and lies against Him with a sharp metal yoke he found by him, jabbed at His throat. "One false move and You get this in the bleedin Gullet." Lucineide smirked at the refound Dublin twenty four or more of his. Anto was so tired of well-behaved; time to uncoil his own civil serpent.

Anton thought if they survived this very unlikely moment what a future for Ireland with its swagger of petrodollars about Herself. Ireland would be seven star duty-full Dubai and the Saxon lands would be just...... sunder lands; the fairways 'n' links of Weybridge'd be briars on briars, the tills at Waitrose'd jam. Napoleon's so-called shapeshifters would get ASBOed, the key trun faraway beyond the Silly most isles. All Sue Ryder's widows sorting DVDs of Morse 'n' ole frox will crimple, their

Brexeunt fine comeuppance now. All the gas peoples of the Western World would be more than grant aided to utter the most melodious of Irish so gorgeous. Jump an aeon and the gists of English will be just ole scratchy jots on Rosetta stones. History knows no logistics hiccups; award winning or not. For the record Anton's Irish extends to *LAW BRA EH*!

CHAPTER THIRTY ONE

The Century of Self procession to give it its due went ahead 'spite of the civil furores. There were floats sponsored by ESB, by Ogygia *Teoranta*, Aer Lingus, by Sutherland Outcomes. MyFace and AppleEye pulled out - they didn't want to be seen dead with the d-tested King or so they claimed.

The Chief seaters in the rain-proof stand in front of Dublin's General Post Office were not the usual top brass. It was like all the chattering classes had been sent for re-education to God Knows, Term-in-feckin.' It was the most glorious triumph of innocence over middle-of-the-rotary. Taking their place half of Clondalkin garish cheering and Rothmann's reds glow on glow; third cousins even of Anton had gotten a seat. There was a multi-screen set of giant screens hanging mid the GPO six pillars of wisdom, behind that an awful amount of squareens of glass were still smashed from the Insurrection whose last plumes were hardly above the city now. There'd been a westerly squall all Monday, minus nine one night in Brrrr. The radio stations were playing Damien Dempsey, Christy Moore. Dublin was blue in the face. Enja and U2 were banned. Sinead O'Connor made her stand, fisted some air at a reckless press conference outside Wynn's Hotel that'd become Revolution Centre; they'd not quite gotten their Robespierre voted yet but there was a wide choice of also rans. Presenters The O'Rourke, le Darcy Ms. Finucane, an Ivan, terrible, dead to the world; their and all clever talk garrotted be *sugawn*. Pictures of new found collaborators were hourly peopling the multi-screens, their flashes 'flecting over what'd once been British no-Home-togoto Stores. Due hate and orchestrated hissing for images of Nige 'n' Victor, for Ceretic di Lemoncello, for various versions 'n' costumes of the Pender Joneses Dinghams or whoever he/ they was. The fingering puppet 'government' of the second Republic renamed the main street of *Das Kaptial*, provisionally translated from the rich Irish as 'Avenue of the Fulfilment,' formerly O'Connell Street. There was finally a proper use given to the Spike. She got a tricolour flag, camogie field sized and it blustered by its own might, wavin' Connolly Station-wards and then with a wind shiftlette pointin' towards the 'Custom's House of the People.' Sat on the Spike-top upside down Britannia's stoned head. The first act of the Second Republic was behead Britannia Commerce off dome-top of 'the 'Custom's House of the People,' stop her sneering that way. Since 1790 her female-ish gaze'd been looking south east sorta Bristol-wards; her pockéd rock-face hardly takin' in the dockers and inclined as said UKwise like she was beaming Ireland's customs or checks and balances that-ways. She was a lot less relentless now, scured on the Spike, itself, a municipal acupuncture visible from all about Dublin, which herself for that week at least might've been renamed San Antonio. 6 December, 2022. Finally the Nation'd zimmered herself 'cross the 100.

George Lee had sworn allegiance to the Second Republic and so kept his job at National Telly (NT) everything became of the People. He was the Nation's eyes, ear, nose and throat during those mo'mental days. Before the dignitary stand he held his big blue mic sponge, a Grover-muppet bent double. Lee was speaking "there is no way to really dig the change that is so felt, so everywhere. We have lived beneath an hidden enemy for the past decades. Our railroaded "re-unification" was like 'auh Mick - have that back - Sly for gizz dat back.' Our reconnection to the Commonwealth, double edged as Brexit compromises finally got shown to be grotesque time-wastings, biggest two fingers to intrin-sick Democracy ever. We were being railroaded into a new feudalism. English workers also and always duped. Estimates rise as to how much the gas 'n' oil heist had meant to them Royals: something between some one point something much trillion and a gazillion former euros." George looked like he'd get a heart attack. People-B4- Prophets got interviewed then swing frame and it's former Secretary of NRG, Light and Entertainment, Duhallow, unused to glow of fame. He'd turned his plaid coat inside out - he was like Pope Francis on steroids, such was his leftward putt-option for the Poor. He explained that the concelebrants in the conspiracy to defraud were like so many statistics ratio-wise: he placed himself with the woebegone majority. "80/20," he said, "80% terrorised into compromising their nation, 20% did it for the sheer joy of treachery and the top dollar." He implied that the young in particular could not resist the shillings of the "Anointed," that under 35 cohort about the Grand Canal Dock. "No loss their round-up," and down along the Dodder they got marched into the *Viva la Revolution* stadium where they await trial by rain.

George Lee: "Let me introduce, People, former Secretary in the Department responsible for oil exploration. Professor...."

Duhallow " Doctor'll do. Actually Jarlath, Jar's sufficient."

George Lee: "Whatever you're havin'."

Jarlath Duhallow does an emphysemack cackle that'd be best heard among the spittle and sawdust of the rare-auld pubs of Dublin 7 or 8 or even 5. There is such pressure to be as ornery as once there'd been to be iPaddySmart. Case in point The Newstalk building had been firebombed. Ireland was withdrawn from the Six Nations Championship. Nobody felt free to commentate in case they'd've their spectacles ground into the ground, Polpottwise.

GL "You've survived."

JD: "I did. I did my bit."

GL: "Jarlath. They threatened..... Tell us precisely how were you controlled."

JD "My children." and he nods and his eyes widened then shut, then welled, then blunk, on open blink his voice said: "they "car accidented" my favourite cousin. Aren't they the great researchers that they'd know the likes of my favourite first cousin; the one that was most the sister to me. Then in no uncertain terms they made it very, very clear that my children would be next if I did not do what they wanted."

GL "Well that pattern is becoming more clear. Can you prove....?"

JD "Not at all. Not at all." and his blustery 1st in history of geology Maudlin College came back so he countered: "but Jezus, Anton. He was the worth effected. The two main men in his life; his husband and father both taken from him. Imagine. I simply can't. I can't fathom that depravity......Speak of the return-of-the-hero or the what-ever-you're-havin' Mister-Spy -who-cam-in-from-the-cold......"

With that the classic out-stretched Austin Princess baring the guests of honour arrived. Anton John Sullivan Fruen, his Mother, his Mother in Law, his favourite sister. Tanya done up to the nines; why not? The clamorous crowd boolybusted the sky with their liberties and west of them. The clapping was that vigorous that the flag o' the spike had a waft of her ownio just as the necks of the latest e-lite craned higher as a guard of honour air corps fly past sprayed trick colour chemtrails declaring the new and heavily made-up Republic. When their napes relax another car slinks to the genuine red carpet of the people. It is some class of an Audi, Leitrim colour coded, no Brasilian but the local gurriers think its Kingdom-coloured but boohs quicken to cheers as stiletto then ankle then choice knee then not childbearing hip then

354

the full of herself exits the vehicle: Lucineide and from the passenger side Clivenden. Specious roaring as they conjoin with the famous five besitting themselves where heads of state ought, at the place where the green 'n' gold rosettes 'n' buntings are densest and the seats soft as Protestant pews.

First in the parade was not so appropriate; Aer Lingus with their open skies theme, all too overfunded and neoLiberal, a byproduct of what'd be formerly be known as "joined up thinkin.'" But they'd had no time to adopt to the new west of west left-a-bit mores. Girls dressed as Aer Lingus coloured macaws threw sugarless sweets to inner city children in their droves, their worms crying out loud. The entire parade could've collapsed into chaos with the greed and glee. Next the reformed *Garda* Band played oddly an upbeat *Yesterday*. Then there was instead of the cancelled Royal Grenadines, a noddy to the Commonweal, there was the Ronanstown Samba Band, two hundred bright people banging bin lids, bugles ushering in a new state-of-yiz. Then there was a double decker sized Gulliver puppet with strings attached pulling shiplettes that had hastily been altered so as they were clearly enemy hydrocarbon prospector 3D analysis vessels to those half in the know or could appreciate the extent of knee-high know-how and clapped their recognition. Then the Union of Midwives, then the Nurses of Terminations Corps, then in lines the prison officers in the different four cuts of uniforms going back to 1922. Latter planned and allowed to go ahead as long as *Fields of Athenry* was played by their trombone band. Seems in the 1950s even men looked like *Bean Gardai*. Giantess Countess Goreboot was next, huge with gunslingin' arms, then even more outsized, really for the kids a re-purposed B.F.G. with wobbling eyes that could find children, this time one time Minister for Adoptions, none other than Noel Browne every bit the gangly Giacometti. Then there was the Midlands gymnasts -

their club made a great people pyramid with a golden zenith with *In Memoriam: Padraic Dempsey* made be letters on their t-shirts. It walked in silence and was meant to be the pyramid that represents one of the Siriuses, earth's rendition of that point of the Sky. There was a grotesque of Eamon Devalera and Archbishop John Charles McQuaid on the back of a Scania writing the constitution in the latter's parlour. His Grace's muppet was so big that his lace yerk was as wide as a Howth net and rent buoys clinging to it for dear life. On and on went the parade and disrespect after disrespect for the old order. The Church got another cheap dig and the older fruitsellers boohed it, another repurposed float from Paddy's Day, a giant twelve year old Patrick in a skimpy sackcloth kilt sucking bejaziz out of the nipples of rough as guts sailors, themselves personifications of Rectitude, Compromise 'n' Gold-diggin.' To put that in proportion a given nipple was the size of a bucket. Remember St. Patrick ran off from the sheep plantation near Crossmaglen then hadn't the reddies for passage back home - so he offered the ferry owners Talent in kind. Next and in honour of fresh deceased Cher, a Cher-a-like sphinx kind of, done out as a roughly mermaid Hibernia and her bare breasts hard pressed by wild cats shedding, not milk but clampit's o' black treacly oil. The Leeds Irish Association were on an arctic playing I DREAMT I DWELT IN MARBLE HALLS on fifty harps of various eptitude and a-tones. The Norwegian Embassy sponsored a hologram of a Viking aiding a naked blue Celt in her fight to extract fire from the throat of a sea dragon who lived more than five kilometres beneath the seabed. Their tanoy blared Aha's TAKE ON ME. Downtown Antonoöpolis was one ravin' ground zero that hi noon.

Then there were ten thousand *brasileiros* in puffer jackets; they'd just spilt out from all the language schools bound by the canals - they were a 5th column awaiting Clivenden's command to unite and take over. They'd been lying and waiting for their command and were all empathisers with Hybrasil, with People Ownership. Their idealisms put Celtic snowflakes to shame. History was being rewritten on the doubly. Then those bound for re-education were paraded in magnolia coloured boiler suits, tethered at the ankles. Then those who'd been on Marian Finucane more than once, with damn fine pension entitlements as fat as Walmart Arse-of-the-Year nominees. Then came the stun grenade, the King of England hands and feet bound and stepping in tiny slave gingers, samba-like, a chain about <u>h</u>is neck attached to a blind donkey. That drew a stunned who'd've-thought silence. Not a jeer nor a rottéd egg.

In the stand two rows down from Anton's family holding hands Lar 'n' Flo. Lar actually had a bullet proof shield in front of him in case a nut in the crowd or a nut on parade took a potshot at him 'cause he was far from done. Flo asks Lar touching his wide knee: "are you glad it is over love?"

"I am. It feels great to be useful."

"Feels great to be believed more like, " and Flo feels a passing telly camera log her words.

Anton tells his Mother about Lar: "See him there. He's a genius, he's chartered half the counties, if the ocean had same. If oil 'n' gas in the ground were seen in money-in-the-bank terms then he has only done say KBC, PTSB and a quarter of Ulster, not a sausage of A.I.B or Bank of Ireland let alone the inshore."

"Really," says Mrs. Fruen née Spenser. "You've learnt a lot from him."

"He and I'll lay some eggs yet; big golden ones for our future lookouts 'cause....." Anton is sat to her hard of hearing side and listening exhausts her so he gives up. Then he gets that awful shudder when you misplace a valuable but then he pats his anorak breast pocket; the Master Bourneses title deeds are safe 'n Superdry.

CHAPTER THIRTY TWO

The search in his breast pocket woke him. Anton awakes - that sharp implement fallen from the throat of the King, that haddock whiff about His anointed Head, yet sack-clothéd, Dingle within ken but why the *Angelus* so early from Saint Brendan the Navigator's ding-dong-God-dangen, not an *Angelus*; it is the joys of dotage ringing out: The HUNDRED, Tuesday 6th December, 2022, one hundred years since the Irish Free State put itself about, rose up on its hobbly straw sugawn o'legs and strutted, then skipped out the road, seeking her cut-thrice Heart in the Emerald City. It is not bang on the hundred, some peals remain. The State appealed for each parish for one hundred slow ones and the hundredth peal lands on the Hundredth to the second. Some peals in, that Black Hawk contraption that'd been fairly gyring herself about the hooker with such a racket as a mortal would not hear the self tinker lowers and some SAS sorts as wee yet as KenDolls preparing harpoon and zipits: Operation 'Blondel' is on starting orders. Anton picks up, in the cold blooded light of day, what turns out to have been a tin opener and puts it back a piece into the King's Adam's apple, dimpling it sharply. The Hostage has rallied, has His eyes on long Reign forecast and struggles. Clivenden wakes up Lucineide who binds Royal hands with bailing twine and attaches him to the oar ring. Lar's just there acting the mermaid mascot be the bow. In the warning light of morning Anton wants to kill the King despite remembering his Communion vows with regard to 'Thou Shalt' etc. The Black Hawk or Apache or Squamish or chopper affair is so low now it is making its own unnamed tornado. The clearly gorgeous assault team have rifles and sten guns and grenades. They've practiced all their lives for such a chance; not in their wild imaginings did they weigh it'd be redeeming their Lion Heart. Startling Lar, their harpoon hits home spot on bow. Hooker is pulled by her prow, by the taut cable, nauts, more nauts of drag and gain, like some newfangled unnecessary water sport. The party are being taken back to sea, back towards *HyBrasil* which means the 'Island of the Once + Great King,' give or take. Anton gets up to unfix the spearhead from the hooker for'head and King William tries trip him overboard just as an warranted rat-a-tat of bullets miss everybody. Anton looks up sees five typical SAS commence their zipit. Half way down their shallow 'U' from the chopper, Anton flips his lid, a thousand year flip, and rips then rents His bleedin' gullet. Quickly the temple of the anointed with a small 't' and a small 'a' is no more, no greater than an old and bloody blue tuna aslump on boat bottom. Right on time the ninety ninth then hundredth knell, faint on faint, tolls - for what ? the leaving of the not-king, cold. Like the Sun King going to bed, the whole of royal Trumpton seemed to be going domino empathy-wise. 'Blondel's' craic troop o'five kaput before legs even board. Anton feels, then sees the taut cable sunder and five loud enough screams then plops into the sea. Looking up there is a silhouette visible at the chopper gantry, shortish and wide. 'Must have some serious bike lock cutters that fellah,' believes Anton. The freed hooker glides to a halt. Clivenden rearranges for eastward ho. Anton detachs the heavy harpoon and takes two lobster pots floored with a skim o' fifteen newton concrete and binds it all to the legs of the king, 'go chuck yourself, hubby-killer.' Gravity takes him to beddy byes. Flung out like illegal catch, there at the south west inlet approach of the wee isle of Tearaght and to this day the place is called out as *Polliam*.

Inny McGeown noted the sea battle result, stepped back from the open chopper door into the pilot zone, mauser dead hot. Taking advantage of the pilots being so buckled. Inny shot chief wing commander Pender Dot Jones in knee one (actually above it through the fleshy part) but it looked not unlike a traditional Ulster kneecapping. That was not sufficient in making his self clear. Shouted demands because of the racket got pared back simply to Inny hollering "obey me" to one and both of the pilots Pender Jones right knee's "shattering" did the trick. Co-pilot Singh obeyed for the sake of his family and squash. He asked the oil exec turned hijacker "what must you be thinking" and Inny shouts, barely audible "long time coming." Next thing he shouts "see that Dingle. Land there anywhere or you share Mister Dot Joneses pain." Singh made more objections so Inny shrieks "mercy me, I best shoot your boss." He placed the barrell to Pender Jones's dapper nape and prepared to execute. Singh pleads: "don't" and McGeown responds "trade you; land uz on that pier there; it'll do dandy." Pender Jones Junior fell forward, went quiet, slumped from bloody loss. "What say you we welcome them patriots ?" Singh with no clearance landed and the swish o'blades put gulls off their second breakfasts.

McGeown made his statement to the Dingle guards and as the young constable was scribbling one outrage after another McGeown noted the ruccous of the RAF chopper taking off: 'sound enough before he'd get his vehicle confiscated or worse' and then it was lunch time and Inny had lamb shank at Drury's Traditional teal-painted pub of the year, 2015. From there he placed a call, a whatsapp of a one.

"Hey Clivenden; what'sahhhhhppp ?"

"Me and my buddies are nearly landed."

"That so. Well; you missed lunch."

"Afternoon tea for four then ?"

"I'll call it; tea by four and clotted whatnots 'n' full-on jam. Do you want it on scone or scon?"

"No matter."

"Scones and scons'll break my bones........"

"Sure thing Inny."

"Hey I thought I had bounty on that there King Willybilly but seems our Dublin 24 could not keep his criminal passions to his self. Congratulate him from me for concludin' that eppy-soda o'*Dynasty*."

Clivenden has his phone on speaker but hard to grasp the words. Lucineide was lying to his left shoulder and Anton on his right, a group huddle against stern and cold. Clivenden is Crist Redemptor holding them to him and he says: "Hey Antonino, the fat one says well done." Anton bewilders and blinks; Clivenden says to the phone. "Mack; talk to him yourself." Anton waves his hands for 'no.'

An hour after, reduced to last chug 'n' glide, the heroes gain the harbour of Dingle, all squawks and smells o'things fishy. Lar recognises Inny on the west pier and waves to him. There is a Garda Sergeant to his left. Inny shouts "oy Swing Man."

As they are lightly debriefing, chortling, A-teaming their way along the pier Lar says with McGeown holding him tight about the shoulder: "Oy big fellah. I thought you were the dog's bollocks." Lar somewhat out of context believes that to mean 'I thought you were with the enemy.'

"Ahar juggle me neighbour," answers The McGeown, "I had my hands full getting Brasilians to seduce Dublin desperate housewife of the year so that Chinese could get their hands on the World's most spot on pendulambulist that way we'd assure their majesties we had a safe idiocy of a fake enemy so they could go display centuries old disregard for other people's otherness and invade the sly fuck out of Ireland for the nth and halfth time. I've a Hoover damnantion o'dodge info on those Plumsteads, enough to keep you Padwax porned up on victimhood till the 29th effin' century."

"I sorta kinda follow," says Lar deferring to the pier granite, itself award winning, Best Ashlar Hew 1878, if they had some degree o' Masonic awards that far back.

"When did you get involved ?" Anton interrupts point blank to McGeown. He has never met such a man before, so brash and caring and confusing.

"They approached me."

"Made the ruse more perfect." Clivenden puts out. Anton is surprised by the Brasilian's familiarity with the Irish extraction of a Texan.

"Why didn't you stop it all earlier," Anton scowled.

"Let all the last puss rise to the top; then squish......" Inny clacks his thumb nails together to indicate the air drawn pimple burst.

"I hope my husband's death was not 'lateral damage."

"Anton I am so sorry about your guy. I was in bed with the enemy; sure and quite a fivesome some times but I did not keep intimates on each 'n' all their sordids. To cover my tracks; understand; I had to not know everything, nor appear to care."

With that a woman from The Kerryman came at them and she was particularly interested to get the woman's take, Lucineide's version of "the devastating ordeals. From the top," she said and before Lucineide had time to blush her modestest they got interrupted by the not yet disgraced Irish Daily Male man. The Male's sub-editor-in-charge charged with Emotion said they'd love a paparasher of Lucineide and Anton having a sloppy snog but Anton was yet in his fashionable, black, appropriate widower-wedes. The cheek anyway; 'as if adventure would straighten the man.'

EPILOGUE

It's just 451 English miles from *Polliam* to SW1. Mid morning weekdays four year old Prince Louis Battenberg iii should be at *Not-Herd*, a kindergarten within Pimlico. The whooping has him abed, seeking one moment sheet coldness, the next heatedness. He feels the house empty or emptying. He is in, then out o'dreaming. Third born of the King, the long awaited, the Culmination, the Longterm Arthur, the Shorterm Louis now startled awake in the North West corner of Buckingham Palace, SW1. On his wall there are no child pictures of mum and Dad but there is of his forenamesakes. One jumbly crayon scrawl has *ahar-ahar-oh* from the crow's nest Louis Battenburg i, First SeaLord. Below dex having a welcome pugwash great uncle Louis ii, self-styled 'Princess of Connaught' whose sea-shadowy yarns and more yarns begat this fiction; Louis Battenberg ii, keeper of his own imaginary Schloss Heiligenberg Battenberg *am See*, or a gothic of it proud 'bove the Atlantic. From its ramparts recall, Louis ii, how he spied then descried MiddleEarth-neath-Sea, that continent, that vast tumblety handmedown o'Yarnia and the gazillion troubles it bad.

That boy prince right then feels the fail 'n' death of the Father, sees his nursery florid curtain not quite renting but a definite tousling, some sprite broadarming. What might the Future be up to if it is down to wee Louis, Louis, Louis to take command o'HMS *Songs of Blinkin' Praise*. The princely, ikey tot wondered at portend and window rattle, felt the Fortytude as his Father part waves; 'the Line will neither be quiet, nor stay Dead.'

About the Author

Colum Stapleton began as a writer, got distracted for two decades into making documentaries and retreated back to the 2D of the blank page to create GAZILLION as a doco couldn't dent the core wonder of the subsea story with all its rumours & maybes.

Director/ Producer of Documentaries

TEAMHAIR/ TARA TG4/ BAI How did Tara become her mythic self. Also stars a reluctant motorway.

TRICK OF THE LIGHT: An Irish-Norwegian Co-production. Why do the "professional" classes: doctor, mayor and vicar not see the UFOs in the Hessdalen Valley, while the local farmers and UFOlogists do.

EMPIRE OF JURAMIDAM: IFB/ NIFTVC/ TELESUR An anthropological journey to the heart of *Amazonas* that charts the evolution of a community that fuses Christianity & plant hallucinogens. (Winner of Grand Prize Documentary Feature 2004, San Francisco GreenCine Festivall)

TELL ME CAPTAIN STRANGE: RTE/ IFB Why does seeing UFOs cause so much trouble amongst loved ones and why are there so many up about North West Ireland ?

HOLY HIJACKER - SEEKING THE THIRD SECRET OF FATIMA RTE/ IFB/ SBS Australia. Perth-man explains why he hijacked an Aer Lingus plane back in 1981. In the process learn among other things how Pope John Paul II became the secret prophecy's protagonist - and said as much. Also stars former *Taoiseach* Albert Reynolds

SAI BABA - STRANGE AVATAR IFB/ FA Berlin/ RTE/ Arts Council of Ireland A village magician declared he was god "in an instant I could make the entire universe disappear" - how he created a Neverland of his own in South India and had the President and Prime Minister of India visiting to kiss his very feet.

Colum designed and built The Gyreum, an 100 foot diametre wooden edifice for workshops and retreats in rural South Sligo, Ireland. www.gyreum.com

GAZILLION 2

…..to …..follow

Lightning Source UK Ltd.
Milton Keynes UK
UKHW011150010319
338265UK00001B/10/P